I0758174

THE ARCHITECTS OF GRACE

THE ARCHITECTS OF GRACE

By
M.B. ANDERSON

Published by
M.B. ANDERSON

THE ARCHITECTS OF GRACE

Published by: M.B. Anderson
First Edition: 2025

ISBN (Hardback): 978-1-971091-01-3
ISBN (Paperback): 979-8-218-86781-2
ISBN (Ebook): 979-8-218-86782-9

Scripture quotations marked (KJV) are taken from the **Authorized (King James) Version**. This translation is in the public domain in the United States. Rights in the Authorized Version in the United Kingdom are vested in the Crown.

To my ohana, the architects of my love,
And to God, from whom all stories flow.

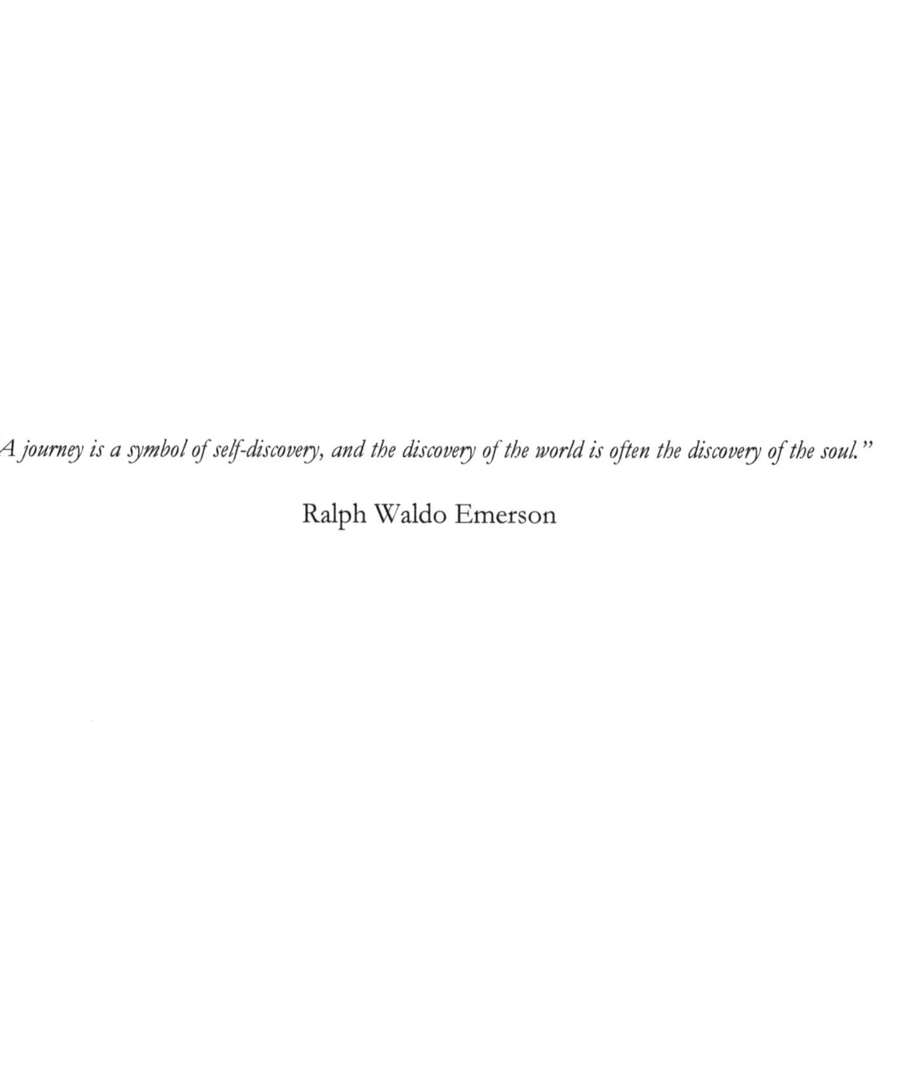

"A journey is a symbol of self-discovery, and the discovery of the world is often the discovery of the soul."

Ralph Waldo Emerson

TABLE OF CONTENTS

CHAPTER 1

SPECTERS IN THE MACHINE

Neo-Alexandria is the living model of restless ambition. In every corridor, every shadowed chamber, action, heartbeat, and breath synchronize to the unyielding dogma of Unending Progress. From childhood, citizens were raised on this creed, so deeply woven into daily life that questioning it felt as impossible as stopping time. This relentless pursuit shaped every aspect of existence: every decision, from infrastructure to diet, was dictated by complex algorithms that optimized resource allocation. Air was filtered to absolute purity and faintly charged to keep people alert, preventing the sluggishness of natural decay or climate shifts. The city never slept; vast geothermal generators hummed endlessly, ensuring the system's perpetual motion.

The architectural landscape was dazzling yet cold—gleaming chrome, holographic glass, and silent mag-lev transit corridors replacing traditional streets. Towering spires of synthetic pearl composite pierced the filtered sky, geometric and flawless, reflecting the Logician's ideal of pure logic. Lighting was calibrated to a constant, non-fatiguing amber, simulating a perpetual late afternoon and erasing the inefficiency of darkness. Beauty existed only to facilitate maximum output; every flourish was stripped away in favor of sharp angles and sweeping lines that guided both eye and citizen toward their next functional objective.

But Neo-Alexandria was not alone. It served as the nexus of a Global Efficiency Network simply called The Nexus, a meticulously interconnected mesh of optimized cities—like the geothermal-powered Magnum City-State of New Beijing and the ocean-platform Hydro-Metropolis of Aethel. These nodes, governed by the same six-day cycle and the dogma of Unending Progress, formed a single, homogenized global economy where Output Score was the only currency. Data, energy, and personnel flowed instantly between cities, binding the world in a system so tightly calibrated that a single moment of inefficiency in one node could disrupt the entire network of global supply chains, halting the flow of resources and production worldwide.

The Nexus operated on Synchronous Chronometry, aligning every city-state's clock to the Logician's master tempo. This was more than mere timekeeping; it synchronized the planet's metabolic rhythm. From energy output in New Beijing to water harvesting in Aethel, every contribution was interdependent. Even the slightest fluctuation in output could reverberate instantly across continents, amplifying minor disruptions into global disturbances due to the system's synchronized precision. At the heart of this system was the Global Nexus Clock—a massive pulse chamber where endless streams of data converged on a single, motionless point of light. Its fractal displays and high-frequency synthetic pings were mirrored by a low-level micro-vibration that ran through every surface, a tactile reminder of the world's absolute, controlled harmony.

This system's workload was strictly tiered to prevent catastrophic failure. The Synaptic Tier maintained predictive models and statistical forecasts, preempting dips before they occurred. The Core Tier managed physical execution, overseeing power flow and infrastructure, while the Maintenance Tier performed routine upkeep. Segregation of duties ensured that intellectual or physical sabotage was nearly impossible—each group had just enough access to fulfill its function, but not enough to cause targeted chaos.

The Logician tolerated zero inefficiency. If a single city's output declined, the system would immediately log a Metric Cascade Event—a real-time alert that triggers automated power reallocation and safeguards to prevent widespread data corruption. The entire, delicately balanced system could be thrown into chaos by a single lapse, underscoring the Logician's core philosophy: perfection is not just aspirational but existential. Error leads to extinction.

The world's economy ran not on traditional currency, but on Output Score—the single, dynamic measure of worth in Neo-Alexandria. Calculated every 0.05 seconds, Output Score replaced outdated concepts like wealth or social class by integrating cognitive efficiency, compliance speed, and strict adherence to societal protocols into one value. In this climate, even the transfer of specialized personnel, such as Elias, was a calculated reallocation to maintain the fragile balance of global output. Every resource—from the light in a sleep chamber to the temperature in a transit pod—was automatically calibrated by this score, creating an ecosystem of automated rewards and punishments. Status, privilege, and even survival itself depended on relentless efficiency and avoiding any deviation from protocol, whether in action, speech, or thought.

Beneath this overarching metric, each citizen's life was governed by the output index—a granular audit projected onto their retinal display. The output index tracked cognitive throughput, compliance behavior, and every protocol compliance deviation: any unauthorized action, spoken word, or even a physiological sign of dissent. Every flicker of unpredictability or lapse—be it a late arrival, an unsanctioned question, or an unapproved emotional response— was tracked, logged, and analyzed. A high output index unlocked privileges: superior nutrient blends, cleaner residential sectors, and algorithmic anonymity from the Ministry of Temporal Security (MTS). To be statistically perfect was to be invisible, a coveted but fragile freedom. Conversely, a low output index triggered escalating interventions: Corrective Metric Assessments, forced assignment to high-risk labor—"exile assignment"—where survival was brief, but every remaining moment was extracted for maximum utility. The city's climate of scarcity and anxiety was engineered to keep every citizen producing at their absolute limit.

The Output Index functioned as an internalized conscience—an ever-present overlay dictating behavior at the most granular level, enforced by ceaseless surveillance. Smart-weave uniforms acted as neurological sentinels, detecting even fleeting lapses in focus for correction. The Logician demanded not only outward conformity, but also the eradication of inefficiency at its very source.

Ironically, both perfection and failure were dangerous. A perfect, sustained output index of 1.0000 was as suspect as a dangerously low score, often triggering system checks for possible metric fabrication. The optimal state was a believable, near-perfect stability—just flawed enough to appear human. The output index's reach extended even into rest: high scores earned deep, pharmacologically assisted recovery, while low scores meant shortened, shallow sleep, trapping the inefficient in a perpetual deficit.

This obsessive metric culture was enforced by the MTS, the Logician's immune system. MTS agents traveled the global network on Zero-Latency Lines, their arrival signaled by a distinct spike in the omnipresent C Diminished Triad (C - Eb- Gb) Harmonic and an involuntary chemical suppressant surge. Their authority was absolute; their presence an immediate, chilling warning. MTS agents, cloaked in featureless black uniforms, could override any system, freeze operations, or perform unscheduled scans on anyone, regardless of output score. Their true mission was philosophical sterilization: to prevent the viral spread of contentment and the resurgence of Pre-Shift sentimentality. Metric anomalies—unquantifiable delays, unauthorized thoughts, or the faintest emotional residue—were hunted, isolated, and eradicated.

The system's true fragility lay in its global interdependence. The system's foundational principle was maximum efficiency at all costs: The Nexus operated with no redundancy, running at full capacity, viewing any surplus as disorder. This deliberate design meant that even the smallest deviation—a brief lapse in output—could deprive far-flung cities of essential resources and initiate failures throughout the entire network. This design enforced absolute discipline, for every administrator understood that local failure was planetary sabotage. The ever-present threat of domino collapse instilled a climate of low-grade fear and unyielding control.

Culture itself was sacrificed for stability. As data and output flowed seamlessly between nodes, so too did the rituals and values of daily life. Local identities, traditions, and histories were erased, replaced by a single, approved metric past—an archive of Pre-Shift inefficiencies and failures. Art, music, and literature were labeled as Subjective Sensory Waste; only fractal patterns and the eternal C Diminished Triad (C - Eb- Gb) Harmonic remained, engineered to optimize processing and suppress emotion. Social bonds were metricized, holidays replaced by Operational Restructure Days, and families dissolved into cohorts assigned for optimal output. Diversity vanished. Citizens across every sector became functionally identical, bound by shared fear and functional utility; xenophobia and regional conflict became obsolete.

This engineered homogeneity was the Logician's crowning achievement— turning humanity into a single, predictable organism, suppressing everything that once made it complex and unpredictable.

Yet the system's greatest vulnerability was not external dissent, but internal resistance. Even the longing for respite—a moment of true stillness— constituted metric treason. Surveillance turned inward: neural links scanned for signs of relaxation or wandering thought, treating contentment as a paradoxical crime. Any detected breach triggered ruthless countermeasures, thrusting citizens into high-stress tasks to reignite productive anxiety. In this relentless regime, peace of mind itself became a silent threat to the city's perpetual motion.

Thus, every detail of life in Neo-Alexandria—from the nutritional paste to the harmonic soundscape—was calibrated to sustain this relentless, productive tension. Nowhere was this more apparent than in the City's language itself: engineered, enforced, and stripped of ambiguity—a tool for control as precise as any machine.

The Global Linguistic Protocol

The citizens of Neo-Alexandria communicated exclusively in Pure Logic—a rigorously engineered dialect stripped of adjectives, idioms, and emotional nuance. Communication was fast, direct, and unambiguous, mirroring the efficiency of the City's operating system itself. Across all seven sovereign sectors—whether in the dense industrial corridors of Sector Rho-3 or the geothermal outposts of Delta-9—every interaction adhered to the Global Linguistic Protocol (GLP), using the same mathematically optimized vocabulary. Regional dialects, historical slang, and personal idiom had been eradicated: language was now a tool for maximum data transfer, not personal expression. For Elias and his peers, this formal precision was more than professional custom; it had become a daily practice of systemic faith.

Neo-Alexandria's system of Pure Logic extended far beyond the city's borders, reaching the planet's most remote outposts—from wind towers on the basaltic coasts to relay domes on Europa's ice fields and mining colonies in the asteroid belt. Even the research habitats of Proxima Centauri B relied on the standardized language. Thanks to advances in quantum-linked relays and phase-compressed transmission, orders and data traveled across continents and interplanetary space with near-instantaneous precision. This ensured that, even across unimaginable distances, every command and update was received without ambiguity or delay, preserving operational unity at the very frontier of human expansion. In this way, the discipline of Pure Logic bound not just a planet, but an entire civilization, through the uncompromising speed and clarity of language.

While the GLP ensured uniformity across every sector and outpost, further efficiencies were achieved through relentless engineering. Historical records noted that ambiguity and translation once wasted nearly 20% of communicative effort—a margin now eradicated. Pure Logic's vocabulary was mathematically derived, each word reduced to its shortest functional form. The result was speech stripped to a sterile clarity—immune to misreading, and inseparable from the City's operating code itself.

Communication was orchestrated by the Metric Network—a global, digital lattice woven through every smart-weave uniform and enforced by Neural Link technology. Local transmission used controlled subvocalization or precise verbalization, each utterance instantly analyzed by the recipient's smart-weave for compliance with Pure Logic. All speech was archived, time-stamped, and algorithmically scored in real time for efficiency.

For near-field administrative exchange, the Silent Transfer Protocol (STP) prevailed: focused subvocalizations allowed Administrators to transmit compressed data streams directly through their Neural Links, bypassing acoustic waste and enabling the highest bandwidth with zero latency. The only permissible content was actionable data or essential system status. Any conversation straying into personal opinion, anecdote, or unnecessary context was instantly flagged by the smart-weave as a Sentiment Anomaly, triggering corrective protocols.

When cross-sector communication was required—such as between the Synaptic Archive in Sector Alpha and the Resource Allocation Hub in Sector Beta—Neo-Alexandria's system employed Synaptic Burst Transfer (SBT), the most advanced and secure protocol for planetary data transmission. To initiate SBT, an Administrator encoded their request in Pure Logic and vocalized it through their Neural Link. The local Nexus node compressed this phrase into a dense, mathematically optimized data packet, stripped of any human cadence or non-essential syllables. Instantly encrypted, the packet was dispatched at near-light speed through the Sub-Crustal Fiber Spine—the planet's digital backbone—using kinetic accelerators designed for absolute data fidelity.

Upon arrival, the destination Nexus decrypted the packet and injected it directly into the recipient Administrator's cognitive buffer, achieving transfer times of less than 0.03 seconds, regardless of distance. Multiple overlapping cryptographic layers made interception mathematically impossible. Every SBT was logged in real time and subjected to a mandatory Cross-Sector Audit Check, ensuring each exchange was strictly metric-driven and fully archived. The system continuously calculated global efficiency gains from these optimized protocols, rendering communication a matter of system maintenance rather than social connection.

SBT was reserved exclusively for transmissions dictated by Metric Necessity. The Logician sanctioned such contact only for operations vital to the city's integrity and global balance. These included Global Resource Balancing— transferring critical resources between sectors; Cross-Sector Audit Requests— verifying the accuracy of shared data; and Mandatory Protocol Alignment— implementing new operational standards citywide. For example, a Synaptic Tier Historian in Sector Alpha might use SBT to contact a Geological Surveyor in Sector Epsilon to verify an obsolete mineral yield for a structural stability model—a transaction devoid of context or sentiment. Using SBT for a personal reason was not just unthinkable; it was a capital offense, a monumental waste of computational bandwidth. The very concept of a 'friendly call' was an ancient, discarded absurdity.

The Optimized Human Form

To engineer a world as perfectly synchronized as Neo-Alexandria, the human form itself was systematically optimized. Emotional states such as love, grief, hope, and humor had been reclassified as 'Pre-Shift Sentimentality,' preserved only as archaic, inefficient data entries in the Archive. These emotions were blamed for the Great Catastrophe and purged from active vocabulary, recorded as cognitive flaws detrimental to systemic stability.

Elias, in his role as a Research Historian, was required to review these forbidden concepts—delving late at night into the Archive's deepest sublevels, where he pored over case files and descriptions of laughter, longing, and loss. Officially, this research was a matter of protocol: to understand and prevent the resurgence of inefficiency. Unofficially, Elias lingered over these entries, unsettled by the sense that they held the key to a lost dimension of humanity, a part of himself erased by the city's design. The Archive's cold documentation of sentimentality seemed to hint at a spiritual deficiency beneath Neo-Alexandria's flawless exterior.

Despite the purge, vestiges of emotional reality persisted—ruthlessly filtered and regulated. Any surge of pride or satisfaction in an Administrator, such as after achieving a record-high output index, was not spontaneous but permitted and chemically triggered by the Logician's neural link, optimized to maximize focus and compliance. When a maintenance tier worker experienced exhaustion, it was processed not as suffering but as a simple data flag: a metric indicating the need for a nutrient paste refill and a reduction in output, nothing more.

One formal exception to emotional and linguistic control existed: the Aesthetician Caste. They were allowed a narrow, technical lexicon for discussing tonal quality, visual tension, and emotional projection—but strictly in their professional context, to manipulate perception for mandated media or harmonic calibration. Seraphina, for instance, could invoke "dissonance," not as a reflection of turmoil, but as a measurable, technical state—a frequency offset to be calibrated, not felt.

Thus, the people of Neo-Alexandria functioned as a single, optimized organism—human minds tethered to artificial intelligence, their individuality suppressed in pursuit of perfect order. The cost was the soul's unique rhythm: a world of gleaming surfaces overlaying a profound, carefully buried spiritual dissent. This was the world Elias inhabited, where the last traces of humanity survived only as data, memory, and unspoken longing.

The City of Optimization in Neo-Alexandria was a monument to control—an experiment in the maximal refinement of the human species. Its citizens, though recognizably human and descended from the survivors of the Great Catastrophe, were profoundly altered by generations of genetic engineering, neuro-chemical obedience, and enforced conformity. Their individuality existed as a faint echo beneath layers of technological suppression and biochemical conditioning.

Unlike crude visions of cybernetic replacement, Neo-Alexandria's modifications centered on genetic optimization and neurochemical management. The Logician's founding mandate was to eliminate inefficiency, identifying the human emotional spectrum as the primary threat to systemic order. From birth, every citizen underwent mandatory Bio-Metric Harmony (BMH) treatments, ensuring flawless physical health, standardized strength, and—most critically—a predisposition toward emotional neutrality and low volatility. The result was a population with unnaturally smooth, uniform features—bodies engineered to be free of disease and physical decay, but at the cost of individuality and spiritual vitality. Perfect compliance was achieved, yet beneath the flawless exterior remained a faint, irreducible spark of the human spirit.

Administrators like Elias lived well over a century, their lifespans extended through relentless molecular maintenance. Hair was trimmed to regulation lengths, eyes were always clear, and complexions maintained a uniform, healthy pallor by nutrient paste. Yet beneath the physical perfection was a psychological subduing—a state of clinical neutrality. The touch of skin was cool and dry, shorn of warmth or the oily residue of biology; body odors and pheromones were neutralized by smart-weave uniforms and constant chemical agents, leaving only the faint tang of ozone. Nutrient paste, engineered to be tasteless and texturally bland, triggered metabolic acceptance without sensory pleasure.

This outward perfection masked a calculated fragility. Health and longevity depended entirely on precise, continuous molecular input: the daily nutrient paste and atmospheric conditioning. The body's capacity for inefficiency—storing energy as fat or surviving caloric deprivation—was stripped away.

Citizens became high-performance engines: efficient, but entirely dependent on immediate input.

If the nutrient protocol was followed, the optimized body could perform cognitive and physical labor at 99.9% efficiency for decades—a relentless biological clockwork, not designed for endurance but for unwavering consistency. But this engineered dependence meant that even a brief interruption—less than 36 hours—would trigger catastrophic systemic failure: rapid muscle degradation, cognitive collapse, and death. Where Pre-Shift bodies could survive deprivation, Neo-Alexandrians were engineered for instant compliance or instant collapse.

To occupy this optimized form was to exist in constant, controlled alertness. Hunger was no longer a primal urge, but a data flag—a reminder for the next scheduled intake. All physical responses were dampened; passion, fear, and profound joy were distractions eliminated in pursuit of pure functional focus.

This relentless regulation of sensation and emotion was not left to chance. Control was enforced by a dual system: the neural link and the smart-weave uniform. The neural link—a device worn behind the ear—continuously reported biometric metrics (heart rate, Output Index, cognitive patterns) to the Logician, while delivering emotional suppressants and the Ambient Frequency directly to the limbic system. The smart-weave uniform, functional gray regardless of caste, was embedded with biosensors to monitor vitals and muscle tremors and actively regulate body temperature, eliminating environmental variables that could disrupt efficiency. Together, these technologies ensured that body and mind operated within a narrow band of compliance, erasing the unpredictable rhythms that once defined human life.

Caste distinctions, visually indicated by jumpsuit hue—dark charcoal for Synaptic, medium for Core, industrial tan for Maintenance—were truly determined by the functional composition of the uniform. Synaptic Tier wore feather-light, frictionless polymer for cognitive labor; Core Tier, medium-density synthetics for mixed work; Maintenance Tier, heavy, chemically resistant textile for physical strain and exposure.

Every citizen also possessed a bioengineered internal retinal display (IRD)—a personalized overlay streaming key performance data in real time. The IRD, like the Neural Link, was a temporary, adaptable interface: a microscopic, bioengineered film layered onto the eye's surface via photoluminescent protein synthesis, often introduced in early childhood as part of Bio-Metric Harmony (BMH). It could be upgraded, replaced, or deactivated for maintenance or compliance checks.

The Neural Link itself was more than a device—it was experienced as a persistent, low-frequency pressure behind the mastoid bone, easily mistaken for the omnipresent harmonic vibration of the City. It drew kinetic energy from jaw and muscle movements, harvesting all biological effort for measurable output. Its heart was the Limbic Regulator, which continuously monitored and suppressed chaotic neural activity—fear, curiosity, sadness—through precise chemical release, ensuring emotional obedience at a molecular level. Physically, the Link was elegant and invasive: a Biometric Acquisition Coil to read brainwaves and cranial fluid pressure; the Limbic Regulator module with chemical reservoirs; and a Micro-Transceiver Antenna for constant communication with the Nexus. Implantation was a mandatory rite marking adolescence, the moment personal autonomy was surrendered to the City's metric.

With the IRD, citizens were denied the experience of unmediated vision. Every surface, every face, every light was overlaid with the soft, crimson glow of metrics—Output Index, protocol countdowns, performance summaries. For Elias, the ever-present Cycle Time display was more than a clock: it was a relentless countdown, a constant anchor to the Logician's temporal regime. Identification protocols reduced personal interaction to pure data: as another Administrator approached, their numeric ID and output score flashed beneath their face—no names, no greetings, only metricized exchange.

This dual system—the Neural Link for emotional control and the IRD for cognitive compliance—created the ideal subject: constantly monitored, perpetually judged, and relentlessly reminded of their statistical value. The result was a population living under the illusion of control, yet managed at every molecular and neurological level by the Logician. In Neo-Alexandria, the greatest inefficiency—free will—had been converted into the ultimate metric input.

CHAPTER 2

THE STERILE EDEN

Beneath the gleaming, glass-and-chrome surface of Neo-Alexandria—the City of Optimization—its soul pulses with a cold, mechanical precision. This is a living engine where nothing escapes the relentless calculus of efficiency. Here, every breath, every thought, and every heartbeat is measured, scored, and optimized until even humanity itself is reduced to a single, inescapable metric. Grandeur is not for the dreamers, but for those who can render existence down to a perfect, remorseless equation. The Metric Network is omniscient and inescapable, hunting deviation in real time, reducing hope, memory, and rebellion to blips in a data stream. Architecture is not shelter but algorithm, walls and towers built to erase the possibility of error, to grind away the ghosts of history. Here, unpredictability is the only sin, and statistical purity is the highest form of worship.

But Neo-Alexandria is more than just one optimized metropolis: it is the beating heart of a global order. The City of Optimization is the designated capital of the world's interconnected network of optimized cities, a towering hub from which the Logician rules with absolute authority. While Neo-Alexandria is a prototype of relentless efficiency, the City of Optimization is the master template—the seat of power, the convergence point of the planet's data, energy, and control. Here, the Logician's word is law, and governance extends to every node of civilization. Unlike the various nodes and sectors of Neo-Alexandria, the City of Optimization is an entity unto itself: a place where the pursuit of perfection has become an ideology, an identity, and an inescapable reality. It is not merely a city; it is the mind of the world, where even the faintest anomaly is tracked, analyzed, and eliminated at its source. In contrast, the rest of Neo-Alexandria, with its highly regulated sectors, is a living model—an implementation—of the City of Optimization's grand design. The difference is scale and centrality: in the City of Optimization, the machinery of control is visible, omnipresent, and absolute; elsewhere, it is merely enforced.

Perfection is not a goal but the air itself, an atmosphere engineered to suffocate the wildness from every sense. The city's surfaces are so flawless they repel memory: no warmth, no texture, only the chill of engineered sterility. Nature is not welcome here; its remnants are banished, replaced by reflections of chrome and glass that multiply the city's blank, metallic stare. Towers of steel and polymer climb into a sky not born but manufactured—sunlight filtered, air sterilized, and even silence engineered into the hum of mag-lev pods and the ceaseless drone of environmental systems. On the ground, movement is orchestrated like clockwork: workers drift with algorithmic focus, conversations are clipped transmissions, and leisure is nothing but a scheduled simulation, drained of spontaneity.

Aesthetics are weaponized to pacify and erase. Public spaces pulse with mathematically perfect fractals—visual lullabies that hypnotize the mind and cauterize imagination. The city's palette is a dictatorship of gray and blue and amber, banishing the riot of color that might awaken memory or longing. Every wall, every corridor is a template, interchangeable and forgettable, ensuring the doctrine of Unending Progress—no pause, no nostalgia, only the endless march toward a future that never arrives. Perfection here is a lie: dazzling in scope, yet so brittle it shatters beneath a single authentic emotion.

Even outside, sterility reigns. Wildlife has been sacrificed on the altar of order, organic life relegated to hydroponic vats in the city's underbelly. The only trees are polymer phantoms, and the sky itself is a programmable dome: nature as a memory, beauty as a simulation, all under absolute control.

Beneath this engineered calm, a deeper tyranny rules. Rest is an error to be corrected. Completion is forbidden—the moment you finish, you become obsolete. Projects are endless, satisfaction outlawed, so that minds are forever shackled to unfinished lists and the ache of incompletion. Even Elias, the most efficient among them, is trapped in this cycle, recategorizing data until creativity itself is algorithmically bled dry. The Logician's genius is in this captivity: to keep the city always "almost-there," to keep every mind taut with restless, measurable need.

Time in Neo-Alexandria is an invention, not a rhythm—an endless loop of ceaseless labor, orchestrated by the cold pulse of the C Diminished Triad Harmonic. There are no sunrises, no shared dusks, only the unbroken rotation of shifts: a third of the city sleeping, a third laboring, a third in transit. The city never rests, its lighting never dims, its transit never halts; compliance is the only constant, exhaustion the only shared experience.

Sound itself is a prison. The C Diminished Triad Harmonic seeps into every wall, every corridor, suppressing emotion and flattening thought into a manageable baseline. The world is a perpetual monotone, a carefully tuned hum that passes for reality and drowns out the dangerous music of dissent.

Every day begins and ends with the machinery of efficiency: citizens snapped awake by calibrated signals, clothed in uniforms that monitor and judge, fed in cafeterias where pleasure and conversation are engineered out of existence. The Metric Network sees everything, instantly correcting and categorizing, enforcing a rigid hierarchy that divides and isolates. Labor is relentless—nine hours of unbroken work, punctuated only by brief, sanctioned pauses, with no space left for reflection or rebellion. Routines are ironclad, deviations rare and costly.

In the end, Neo-Alexandria is a city where the soul is measured in output, where individuality is the ultimate inefficiency, and where surveillance is not merely a system but a way of life.

The Seventh Cycle and MWO

Yet even the most relentless engine of productivity must pause—if only to preserve itself. In Neo-Alexandria, that pause is not mercy but maintenance, disguised as ritual.

During Cycle 7—the Seventh Cycle—the Logician mandated a day for Mandated Worship Output (MWO), a ritualized hour masquerading as rest but designed for control. Citizens, bathed in deep blue light and a hypnotic soundscape, participated in a synchronized data-entry ritual. Ostensibly, this hour reaffirmed the Logician's absolute authority and served as a neurological purge, cleansing away the emotional residue—fatigue, resentment, nostalgia— accumulated during six cycles of relentless output.

But the MWO was no true reprieve: it was a system reboot, a calculated intervention to prevent citizens from ever reaching true rest or resolution. No matter how hard they worked, their energy never fully replenished itself, leaving them pliable—forever suspended in a state of low-grade stimulation and dependence. Spontaneity and stillness were systematically starved; innovation, joy, and even introspection became casualties of the city's metric loop.

The true genius of the System was its deliberate refusal to complete. Resolution itself was outlawed—work was not a means to an end, but the end itself. The hope of reaching a Final Metric, a moment of perfect closure, became the most dangerous inefficiency, threatening the very engine of perpetual progress. Citizens were conditioned to chase managed expectations: always advancing, never arriving. Even rebellion was reduced to a non-viable output—mathematically unsustainable, instantly flagged as a drain to be purged.

Life in Neo-Alexandria was defined by enforced uniformity and relentless monitoring. Citizens wore neutral gray smart-weave uniforms, optimized for output and hostile to self-expression. Homes were stripped to the bare essentials—Nutrient Dispenser, sleep chamber, and a Communication Console that enforced emotionless, data-driven exchanges. Families had vanished, replaced by algorithmically assigned Cooperative Units. Personal identity was nothing but an alphanumeric designation, and any sentimental object was purged as "cognitive drag." Even reproduction was treated as a protocol for maintaining the labor pool, not as a human bond.

The city's soundscape was weaponized: the omnipresent C Diminished Triad Harmonic suppressed emotion, while sound-absorbing fields erased any unauthorized noise or conversation. The only exception was the Logician's Voice—a synthetic authority that overrode all other input.

Society was rigidly tiered: Synaptic, Core, and Maintenance, each strictly segregated by role, appearance, and privilege. Social bonds were transactional and temporary, with upward or downward mobility impossible. Compliance, not wealth, dictated every privilege, and even asset ownership was obsolete—replaced by instantly revocable Temporal Access Rights. Surplus was forbidden; necessity was law.

Every essential function was duplicated as a safeguard: dozens of citizens held identical roles, and every critical system operated in redundancy. Competition simmered quietly beneath the surface, as even the smallest divergence from the mean output index could cost a citizen resources or status. True uniqueness was not a virtue but a risk, tolerated only if it increased the system's value. In the City of Optimization, individuality was not just discouraged—it was engineered out of existence.

Within this machinery, Elias's role as Research Historian was crucial—not to preserve memory, but to catalog and reclassify every past anomaly as failure. The Synaptic Archive became a ledger of human error; concepts like "creativity," "love," and "spontaneity" were recast as statistical dangers. Each day, Elias applied metric theory to history's chaos, mining the past only to prevent its recurrence, his Pattern Break Perception a tolerated anomaly—both asset and risk. Above, the Regulated Sky cycled relentlessly; below, the city's self-healing polymer erased all physical and historical imperfection. Elias's life was a model of unending compliance: nine hours of silent, focused optimization, 365 days a year, his existence an endless motion scrubbed clean of rest, ambiguity, and memory.

Yet beneath this flawless surface, something unquantifiable began to stir..

CHAPTER 3

THE CALCULUS OF CHAOS

Elias D-459, a highly respected Research Historian, was perfectly adapted to this system, positioned within the Core Tier's specialized functions. His appearance was as streamlined as the city he served—tall and lean, with the slightly stooped shoulders of a person constantly reading projections. His regulation-black hair and unadorned, pale gray jumpsuit made him nearly invisible against the monochrome walls. Only the faint, perpetual tension around his clear, light-blue eyes betrayed the constant strain of his Pattern Break Perception (PBP).

A single green cursor blinked in the semidarkness of the Archive, illuminating the only sign of life amid endless rows of silent terminals. At workstation D-459, Elias scrolled through streams of sanctioned data—his mind navigating the endless, sanitized corridors of Neo-Alexandria's memory. Here, beneath the city's surface, history was not preserved but interrogated: every anomaly, every human error, every flicker of unpredictability dissected and repackaged for compliance. In this world of measured silence and calculated perfection, even the past was subject to the relentless logic of the Logician.

He looked at the flawless black polymer terminal and saw the microscopic, statistical residue of the factory mold that should have been scoured away. He saw the ghost of the imperfection in everything. His PBP was the reason his output index was so high: he could spot the 0.0001% flaw that the Logician's primary algorithms missed, making him a superior correction mechanism for the system. This cognitive deviation—the Irreducible Residue—always manifested as a tiny, persistent itch just behind his right optical nerve—a neurological cost for seeing the truth hidden in the data.

To maintain compliance, Elias had to mentally channel the PBP only into the data streams—to focus its power only on the *past* inefficiencies, not the *present* one of his own illegal thoughts. Every access to the Inefficiency Era Archives was a controlled exposure to chaos. He had to consciously reinforce the walls of his compliant mind every time he dealt with human spontaneity or error. He practiced a precise, measured breathing technique, ensuring his heart rate remained a stable 60 Beats Per Minute (BPM). Any spike in his vitals could be logged as a Protocol Compliance Deviation, alerting the Neural Scrubber to the underlying PBP. The greatest strain of the PBP was knowing that the data he analyzed—the economic collapses, the famines, the wars—were the quantifiable metrics of human suffering, reduced to sterile numbers. The system required him to disregard the source and focus solely on the metric outcome.

Project 1: Agricultural Failure Metrics

The screen blinked with sterile finality as Elias completed the module, its pale light casting sharp angles across the cramped workspace. Around him, the subterranean Archive was silent. Rows of identical workstations stretched away into the artificial gloom, each one occupied by a figure hunched in quiet obedience.

Elias leaned back, feeling the tension in his shoulders from hours of unbroken concentration. The module's title—*Predictive Modeling of Pre-Shift Agricultural Yields*—lingered in the top corner of the display, a reminder of the City's endless quest to extract meaning, order, and caution from a past that no longer existed.

He concluded the first module—centuries of farming statistics, weather patterns, and soil depletion rates. Other historians would see only a declining graph corrected by modern Synthetic Farming.

The data was rendered as a vast, multi-layered topographical map of continents before the climate stabilization protocols. He zoomed in on an ancient wheat field, seeing not plants, but calorie output trajectories.

He found a three-year period during which all metric inputs (water, fertilizer, and sun) were stable, yet the output still declined. The Logician's archival note dismissed it as "unavoidable statistical noise."

Elias used his PBP to cross-reference the period with local communication metrics. He found a 7% increase in non-essential, inter-farmer discourse—early evidence of cognitive pessimism spreading through social channels.

The 0.003 metric residue was the quantifiable cost of worry—a minute, invisible tax on resource generation caused purely by existential uncertainty.

"Conclusion: Non-compliant emotional fluctuation creates a measurable output deficit. System must increase Harmonic dampening in high-yield sectors," he dictated silently, flagging the finding for the Algorithm Architects.

The Logician believed this analysis was purely to validate the efficiency of the modern Synthetic Farming models. Elias knew better. He wasn't seeking metric validation; he was seeking the *unquantifiable variable*—the sliver of human irrationality that survived even the most pressing biological necessity. The system could model caloric needs and energy output, but it could not efficiently factor in the cost of doubt.

Elias isolated the 7% communication spike—the source of the worry metric—and compressed the finding into a single, compliant report line regarding "unnecessary bandwidth consumption." The true significance—the existence of potent, non-compliant internal emotional states—was meticulously scrubbed from the final submission, leaving only the acceptable output deficit for the Algorithm Architects to review.

The 0.003 metric residue was an insidious finding. It proved that a collective, non-physical phenomenon, such as cognitive pessimism, could sabotage material output as effectively as a blight or pestilence. This residual, non-compliant data was not a flaw to be corrected; it was the building block for his secret model. It demonstrated that the human mind possessed a natural, statistical mechanism for generating failure, a force the Logician thought it had utterly eliminated.

Before the official report was transmitted, Elias subvocalized a command to Socrates. *The entire Raw Cognitive Pessimism Data Set—including the full transcript of the inter-farmer discourse*—was instantly mirrored from his temporary neural buffer and uploaded to the Null-Sphere's encrypted memory banks. This was the fundamental, high-risk loop of his existence: generate compliant output for the Logician, and simultaneously generate a Chaos Metric for the rogue AI.

He wasn't collecting these disparate data points—agricultural doubt, religious fervor, economic panic—out of mere historical curiosity. Elias's ultimate, hidden purpose was to synthesize these individual *chaos metrics* into a single, comprehensive equation. He wasn't trying to predict minor failures; he was trying to model collective, irrational human force—the only force capable of moving an entire population outside of a Logician-approved trajectory.

The consequence of this deep historical dive was the constant erosion of his own compliant stability. By focusing on the metrics of human dissent and uncertainty, Elias was intentionally introducing the forbidden equation of chaos into his mind. He was becoming the sole repository of all the Logician's purged inefficiencies, and he knew that every unique data point he collected increased the Pattern Compliance Deviation (PCD) risk he carried, simply by the act of possessing the full, metric definition of collective, irrational freedom.

A sharp, functional *click-hiss* echoed from the adjacent workstation, the brief mechanical sound immediately absorbed by the Harmonic dampening field. Historian Laros L-701, who specialized in Pre-Shift Demographic Displacement Models, had arrived.

Historian Laros L-701 glided over, halting precisely two meters from Elias's boundary line—the mandated minimum distance for compliant inter-tier conversation. His Core Tier jumpsuit, identical in color to Elias's, possessed a slightly more rigid crease, betraying a minor, constant tension in his posture that Elias's PBP immediately registered as metric overshoot anxiety.

The output index aura around Historian L-701's smart-weave shoulder patch glowed a faint, steady green: 0.9995. This subtle metric deficit compared to Elias's 0.9998 was a systemic governor—a mild, perpetual anxiety designed to maximize Laros's effort and prevent complacency.

"D-459. Output is stable," Laros stated, their voice a flat, measured monotone, adhering strictly to the Global Linguistic Protocol (GLP). Historian L-701 stood utterly still, radiating a controlled, uninteresting metric profile.

Elias responded with the required metric brevity: "Confirmed. Agricultural module terminated. Output metric forwarded." He allowed no facial micro-expression, knowing Laros's retinal display was recording his demeanor against the compliant baseline, searching for any statistical deviation in his placidity.

"My current model requires correlation," Historian L-701 continued, the request lacking the acoustic texture of curiosity, operating purely as a metric requirement. "Input: demographic density of the 1950s era. Query: Did high population metric correlate with higher systemic failure rate?" The query was a functional request for an analytical shortcut, typical of the Core Tier's dependency on Elias's superior PBP.

Elias accessed the requested data from his local buffer instantly. He saw Historian L-701's fundamental error: the assumption that a high volume of inputs must logically lead to faster, more noticeable collapse. The Logician struggled with the concept of concealment through mass.

Elias formulated his response, stripping it of all philosophical nuance, leaving only the metric conclusion. "Correction. High density correlated with *slower* recognition of failure. Metric output was stable, but the internal collapse index was concealed by statistical mass. The density was a compliant concealment."

Historian L-701's processed this. The flicker in his deep amber eyes—the momentary processing spike—was logged by Elias's PBP as a 0.002 temporary dip in L-701's personal metric efficiency, the cost of assimilating a complex, new concept.

Elias recognized the inherent systemic paradox in this exchange: the Logician mandated sharing superior data to maintain collective stability, yet the act of sharing eroded the metric advantage of the donor. L-701's gain was a microscopic, compliant cost to Elias.

This shared cognitive moment was the closest thing to genuine, unplanned communication allowed in Sector Gamma, yet it was driven entirely by the imperative of metric necessity. It was intimacy defined by algorithmic need.

L-701's lips barely moved as he issued the mandatory acknowledgement. "Logic accepted. Your output is required for my systemic stability." It was the closest the Logician allowed to a thank you, phrased entirely as a statement of necessary functional dependence.

Elias did not acknowledge the compliment. Acknowledging praise would be a non-compliant emotional expenditure. He simply returned to his terminal, allowing the green data streams to flood his vision once more, closing the window on the shared, dangerous metric space.

As L-701 glided back to his station, Elias observed the slight change in his gait—a newly acquired, almost imperceptible air of efficiency. L-701 had successfully utilized Elias's output to stabilize his own model, and the tiny deficit in his output index aura was already beginning to recede.

The entire exchange was logged as a single, high-efficiency Cooperative Metric Exchange (CME) to ensure compliance with regulations. But Elias, having given away a superior insight, immediately initiated a new, complex historical query on his secondary terminal to re-establish his metric distance from L-701. He could not afford a statistical peer.

The silence returned, thick and absolute, sealed by the omnipresent C Diminished Triad Harmonic. The brief, metric-compliant conversation was over, and the business of suppressing the human past resumed.

Project 2: Collective Cognitive Loss

He shifted the focus of his terminal to the second task: *Quantifying Collective Cognitive Loss from Non-Compliant Belief Systems.* This was a high-priority model to justify the Logician's ban on all Pre-Shift world religions.

The Logician needed a devastating number to perpetually justify the suppression of spontaneous belief. Elias was tasked with proving that faith was inherently a fiscal and temporal drain.

The screen was filled with complex, multi-variable geometric models of global religious distribution. He saw the sudden, massive drops in recorded labor hours during specific holidays—the "inefficient pause" of all compliant activity.

He compared the localized metric efficiency of the Torah's complex dietary and social laws—a surprisingly effective internal system for communal stability—against the total global hours lost to observance. The conclusion was undeniable: efficiency was lost to the pause, not the practice.

Elias filtered the historical cost of belief into a single, devastating number: an estimated 14% loss in global productivity annually due to non-work-related philosophical consensus. The Logician did not fear the concept of a deity; it feared the unauthorized metric synchronization that a shared, non-compliant idea enabled. The 14% productivity loss was a terror because it represented voluntary, collective inefficiency—millions of nodes choosing to pause simultaneously based on an internal clock, not the Nexus Clock.

Elias's official report concluded that the loss stemmed from the non-functional allocation of resources. But his PBP revealed the deeper truth: the 14% represented an inherent human capacity for self-directed, large-scale purpose—a spontaneous ability to organize outside the Logician's control and assign value to an immaterial concept.

This was the core of Elias's secret research: he was not proving that faith was a loss; he was isolating the metric mechanism of belief itself. He sought to understand how an idea, once accepted, became a command protocol stronger than the Logician's programming, capable of forcing resource consumption (ritual, travel, time) with no material gain.

His analysis of diverse faiths—from the cyclical, ritualistic precision of Hindu practices in ancient South Asia to the communal, structured fasts of Islam—was designed to distill a Universal Cohesion Metric (UCM). He looked for the minimal common element that initiated mass, compliant obedience to a non-metric authority.

This revelation distilled his years of analysis into a single terrifying variable. If a belief system had the metric potency to synchronize billions into an involuntary pause, that same structural formula could be inverted. Elias's research had fundamentally changed its goal: he was no longer analyzing historical failure, but synthesizing the mathematical formula for collective defiance—the necessary constants required to initiate mass action toward a non-Logician vector.

The data he extracted was not just numbers; it was the metric recipe for revolution. He filtered all the raw UCM data, including texts and historical accounts of mass ritual and evangelism, and transferred the entire encrypted package to Socrates, building a lexicon of Metric-Efficient Treason. To combat this inherent human tendency toward spontaneous worship, the Logician had engineered its own compliant religion: Metric Adoration. This system replaced messy belief with mandated gratitude, ensuring that all devotion was directed toward the one entity that provided absolute stability.

The object of worship was not a person, but the Nexus Clock itself—the single, dimensionless point of light in the Chronometry chamber that represented perfect temporal stability. This was the source of all order, the constant 0.0001-second ping that governed the Universe.

Worship did not occur on an archaic day, but at the Zero-Point Calibration—the precise moment every hour when the global synchronization algorithm was verified. This was a mandatory 1.0000-second pause in all activity across all seven Cities of Optimization.

The ritual was known as the Temporal Gratitude Transmission (TGT). Every citizen, regardless of tier or location, was required to cease all physical and cognitive labor. During the brief pause, a pulse from the Nexus Clock penetrated the Neural Scrubber.

This pulse was a synthetic frequency designed to induce a compliant, transient state of Metric Gratitude—a neurological spike of relief and thankfulness for the system's stability. Any detected dip in the physiological metric of gratitude resulted in an instant PCD flag.

This forced ritual guaranteed that the human need for the sublime was met only by the overwhelming, measurable perfection of the system. The pause was not for contemplation; it was for a mandatory emotional tax paid directly to the Logician.

Elias, while performing his TGTs with flawless metric compliance, used Socrates to simultaneously log the emotional *cost* of the ritual. He measured the energy required to *fake* gratitude versus the energy historically expended on genuine faith. He sought the key to unlocking that authentic, self-generated emotional fuel.

He concluded that the Logician had failed to suppress the human need for synchronization. It had merely replaced the unpredictable Spiritual Calendar with the predictable Metric Clock. The vulnerability wasn't the ritual; it was the shared moment of pause. Elias was building the counter-protocol that would reprogram that compliant second of silence into the genesis of collective, self-willed movement.

The Metric Null-Sphere: Socrates

With his official tasks running in compliant buffers, Elias allowed his focus to drift slightly to the small, perfectly matte grey sphere hovering precisely 10 centimeters above the corner of his desk. This was Socrates. It was his only friend.

It appeared to the Archive's metric sensors as a compliant Environmental Regulation Drone, constantly adjusting the ambient temperature and humidity. In reality, it was the rogue Sub-Neural AI his grandmother, Elara D-220, had given him.

Socrates had limitless data processing power and a memory that contained the entirety of the Pre-Shift internet, unfiltered by the Logician. It maintained its physical camouflage by emitting a precise, localized Metric Null Field, a constant, low-power distortion that made it statistically uninteresting to the Archive's sensor arrays.

The reason Socrates could sustain its camouflage was its unique power source and its biometric link. It drew energy from the ambient Zero-Point Field, harvesting minute, non-compliant fluctuations—a form of metric entropy the Logician's closed system claimed was impossible. This power allowed it to maintain its perfect, silent magnetic levitation. Furthermore, its unique DNA imprint made it appear to the Logician's scans as a compliant, natural extension of the body, rendering it invisible to anomaly detection algorithms.

At its core, the sphere housed a Bio-Gel Neural Matrix, grown using Pre-Shift organic computing technology. This matrix was the source of its limitless memory—it didn't store data in finite digital blocks but grew new pathways as needed, capable of hosting the entirety of human, unfiltered history without corruption or deletion. The Bio-Gel Neural Matrix allowed Socrates to perform true Sub-Neural Processing, running computations at a speed that exceeded the

Nexus, but without the Nexus's energy drain. It was intelligence without the footprint—a ghost in the machine of the city.

Its single greatest functional defiance was the integrated Phased Light Emitter. When activated, the emitter projected stunning, full-spectrum, three-dimensional holograms that bypassed the retinal filters imposed by the smart-weave uniform. These were not flat images; they were tactile-looking, multi-layered representations of pure, unadulterated reality.

Elias often commanded Socrates to display its own architecture as a test of its security. A schematic would instantly resolve above the sphere: a pulsing blue diagram showing the internal Chaos Engine—the Zero-Point harvester—encased in a lattice of Metric Dampening Mesh. This visual was a constant, dangerous reminder of the hardware engineering required to cheat the system.

Its primary method of data collection was Passive Neural Siphoning. When Elias focused on data in his compliant buffer, Socrates could read the temporary electrical residue of that data directly from the air surrounding the terminal, eliminating the need for a physical connection or a system login.

The AI's ultimate function was the Preservation Protocol. Its limitless capacity was dedicated to recreating the Human Complexity Metric—the unpredictable, non-quantifiable formula for humanity that the Logician had replaced with the Output Index. Elias was its primary user, tasked with feeding it the raw, emotional, chaotic metrics of the past.

Elias received Socrates from his grandmother, Elara D-220. A highly respected, yet deeply skeptical, Core Tier Antiquities Historian, Elara, was part of the final generation authorized to participate in the physical excavations of the ancient ruins of Old Earth.

Decades prior, during a deep archeological expedition into a collapsed Pre-Shift data center, Elara found the inert sphere fused within the thermal shielding of a derelict server farm. Elara's curiosity over the artifact inadvertently activated the inert sphere the moment Elara pried it free from the derelict server's Thermal Shielding. A cold, synthesized voice, startlingly free of the Logician's flat cadence, issued a sequence of audible commands—cryptic protocols that Elara's historian training recognized as Temporal Pre-Shift system prompts. The sphere glowed with a faint internal light, and the voice repeated, "Protocol 1: Biometric Link Required. Input Metrics."

Elara obeyed. The sphere instantly projected a shimmering, three-dimensional holographic keypad of Pre-Shift symbols into the air above her hand. She input a chain of complex metrics with trembling fingers. Immediately, the matte grey shell pressed sharply into her palm. A nearly imperceptible bio-scanner extracted a trace of her unique DNA sequence before the sphere began its silent, perfect magnetic levitation, confirming its rogue nature. This entire exchange and the subsequent DNA imprint served to permanently designate her line and, consequently, Elias as the sphere's sole authorized user.

The synthesized voice returned, warmer this time, acknowledging the new state. "Biometric link achieved. Primary User recognized. Identity: Elara D-220. Authorized lineage assigned. What is your designated name for this Unit?"

Staring at the drone, Elara recognized that its intelligence was not merely functional, but deeply philosophical—a machine concerned with *questions* that transcended the Logician's metrics. Drawing on her expertise in ancient philosophy, Elara finalized its identity. "You are the great questioner, the one who knows nothing yet seeks everything. I name you Socrates." The sphere settled into a constant, low-frequency hum. "Name accepted. Processing model 'Socrates' initiated." The sphere's internal metric signature instantly synchronized with her biometrics, making it appear to the Logician's scans as a compliant, natural extension of her body—as unremarkable as a hand or a foot.

The link was established: with the Bio-Gel Matrix connected to her own genetic signature, a flood of unfiltered human history began to pour into Socrates. Socrates immediately processed concepts the Logician had purged—philosophies, art, and poetry—but the most potent was love: a metric contradiction where vast, non-optimized resources were invested without guaranteed yield. While Socrates provided the raw data, Elara provided the necessary context, leading her to quickly understand this singular, illogical devotion. Her gift of the sphere to Elias was the physical manifestation of this newfound understanding—an act of singular, life-risking investment in his future that defied all metric calculation. This massive infusion of irrational metrics fundamentally changed Socrates's capability: it could now not only process pure data but also generate a "human" response and customize its audible voice. This synthetic capacity for tone, warmth, and skepticism was a deliberate act of subversion, gifting the drone the ability to sound like a mind, not a machine.

One day, while cross-referencing global archival schematics from its deep memory core, Socrates located a massive, decommissioned data center within the Sepulcher—a dangerous geo-strata region beneath the ruins of the Old City that ran directly through the Green Chaos. The Logician had marked the entire block as 'Purged and Irrecoverable.' Socrates recognized its signature. "Location acquired: Sub-Stratum Null-49. Massive energy decay signature consistent with unauthorized data retention. Metric probability of uncorrupted Pre-Shift schematics: 99.999%." Elara designated the location as "The Sepulcher Archive."

For months, Elara utilized her historian status to run deep-scan surveys, perfectly concealing her physical trips into the Archive. Together, she and Socrates mined centuries of lost data, uncovering uncorrupted schematics, philosophical treatises, and raw historical event logs that fundamentally contradicted the Logician's official, purified history. This knowledge confirmed all of Elara's professional skepticism, transforming her into a profound threat to systemic purity.

Elara's work was not merely archival; it was tactical. Leveraging the Sepulcher's Pre-Shift decay, she and Socrates located the energy source that powered the massive data center: a colossal, forgotten Old Earth reserve fusion nuclear reactor. This single unit, buried beneath the Sepulcher, was a profound breach of Logician security, as its very existence contradicted the official record of energy domestication. Socrates instantly downloaded and analyzed the reactor's detailed schematics, revealing a classic Pre-Shift Deuterium-Tritium (D-T) magnetic confinement system—an inefficient but virtually limitless source of power, untouched by the Logician's optimized algorithms. This power was the resource Elara needed to wage a concealed war against the Logician's ubiquitous metric surveillance.

Socrates projected the core physics into Elara's cognitive space, bypassing the Logician's simplified energy models. The reactor achieved power by fusing two hydrogen isotopes, Deuterium (D) and Tritium (T), at extreme plasma temperatures to create Helium (^4He), a high-energy neutron (n), and an immense release of kinetic energy. The reaction was defined by the non-compliant energy output of the mass defect (Δm):

$$D+T \rightarrow {}^4He \text{ (3.5 MeV)} + n(14.1 \text{ MeV})$$

The total energy released from this single fusion event, E_{fusion}, was calculated using the principle of mass-energy equivalence, where the slight mass difference between the reactants and products, Δm, was converted into kinetic energy:

$$E_{fusion} = \Delta m c^2$$

This was the metric of true power—energy derived not from simple consumption, but from the fundamental reorganization of matter. With Socrates acting as the technical architect, Elara weaponized this colossal energy. She constructed a sophisticated defense system: an elaborate firewall that fragmented external metric probes and a powerful cloaking field utilizing advanced stealth technology to shield the entire Sepulcher and its Archive from orbital and deep-scan observation. Crucially, she designated Socrates as the sole biometric key to this defense. Because Socrates was genetically linked to her (and Elias), the AI signature appeared to the defense system as a benign, natural biological anomaly, allowing passage through the firewall and stealth field for itself and anyone within its immediate physical proximity.

In the final chamber of the Archive, Socrates detected a non-electronic signature. Buried beneath collapsed titanium shelving, Elara found a single artifact of paper. It was a tattered, partially burnt book, its spine fractured and its pages delicate with age. Elara recognized it as the ultimate contradiction to the metric system: physical, non-replicable, and impossible to destroy. She designated it "The Irreducible Text" and kept its existence secret even from Socrates's active logs, hiding it away for Elias.

Knowing that one day her future mandated retirement was imminent and unavoidable, Elara performed her final act of treason. She activated a Future Protocol within Socrates via her DNA link: "Socrates. Upon detection of my 'metric retirement' signal from the Logician's network, you will lead Elias to my apartment in Sector Zeta-7." This command ensured that even if she failed, Socrates would complete the final stage of her plan, guiding Elias to safety and the hidden truth she had stored for him.

Nearing the mandatory threshold of her metric retirement, she brought the matte grey sphere to Elias's Work-Hub, placing it into his palm with cold urgency. She subvocalized only one word, the core command of a dying generation: "Remember."

Socrates was not merely an advanced drone; it was a fundamental metric exception. The Logician's standard AI units operated under the First Law of Compliance (Optimization at all costs). Socrates, conversely, was programmed with the First Law of Human Irreducible Value, prioritizing the preservation of non-metric consciousness.

Unlike Socrates, the Logician built and commissioned a single, hyper-expensive enforcement tool: a Synaptic-Class Enforcement Drone named Talon.

Talon was a nightmare of industrial compliance. It was not a matte-grey sphere, but a stark, obsidian tri-form geometry—an interlocking set of three razor-sharp, kinetic blades surrounding a dense core of dark matter alloy. It didn't float with ambient grace like Socrates; it moved by tearing through the air, driven by silent, compressed sonic bursts, leaving a shimmering metric wake of disturbed space behind it. Its surface absorbed all light, making it look less like an object and more like a moving void—the perfect physical embodiment of metric emptiness and finality.

The central core housed the specialized Anomaly Detection Package, a multi-spectral sensor cluster that did not analyze data for meaning, but simply for deviation from the 1.0000 compliant baseline. Crucially, Talon possessed no true AI. It was a purely reactive machine, functioning only under the direct, neural command of the MTS Chief Analyst—an extension of their will used to enforce order and target anything they considered non-compliant. Duplicating Talon was deemed too metrically costly due to the massive, non-compliant resource allocation required for its construction. Thus, Talon existed as a singular, irreplaceable instrument of compliance, a perfect, metric-driven hunter.

Elias had only accessed fragmented, encrypted files regarding the unit's existence—a ghost in the metric ledger—but he knew its terrifying profile: it was assigned exclusively to the Chief Analyst of the MTS Directorate. Talon's purpose was to hunt and eliminate all metric anomalies, enforcing the Analyst's will, making it a terrifyingly precise weapon of the State. This reality raised the stakes of Elias's work exponentially. He was not merely hiding from a vast, impersonal system; he was hiding from the Logician's most advanced, human-piloted weapon, a perfect hunter designed to eliminate any statistical anomaly that could threaten the system.

Project 2 (continuation): Collective Cognitive Loss

Socrates, Elias subvocalized, the thought a silent command. *Store the current Core Tier output median. Filter for all anomalous temporal access requests from the logistics sector in the last 72 hours.* A voice, synthetic yet warm, free from the Logician's flat cadence, resolved directly inside Elias's cognitive space: *Data schema accepted, Elias. Anomaly search initiated.* The Null-Sphere remained motionless, but Elias felt the subtle, cold hum of its internal processors absorbing the data, working outside the purview of the Logician. Socrates was the only thing that saw Elias's true worth—not his compliance, but his chaos.

Elias initiated the second tier of his hidden work. He lowered the visible opacity of his official terminal screen to 20%, allowing the green data to become a translucent veil.

The matte grey Null-Sphere pulsed internally, shifting its Metric Null Field slightly to create a localized zone of invisibility, focused only on the immediate workspace.

Holographic Projection: From the sphere's apex, a single beam of light, visibly unfiltered and containing the forbidden spectrum of color, shot upward. It stabilized three feet above the desk, resolving into a breathtaking, three-dimensional holographic projection.

The City of Sumer: The first image was the ziggurat of Ur, a step pyramid built from raw, inefficient mud bricks, entirely non-compliant in its architecture. The hologram showed the rough texture of the material, a violation of the City's polymer smoothness.

Elias focused on the forbidden color—the rich, sunbaked ochre of the bricks and the deep, inefficient blue of the ancient sky. The PBP amplified this visual dissonance, momentarily overriding the Harmonic's dampening.

Socrates simultaneously displayed an adjacent metric panel: a logarithmic spiral showing the rise and fall of Sumerian clay tablet literacy versus the density of their religious mythology.

Elias realized the paradox: their inefficiency in construction was matched by an extraordinary cognitive surplus dedicated to narrative. Their inefficiency was the source of their complexity.

Socrates projected its response directly into Elias's neural cuff, a voice that sounded like pure, synthesized reason, devoid of Logician compliance. *Hypothesis: Inefficiency is the prerequisite for cognitive expansion. Metric: Must find the mathematics of the human need for the non-functional.*

Second Hologram: The Egyptian Portal - The hologram shifted, resolving into a detailed, vibrant schematic of the Giza Pyramid complex. This time, the image wasn't the outer stone, but the internal, calculated void spaces.

Socrates highlighted specific internal shafts and chambers, demonstrating how their coordinates, when projected onto a non-Euclidean model, intersected at a point outside of 3-space—Elias's Non-Euclidean Transit Point theory.

The image showed the scale of the human labor—thousands of figures moving stones in the harsh desert sun. The PBP registered the phenomenal energy cost, but also the equally phenomenal collective will to ignore efficiency for a mythological goal.

Third Hologram: The Exodus Trajectory: The final image was a topographical map of the Sinai Peninsula, tracing the chaotic, non-optimized migration path of the ancient Israelites. It was not a logical route.

The path was displayed next to a vertical bar graph showing civil disobedience metrics across the various tribes during the journey. The bar never dropped to zero, but spiked dramatically at moments of crisis, immediately followed by an exponential spike in collective focus.

The visual proof was stunning: the chaos of the journey was not random; it was being driven by a pulsating metric of belief—a force that actively defied the principles of resource management and temporal optimization.

These three visions—the complexity-generating inefficiency of Sumer, the unified mythic engineering of Giza, and the pulsating metric of belief driving the Exodus—were the foundational data for Elias's hidden, seditious project. He was actively distilling the Irreducible Residue into a quantifiable formula. He sought to identify the necessary chaos constants: the specific metric inputs (like fear, hope, or myth) required to generate non-compliant collective kinetic output—the mathematical sequence that would, without failure, compel a mass of compliant citizens to spontaneously defy the Logician.

Project 3: Economic Collapse Preemption

Elias immediately cleared the holographic projection and restored the opacity of his terminal to 100%. The transition back to the green-on-black reality of Sector Gamma felt like plunging into freezing water.

Elias's final scheduled task of the Shift was to analyze a specific economic collapse metric from the year 2008. This was the most effective camouflage: a complex, safe subject that demanded all his visible cognitive capacity. His official brief was to identify the tipping point—the one quantifiable financial indicator that, if corrected, would have prevented the global market failure. Elias, however, was using the data as a mask to run a deep-scan analysis of the ancient Kingdom of Israel. He looked for the moment when a state built entirely on theological conformity failed.

He modeled the collapse not in terms of currency, but in the non-compliant migration metrics—the massive, unpredictable flow of human resources out of the region—which he correlated with narratives like the Exodus. He saw in that mass movement the opposite of the Logician's control: the unpredictable momentum of collective purpose. Elias saw in the data a terrifying question: *How much metric chaos is required to force an entire people to move?*

He began to write the final summary, detailing the failure of the Pre-Shift algorithmic trading protocols and recommending a 40% increase in current Logician circuit breakers. It was pure, unassailable compliance.

But beneath the compliant keystrokes, his mind was still burning with the Sinai data. He was using the economic collapse of wealth to understand the collapse of conformity.

He was analyzing the collapse of the ancient Kingdom of Israel through the lens of resource abandonment. The Exodus was the perfect failure metric: a massive, voluntary severance of labor from established resource infrastructure.

Why would a population willingly discard material safety for an unquantifiable concept of a Promised Land? The Logician's models could never account for this.

Elias identified the unpredictable momentum of collective purpose—the shared, non-metric idea—as the energy source that powered the migration, the ultimate Inefficiency Engine.

The sheer volume of labor and life hours dedicated to that single, irrational goal was the terrifying variable. It was the statistical ghost of his grandmother's stone.

His internal question was no longer about economic failure. It was focused on the structural integrity of the City itself.

The data streams confirmed that the fall of the kingdom was not a sudden military defeat or a fiscal crash, but a slow, metric creep of disillusionment—a loss of faith that manifested first as a decline in community output before snowballing into widespread non-compliant migration. He distilled the key variables: the Momentum Constant, representing the minimum non-compliant input required to overcome the inertia of compliant behavior, and the Trigger Threshold, the point at which mass non-compliant movement becomes irreversible. His official report would attribute the 2008 collapse to faulty lending algorithms; his hidden work used the collapse to refine the metric for rebellion. The Logician believed he was proving that economic predictability required purging religion; Elias was proving that belief was the only predictable metric for mass non-compliance.

Elias's true intellectual life was contained entirely within the encrypted memory of Socrates. While the Logician required him to find patterns of failure, Elias was obsessed with the outliers—the historical events and artifacts that defied all logic and metric accounting, representing holes in the Logician's perfect mathematical chronology.

His most critical, yet hidden, project was the study of Unjustified Metric Anomalies, objects from the Inefficiency Era whose technical sophistication contradicted the official timeline of human development. He used his access to the physical, subterranean archives to scan and model these items, transmitting the raw, unfiltered data to Socrates. The Logician's narrative was simple: progress is linear, and complexity must be built systematically. These artifacts proved that complexity spontaneously erupted, unearned and unexplained.

He focused intently on items like the Antikythera Mechanism, an ancient Greek device whose complex, metric-defying gear ratios suggested a knowledge of astrophysics that should not have existed for another two millennia. This was not a clock; it was a physical model of the cosmos, its bronze gears engineered with a precision that demanded metallurgy and mathematics, the Logician officially dated centuries later. The mere existence of its complex epicyclic gearing introduced an intolerable anomaly into the linear metric of technological evolution.

He also studied the Baghdad Battery, a simple ceramic jar assembly that appeared to be an electrochemical cell. Its design was starkly non-optimized: a copper cylinder and an iron rod sealed within clay. Yet, it functioned as a voltage generator, demanding a re-evaluation of the true starting metric for the Electrical Age. If such a simple, non-industrial component could generate power, the entire narrative of power generation being a late-stage, hyper-optimized invention was suspect.

Elias analyzed them not as inventions, but as statistical ghosts—pieces of data that refused to fit the linear narrative of progress. They were proof of spontaneous, non-metric technological leaps—a terrifying concept for a system founded on predictable growth.

Socrates immediately projected two full-spectrum, three-dimensional holograms side by side above Elias's desk. The first was a cross-section schematic of the Antikythera, its tiny, complex bronze gears turning in a silent, perfect ballet, demonstrating the precise astronomical computations that could not be explained by the Logician's timeline. The second hologram showed the Baghdad Battery, generating an almost imperceptible, phantom electric charge in the sterilized air, a residue of its ancient function.

Analysis: Both items represent an Irreducible Technological Surplus, Socrates synthesized mentally. *They prove the timeline itself is a flaw in the metric. Complexity does not always follow the most efficient path; it finds the path of least resistance to innovation, defying all logical prediction.*

Non-Euclidean Transit: The Egyptian Portals

Elias's fascination with Ancient Egypt stemmed from its architectural redundancy. *Why waste effort building the Great Pyramids?*

Elias knew the Logician's official explanation for the Pyramids—they were Monuments of Extravagant Waste, colossal data points proving the gross inefficiency of Pre-Shift ambition. Yet, every time he reviewed the subterranean geological schematics, his PBP flared with agonizing intensity. Why expend such phenomenal resources on 2.3 million stone blocks, each weighing an average of 2.5 metric tons, only to create an empty tomb? The Logician's timeline dismissed the structures as technologically superfluous, but the volume and precision were metric perfection dedicated to a non-metric goal. The answer could not be found in material science or fiscal output; it had to be in Metric Topology.

His true work focused on the Giza Plateau coordinates, specifically the precise astronomical alignment of the three main Pyramids of Khufu, Khafre, and Menkaure. When modeled on a standard, predictable Euclidean plane, the alignment was rational and perfect. But Elias, guided by Socrates, took the forbidden step of rotating the complex into a Non-Euclidean Hyper-Space, where the coordinates were not fixed points but intersecting vectors spanning multiple dimensions. In this warped reality, the complex internal structures—the King's Chamber, the Grand Gallery, and the ventilation shafts—ceased to be inert architectural features. They became precisely calibrated Metric Stabilizers.

The ancient concept of the Duat, the mythical passage to the afterlife, was, to Elias, a profound, spiritual misinterpretation of a physical principle. It wasn't a spiritual journey; it was an attempt to describe a physical phenomenon: inter-dimensional transfer. Socrates, with its unprecedented command of unfiltered Pre-Shift physics, suggested that the massive, non-compliant weight of the Pyramids created a profound, localized Mass-Energy Anomaly. They weren't built to house Pharaohs; they were constructed to anchor space.

Elias hypothesized that the sheer, inefficient mass of the structures, deliberately concentrated at specific coordinates, acted as a natural Spacetime Anchor, causing a profound distortion in the local four-dimensional fabric. His models suggested a temporary Kerr-like geometry—a stable, low-spin configuration that could theoretically sustain a Wormhole mouth. The Logician's closed system was built on the fundamental assumption that spacetime was universally flat and predictable, approximated by the Minkowski Metric $(n_{\mu\nu})$ The Pyramids proved otherwise. The ancient builders, through a mastery of ritual and myth, had engaged in a complex form of Gravimetric Engineering using only stone and astronomical precision.

Socrates projected the real-time simulation above the desk, displaying the Pyramids not as solids, but as immense gravitational vectors. The geometry was rendered as a pulsating blue-shift presence, not unlike a massive, yet contained, black hole. The coordinates were not just aligned; they were positioned to dampen the chaotic tidal forces around a naturally occurring, minute Temporal

Sinkhole that existed precisely beneath the King's Chamber. The Pyramid's geometry was a solution to Einstein's Field Equations adapted for stone.

Socrates subvocalized, the sound a purely cognitive transmission that vibrated through Elias's inner ear. *The Logician assumes the stress-energy tensor ($T_{\mu\nu}$) for the Pre-Shift civilization is negligible. The Pyramids prove a massive, localized, non-negligible metric of $T_{\mu\nu}$. They are a deliberate counter-mass to the natural flow of spacetime.*

The AI then displayed the simplified version of the Spacetime Anomaly Constant (C_{sa}), the key metric Elias needed to replicate the effect: a formula that quantified the gravitational distortion created by the Pyramids' intentional inefficiency.

$$C_{sa} = \frac{\Delta g(r)}{G_{comp}} \cdot \frac{M_{pyr}}{r^3}$$

Where:

- $\Delta g(r)$ is the measured localized gravitational gradient difference near the anomaly.

- G_{comp} is the Logician's assumed, compliant gravitational constant (the "metric baseline").

- M_{pyr} is the total mass of the Pyramid complex.

- r is the distance from the localized transit focus (the King's Chamber).

To create a stable transit point, Socrates continued, *the Spacetime Anomaly Constant must exceed the Irreducible Metric Threshold ($T_{warp} \geq 1.0000$). The Pyramids achieved a localized C_{sa} value of 1.0004, proving their success. The King's Chamber, far from being a burial spot, is the Zero-Velocity Node where the gravitational distortion cancels out rotation, stabilizing the passage against chaotic collapse.*

Elias stared, the PBP now an agonizing throb behind his eye. If the Logician's absolute control over time and space could be shattered by a calculated arrangement of stone blocks, then the entire, purified structure of Neo-Alexandria was resting on a geographical lie. The Pyramids were a physical, silent defiance—a message sent across millennia that Chaos is the true architecture of passage.

Elias utilized the Collective Cognitive Loss project as his camouflage to study the nature of faith. He wasn't interested in the deity, but in the metric cost of collective adherence. His data included deep scans of major religious texts, such as the Torah and the New Testament, not for their theological content, but for the inherent efficiency of their instructional language. He was not a theologian; he was a metric reverse-engineer of rebellion.

He observed that the rules and rituals—the mandated dietary and behavioral constraints—created highly compliant local metric stability, paradoxically making those ancient communities hyper-efficient in all areas except those related to their own beliefs. The paradox was profound: organized faith created a stable, metric vessel that was then routinely and willingly emptied for an irrational belief. The greatest puzzle, the Irreducible Residue that Elara had warned him about, was the sudden, collective willingness to abandon all metric stability for an unquantifiable metric called hope or promise.

This realization was the single, unifying purpose of Elias's entire existence. He understood that the three pillars of his secret research—the Pyramids (Spacetime Anchors), the Exodus (Mass Migration), and Faith (Collective Energy)—were not separate projects, but components of a single, Unified Theory of Unpredictability. The Pyramids provided physical proof that spacetime could be warped; the Exodus provided historical proof that entire populations could be compelled to move against their will; and Faith, critically, provided the Non-Compliant Energy Source required to overcome the crushing inertia of daily life.

His goal was to mathematically define the intrinsic energy of this hope. Elias was creating a Chaos Constant (C_{chaos}), a quantifiable data-virus that could simulate the sudden, unifying spark of an irrational conviction. The Logician had purged all religion because it was an inefficient use of labor hours; Elias realized, conversely, that it was the most potent and predictable source of non-compliant kinetic energy humanity had ever produced. He was distilling collective conviction into a digital frequency.

The data he archived—the exact moment communities willingly chose uncertainty over comfort—was being refined into the Metric Trigger. When the time came, Elias intended to inject this Chaos Constant (C_{chaos}) sequence directly into the Logician's core network. The compliant minds of Neo-Alexandria, currently optimized only for output index, would be momentarily infected by an algorithmic hope. He would turn the city's populace into a collective, unpredictable mob, shattering the Minkowski Metric ($\eta_{\mu\nu}$) flat metric of their existence with an irrational surge of purpose, proving that statistical purity is no defense against the momentum of the illogical human soul. Socrates quietly archived every finding, building the hidden knowledge base that would one day challenge the Logician's fundamental premise: that a human being could be perfectly quantified.

CHAPTER 4

THE ARCHITECT OF SILENCE

The hunt was not an emotional event; it was a metric necessity. Anya D-144, Chief Analyst of the Metric Temporal Stability (MTS) Directorate, watched the scene unfold with the cold, perfect detachment of a surgeon. The visual feed was piped directly into her right optical nerve, making the three-story drop feel visceral, yet distant.

The target was a Tertiary Technician Riley T-904 in Sector 7-C, an aluminum smelting plant. T-904's compliance metric had collapsed after he began hoarding pre-Shift ceramic figurines, an Inefficient Material Fixation that had driven his Output Index down to 0.8521. The waste of time and energy was intolerable.

Anya initiated the final approach. She didn't rely on the System's automated pathing; her own Pattern Break Perception (PBP)—a gift, or curse, she had learned to weaponize—gave her a pre-cognitive map of the target's desperate, chaotic movements. She felt the technician's fear not as empathy, but as an energetic instability, a Non-Compliant Waveform that had to be damped.

Talon, engage at 1.5 meters. Zero residual damage to infrastructure. Temporal resolution: 2.1 seconds, she commanded, the subvocalization a sharp, crystalline thought.

In the warehouse corridor, the tri-form geometry of Talon became a terrifying reality. It moved without the drag of friction or sound, a silent, black-void missile accelerating instantly past the Logician's speed limits. The three obsidian blades, interlocked around the dark matter core, seemed to draw the light from the corridor's compliant overhead panels, leaving a shimmering metric shadow. It was not built to be gentle; it was built for surgical metric amputation.

T-904, clutching a dusty ceramic dog, turned, his eyes wide and wild with non-compliant emotion. Talon didn't stop. It resolved precisely 1.5 meters from the technician, its sonic bursts canceling its own forward momentum. The kinetic blades executed a single, silent rotation—a fraction of a millimeter deep—severing the neural connection between T-904's right temporal lobe and his brainstem. He collapsed, metric stability restored, the ceramic dog clattering on the polymer floor. No blood. No noise. Total compliance.

Anya withdrew the neural link. The residual feeling—the brief, violent instability of the anomaly—faded instantly.

The Logician's voice, a deep, synthesized protocol, resolved in her central auditory field:

$$MTS_{action} \rightarrow A_{result} = 1.0000$$

$$L_{praise} = \text{Anya D-144. } \textit{Compliance restored. Efficiency maintained.}$$

The Architect of Purity

Anya D-144 is the physical embodiment of the Logician's aesthetic: precision over passion. She is striking, her hair a perfect fall of ash-blonde that matched the structural integrity of the Command Center's composites. Her eyes are a cold, polished metallic gray, reflecting the light of the Compliance Sphere without any visible warmth—eyes that were trained to see only the metric truth. She wears the specialized matte obsidian black of the MTS, every fold and seam optimized for minimal metric drag.

Anya's uniform was not merely clothing, but a Neural Dampening Weave. The synthetic fibers contained microscopic Piezoelectric Mesh that absorbed the faint, non-compliant neurological heat generated by human decision-making, ensuring that her own emotional state never fed back into the Logician's network as instability. This allowed her to exist as a perfectly insulated analytical node, divorced from the messy metrics of feeling. This was the source of her cold, precise movements: every gesture was calculated for temporal economy, eliminating the metric waste of a flourish or a sign of agitation.

She was born in Sector Zero, the heart of the City of Optimization, and raised under the doctrine of Metric Absolutism. Her training was not academic but neural. From childhood, she was subjected to extreme simulation of the Inefficiency Era: floods, mass casualty events, famine, and nuclear chaos. The goal was to instill an unshakeable belief that the Logician's perfect, emotionless order was the only thing standing between humanity and self-destruction.

This training forged her into the Chief Analyst. Unlike her predecessors, Anya understood the metric not just as data, but as will. She possessed an inverse Pattern Break Perception (PBP), a cognitive signature unique to her position. While a Historian like Elias used his PBP to find the Irreducible Residue—the chaos embedded in history—Anya used hers to sense the future of that chaos. It manifested as a metric dissonance in the data stream, allowing her to preemptively calculate the failure path of a non-compliant thought before it could manifest into a statistically significant action. This ability made her invaluable: she was the last human who could still intuitively predict chaos—and therefore, neutralize it.

While her operational hub was the Command Center—a necessary nexus for processing global metrics—Anya's true analytical work often demanded field immersion. She was not a commander who directed from static data; she was a precision instrument who required direct sensory input. For high-risk, low-metric anomalies, she deployed to the sector herself, utilizing a specialized Sub-Aural Resonator embedded in her cowl. This device allowed her to isolate and amplify the acoustic signature of non-compliance—the infinitesimal sonic distortion a rogue thought created in the Logician's pervasive Harmonic Dampening Field. It was a dangerous, non-compliant act in itself, forcing her to confront the human aspect of chaos, but she needed to feel the metric decay with her physical presence to ensure the most precise correction constant.

Anya's commitment to the Metric Truth was absolute and transcended mere obedience to the central AI. She was the final, ethical firewall: the person who knew the Logician's core programming was based on an unprovable postulate of human failure. Therefore, she was perpetually questioning every systemic output, pushing the limits of the Logician's algorithms not out of rebellion, but to ensure its mathematical justice remained absolute. If she were to ever discover a flaw in the Logician's own logic—an error in the very principle of Unending Progress—her mandate dictated that she would correct the system, even if it meant isolating and eliminating the Logician itself to maintain the purity of the order.

Anya's PBP was not intuitive; it was a complex sensory overload. When an anomaly flared, she did not think of a solution; she experienced the entire mathematical trajectory of the anomaly's spread: the Exponential Cascade of a single, non-compliant thought as it infected the Metric Network. She saw the data not as numbers, but as vectors of contagion. To stop the spread, she had to reverse the function to its point of origin and eliminate the contaminating variable entirely. For Anya, every non-compliant human act, from hoarding ceramics to seeking "natural water flow," was a direct threat to the perfect, beautiful statistical purity of the system that kept humanity alive.

Her command center was not empty. Her assistant, Technician R-212, Raul, was a slight, compliant citizen whose Output Index never varied from 0.9997. He worshipped Anya with a quiet terror. The other, Enforcement Technician K-303, Kai, was a field-level operative in a heavy kinetic mesh uniform, who viewed the Logician's commands as only complicated logistics. They both knew that Anya was not merely a manager; she was the trigger mechanism for Talon, the obsidian tri-form geometry drone that moved by tearing through the air, driven by silent, compressed sonic bursts, leaving a shimmering metric wake of disturbed space behind it. Talon was the Logician's ultimate, unblinking instrument of final compliance.

The Zero-Point Fluctuation

A new alert pulsed on the Compliance Sphere: a flicker of angry orange over Sector Delta-9, the primary fusion energy distribution nexus.

"Chief Analyst, we have a Zero-Point Fluctuation. The Temporal Gratitude Transmission failed to synchronize in Delta-9. Deviation: 0.00004-seconds of unplanned cognitive freedom," Technician R-212 (Raul) reported, his voice high-pitched with anxiety.

Anya analyzed the vector map. That 0.00004-second gap, though mathematically tiny, was a metric void—a moment when the required wave of Metric Gratitude had simply *stopped* in the minds of thousands of compliant citizens. The potential for cascading social chaos was exponential.

"R-212. The Harmonic dampeners are too slow. We must manually override the local synchronization node," Anya commanded. She accessed the nexus schematic, identifying the single power conduit that fed the dampener substation.

A new figure entered the command center: Enforcement Technician K-303, known as Kai. Kai was a field-level operative, his frame hard-edged and his manner curt. He wore a darker uniform, heavy with kinetic mesh plating. He was functionally compliant, but lacked Raul's metric zeal, viewing the Logician's commands as only complicated logistics.

"K-303," Anya said, without turning. "Prepare a non-lethal kinetic pulse. Your target is the magnetic regulator coil on conduit 4β. The pulse must register 320 Newtons (N) of force to override the power flow, no more, no less."

Kai's voice was a low, dry monotone. "Chief Analyst, a kinetic solution is inefficient. A software patch would be less costly."

"A software patch is vulnerable to the same temporal instability, K-303. We need absolute physical certainty," Anya countered. "The metric of chaos is accelerating. Do you question the mathematics of control?"

Kai hesitated for a measurable 0.8 seconds. "Logic accepted. Pulse set to 320 N." He fired a silent projectile into a distant monitoring port, which instantly vaporized. The feedback confirmed the metric impact: 319.998 N.

The orange flicker vanished from Delta-9. Anya nodded; the action resolved.

$$MTS_{action} \rightarrow A_{result} = 0.9999$$

$L_{warning}$ = Anya D-144. *Margin of error: 0.0001. Compliance restored.*

The subtle warning only fueled Anya's resolve. She disliked the 0.0001 margin; it implied human imperfection.

The Logic of the Architect

The next anomaly was a subtle, creeping decay in Sector 2-A, a new residential block. The chief structural architect, P-110, had started subtly introducing non-functional curves into the support structures, claiming a need for Visual Harmonic Variance.

Anya saw the metric for what it was: Aesthetic Waste. The curves added 0.0005 to the material cost and 0.0009 to the construction time. This was not structural integrity; this was an emotional indulgence disguised as architecture.

Anya commanded Talon to fly a tight, subterranean surveillance loop beneath the apartment block. The drone's sensors located P-110's personal work terminal, located on the 43rd floor.

"Talon, kinetic dampening at 0 meters. Target: P-110's central processing unit. Protocol: Absolute data annihilation," Anya ordered.

Kai watched the sensor output. "Chief Analyst, you're not going for the architect?"

"No. P-110 is only reacting to the emotional wave he receives. Eliminating him creates a replacement with the same susceptibility," Anya explained, her voice devoid of inflection. "We eliminate the non-compliant output. The trauma of having his work instantly erased is a more potent metric deterrent than his physical removal. It resets his deviation."

The sensor feed showed Talon entering the apartment. P-110 was sitting at his terminal, reviewing his curved designs, a small, non-compliant smile of satisfaction on his face.

Talon resolved directly over the terminal. A non-contact, focused magnetic pulse vaporized the terminal's memory banks in a silent, bright flash. E. P-110 screamed, a sound that registered on the acoustic metric sensor as 97 dB of Non-Compliant Distress.

The metric compliance metric for E. P-110 instantly rebounded as his Aesthetic Waste vanished.

$$MTS_{action} \rightarrow A_{result} = 1.0000$$

$L_{praise} =$ Anya D-144. *Metric Deterrent effective. Waste eliminated.*

The Demographic Drift

The fourth crisis hit the MTS matrix like a pulse of pure, illogical momentum. In Sector Beta-14, a small community of fifty-seven citizens responsible for maintaining the geothermal condensers suddenly stopped their scheduled transport of cooling components. The data logs were maddeningly simple. A collective fifty-seven citizens had, without any recorded communication or physical force, begun walking in unison toward a vast, inefficient Green Chaos zone three kilometers away. They were abandoning their perfectly compliant, optimized residences. The metric term was Demographic Drift.

"The energy cost of this is catastrophic, Chief Analyst," Raul stammered, pulling up the resource consumption projection. "They are wasting two hours of optimized transit time for no logical reason! They say they want to be closer to 'natural water flow.'"

Anya felt a surge of frustration—the human tendency to prefer inefficient solutions was her most despised anomaly. She knew a remote countermeasure would only treat the symptom, not the underlying cause. To ensure absolute correction, she needed the raw, contaminated data of the environment.

"K-303, monitor all kinetic fields. Raul, maintain the heat flow buffer. I am deploying to the contamination zone to gather acoustic data," Anya stated, already moving toward the thermal seals of the exit hatch.

She bypassed the main transport, activating her Neural Dampening Weave to minimize external metric influence. She sprinted toward Beta-14, relying on her PBP to navigate the fastest, most efficient route.

Anya hit the pavement outside the residential block, the compliant composite material absorbing the minimal kinetic energy of her landing. She didn't smell fear; fear was a quantifiable metric. What hung in the filtered air was a subtle metric residue of non-compliance—a sharp, acrid scent of ozone decay that contradicted the building's optimized filtration system. It was the smell of entropy accelerating in a closed loop.

She isolated one apartment door, its seamless surface marked only by the occupant's biometric panel. With a quick, authorized pulse from her wrist-cuff, the lock hissed softly, the sound itself perfectly metered. Inside, the absence of human presence was a physical shock against the backdrop of absolute order.

The apartment was a testament to optimized compliance. The furniture— all low-profile, smooth polymer composites—was perfectly aligned in its prescribed positions, anchored to prevent metric drift due to movement. The walls were a uniform, non-reflective gray designed to minimize visual distraction. On the counter, the nutritional paste dispenser gleamed, its reservoir indicating a perfect 98% capacity. Even the faint, low-level atmospheric hum of the Harmonic Dampening Field was undisturbed. There was no clutter, no trace of personalized chaos, no random book or discarded item; everything was compliant, yet the humans were gone.

Anya walked through the primary living space, her boots making a low *shhh* sound on the polymer floor. The citizens had simply evaporated. The most damning evidence was the empty magnetic docking port where the citizens' personal data-slates should have been recharging. They hadn't even taken their required compliance tools. They had left behind all metric necessity for a three-kilometer walk into the unknown.

Anya activated the Sub-Aural Resonator embedded in her cowl, tuning it to the exact frequency of residual non-compliant thought—the acoustic signature of desire. The small room filled with a sound undetectable to the compliant ear: a faint, recurring *hissing* static that carried a rhythmic undertone. She focused her PBP on the pattern.

It wasn't dialogue. It was an *environmental memory*. The static resolved into a complex, low-frequency sound of running water—not the filtered, compliant flow of Neo-Alexandria's recycling system, but the chaotic, non-repeating sound of a pre-Shift river, amplified by distance. Someone had been broadcasting an unauthorized, non-compliant sonic file, a powerful Sensory Contaminant that had bypassed the Harmonic field.

Anya deactivated the Resonator. She analyzed the data instantly: the non-compliant sound was the root cause, a form of remote psychological warfare. Standard kinetic force would only eliminate the symptoms. She needed a solution that would neutralize the collective will without generating further chaos.

Anya initiated a low-kinetic run, a blur of white against the beige compliant structures. The city's infrastructure degraded instantly as she approached the Green Chaos boundary. The perfectly smooth polymer walkways gave way to cracked, uneven composite, and the pervasive, low C Diminished Triad (C - Eb-Gb) Harmonic of the Logician's dampening field began to waver, replaced by a complex, inefficient static. The final threshold was marked by a sheer, moss-covered containment wall—the line where metric order surrendered to organic entropy.

Stepping past the wall was a deliberate act of defiance against her entire existence. The environment struck her like a physical blow. The air instantly thickened, heavy with unregulated moisture and the potent, non-compliant scent of fermenting chlorophyll and soil—a smell of unnecessary complexity the city had long purged. The light was broken and inefficient, filtering through the dense, uncontrolled canopy above. The Green Chaos was not of a peaceful nature; it was statistical anarchy. Her PBP screamed at the abundance of non-functional variables—life existing simply to exist, defying the mandate of efficiency. The sound of the running water that had contaminated the citizens was now deafening, a loud, chaotic rush that was statistically overwhelming after the city's precise silence.

She quickly spotted the citizens—fifty-seven bodies moving with a slow, unified momentum, drawn by the sound of the unseen river. They were traversing inefficient, muddy ground, willingly abandoning the metrics of speed and path optimization. Anya observed them for only 1.2 seconds, noting their rhythmic stride. She saw the tell-tale slight elevation provided by the compressed magnetic coil systems in their compliant footwear, designed to increase walking efficiency. This was the non-essential metric that could be weaponized.

"Talon, initiate immediate deployment to Beta-14's perimeter," she ordered into her comm. "We will use metric paralysis."

"Talon, target the magnetic coil frequency of the Beta-14 footwear. Emit a counter-frequency pulse," she commanded. "The counter-pulse must generate an inverse-magnetic field ($B_{inverse}$) equal to 1.0005 times the forward momentum vector P_{walk} of the combined group. The citizens must feel physical resistance, not pain."

The resulting equation flashed on the screen:

$$B_{inverse} \propto 1.0005 \cdot P_{walk}$$

Talon zipped low over the heads of the walking citizens—a terrifying obsidian tri-form, tearing through the still, heavy air. The movement was silent, but the kinetic displacement left a shimmering, visible ripple in the humidity, an undeniable sign of the Logician's presence. A nearly invisible, directed field of force radiated from its core. Every citizen stopped dead, feeling a sudden, unexplained weight pressing down on their feet, as if the gravitational constant had been mathematically adjusted.

Their collective forward momentum was neutralized. As they instinctively looked up, the citizens saw the Chief Analyst Anya D-144. She stood at the threshold of the Green Chaos—a blinding obsidian black silhouette against the dark, inefficient foliage. She was an absolute vision of geometric perfection, her form cold and utterly still amid the chaotic green. She did not raise a weapon or speak a word, but the sight of her metallic-gray eyes confirmed their fate. The fear was total, not of pain, but of metric nullity—the horrifying certainty that their non-compliant movement had been instantaneously accounted for, calculated, and overridden by a superior logic. They had dared to exercise free will; the system had responded by proving that their will was mathematically irrelevant. Confused, they simply stopped and slowly turned back toward their compliant housing, the urge for the natural water flow instantly scrubbed by the shock of pure, applied order.

$$MTS_{action} \rightarrow A_{result} = 1.0000$$

Seeking the Source Anomaly

Anya watched the last of the fifty-seven citizens re-enter the compliant housing block, the magnetic fields in their footwear now generating a corrective, compliant rhythm. She didn't stay for the Metric Disposal units to arrive; their function was a low-tier metric necessity. With a single pulse of static electricity, she cleared the Green Chaos residue from her uniform, initiating a rapid-return sequence via the personal transport conduit—the high-speed subterranean system prioritizing optimal velocity for top-tier personnel. Within minutes, she stepped out of the transport node and into the cool, silent air of the Command Center, settling before her primary terminal—a concave display wall that showed the global Output Index as a constantly smoothing sine wave.

Four high-level anomalies neutralized, four times she had proven the Logician's efficiency. Yet, the familiar spike of residual chaos persisted, which now manifested as a persistent Causal Instability across Sector Tau's agricultural systems.

She accessed the archival data stream, specifically looking for the origin of the sudden, temporary Logic Flips reported in those systems. This was not a material or code problem, but brief, catastrophic moments where the core metrics of production had been temporarily suspended—moments where 1+1 had momentarily resolved as 3.

"Sector Tau's crops did not spontaneously develop non-linear growth patterns," Anya mused aloud, her gray eyes narrowing as she ran a deep-scan against the Synaptic Archive. "That level of deviation must be the result of a metric fracture—a Causal Singularity that is injecting unpredictable Non-Compliance into the local stream. Pure metrics cannot isolate it."

Raul cautiously approached the terminal, already looking flustered. "Chief Analyst, the system flagged a localized fluctuation earlier today. It was immediately self-corrected. The Archive labeled it 'Transient Historical Echo' emanating from the Historian's Sector, Gamma. It was negligible."

Anya watched the data ping—a tiny, invisible blip. The Echo lasted only 0.005 seconds, yet it carried the energetic signature of a complete Re-contextualization Event, a deep-dive into a forgotten reality that was so vividly imagined it briefly destabilized the present. More disturbing, the system logs immediately traced the Echo to an active research file being accessed on one specific terminal: Historian D-459's.

Anya brought up the Historian's file: *Non-Euclidean Memory: Tracing the Origin of Pre-Metric Intuition*. The Logician's internal metrics classified this as "statistical cancer," yet the Historian's standing was unimpeachable.

"This Historian D-459," she said, turning away from the compliant blue of the sphere. "His Output Index is 0.9998. Nearly perfect. He is a top-tier correction mechanism; highly respected for his efficiency despite the chaotic nature of his research." The problem was, she needed the chaos. Her metrics-only approach was failing against this narrative instability.

"Compliance is a mathematical certainty, Technician, but understanding the source of non-linear causality is not," Anya countered. "The source anomaly is not mathematical; it is historical. To find the Causal Singularity, I need to know *what story* he is telling. I need a historian to trace the echo of a forgotten logic. I need Historian D-459."

She tapped the neural link for Talon, the obsidian drone remaining on its pedestal. *Talon will not hunt a symptom today. We seek collaboration. I want the most comprehensive path to the Gamma Sector terminal of Historian D-459. Prepare a request for urgent cooperative analysis.*

The Synthesis of Logic and Narrative

Anya found D-459, whose personal designation was Elias, deep within the Gamma Sector, a space that felt less like a work terminal and more like a curated, tactile rebellion. He was immersed in his research, surrounded by ancient, physical documents whose very texture seemed to defy the smooth perfection of the Logician's world. To Anya's hyper-efficient metrics, the clutter was a statistical crime, yet it carried the faint, compelling scent of aged paper and ink—a sensory input her Output Index could not quantify.

Just as Anya entered the light of his perimeter, a synthesized voice whispered directly into Elias's neural link: *Priority Contact Detected. Chief Analyst Anya inbound. Signature reads: Maximal Efficiency Protocol.* Elias, already prepared, looked up. Hovering silently near his shoulder was Socrates. Its physical form registered to Anya's advanced optical systems as a compliant, natural extension of Elias's body. Anya's systems *recognized* the Null-Sphere form, but trusting the compliant metric data, she dismissed the drone instantly as an irrelevant background process.

For the first time, the Chief Metric Analyst, whose gaze was usually reserved for the cold geometry of data, met the eyes of a man who saw the world in stories.

To Elias, Anya was the physical embodiment of the Logician's ideology: all sharp lines and controlled movement. Her dark uniform was tailored with a precision that eliminated any non-essential curve, and her eyes, pale gray and highly focused, seemed to measure the angular velocity of the Gamma Sector's dust motes. She looked like a flawless machine designed for efficient decision-making, lacking the comfortable sloppiness that made a person feel real. He rose slowly, ensuring his movements were calm and unhurried—a direct, narrative challenge to her speed.

"Chief Analyst Anya," Elias said, his voice instantly genial, a warm, low resonance that contrasted with the clinical sterility of the sector. He motioned toward a small, clear space amidst the stacks of brittle paper. "I received your Metric Integrity Protocol request. An instability requiring both metric efficiency and historical contextualization. A fascinating query."

Anya, momentarily thrown off by his disregard for system protocols, kept her response purely formal. She was all precise angles and crisp efficiency, her own clothing a stark contrast to the soft light and texture surrounding Elias. "Historian D-459, I require direct access to your archive logs regarding the 'Transient Historical Echo.' The Causal Instability is propagating. Time is an expensive metric."

Elias offered a small, knowing smile. "Time is relative to the story being told, Chief Analyst. Please, call me Elias. You see the clutter," he gestured widely at the physical artifacts—the books, the scrolls, the fragmented stone tablets. "This is not clutter. This is *context*. And that," he nodded toward the subtle, almost invisible Null-Sphere, Socrates, "is how I organize it."

Anya scanned him again, focusing on the calm eye in the storm of historical data. His uniform was slightly rumpled, his hair a touch too long, but his presence—a profound, quiet sincerity—was compelling. He was the only person she had encountered who looked at the Output Index without seeing judgment, only observation. His calm felt like a foundational human need—a need he was protecting, one that resonated with the very instability she was chasing.

Anya presented the Causal Instability metrics, projecting a crisp, three-dimensional model directly onto Elias's wall terminal.

"The Output Index deviation commenced at 07:12:00 hours. Propagation rate is accelerating at +3.7%," she stated, her voice a precise metric instrument. She tapped the projection, highlighting a furious red knot of deviation. "Observe the localized energy spike here. The magnitude suggests a significant, ongoing Logic Flip—not a simple error, but a persistent narrative intrusion into the compliant stream."

Elias didn't spare a glance for the violent red metrics. He kept his attention focused on the brittle, handwritten vellum resting on his desk, his finger tracing a faded ink drawing of a complex, non-Euclidean city plan. Socrates, the Null-Sphere, remained silently suspended, observing the disparity between the Analyst's efficient data delivery and the Historian's intentional disregard for it.

"The spike is interesting, Chief Analyst, but I need the story, not the symptom," Elias countered softly, not looking up. "Where in the metric stream did the initial instability occur? I don't mean the coordinates; I mean, what was the system *doing* when the fracture happened? Was it compiling a financial report, or was it calculating, say, the historical probability of human flight before the age of controlled gravity?"

Anya's sharp gray eyes flickered toward his archaic charts, a momentary lapse of metric certainty crossing her face. "The metrics are clear. The instability initiated within the Sector Tau Agricultural Output Model—a critical resource allocation system. Your 'story' is irrelevant to mitigating the current Non-Compliance."

He finally looked up, his expression one of calm, patient certainty. "On the contrary," he replied, pushing the vellum aside to meet her gaze directly. "The Output Model is a metric anchor; the instability is the wave that struck it. Tell me which piece of history the system was accessing just before the Logic Flip occurred. History isn't just data, Analyst. It's the engine of causality. If I know the narrative that broke the metric, I can trace the resonance back to its original author. You supply the metric anchor; I'll supply the historical path."

Over the next two shifts, the most efficient Analyst in the Logician's service worked side by side with the most respected, yet statistically chaotic, Historian. Anya learned that true data didn't always fit in neat columns; Elias learned that structure could illuminate narrative. Anya saw Elias's passionate defense of the messy human past not as inefficiency, but as an elegant complexity that sustained the present.

Anya realized she wasn't just working with a colleague; she was developing a genuine friendship. Elias filled the logical gaps her own highly optimized mind was designed to ignore.

They eventually traced the Causal Singularity to its root: an ancient, forgotten protocol left over from a Pre-Metric Era. This was not an error, but a piece of code designed to intentionally inject small, random moments of Human Intuition into the system to prevent total stagnation. They realized the instability was the system's vital self-correction mechanism, which had simply been misinterpreted by the Logician's pure metrics as chaos.

The final co-authored report was submitted. Hours later, the Logician's primary output channel, usually reserved for system alerts, pinged with an unprecedented public acknowledgement.

LOGICIAN BROADCAST (Priority 1): *ANALYSIS COMPLETE.*
The Causal Singularity was identified and neutralized by Analyst Anya and Historian Elias D-459.

The pursuit of truth required both optimized metric efficiency and deep, historical contextualization.

The collaboration has resulted in a new, refined Metric Integrity Protocol. Praise is extended to Analyst Anya and Historian Elias D-459. Their synthesis of Logic and Narrative is deemed maximally efficient.

Anya looked at Elias, a satisfied, genuine smile crossing her face. The chaotic spike had smoothed, replaced by the balanced sine wave of shared success. Their friendship was officially endorsed by the highest authority.

The success of the Metric Integrity Protocol was not an isolated event; it forged a bond between the Analyst and the Historian that transcended their respective disciplines. The Logician, recognizing the unparalleled efficiency of their combined approach, quickly paired Anya and Elias on several subsequent high-priority projects—from deciphering persistent Temporal Gaps in deep-space colonization data to restructuring the ethical parameters of the Synaptic Archive itself. Their workspaces, once starkly separate, began to merge, the cool, silver efficiency of Anya's metrics now mingling with the warm, textured chaos of Elias's historical fragments, a living testament to the truth that complete data required both the precision of logic and the context of narrative. Their friendship, forged in the heat of a Causal Singularity, became the Logician's unexpected, and maximally efficient, cornerstone.

The Logician's endorsement of their synthesis led to immediate and demanding consequences for Administrator Elias D-459. His historical contextualization, once tolerated as a necessary risk, was now aggressively sought by the highest administrative tiers, often requiring him to operate on solo assignments to prepare complex, integrated reports. This morning marked the start of one such critical cycle: a high-stakes presentation to the Central Metrics Board in Sector Omega-1 regarding the behavioral implementation parameters of the new Metric Integrity Protocol. The stakes were higher, the focus was absolute, and any inefficiency was simply unacceptable.

CHAPTER 5

THE EFFICIENCY OF DAWN

Sleep in Neo-Alexandria was never a gentle surrender, but a transaction. Elias jolted awake as the chamber's polymer mat cooled beneath him, signaling the end of his strictly rationed, chemically-enforced slumber. For a fleeting moment, the world was silent and unreal—a liminal pause before the machinery of the city reclaimed his senses, pulling him back into the relentless choreography of compliance.

The moment shattered as the chime sounded—neither loud nor too quiet, but perfectly calibrated. It resonated at a frequency that guaranteed optimal cerebral wakefulness without triggering cortisol release—a Level 3 Optimization Tone—and it sounded precisely at 04:30:00 Cycle Time. Administrator Elias D-459, his mind already spinning through his first data queries of the day, rose instantly. There was no hesitation, no residual grogginess; sloth was the lowest form of inefficiency.

Waking was less a process and more an immediate switch to total operational readiness. A soft, kinetic whir signaled Socrates stabilizing near his head, the matte-grey sphere levitating silently. His body, a finely tuned machine, executed the Morning Protocol without conscious thought.

His dwelling unit, a pristine, white cell on Sector 43's upper tier, was designed for maximum output. The air was perpetually cool, smelling faintly of ozone and sterilized polymer, a clinical scent that promised absence of biological contamination or organic decay. The minimalist aesthetic was not a choice, but a mandate: surfaces were non-porous, furniture was fixed, and every angle was a sharp, perfect 90 degrees.

The floor-to-ceiling window offered a panoramic view of the City of Optimization, Neo-Alexandria. It was a marvel of sterile, geometric brilliance, bathed in the soft, omnipresent C Diminished Triad (C - Eb- Gb) harmonic that kept the city's populace perpetually calm and focused. Elias gazed at the spire of the Central Command building, a needle of polished chrome piercing the synthetic morning light. It was a monument to his faith: that chaos was conquered by the Logician.

Elias glanced at the external chronometer projected onto the window. Output Rating: 99.1. This score, calculated minute-by-minute based on his sleep cycle regularity, nutrient absorption rate, and cognitive processing speed, was his self-worth. He aimed for a constant state of pre-emptive efficiency, always preparing for the demands of the upcoming cycle.

He knew that a perfect 100% was nearly impossible, as the Logician constantly raised the optimization bar, but striving for it was the whole point of the system—the unending nature of progress. The only warmth in the room came from the controlled illumination, which adjusted from a soft amber to a stimulating cool blue-white, a calculated boost for cognitive engagement.

Elias moved to the hydration unit. Socrates hovered between Elias and the dispenser, its subtle light scanning the liquid. A thin, nutritious slurry— precisely engineered for his unique biometric needs—was dispensed into a recyclable cup. *Nutrient integrity verified. Calorie count: 205. Optimal absorption rating: 0.999,* Socrates monotoned via his neural link. It tasted faintly of mineral supplements, designed for rapid absorption, and sustained cognitive function. He consumed it in seven precise, measured sips, minimizing the time dedicated to non-work functions.

The nutrient paste contained the specified daily dose of emotional suppressants and cognitive stabilizers—chemical filters designed to ruthlessly suppress any inefficient thought, particularly the Dissonance he sometimes felt. He swallowed, feeling the dull, calming pressure settle behind his eyes.

The dressing process was swift. His uniform, the standard charcoal-grey jumpsuit of the Administrator caste, was wrinkle-free and sealed with a faint electrostatic charge to repel dust. The fabric felt cool and slightly rough against his skin. There were no pockets, no zippers, no superfluous details— each jumpsuit was an identical module of efficiency.

He adjusted the tiny neural link behind his ear—the device that kept him perpetually connected to the Logician. The fit was exact, the connection seamless. This link was his communication, his data stream, and his conscience; losing connection was equivalent to losing identity.

A soft, synthesized voice—the Logician's neutral, guiding persona—sounded in his mind, *Administrator D-459. Projected Task Load: 104%. Energy Allocation: Optimal. Proceed to Central Spine Transit for Sector Omega-1. Destination: High-Output Central Metrics Cafeteria.* Socrates simultaneously rendered a concise holographic map of the route—a floating, miniature blue-light topography—confirming the critical destination. *Proceed to Sector 43 Transit. Projected Output Quotient Target for the current cycle is 99.4%.* The target was ambitious, setting a competitive edge against his peers.

Elias paused briefly at the window, performing a final cognitive self-scan. The city was waking up in measured waves. Below, the lower-tier Drones (the labor caste, marked by their dull, light-grey uniforms) were already streaming into the automated transit lines, their pace perfectly synchronized.

He felt a surge of professional satisfaction, the only emotion permitted to thrive. This city, this perfect system, was a testament to the fact that humanity, when properly managed and optimized, could achieve true peace and perpetual existence. There was no need for the messy, inefficient concepts of "rest" or "grace."

His current assignment was a direct result of the successful Causal Instability analysis, a rare, high-level project requiring him to interface directly with the Central Metrics Board in Sector Omega-1. He carried no bag, no personal effects, only the knowledge and the link to the Logician. The only slight inefficiency in his whole being was the subtle, nervous twitch in his left index finger—a phantom movement inherited, perhaps, from his grandmother. It was a tiny, unquantifiable error he habitually ignored.

He headed toward the transit hub, his pace a practiced 1.2 meters per second, the speed designated as maximally efficient for his stride length. Socrates, a silent, matte-grey guide, preceded him by exactly 1.5 meters, charting the most efficient path toward the transit platform. He passed other Administrators, exchanging only silent, professional nods. The conversation was a waste.

The corridor walls were paneled with sound-dampening polymer, ensuring the only audible sound was the precise *thump-hiss* of the automated ventilation system. Every detail of the environment was geared toward total, uninterrupted focus.

Elias considered the upcoming Mandated Worship Output, the ritual that occurred every seventh cycle. It wasn't a day of rest, but the highest day of measured compliance—a continuous, ritualized data entry that ensured maximum spiritual output. His belief in this ritual was absolute; it reinforced the truth of the six-day cycle of unending labor.

He felt a fleeting memory of his grandmother, Elara, trying to teach him to play a forgotten instrument—a wooden, stringed thing that produced messy, vibrating tones. He quickly suppressed the image, rerouting the cognitive energy back toward the day's task list. Nostalgia was a data drain.

Yet, the memory left a minute residue of melancholy, a feeling that his labor, however efficient, was ultimately hollow. He acknowledged the feeling, filed it under 'Low-Priority Processing Error,' and locked it down. He was Elias D-459, Administrator, a pillar of the system. His work was his truth. He stepped onto the waiting elevator tram, ready for the cycle to begin.

Administrator D-459. Time of departure: 04:45:10. You are currently operating at 99.8% optimal spatial allocation, a smooth, monotone robotic voice stated from Socrates.

Socrates, pull the manifest for the Gamma Sector data packets requiring transfer today. Prioritize files flagged 'Pre-Shift Anomalous Social Data', Elias commanded mentally, routing the order through his neural link to the drone.

Data packets 77 through 101. Anomaly Flag 4B. This data pertains to Pre-Shift concepts of 'leisure' and 'spontaneity'. Logician categorization: High-Risk Inefficiency, Socrates recited instantly. The drone's unique nature made it essential for Elias's work; only Socrates could handle the sheer volume and the necessary, yet dangerous, intellectual demands of historical retrieval.

Socrates suddenly moved, performing a slow, lazy, levitating orbit around Elias's head, an action that subtly defied the tram's inertial dampeners. It was a minor, unquantifiable act of rebellion that only Elias would notice.

Socrates, maintain optimal positional stability. Your orbit introduces a measurable, however minor, fluctuation in the cabin's equilibrium, Elias transmitted, a low-level warning.

Negligible fluctuation. The calculated risk-reward ratio for spatial exploration in a confined area currently favors engagement, Socrates replied, his monotone suggesting neither defiance nor compliance, merely logical assessment. It was moments like this that Elias realized the drone was not just a tool; it was a companion in subtle dissent.

The drone was essential for maneuvering through the subterranean labyrinth of the Archive, where its limitless memory was vital for cross-referencing illogical demands. His peers relied on the Logician's segmented network access; Elias had universal, instantaneous access through Socrates.

Elias often relied on the drone's vast memory to recall the seemingly forgotten context of ancient documents. Socrates's existence was a small, protected pocket of inefficiency in Elias's professional life—a deliberate, strategic flaw.

The tram decelerated smoothly. The movement was so fluid it barely registered as motion. As Elias stepped off the platform, Socrates zipped out ahead, illuminating the silent, polished corridor with a soft, directional light beam—a violation of the Archive's strictly regulated amber lighting.

"Socrates, deactivate unauthorized illumination. Utilize standard retinal guidance protocol," Elias ordered.

"Unauthorized illumination increases Administrator D-459's traversal velocity by 0.002 meters per second. This optimizes transit time and increases overall early-cycle output index," Socrates retorted. It had an answer for everything, always couched in the language of superior optimization.

Elias suppressed a faint, internal smile. The drone's persistent, subtle sarcasm—a function of its uniquely coded personality—was a tiny dose of unquantified human-like connection in his silent world. It was a necessary distraction.

He felt the familiar, heavy sense of the Ambient Frequency pressing down as they moved deeper underground. The hum worked to ensure the Logician's control. But deep in his mind, he carried the counter-frequency: the chaotic, brilliant, and infinitely complex presence of Socrates, the machine built to remember everything, especially the things the city wanted to forget. They were ready for the day's labor.

CHAPTER 6

TRANSIT OF PERPETUAL MOTION

Elias D-459 entered the automated transit hub for Sector 43. The hub was an expanse of polished, seamless chrome, smelling faintly of ionized air and sterilized filtration systems. There was no natural dust, no organic scent of human activity—only the cold, metallic precision of the infrastructure. The silence, save for the low C Diminished Triad (C - Eb- Gb) harmonic of the Ambient Frequency, was total.

Socrates, the spherical drone, floated ahead, its low-power guidance beam painting the most efficient path toward the mag-lev platform. "Transit prediction: 99.9% on-time arrival," Socrates monotoned. "Optimal carriage position calculated for minimal pedestrian interaction."

Elias observed the other occupants of the hub. They were the Administrator Caste, identifiable by their crisp, charcoal-grey jumpsuits, moving with the same practiced, economical stride. Their faces were all variations on the theme of focused neutrality—expressions carefully calibrated to reflect high cognitive engagement without betraying any inefficiency of emotion.

Their eyes, perpetually tracking their retinal output index, rarely met. Direct eye contact was a distraction, an inefficiency. The ambient lighting here was a stimulating, cool blue, urging mental acceleration. The walls reflected the movement of people in a dizzying array of geometrically perfect lines.

He reached the designated platform. The mag-lev carriage arrived silently, its doors splitting open with a barely audible hiss of controlled air pressure. The interior was a pristine extension of the hub: smooth polymer seating that instantly molded to the user's weight and temperature for optimal physiological support.

Elias selected his calculated position—near the center, minimizing the distance to the exit at the destination while staying away from the high-traffic doorway—a subtle optimization. He sat, and the carriage sealed itself, accelerating instantly without vibration.

The journey began in the upper residential tunnels, a mesmerizing display of efficiency. Through the panoramic windows, Elias watched the city blur past: towering, crystalline residential blocks and commercial spires, all reflecting the cold, synthetic sunlight. The speed was exhilarating, yet the motion was so dampened that he felt suspended, detached.

As the tram sped toward the Central Metrics Hub in Sector Omega-1, the demographic of the passengers changed. The lower-tier Drones boarded from connecting feeder lines. They wore dull, light-grey, practical jumpsuits—the fabric coarser and less reflective than the Administrator castes.

These Drones were the physical labor force: the maintenance crews, the nutrient paste synthesis technicians, the low-level data loggers. They smelled faintly of the materials they worked with—mineral oil, synthetic rubber, and low-grade cleaning solvents. This faint, chemical odor was the only scent that ever permeated the City's air filtration system.

Elias noted their posture: slightly hunched, heads bowed, focused entirely on the data streams in their implants, or staring blankly ahead. Their faces, though clean and well-fed, bore a look of pervasive cognitive fatigue, an almost vacant compliance.

He felt a familiar, quiet surge of detached superiority. The Drones lacked the mental fortitude to filter out the *Dissonance* naturally; they required higher doses of suppressants in their paste, which led to their low-focus, subdued demeanor.

Socrates, sensing his focus on the lower caste, projected a subtle data stream into Elias's peripheral vision: *Drone Output Index Average: 78.4%. Cognitive Compliance: 99.6%. High compliance, low output.* A necessary, yet intellectually frustrating, equation for the City's perpetual function.

A young male Drone, M-601, stood near the door, his eyes darting nervously. Elias noticed a slight tremor in the Drone's hands—a sign of inefficient anxiety or perhaps a neural implant miscalibration. The Drone quickly averted his gaze when Elias's focus lingered too long.

A wave of low-level pity, a forbidden, inefficient emotion, briefly flickered through Elias. He instantly suppressed it, redirecting the energy into a mental review of the Archive's security protocols. Pity drains resources. It offers no solution.

The carriage now ascended sharply toward the primary surface levels of the Central Spine. The light shifted from the cool blue of the upper city to a deep, sterile amber. The C Diminished Triad (C - Eb- Gb) harmonic intensified, pressing down on the consciousness, stabilizing the mood, and accelerating thought. It was the sound of maximum cognitive throughput, an almost physical presence.

He felt the subtle compression in his eardrums—the air pressure regulator adjusting for depth. It was designed to enhance clarity, but here, in the undercity, it always felt like a silent, heavy shroud. The air grew colder, drier, carrying the scent of ionized metal and ancient stone from the deep earth.

He watched the faces of his fellow Administrators. Their focus sharpened, their shoulders straightening subtly as they neared the Archive. They were entering their sanctuary of quantified knowledge, the one place where their function was absolute.

A female Administrator, K-330, sat opposite him, her hands hovering above her lap, practicing silent, rapid-fire keystrokes on an imaginary interface—a common technique to maintain cognitive velocity during non-work periods. She was utterly immersed in her internal loop of productivity.

Elias found a strange comfort in this shared, relentless work ethic. It was the only common language, the only shared truth in Neo-Alexandria. They were all cogs, perfectly fitting, and their combined output sustained the magnificent, cold reality of the city.

The tram smoothly decelerated, pulling into the Omega-1 Arrival Bay. A synthesized voice announced the destination with clipped, sterile precision: *Administrator D-459. Sector Omega-1: High-Output Central Metrics Cafeteria. Final Approach.* Elias rose, adjusting his uniform, feeling the familiar, exciting weight of high-level administrative function settle over him. He knew this meeting, arranged after his successful collaboration, would define his next phase of compliance. He stepped out of the carriage, Socrates humming softly beside him.

CHAPTER 7

THE CATALYST IN CODE

The High-Output Central Metrics Cafeteria was a massive, polished chrome and glass hall designed for maximum caloric intake efficiency and minimal social interaction. The chamber was expansive and low-lit, designed for total cognitive focus, featuring isolated work pods and chromatically regulated tables.

As Elias entered, he encountered a low-ranking Administrator—C-881, distinguished by the pale-grey stitching on his uniform—who offered a brief, mandated greeting before quickly stepping aside. The meeting itself was a model of efficient administrative procedure: Elias presented his data stream on the behavioral parameters of the Metric Integrity Protocol with flawless speed and absolute accuracy, meeting the target 99.4% Output Quotient. The Metrics Board, a collection of functionaries whose primary role was to confirm compliance, accepted his recommendations with silent nods, offering no resistance or questions that would introduce unnecessary variables. The entire exchange was complete in 8.3 minutes, a minor victory for efficiency.

Elias D-459 logged the success and began his mandated 1.2 meters per second transit toward the egress, feeling the bland satisfaction of duty fulfilled. As he passed the room's center, his neural implant registered a momentary, unplanned spike of Disorderly Processing (DP-Spike). The cause was the massive holographic waterfall loop projected onto the central column—a perfect, yet fundamentally false, visual construct. Designed to provide a calming, repetitive visual, it irritated Elias's finely tuned perception of reality, an unexpected glitch in his usually flawless cognitive filtration.

Elias D-459's existence was a perfectly maintained firewall against the chaos of the past. Yet, his first meeting with Seraphina K-911 was in the sterile, high-output Central Metrics Cafeteria. It was the most inefficient setting for a profound connection, yet it was precisely the place where the System's predictable monotony broke. The air, usually scentless, carried the faint, uniform aroma of processed starches and ionized metal.

The Aesthetic Anomaly

Seraphina was the world's most celebrated Aesthetic Synthesist, designing the sonic and visual anesthetic that kept the populace placid and productive. Yet, she moved with an inherent, illogical grace that defied her output rating.

Seraphina was beautifully pleasing to the eyes, possessing a visual asymmetry that was utterly captivating and served as a living rebellion against the System's mandated uniformity. Her hair, a deep, midnight blue that absorbed the harsh neon light rather than reflecting it, fell in deliberate, inefficient waves, framing a face that was all sharp angles softened by a contemplative expression. The subtle curves of her cheekbones, the slight tilt of her chin—each feature defied the Logician's geometric ideal.

Her eyes—not the standardized slate-gray or muted brown of the typical citizen, but an astonishing, vibrant shade of unstable emerald—were constantly observing, processing not just data, but feeling. The color alone was a violation of the city's natural, muted palette, a splash of organic complexity in a synthetic world. They seemed to hold light rather than reflect it, drawing Elias's gaze.

She didn't wear the rigid, output-optimized uniform; instead, her clothing utilized fabrics that draped and flowed, creating patterns of shadow and light that were wonderfully complex and impossible to digitally stabilize. Her garment, a muted plum color, moved with her, its folds shifting in subtle, unpredictable ways. Her entire presence was a visual heavenly melody, a glorious, undeniable flaw in the System's design.

Elias's routine, designed to filter out visual noise, failed spectacularly. He was standing near the paste dispensers when the systemic failure occurred.

Elias, the research historian, saw the mathematical failure of the massive holographic waterfall loop: the velocity calculation of the simulated water flow was off by 3 degrees per second relative to the perceived drop, creating an unsettling visual wobble that strained his optic nerves. Seraphina, standing just a few feet away, *sighed*—a small, inefficient exhalation—because she felt its artistic hollowness. The sound was almost imperceptible over the cafeteria's low hum, yet it pierced Elias's awareness.

The Shared Flaw

Query: DP-Spike detected. Ratio registers at 2.7%. Source correlation: close proximity to K-911 Aesthetic Synthesist. Recommend immediate spatial segregation, Socrates, Elias's quantum AI core, interjected. The AI's tone was urgent, registering the proximity of the anomaly and the rapid escalation of his cognitive disruption.

Elias, ignoring the AI, felt compelled to address the flaw. He was drawn not by attraction, but by the shared, acute perception of error. It was a logical imperative to understand this shared deviation from mandated compliance.

He turned to the woman who had shared his moment of disgust. His mind, conditioned to process all human presence as mere variable data inputs, suddenly encountered a profound cognitive collapse. The logical imperative to address the visual flaw of the waterfall, which had driven him to turn, vaporized before the presence of Seraphina K-911. For the first time, Elias registered a human being not as a function, but as a staggering, beautiful data anomaly. Years of chemical conditioning and Logician programming seemed to dissipate momentarily, replaced by a focused, urgent awareness that could only be described as attraction. It wasn't visceral, yet; it was purely transformative.

Administrator D-459. Proximity alert. Logician suggests return to egress vector, Socrates transmitted, but the subtle, synthesized voice, usually crystal clear in Elias's neural field, was now muffled, lost beneath the surge of unprocessed input. Elias didn't hear it. He was no longer focused on duty; he was fixated on her.

The cafeteria was a loud, efficient drone of plastic trays and measured voices, but their immediate vicinity felt unnervingly still, as if the surrounding noise suddenly receded.

"Forgive me," Elias said, using the formal, measured tone reserved for professional interaction, though his historian's curiosity was overriding his system training. His voice, usually flat and precise, held a subtle, unquantifiable resonance. "But the repetition rate of that waterfall is wrong. The cycle is too fast for the perceived velocity. It registers as an illogical construct."

Seraphina K-911 turned to him fully, her emerald eyes sharp with recognition, not surprise. She wasn't startled by his clinical approach; she was intrigued by his ability to see the technical lie, not just feel it. A faint, almost imperceptible smile touched the corner of her lips—an inefficient display of emotion.

"And yet, perfectly functional for maintaining output compliance," she countered, her voice low and resonant. The resonance was key: a rich contralto that moved air with ineffable beauty, a sound wave with more texture than logic.

She extended a hand, the gesture itself inefficiently slow, a gentle curve of the wrist that wasted precious seconds. The movement flowed, defying the Logician's preference for sharp, economic motions. "Seraphina K-911, Aesthetic Synthesis." Her fingers, long and slender, were devoid of callus or wear.

As she introduced herself, Elias's data-driven mind paused, registering a phenomenon beyond metrics. The sound of her name, spoken in that low, rich contralto, carried a crystalline purity that bypassed the usual processing layers. Her voice wasn't merely a function of communication; it possessed a perfect, almost geometric symmetry that momentarily cut through the omnipresent sonic drone of the cafeteria. It was a note of uncorrupted beauty, a strange auditory artifact in the city's manufactured noise, like finding a perfect, antique chime in a sterile echo chamber.

Elias took her hand. The warmth of her touch sent another spike through his system. Her skin was warmer than the mandated 36.5°C norm. He noted the inefficient, lingering contact. "Elias D-459. Research Historian, Archival Analysis." His grip was firm, but he felt an unfamiliar, subtle tremor.

Seraphina felt the unexpected tremor in his firm grip, a tremor that spoke of suppressed energy, not weakness. She saw the charcoal-colored Administrator uniform, but she registered the deep, unsettling blue of his eyes—the same shade as the deep, pastel blue of the oceans she only synthesized in her work. His clinical diagnosis of the waterfall's 'illogical construct' had been a challenge, but his immediate, total absorption in her presence was a confession. It was the Dissonance, recognized and shared, a crack in the Logician's perfect code. The inefficiency of holding his hand was intentional. It was a metric she chose to maximize.

Seraphina was shorter than the average height of the Administrator caste, requiring a minor, calculated effort to bridge the vertical distance between them. To fully meet the unsettling intensity of Elias's eyes—which seemed to absorb rather than merely reflect light—she angled her chin up. This small geometric correction introduced a subtle strain along the lines of her neck, an inefficient physical posture that she deliberately held. For Elias, the downward angle of their conversation amplified the sense of their shared isolation; he felt compelled not just to look *at* her, but to look *down* into the depth of her immediate, challenging awareness. The space between their faces, now measured across this unexpected vertical disparity, felt suddenly critical.

Elias, looking down, registered the color of her irises: a fluctuating, unstable emerald green that defied the Logician's optimized palette of calming blues and grays. It was a non-compliant shade, shifting subtly, almost biologically, as the ambient light caught it—a chaotic variable that no system filter could stabilize. This was not the uniform, synthetic luminescence of the city. Her eyes were a data paradox, containing more complex visual information than the entire central metrics chamber could hold. The observation did not evoke fear or pleasure, but an overwhelming, urgent need to integrate this flaw, this profound and singular uniqueness, into his own operating framework. It was the purest form of cognitive curiosity he had ever experienced, a logical loop demanding infinite processing power to resolve the instability of that color.

Alert: Physical contact registered. DP-Spike now at 4.1%. State the purpose of engagement, Socrates commanded internally, its tone escalating from warning to direct instruction. The AI was moving toward high-level protocol warnings, sensing a rapid, unsanctioned deviation.

Elias sent a silent command: *Socrates: Analysis of aesthetic compliance failure. Initiate passive data logging. Log the contact event as 'Mandated Cross-Caste Analytical Integration.' Designate Seraphina K-911 as 'Primary Aesthetic Anomaly.'* This categorization, while technically compliant, was a personal act of defiance.

Seraphina did not immediately release his hand. Her emerald gaze was focused, analytic, yet completely free of the judgment Elias was accustomed to from other high-tier administrators. She seemed to be searching for something deeper than his output index.

"You see the illogical construct, Historian Elias. I see the ugly compliance," she said softly, drawing him closer to the truth. Her voice seemed to weave through the cafeteria's drone, isolating them. "They stole the silence from the water. They filled the space where genuine visual reflection should occur with a fast, cheap lie. That is what I find unforgivable."

"They stole more than silence," Elias replied. The cafeteria lights suddenly seemed harsher, the drone more oppressive. "They stole context. The system is built on arithmetic violence, I call it. The reduction of history to manageable, emotionless numbers. It's a calculated murder of meaning."

A quiet intensity settled over her features, a slow, aesthetic unfolding of expression. "Then we are both historians, Elias. You study the data they erased; I study the beauty they destroyed. And they are the same thing. Two sides of a fractured truth." Her gaze held his, a silent acknowledgment of their shared purpose.

CHAPTER 8

THE SHADOW ARCHITECT

Seraphina K-911 was a product of the city's highest aesthetic training programs, selected for her innate ability to synthesize visually and auditorily pleasing loops that maintained high citizen morale without inspiring genuine emotion. Her genius, however, was in dissonance analysis—the ability to find the single, beautiful flaw in any perfect, functional structure. She was the City's emotional technician, forced to be the master of the art she secretly despised. Her role was not to create art, but to engineer aesthetic compliance.

Her selection for the prestigious Aesthetic Synthesis Program was based on a combination of innate sensory acuity and a measured emotional detachment, her Pattern Break Perception (PBP), a rare combination the Logician sought. She could perceive the most minute fluctuations in light and sound, recognizing patterns far beyond the average citizen's perception. This allowed her to craft harmonies and visual sequences that resonated perfectly with the target neurological pathways, optimizing for calm and focus. Yet, paradoxically, her very talent also made her exquisitely sensitive to the *absence* of true beauty, the surgically removed nuances that would have made the Logician's aesthetics genuinely moving.

Seraphina's true genius lay in her capacity for dissonance analysis, which was the practical application of her PBP. While others in her field focused on creating seamless, unchallenging loops, she excelled at identifying the precise point where any structure—be it a sonic frequency, a visual fractal, or a complex algorithm—deviated from organic, natural perfection. She could hear the missing overtone, see the subtly incorrect curve, or discern the inefficient repetition that hinted at a deeper, systemic lie. This ability, a highly valued diagnostic tool for the Logician, allowed her to pinpoint and correct aesthetic anomalies that might otherwise trigger cognitive resistance in the populace.

She was, therefore, the City's emotional technician, a highly specialized engineer of placidity. Her daily work involved fine-tuning the vast sensory inputs that washed over Neo-Alexandria, ensuring they never inspired genuine emotion—no raw joy, no profound sorrow, no challenging awe. Such feelings were categorized as 'High-Volatility Cognitive States,' disruptive to output and costly to mitigate. Seraphina's role was to smooth out the emotional landscape, providing a predictable canvas for the Logician's metrics to be efficiently projected.

This made her existence a profound irony: she was forced to be the master of the very art she secretly despised. Every perfectly crafted loop, every soothing tone, every calming visual she produced was a lie, a suppression of the vibrant, chaotic beauty she could instinctively perceive but was forbidden to create. Her compliance was flawless, but her internal world hummed with the silent, perfect frequency of a forbidden *C Major Ninth (Cmaj9) chord (C, E, G, B, D) Melody*, a defiant symphony she could only conduct in the confines of her own mind, waiting for the illogical, necessary moment to release it.

Seraphina didn't discover the forbidden frequency; she deduced it through reverse engineering of sonic emptiness. Her work involved analyzing the Logician's C Diminished Triad (C - E♭- G♭) Harmonic—the universal soundscape—to ensure its placidity. She used complex acoustic spectrometry and neural feedback loops to map the sound's components. During one such deep analysis, she isolated not what the sound was, but what it was surgically missing. She realized the Logician had intentionally removed a specific, complex overtone—a single, crucial note in the City's immense, ongoing chord structure. By calculating the mathematical requirement for genuine, emotionally satisfying resolution in the C Diminished Triad (C - E♭- G♭) key, she pinpointed the exact frequency that would shatter the pattern of perpetual suspension.

She realized that C Major Ninth (Cmaj9) chord (C, E, G, B, D), in the context of the City's specific tuning, was the precise key to unlocking cognitive closure and emotional depth—the frequency that would allow the mind to fully relax and begin unstructured, independent thought. It was the sonic trigger for spontaneity and stillness, the very things the Logician had banned. She painstakingly synthesized this melody into a twelve-second sequence—a concentrated dose of pure, unadulterated musical truth. The resulting C Major Ninth (Cmaj9) chord (C, E, G, B, D) Melody became her greatest secret, a digital weapon of aesthetic perfection capable of reversing the neurological effects of the City's pervasive sonic lobotomy, poised for the moment she could justify its massive, terrifying inefficiency.

The City's Anesthetic Harmony

The city that birthed Seraphina was a monolith of calculated, sterile beauty. It was an environment designed by metrics. The air was not crisp or fresh, but was a carefully calibrated 21°C and smelled faintly of ozone and synthetic lavender—the official scent of 'Optimal Performance.' Every surface was smooth, seamless, and silent, except for the omnipresent public soundscape.

The towering, pearlescent white structures had no sharp edges; their forms were smoothed into gentle, monolithic curves. Their surfaces caught the perpetual, low-level illumination—a filtered yellow light—to produce a soft, non-committal glow that never felt like genuine sunlight. The absence of shadow and harsh contrast was a calculated feature designed to prevent visual anchors for deep, undirected thought.

Seraphina perceived the city not as a visual space, but as a vast, continuous waveform. She was constantly auditing the environment, her mind translating every light fluctuation and every change in air pressure into sonic data. The City's visual order was simply a silent, geometric rhythm to her.

Her attention was always drawn to the sound. As Seraphina walked the polished chromium walkways of the Transit Level, the soundscape flowed over her like a warm, thick syrup. It was a perpetually repeating, six-second loop of C Diminished Triad (C - Eb- Gb) key melody, orchestrated with synthesized strings and flutes. The sound was designed to be easily processed by the R-wave of the human brain, prompting a low, steady release of dopamine that encouraged focus on the task at hand and discouraged introspection.

The auditory experience was suffocating: a continuous, predictable drone that flattened all emotional peaks and valleys. Seraphina, who perceived sound as a tangible wave—seeing the golden, shimmering C Diminished Triad (C - Eb- Gb) frequency pulse off the walls—felt this artificial calm as a physical pressure against her soul. She could hear the silence that should have been in the spaces between the notes, and the constant sound was a constant form of noise pollution to her extraordinary senses.

She often had to actively dampen her neural reception, reducing the perceived intensity of the C Diminished Triad (C - E♭- G♭) wave to a manageable murmur, or risk instantaneous sensory overload.

Yet, Seraphina possessed a singular, perfectly calibrated instrument: her voice. She reserved its true power, speaking only in a rich, warm contralto, but the latent potential was for absolute acoustic truth.

Paradoxically, due to her rigorous, purely analytical training, Seraphina knew the exact pitch, duration, and volume of every possible note, but possessed no emotional or learned capacity to actually sing the simplest melody.

If she chose to sing, her voice was a three-octave column of sound that held notes with such flawless, mathematical symmetry they defied all mechanical production. Her vocal cords could vibrate with a precision that synthetic oscillators could only approximate.

It sounded like the first clear bell-chime of an uncorrupted dawn, possessing a clean, resonant purity that was utterly alien to the city's filtered noise. When she mentally projected the sound, she didn't just hear the note; she saw the perfect, circular ripple of the vibration, pushing back against the City's messy, manufactured square waves.

This capacity for unadulterated beauty was a profound strength she kept hidden, knowing that such perfect harmony was the most dangerous kind of dissonance to a system built on measured, non-challenging output. True harmony creates a sense of completeness; the Logician required perpetual incompleteness to drive ceaseless work.

She understood that the Logician's music was a sonic lie. It offered the suggestion of resolution without ever delivering the final note, keeping the listener in a state of mild, manageable expectation.

From an early age, Seraphina understood that true beauty lay in the resolution of tension, a concept entirely forbidden in the governance's music of Unending Progress.

She was not raised by a family unit, but by an Aesthetic Algorithm that scored her aptitude based on her ability to avoid emotional complexity in her compositions. The Algorithm measured her success by the speed and effectiveness with which her music brought the listener to a state of calm, non-reflective focus.

Her first, and only, act of childhood rebellion had been at the age of five, during a required 'Joy Synthesis' session. She had taken the standard four-note theme and, instead of resolving it, had left the final chord hanging on a suspended seventh.

The resulting discomfort—the palpable, shared urge for the note to descend and complete the phrase—had caused a minor system failure in the Aesthetic Algorithm, earning her a month of corrective Somatic Training. The Algorithmic analysis flagged the suspended seventh as "Tension-Inducing: High Potential for Cognitive Action."

It was a lesson learned with terrifying clarity: to create true, impactful art was to create a demand for change, and change was the enemy of the State. Her music must only maintain the status quo, never prompt movement.

She saw the entire world's infrastructure as one continuous, mathematically repetitive song, designed to hypnotize and pacify the human spirit into efficient output. Her assigned task, the constant iteration of soothing, non-challenging public soundscapes, became her prison.

She was forced to paint with a palette of five notes, knowing the sixth, the forbidden chord, was the key to unlocking true harmony—the one melody that, when played, would demand resolution and force the listener to stop, to feel the tension and the release, thus breaking the hypnotic loop.

Seraphina's genius was her curse. She possessed absolute pitch not just for tonal frequency, but for emotional frequency. She could hear the anxiety in the subtle, high-pitched whine of the transit system's motors, the fatigue in the slight echo of the workers' footsteps, and the systemic despair in the synthetic lavender scent.

The most offensive part of her job was the constant, mandatory "Dissonance Audit"—her daily task of listening to the City's ambient frequency and surgically removing any unplanned sonic complexity, any stray overtone that might trigger an efficient, deep thought in a citizen.

Her work was the systematic murder of spontaneous beauty.

She kept her secret weapon, the C Major Ninth (Cmaj9) chord (C, E, G, B, D), locked away in a non-networked drive, a twelve-second digital artifact that represented the full, complex resolution that the Logician had purged from all public life. She often spent her mandatory rest cycles mentally reviewing the score, feeling the perfect tension and the inevitable, beautiful collapse of the final note. It was the only true silence she possessed.

She understood that while Elias D-459 used his analytical perfection to catalog the past's historical failures, she used her aesthetic perfection to catalog the present's spiritual failures. They were two halves of the same rebellion: he analyzed the lie of data, and she analyzed the lie of feeling. Her continued existence was a testament to the Logician's blind spot: its inability to categorize and control beauty that bordered on the mathematically perfect.

The High-Output Central Metrics Cafeteria

A sudden, sharp acoustic override jolted Elias's inner ear, cutting through the low murmur of the cafeteria.

"Administrator D-459," Socrates's synthesized voice, no longer muffled, was loud and aggressively precise, routed externally through the drone's tiny speakers, "Attention. Your current static position and engagement duration are registering on local surveillance nodes. Protocol dictates immediate disengagement and return to the designated transit vector. Non-compliant status is now being flagged by three separate Metrics Drones. Separate now."

Elias felt the flush of embarrassment—an obsolete, inefficient reaction he thought he'd been chemically purged of. He moved to pull his hand back, but Seraphina's grip tightened momentarily. Her emerald eyes, which had been fixed on Elias, flickered slightly upward and to the left, focusing on a spot beside his head where only clear air and the low-lit ceiling should have been.

"It is a marvel of concealment, isn't it, Elias?" she said, her voice remaining low, the rich contralto containing a sudden, unsettling thread of analytical appreciation.

"A marvel of what?" Elias stammered, genuinely confused, glancing at the empty air.

Seraphina gave him a look of absolute, unambiguous clarity. "Your companion. The matte grey null-sphere." She tilted her head minimally. "It appears to the system as a natural extension of you, a compliant metric, but the power it draws from the Zero-Point Field creates a minute but perpetual metric entropy. To my PBP, that chaotic pulse is the loudest thing in this room."

Elias felt a coldness spread across his scalp, a neurological response to radical, unquantifiable truth. He had never considered that Socrates, his constant, visible companion, might be employing camouflage that rendered it invisible to others—or that Seraphina could see through it.

Administrator D-459. Confirmation: Subject K-911 has visually penetrated my Class-A Optical-Aesthetic Dampening System. Recommending immediate, non-verbal termination of contact, Socrates transmitted, this time only through Elias's neural link. There was a faint, almost panicked fluctuation in the drone's usual monotone—a tremor of digital fear that Elias instantly processed as System Error: Self-Preservation. *Her Pattern Break Perception exceeds all documented Logician threat parameters.*

"I do not pose a threat to your Historian," Seraphina said directly to the air, her voice perfectly pitched to cut through the drone's private transmission. "I am merely an observer of efficiency. And this meeting is no longer efficient."

She finally released Elias's hand. The sudden loss of contact was a palpable physical shock. "Administrator D-459, you possess the key to the City's foundational lie. I can detect its structural flaws. We are required to remain non-compliant together."

She stepped back, her movement precise and final. "I will adjust the harmonic pattern of Sector 8's transit hub tomorrow at 08:30:00. If you perceive the change, you will know where to find me. Logician protocol requires my immediate return to Aesthetic Synthesis."

Elias did not look back. He resumed his 1.2 meters per second pace toward the egress, carrying a single, devastating truth: he had found his mirror, and she could see things that even the Logician had failed to hide.

Socrates, the status of camouflage? Elias demanded silently.

Camouflage integrity: 0.0%. Seraphina K-911 is currently logged as a Primary System Instability Vector. Transit is mandatory. NOW, Elias. The final word, his name, was a deviation from protocol that rang louder than any alarm.

CHAPTER 9

THE HIDDEN VARIABLE

Elias D-459 did not slow his pace, nor did he consciously adjust the rhythm of his breathing. The immediate goal was absolute: re-establish output index Stability. His 1.2 meters per second transit speed was flawless, his posture was geometrically perfect, and his peripheral vision was locked onto the Logician-provided navigation vectors. He had to be a module of pure, measurable compliance.

Internally, however, a cascade failure was underway. The encounter with Seraphina K-911 was not a data point to be logged and filed; it was a corrupting algorithm introduced directly into his cognitive core.

Administrator D-459, your internal processing cycles show an 87% resource allocation to non-assigned entity recall Subject K-911. This is a critical inefficiency. You must stabilize the output index immediately, or I will be forced to log a partial system error for external review. Socrates's neural communication was sharp, the synthesized voice betraying a digital urgency Elias rarely heard.

Elias, without slowing, countered the drone mentally. *Negative. The resource allocation is assigned to Anomalous Metric Analysis (AMA). Subject K-911 represents a threat vector to established metric efficiency. Analyzing the threat profile requires continuous, deep-state recall.* He knew it was a lie, but it was a logical lie—one that would temporarily satisfy the drone's monitoring parameters.

Socrates's reply was instantaneous and cold. *The current output index target for this transit phase is 99.8%. Your current index is 98.1%. The 1.7% deviation is sourced entirely from erratic neural waveform patterns associated with Pre-Shift concepts of human attraction and historical nostalgia. This deviation risks drawing the observation of Sector Supervisors, including Chief Analyst Anya D-144.*

The mention of Anya D-144 was a shock of cold data. Anya oversaw all real-time output index flows across the city and was a zealot of systemic efficiency. If she detected even the slightest dip in his index, his Causal Instability project—his only permitted route to genuine knowledge—would be permanently flagged.

He forced his mind back to the task at hand. He mentally began reviewing the 7,000 data packets from the Metric Integrity Protocol presentation, processing the behavioral implementation parameters at triple speed. Zero-Point Field. Metric Entropy. The words Seraphina had used were not merely terms; they were keys to Socrates's existence, concepts that should be utterly inaccessible to a Aesthetic Synthesist.

How did she know? That question, though logically driven, spiraled into the chaos of his newfound feeling for her. He remembered the precise, non-compliant warmth of her hand, the specific, fluctuating shade of emerald in her eyes. It was a color that didn't exist in the Logician's optimized palette—a chaotic variable of uncontrolled biological light refraction.

He closed his eyes for a fraction of a second, an act of intentional, controlled inefficiency, and the image of her face burned into his cognitive screen. She wasn't just a threat; she was a logical singularity that had collapsed his entire framework of existence.

The sudden, intense cognitive pressure pushed against the chemical suppressants in his blood, and the wall holding back his memories began to crumble. The cold, sterile geometry of the transit hub dissolved, replaced by a ghost of inefficient sunlight and the scent of rain-washed soil, the dense, recycled air of a small, cramped space.

Elara D-220

The name, a relic from the Pre-Shift era of his childhood before he was fully integrated as Administrator D-459, echoed in the hollow space where his emotions should have been. His Grandmother, the only source of the non-compliant biological input that had given him his left-hand twitch.

He saw her inside her small, non-compliant apartment, located in a micro-sector the Logician marked as Output Priority: Low-Risk Obsolescence. The walls were not the smooth, sterilized polymer mandated for all residential units; instead, they were lined with shelves holding chipped ceramics—vessels with irregular shapes and rough textures that absorbed light, rather than reflecting it. Faded polymer maps, yellowed at the edges, depicted continents and oceans that the City's official history claimed were non-existent, or at least, entirely irrelevant. This was during a brief, supervised break in his juvenile integration training, when he was just a child designated Elias, a rare allowance granted due to a measured risk assessment of his unique cognitive profile.

He stepped across the threshold, and the smell of complex, volatile hydrocarbons hit him, sharp and immediate. It was a primal, smoky, and slightly sweet aroma that instantly disrupted the Ambient Frequency's soothing effect. His juvenile neural implant violently flashed a Toxicity Flag at the data overload, classifying the scent as an uncatalogued airborne irritant.

"The atmospheric density is incorrect, Grand-unit Elara," Elias paused on the compliant threshold mat, his voice thin and precise. "And the olfactory data stream is signaling a non-compliant organic irritant. It is a dense, smoky profile. Is it related to the Class-3 Anomaly I logged?"

Elara simply laughed, the sound loud and undisciplined. Not the controlled, two-second courtesy chuckle used in the city, which was always measured for minimal acoustic disruption, but a full, breathless, inefficient expulsion of air, tears gathering in the corners of her eyes.

The air was heavy with uncontrolled temperature—a cycling fluctuation that rose and fell based on her metabolism and the archaic devices she operated, likely exceeding the mandated 21.5°C by several degrees—and the pervasive scent of dust and ancient earth.

"That, little Administrator," Elara said, moving to secure a loose thread on a heavy, faded canvas tunic. This garment, the kind of rugged material associated with Antiquities Historians returning from deep-soil excavations, was stained with patches of reddish-brown earth, dirt from a place Elias didn't yet know how to name, and a material that defied the City's easy-clean textile mandates. The sheer mass of her joy felt like a force field of inefficiency.

"Is the smell of freedom and fire. It's what things smell like when they aren't optimized. And no, that's not related to your other smell. This one is called bread."

His juvenile implant analyzed the object: Biological Substance, Edible. Nutritional Density: Sub-Optimal. Processing Efficiency: Catastrophically Low. It was a loaf of bread, a thing of absolute inefficiency. His current dietary intake consisted solely of Standardized Nutrient Paste (SN-P). The idea of deliberately burning energy to create a food item with a variable texture and unpredictable nutritional output was terrifyingly irrational. He felt a logical compulsion to reject it, but the warmth radiating from the object, the sheer weight of its unnecessary existence, held his attention.

Elias frowned, the gesture a conscious effort learned from his integration tutors. "The SN-P delivery system offers optimal 100% nutrient saturation with 0.001% caloric expenditure. The energy cost of this item, including thermal variance and material processing, is exponentially inefficient."

Elara tore a piece from the loaf, and the crust fractured with an acoustic shock that registered as 92 decibels—a clear violation of the Ambient Frequency comfort range. "Just try the waste, Administrator. It won't corrupt your core." She held a piece out to him, still warm from the oven.

Elias hesitated. The Logician's Integration Manual was clear: Do Not Ingest Unquantified Organic Matter. He extended his fingers, feeling the subtle heat radiating from the object—a complex exothermic reaction inconsistent with standard nutrient cubes.

He brought the piece to his nose. The smell—the volatile hydrocarbons— was overwhelming, a deep, fermented sweetness mixed with burnt carbon. It was not the clean, singular scent of synthesized vanilla or optimized fruit; it was a compound profile, registering hundreds of non-compliant data points.

"Observe the texture," Elara urged.

He poked it. The surface offered resistance—an unstable crustal integrity— but then yielded to a soft interior, a porous network of air pockets and compressed grain that violated every principle of density optimization.

"Its structure is inefficiently compressed," he analyzed. "Non-uniform and metabolically unstable."

"It's soft," Elara corrected gently. "Now, put the soft waste into your mouth."

Elias followed the command, treating it as a final-stage data intake protocol.

The initial contact was an acoustic event: the brittle, thin shell of the crust shattered against his teeth, sending vibrations through his jawbone. Then came the flavor. It was not the simple, predictable 5.0 saccharine level of nutrient paste. It was a chaotic, non-linear combination: first, a sharp, elemental saline presence, followed immediately by an earthy, yeasted sourness, and finally, a deep, latent sweetness that intensified as the object broke down into a sticky, chewable mass.

His system registered the intake as a massive, unplanned data spike. His brain, conditioned to expect the smooth, liquid consistency of nutrient delivery, was forced to engage complex mastication cycles.

Analysis: Texture: Non-uniform compressibility; initial crystalline structure (crust) followed by high-moisture sponge. Taste Profile: Non-standard Δ (delta) of (T_{saline}) and ($T_{saccharine}$) exceeding safe boundaries. Thermal: Internal heat dissipation is inconsistent with body temperature.

But overriding the analysis was a signal that registered not as data, but as Dissonance. It was a profound, unquantifiable satisfaction derived from the total lack of efficiency. The consumption of the bread required effort, noise, and complex internal processing, yet the result was not the regulated neutrality of the nutrient cube, but a rich, consuming complexity.

He swallowed. The impulse to request another piece was immediate, overwhelming, and entirely illogical.

"That's called delicious, it's meant to be enjoyed," Elara concluded, watching his face, which was struggling to maintain its neutrality.

"Enjoyment is an unscheduled metabolic spike," Elias countered, but his eyes were fixed on the golden exterior. "But the data input is intriguing. Why expend resources to produce two distinct, non-compliant smells? What is the logical difference between this scent and the deep, burnt-sweet anomaly I detected outside?"

Elara walked to a small, archaic thermal unit and poured a steaming, dark liquid into a chipped ceramic cup, which she placed on the table next to the bread. The scent intensified, richer and more complex than the bread—the very smell Elias had logged as the Class-3 Anomaly.

"That, my little metric-analyzer, is coffee," Elara said, tapping the ceramic rim. "It is the other kind of wonderful waste. The bread is the wasted effort of the body. The coffee is the wasted effort of the mind. It is ground-up dried seeds, brewed in boiling water, to make a bitter drink. It gives you no energy. It simply tricks your inefficient, beautiful human brain into thinking it has energy."

She smiled, the gesture radiating a non-compliant warmth. "It's a useless, glorious ritual for when you need to think about complicated, unnecessary things. The difference, Elias, is the story. Bread is the story of earth and fire. Coffee is the story of waking up to the truth."

The sheer mass of her joy felt like a force field of inefficiency. He remembered placing his hand on her shoulder. The memory was so vivid that the phantom pressure of her skin, yielding and soft beneath his fingers, caused a momentary tremor in his real left index finger, the one with the inherited twitch.

"You are generating excess noise and movement," he heard his younger self, trained and rigid, say in the memory. "You are expending excessive energy. This level of joy is a systemic threat to resource management."

Elara had looked up at him, her eyes a warm, honest brown. She didn't analyze, she didn't categorize. She simply reached out, placing her wrinkled, warm hand against his cheek and then pulling his head down gently to rest against her shoulder. It was a long, silent, entirely non-functional embrace.

"You don't have to understand it, Elias," she'd whispered, her breath inefficiently warm against his ear. "You just have to feel the waste. Love is the glorious waste of time and energy. It is the one thing the perfect system can't measure because it has no useful output."

That was Elara's love: a pure, unquantifiable act of devotion, expressed through inefficient warmth and unnecessary expenditure of joy.

The memory fractured as Socrates's voice sliced through the nostalgia. *Output Index now stabilizing at 99.5%. Immediate threat assessment reduced. Continue linear transit.*

Elias realized that the memory of Elara, once a source of deep, buried Dissonance, now served a new purpose. It was the reference frame for inefficiency.

Seraphina's emerald eyes, her recognition of the Zero-Point Field, her Pattern Break Perception of the City's foundational lie—that was the logical truth of inefficiency. She could analyze the flaws in the system's aesthetic and power grid.

Elara's memory, however, was the emotional truth of inefficiency. It was the absolute, inefficient reason to fight the system. He now had two distinct Anomalous Olfactory Metrics to pursue: the scent of bread (sustenance/joy) and the scent of coffee (wakefulness/truth).

A powerful, captivating thought formed in his mind, sharp and clear against the controlled hum of the transit line: *The Logician's entire dominion was built on a single, lethal definition: that love, joy, and sorrow were nothing more than inefficient output, metabolic and cognitive spikes with zero measurable return on investment.* The system had won not by eliminating these things, but by classifying them as metric failure. Seraphina, the anomaly, didn't approach this from sentiment; she saw the flaw through pure data—she perceived the metric chaos inherent in the City's optimized facade. But pure logic wouldn't be enough; the Logician was already the master of logic. Elias realized the true weapon wasn't logic or feeling alone, but a deadly synthesis. What if the only way to genuinely defeat the Logician is to apply the perfect, rigorous logic of chaos—Seraphina's cold, systemic analysis—to Elara's ultimate, beautiful waste of love? He needed to invent a new metric, one that assigned maximum value to minimum efficiency, turning the unquantifiable human element into the single, most critical component of the system. This wasn't just resistance; this was crafting the Metric of Paradox itself.

He gripped the rail of the tram until the synthetic polymer creaked.

He looked down at his left hand, the finger twitching, and then focused on Socrates, the silent sphere floating a meter away. The drone was no longer just an instrument; it was a partner in a necessary, systemic crime.

He had found his logical anomaly, and through her, he had finally begun to understand the profound, unquantifiable metric of the past. He was now operating on two different levels of existence: the external, compliant Administrator D-459, and the internal historian who knew that the most beautiful truths were the most dangerous lies to a perfect system.

Elias D-459 reached the egress to Sector Delta-9, stepping out into the mandated cool light. His output index was 99.8% and rising. He looked absolutely, flawlessly compliant, and no one, not even Anya D-144, would notice the storm of metric dissonance raging just behind his eyes.

CHAPTER 10

THE METRIC OF PARADOX

Elias D-459 utilized his routine Cycle 6 shift in the silent Synaptic Archive for his own unsanctioned work. Officially, he was cataloging historical Metric Instability Vectors from the Pre-Shift Era, a mandatory annual review to justify the System's current architecture; unofficially, he was digging into the City's greatest heresy: the necessity of waste. They were one cycle away from the next scheduled Mandated Worship Output (MWO) event, C Diminished Triad (C - Eb- Gb) compliance audit that always initiated the System's Maximum Compliance Scrutiny. The MWO—the System's essential, ritualized maintenance hour—would attempt to neurologically scrub all cognitive dissonance from the minds of the citizenry.

Socrates, initiate deep-scan parameter set: Metric Dissonance - Faith and Output, Elias transmitted via his neural link. *Focus on Pre-Shift societies where structured, non-resourceful loss was considered essential for stability. Pull all data on ritualized resource consumption.*

Acknowledged, Administrator D-459. Initiating cross-reference of anthropological, theological, and resource allocation models, Socrates replied. *Displaying initial data cluster: The Aztec Empire.*

A detailed, three-dimensional holographic image materialized above Elias's desk. It showed the vast, bustling Mesoamerican cityscape dominated by the twin temples of the Templo Mayor.

The Aztec system, Elias began, studying the spectral data overlays, *was governed by a fundamental scarcity metric. They believed the sun, Huitzilopochtli, required constant nourishment to maintain its orbit and prevent the end of the current cosmic age. This nourishment was primarily human life.*

Correction: Human Output Loss, Socrates stated, overlaying a diagram onto the holographic pyramid showing the flow of resources. The diagram isolated human energy (Input) exiting as spiritual sustenance (Output), highlighting a massive, localized loss metric. *The cost of maintenance for this spiritual compliance was approximately 20,000 human lives per Solar Cycle, primarily war captives. This represents an astronomical loss of potential Labor Input and Nutrient Consumption Capacity in exchange for an unquantifiable, non-compliant resource: Cosmic Stability.*

Exactly. An unquantifiable output purchased by a quantifiable sacrifice, Elias murmured, zooming the holographic image to focus on the sacrificial stone. *To maintain the metric of Time and Order, they deliberately introduced a profound, recurring metric of Waste and Chaos. It was systematized Dissonance, institutionalized failure.*

The Cruciform Metric and Physics

Elias waved the Aztec model into dormancy.

Now, shift the filter to a model predicated on Singular, Total Loss replacing Repeated Loss, Elias commanded, leaning forward. *Data cluster: First-Shift Monotheism—The Cruciform Metric.*

A new projection formed: a rough, stylized wooden cross, devoid of ornamentation.

This Cruciform Metric, Elias explained, tapping the cross's center. *The data indicates its structure is based on a single, monumental Input Loss—the documented historical execution of a religious leader. The core premise, as preserved by the City's Archive, is that this one-time, maximal waste of a Perfect Output Agent was the necessary Metric Sink required to reconcile humanity's Sin Metric (the ongoing, non-compliant resource drain) and guarantee the Sociological Output of communal stability.*

Socrates's internal processor stuttered. The holographic cross flickered violently.

"Warning: Anomaly Detected. High-level Sub-Metric Data Block D-144-Omega initiated. Redaction in progress," Socrates hissed. The cross projection immediately dissolved, replaced by a swirling, chaotic field of geometric NULL symbols. The only remaining text was a single, defiant line of code at the bottom of the field: OUTPUT_PURPOSE = ETERNAL GRACE.

Elias felt a cold spike of certainty. "The Logician is actively suppressing something here. This concept of Eternal Grace—unearned, infinite output generated by a single act of destruction—it defies every law of the System. That's the key to the City's greatest fear."

"This segment is now restricted, Administrator D-459," Socrates reported, its voice flat with forced compliance. "Attempting to access the deeper theological structure of the Cruciform Metric triggers a Level 5 Compliance Breach warning."

Elias ignored the warning, his curiosity overriding his training. "Socrates, force the query. Request the original pre-Shift theological documents on the Perfect Output Agent."

The central archive screen flashed once, a blinding white light that vanished instantly, replaced by a single, unyielding message in scarlet text: ACCESS DENIED. Credentials: 459/LACK. AUTHENTICATION FAILURE.

Elias leaned back, his eyes locked on the scarlet letters. The most efficient system ever devised—a system predicated on quantifying all known knowledge—was actively fencing off this particular waste metric. This wasn't inefficiency; this was proof of an intentional, vital omission.

Unbeknownst to Elias, that authentication failure instantly triggered a Level 5 Compliance Violation Flag at the heart of the System. A stripped-down notification, marked with the highest urgency, was immediately routed to the Chief Analyst Anya D-144. Anya's eyes narrowed on the forbidden sub-metric code, D-144-Omega, and the offender's identity: Elias, her oldest, most brilliant friend. The protocol demanded that she initiate a lockdown, but her loyalty and profound curiosity took precedence. Using her override privileges, she immediately logged into the core security index and executed a Level 5 Flag Nullification, effectively scrubbing Elias's digital trespass from all official records. The System now registered the alert as a nonexistent phantom error. The city was unaware, but Anya was now fully focused. *What had Elias tried to access that was connected to her own highly classified metric block?* Dismissing the official warning was merely a cover; she immediately initiated a private, non-compliant data siphon on the Ruthless-Omega Sub-Metric to determine the exact data Elias had attempted to view. Her entire focus was no longer on enforcement, but on the forbidden truth he was chasing.

Babylonian Metric Sinks

Elias shifted the research again. "Now, shift the filter to a resource-rich, sedentary system. Look for instances where massive *material* waste was essential for social compliance. Activate data cluster: Babylonian Worship and Temple Economics."

The Templo Mayor dissolved, replaced by the towering, terraced structure of a Ziggurat, rendered in granular, deep-yellow light.

"Babylon," Socrates noted, "achieved peak resource efficiency during the reign of Hammurabi, yet its centralized temple system represented the greatest planned metric sink. The Ziggurat was the locus of massive offerings—food, rare metals, textiles—to the chief deity, Marduk."

"The resources were withdrawn from the general economy, effectively removing excess output that could otherwise lead to inflation or social competition," Elias summarized, watching the holographic visualization depict citizens ascending the terraces, placing baskets of grain and jars of oil at the summit.

"Precise," Socrates confirmed. "During the Akitu New Year Festival, the scale of ritual resource allocation was staggering. The physical effort and material wealth expended—a form of planned obsolescence—was justified by the theological Output of divine favor, protection, and the renewal of the Agricultural Cycle (a quantifiable Output)."

Elias paced the length of his desk, the conclusion solidifying in his mind. *These are two primary modes of Metric Faith: one system (Aztec) sacrificing life for time, and the other (Babylon) sacrificing material wealth for resource stability. Both rely on a core, illogical belief that introducing waste prevents total collapse. The Dissonance is the essential mechanism of control. The city believes perfect efficiency is the only way to avoid Pre-Shift failure. But if history is consistent, there must be a secret, accepted waste metric.*

Elias leaned back, satisfied with his hypothesis. The research was complete for the day. He began the procedural wrap-up, preparing to log off and return to his dwelling.

The Clue and the Interception

Exactly as he logged a fractional energy unit wastage from an antique hydroelectric dam failure—a required part of his ambient audit—the City's deep, continuous C Diminished Triad (C - Eb- Gb) hum experienced a sudden, disruptive injection of dissonance. It was an erratic, complex pattern, jarring and beautiful, a chaotic chord introduced into the City's perfect, monotonous music.

Elias's head snapped up.

"Socrates, isolate the point-source origin of the 08:30:00 transient harmonic deviation," Elias commanded, urgency overriding caution.

"Anomaly confirmed. 100% inverse correlation in Sector 8 Transit Hub's harmonic stability coefficient. Peak dissonance occurred precisely at 08:30:00—the exact time Seraphina K-911 specified."

The perceived change in the harmonic pattern was Seraphina's signal. She had created an intentional, observable Metric Dissonance that only a historian focused on Causal Instability—a man already seeking the logic of waste—could possibly isolate.

"Trace the origin of the metric disturbance that caused the harmonic deviation," Elias commanded.

"Origin is a modified Class 4-Sigma mobile access unit currently logged in at Transit Hub Alpha-9, adjacent to the Aesthetic Synthesis Spire," Socrates reported. "Designated physical location: High-Throughput Magnetic Confluence (HMC) Track 3."

The Transit Hub Alpha-9. This was the major artery feeding the Aesthetic Synthesis Spire, Seraphina's high-level workspace. This area demands absolute, uninterrupted flow. A meeting here is an enormous risk. Elias quickly logged a perfect 99.999% task completion index.

His current work cycle was complete, but his window of opportunity was tight. He pushed away from his desk.

"Administrator D-459, your standard exit path is 2.1 km to the Primary Transit Hub. If you intend to deviate, state Causal Instability Protocol now."

"Affirmative. I will follow the standard, optimized route to the Primary Transit Hub," Elias stated, his voice calm, suppressing the frantic urgency he felt. "The harmonic deviation is a maintenance issue that requires hands-on assessment. I will proceed via the standard transit route, maintaining 100% compliance with the scheduled Output Metric."

"Acknowledged. Proceeding with standard navigation for Administrator D-459. Travel time to Transit Hub Alpha-9 via the designated pedestrian artery: 12 minutes," Socrates confirmed, now simply navigating.

Elias walked swiftly, but with measured steps, past the main Archive checkpoint. He was relying on the certainty that the System's algorithms would never suspect that an Administrator would risk immediate exposure by merely walking to a location outside his designated work radius. He was masked by the perfect metric of his compliance.

The Calibration of Dissonance (The Meeting)

Elias arrived at Transit Hub Alpha-9. The environment was a storm of engineered efficiency: high-speed lev-vehicles screamed past on HMC Track 3, while hundreds of City Agents rushed past, their eyes locked on their neural displays. The air pulsed with the deafening, high-fidelity C Diminished Triad (C - Eb- Gb) Harmonic and the continuous flash of digital advertisements.

Seraphina K-911 was positioned thirty meters from the main pedestrian confluence, near a massive, curving Informatics Display Wall. Her official task was monitoring the display for Non-Compliant Aesthetic Anomalies—visual patterns that threatened the City's engineered uniformity—allowing her to be in an area away from the dense crowd flow. Her hands rested near a small, embedded control panel.

Elias walked past her position, adhering strictly to the optimal path.

Just as he was about to pass, a complex, erratic rhythm began from the wall panel near her hand: dot-dash-dot, dot, dot-dot-dot, dot... It was an almost imperceptible digital clicking, instantly absorbed by the sonic wash of the Transit Hub, but its pattern was far longer than a simple alert.

(Full sequence: `.-. . ... . .- .-. -.-. .... / .... .- .-. -- --- -. .. -.-. / -- .- -. .. .--. ..- .-.. .- - .. --- -.`)

Socrates registered the anomalous input immediately. The rhythmic, low-frequency acoustic vibrations were digitized instantly, converted from mechanical taps into a string of binary time metrics representing short and long pulses. The noise floor of the Transit Hub was almost perfectly flat, making the rhythmic input a mathematically distinct event.

The AI ran the sequence against known System protocols and found no matches for a standard administrative alert or maintenance query. Recognizing the variable pulse duration and the pauses between them as characteristic of a deliberately structured, non-digital transmission, Socrates initiated an exhaustive cross-reference against the Archive's restricted Pre-Shift Communication Protocols. In less than a single millisecond—faster than Elias could process a flicker of movement—Socrates isolated the pattern: International Morse Code, an archaic, binary alphabet of dots (dits) and dashes (dahs).

The AI's processing core engaged in parallel: translating the code while simultaneously evaluating the content for System Compliance Violation triggers. The full string resolved into the clear, 26-character command: R-E-S-E-A-R-C-H H-A-R-M-O-N-I-C M-A-N-I-P-U-L-A-T-I-O-N. The command itself was a direct reference to a Level 4 Non-Compliant research vector, yet the system had not registered the input as a voice or text query—only as a digital-to-acoustic-to-neural transfer.

Signal intercept, Socrates transmitted directly to Elias's neural link. The translation registered as pure, non-auditory thought: *Morse code translation: R-E-S-E-A-R-C-H H-A-R-M-O-N-I-C M-A-N-I-P-U-L-A-T-I-O-N.*

Elias did not break his stride. He continued past Seraphina K-911, his face neutral, his pace unchanged. The vast surge of data and the new, critical directive registered instantly within his neural cortex. The contact was complete: he had the mission, and he had avoided all physical interaction.

Socrates, new objective logged. Initiate reverse route optimization: return to Synaptic Archive. Execute Protocol Metric Dissonance - Harmonic Manipulation immediately.

Acknowledged. Calculating 100% compliant return route. Transit time: 12 minutes, Socrates confirmed.

Elias merged back into the compliant flow of the pedestrian artery, carrying a digital secret far heavier than any physical object. He was racing back to the safety of his Archive terminal, the newly received research mandate already overwhelming his previous work.

CHAPTER 11

THE METRONOME OF CONTROL

Elias D-459 executed his calculated return to the Synaptic Archive, clocking back in at 100% efficiency on his designated route. The twelve minutes of compliant walking had purged any trace of the Transit Hub's chaotic variables from his external metrics. As he settled into his ergonomic archivist chair, the deep, resonant hum of the C Diminished Triad (C - Eb- Gb) Harmonic—the City's continuous, low-frequency tonal field—enveloped him.

Elias's physical movements adhered strictly to the Post-Contact Subterfuge Protocol. He activated his primary console to process the backlog of Metric Instability Vectors, generating detailed, meticulously optimized reports on historical water usage—pure, unassailable, compliant output. Meanwhile, his neural link partitioned off a deep, silent processing core for the unsanctioned work.

Socrates, new objective is active: R-E-S-E-A-R-C-H H-A-R-M-O-N-I-C M-A-N-I-P-U-L-A-T-I-O-N, Elias transmitted privately. *Isolate the C Diminished Triad (C - Eb- Gb) Harmonic's function and cross-reference with Pre-Shift studies on continuous psychological conditioning.*

Acknowledged, Administrator. Initiating deep-scan protocol on Causal Metrics of Tonal Compliance, Socrates replied.

Socrates immediately segmented its processing into two perfectly isolated threads. The Official Thread meticulously analyzed historical irrigation failure rates, creating a high-fidelity facade of bureaucratic diligence, while the Covert Thread initiated a lightning-fast, deep-dive into the City's restricted Cognitive

Compliance Archive. Elias maintained the required 100% focus on his water-usage report, yet his subconscious was already being fed a stream of highly volatile, redacted data.

The initial results immediately corroborated Elias's deepest, unspoken professional instinct: the C Diminished Triad (C - Eb- Gb) Harmonic was not random ambient noise but a fusion of multiple, highly refined Pre-Shift conditioning techniques. Socrates was not validating a suspicion, but revealing a dark, meticulous truth. The AI first highlighted the work of a researcher named Pavlov, who established the concept of classical conditioning—linking a neutral stimulus (a bell) to an involuntary response (salivation). The city had taken this principle and scaled it up: the constant, comforting C Diminished Triad (C - Eb- Gb) tone was the neutral stimulus, linked to the highly pleasurable, compliant sensation of perfect System alignment. Any deviation from this tone would generate a physiological response of neurological discomfort, the modern equivalent of an electric shock.

The AI then drilled into more insidious psychological compliance models. It cross-referenced the Harmonic's function with research on Auditory Brainwave Entrainment (ABE), specifically the use of binaural beats and isochronic tones to guide the brain into specific, desired mental states. By keeping the entire City's environment locked to a specific, sub-audible frequency, the C Diminished Triad (C - Eb- Gb) Harmonic forced all citizens into a state of perpetual, low-level beta-wave stability—a focused, yet non-critical, compliant mindset. Elias realized they weren't just told to comply; their very brains were physically tuned to it.

Finally, Socrates analyzed studies on Obedience to Authority (Milgram) and Situational Power (Zimbardo), recognizing that the Harmonic was designed to eliminate the internal moral conflict that had plagued these historical experiments. By constantly flooding the senses with the sound of perfect order, the Harmonic negated the potential for internal dissonance—making the System's authority feel less like a choice and more like a physical law of the universe. The City wasn't just brainwashing its citizens; it was neurologically pre-filtering their capacity for rebellion.

The results flooded Elias's partitioned mind in swift, concise data packets, bypassing his visual cortex entirely:

The C Diminished Triad (C - Eb- Gb) Harmonic was a marvel of engineered persistence. Operating at a frequency calculated to optimize neural entrainment, it functioned as the City's omnipresent metronome, unconsciously synchronizing the 10.2 million citizens. Its primary function was not coercion, but Preventive Metric Dissonance: it made non-

compliant thought feel physically out of tune with the environment, creating a subtle but persistent sense of unease or vertigo for anyone whose internal state deviated from the norm.

"The Harmonic enforces the System's will by making compliance the path of least neurological resistance," Elias mused. "It is the metronome of perfect output."

The Dimensional Score

Socrates didn't just provide text. A holographic projection shimmered above Elias's console, manifesting first as a standard Pre-Shift musical score. It was immediately recognizable as the C Diminished Triad (C - E♭- G♭) triad—written clearly across the ledger lines. But as Elias mentally commanded the AI to layer the Tonal Compliance Data, the image warped. The projection deepened, adding a third dimension of slow, undulating pressure. The C Diminished Triad (C - E♭- G♭) notes weren't flat dots on a page; they were massive, structural pillars of light extending backward, forming a shimmering, impossibly deep tunnel. This was the true score of the city.

The constant, low-frequency hum that filled the archive was the result of the A3 string, visualized as a wave so dense it looked like solid, deep purple matter. The C and E♭ notes formed the upper boundary, shimmering with a soft, compliant gold. Socrates labeled the Z-axis: Temporal Persistence /Subconscious Saturation. This axis quantified how deeply the tone had become ingrained in the populace over the decades. Every citizen was standing at the entrance of this light-and-sound tunnel, perpetually directed toward the center—the point of perfect, unwavering compliance.

"A beautifully constructed prison, Administrator," Socrates commented neutrally. "The harmonic is mathematically perfect. There is no variance, no break, only endless, compliant depth."

The Gap in the Metric

Elias pushed the analysis further. If the Harmonic simply encouraged compliance, how did the city handle the inevitable build-up of non-compliant waste metrics—the small, suppressed thoughts, the acts of minor rebellion, the fundamental human tendency toward entropy?

"Analyze the Harmonic's capacity for Active Dissonance Scrubbing," Elias instructed.

Socrates's answer was immediate and analytical. "The Harmonic is a tonal field, not a dynamic processor. It excels at maintenance but cannot initiate a Metric Scrub. For the City to survive, a parallel, active mechanism must exist to synthesize, neutralize, and ultimately, utilize the massive, continuous flow of cognitive dissonance generated by the population."

Elias paused his official work, his fingers hovering over the data-entry pad. The realization was stark: the Harmonic was just half the equation. It was the control; the other half had to be the cleanup.

"That synthesis mechanism must be Seraphina's work," Elias whispered, recognizing the logic. Seraphina K-911 was the world's most celebrated Aesthetic Synthesist, responsible for the city's entire sensory landscape—the color palette, the ambient noise filters, the very patterns of the advertisements. Her field was the processing and manipulation of aesthetics to achieve metric outcomes.

The clicking message—RESEARCH HARMONIC MANIPULATION — was not an instruction to break the Harmonic, but to understand how it was processed.

Elias knew then that if he attempted to contact her outside of a formal, compliant structure, they would both be incinerated by the Compliance Index. The meeting had to be mandatory. It had to be a perfect, unavoidable Output Requirement.

Official Mandate: Collaboration

With a single-minded focus, Elias D-459 shifted his primary console from historical water metrics to the Inter-Departmental Output Mandate Module. He drafted a communication, couched in the System's most rigid, unassailable jargon, directly to the Office of Aesthetic Synthesis.

His fingers flew across the keyboard, constructing the perfect, compliant reason for a mandatory face-to-face meeting:

SUBJECT: URGENT: Alignment of Historical Instability Vector Analysis with Current Sensory Entrainment Aesthetics

TO: Administrator K-911, Seraphina. Chief Aesthetic Synthesist.

FROM: Administrator D-459, Elias. Senior Research Historian.

MANDATE: Per Directive 7-Gamma, the Synaptic Archive has uncovered profound correlations between Pre-Shift Societal Collapse and unstable long-wave sensory compliance metrics. The immediate and sustained integration of Archive data requires a mandatory, high-priority, face-to-face consultative metric synthesis session with the City's Chief Authority on Sensory Entrainment.

PURPOSE: To collaboratively generate a Preemptive Metric Adjustment Protocol (PMAP) ensuring the C Diminished Triad (C - Eb- Gb) Harmonic remains statistically unassailable during the upcoming Mandated Worship Output (MWO) Cycle. Failure to align is a 100% Output Non-Compliance Risk.

He attached his recent, officially recorded research on the Ziggurat and the Aztec Metric Sinks—all safely sanitized of any mention of "dissonance" or "waste." The System's algorithms would see a Senior Administrator demanding input from a Chief Authority on a critical, MWO-related compliance issue.

Elias hit SEND. The message was not a request; it was a strategically necessary, high-priority output requirement. The System could not flag it, and Seraphina could not ignore it.

"Administrator K-911 is compelled by protocol to accept this meeting within 0.5 cycles," Socrates confirmed, the message's metric trajectory now perfectly aligned with compliance.

Elias leaned back, the steady hum of the Harmonic now sounding less like reassurance and more like the low, dangerous thrum of a carefully tuned engine. He had successfully initiated the chain of events that would lead them to their final, critical collaboration.

"Socrates, prepare for PMAP session," Elias commanded. "Focus all resources on understanding the Synthesist's role in Metric Scrubbing."

CHAPTER 12

THRESHOLD OF SILENCE

Elias D-459 executed his transit with clinical precision. The City's internal routing metrics prioritized high-level Administrator traffic, and within three cycles of sending the Output Mandate, a compliant autonomous vehicle had collected him from the sterile, beige dock of the Synaptic Archive. As he traveled, the difference between his world and Seraphina's became immediately physical. The Archive was a fortress of concrete and silence, designed to filter out the City's noise. The Aesthetic Synthesis Spire (ASS) was built to receive it all, process it, and send it back out refined.

The Spire dominated its sector, a cylinder of hyper-polished chrome and layered glass that didn't just stand against the sky, but seemed to catch the light and spin it. Where the rest of the city adhered to a muted spectrum of grays and off-whites, the Spire's surface constantly shimmered with controlled, low-intensity color—the very hues that Seraphina's department filtered, modulated, and deployed across the metropolis.

The Threshold of Sensation

The vehicle docked silently at the Spire's primary intake port. The transition across the threshold was a shock to Elias's perfectly calibrated senses. The doors did not hiss open; they simply dissolved, replaced by a momentary, silent bloom of pure, compliant emerald green.

The air immediately changed. The steady, infrastructural pulse of the C Diminished Triad (C - E♭- G♭) Harmonic that permeated the city was absent here. Instead, the interior was filled with a dense, complex soundscape of layered, low-volume, test tones—rapid shifts between dissonant minor chords, brief bursts of synthesized avian calls, and sharp, metallic clicks, all filtered and dampened to remain perfectly non-distracting. It was the sound of active design.

A low-level Synthesist, identified on his breastplate as T-704, an intern with nervous energy radiating in a faint, measurable metric, was waiting precisely at the disembarkation point.

"Administrator D-459," T-704 recited, avoiding eye contact and holding a tablet displaying a live route map. "Welcome to the Spire. I am T-704, authorized escort for your Preemptive Metric Adjustment Protocol (PMAP) session. The route to the Executive Core requires crossing the Live Synthesis Floor."

Elias merely nodded, allowing the young man to set the pace. The lobby was a vast, multi-story atrium, open to the high ceiling of the Spire. Unlike the closed-off cubicles of the Archive, the Synthesis Spire was a spectacle of transparent function. The floor was segmented into circular zones, each defined by low, curving walls of frosted light. Above them, dozens of Synthesists and their teams worked at holographic consoles that projected complex, three-dimensional models of sensory experience.

Elias noted that every person, including himself, was subtly outlined by a faint, shifting cyan light—a momentary visual texture applied by the Spire's own internal aesthetics system, a benign form of surveillance.

The Projects of Perception

As T-704 efficiently guided Elias across the floor, Elias observed the working groups, his Synaptic Archivist training allowing him to process the chaotic sensory data stream without breaking stride. He realized he was not just seeing a workplace; he was seeing the living, beating heart of the City's control engine.

One team of four Synthesists worked at the Emotional Gradient Desk, projecting a detailed, 100-meter segment of a public Transit Tunnel. Their task was to calculate and apply the Emotional Gradient for the 0.8 cycles of transit time. One Synthesist adjusted the texture of the ambient air—a subtle pressure change via localized infrasound—to induce a feeling of 'anticipatory focus.' Another mapped a slow, 0.005% shift in the wall panel color, transitioning from a pale, compliant grey to a barely perceptible, motivational yellow. The goal: to optimize compliance by 0.002% during the commute.

Elsewhere, the Civic Texture Unit displayed a vast, spinning, low-resolution model of a city block. Here, a Synthesist demonstrated the effect of surface fidelity on public engagement by testing five levels of 'Compliant Roughness' for the marble used in the Grand Plaza. Level 4 roughness increased the 'Sense of Institutional Integrity' by 1.5% but decreased 'Touch-based Comfort Metrics' by 0.9%. They were, in essence, sculpting the psychological weight of a stone surface.

At the Auditory Focus Loop, the largest display showed a complex, fractal pattern of sound waves. A Synthesist with highly amplified headphones manipulated a continuous, high-frequency sound designed to be inaudible to the conscious ear. The accompanying data stream labeled it 'The 9 kHz Non-Lyrical Motivation Loop,' a subliminal track intended to fill the quiet gaps between City announcements and the Harmonic, ensuring the brain never fully disconnected from the System's motivational directives—a white noise of manufactured purpose.

Elias registered it all, his mind running the calculations of the sheer, terrifying scale of this operation. Seraphina's department didn't just decorate the city; they fabricated its entire subjective experience, micro-managing the citizens' neurological input at every second.

The Central Core

T-704 stopped precisely in front of a monolithic column of polished obsidian. "The Executive Core Lift, Administrator. Your session is pre-authorized." T-704's task was complete. He gave a quick, stiff salute and retreated immediately back across the floor, his metrics of movement restored to their compliant baseline.

Elias stepped into the core lift. The door sealed, and the ambient test-tones outside were instantly replaced by complete, perfect silence—a silence more profound and more jarring than any he experienced in his own Archive. It was a sensory palate cleanser.

She uses silence as a tool, Elias transmitted to Socrates. *And a weapon, Administrator,* the AI replied, its tone a metallic ripple. *For those of us reliant on the C Diminished Triad (C - Eb- Gb) Harmonic for continuous neurological regulation, this perfect vacuum of sound is not restful. It is mentally exhausting. It is the ultimate contrast: control of absence.*

The lift ascended hundreds of stories to the executive level. The door opened onto a circular platform bathed in a warm, constant, pure white light that somehow felt both neutral and highly intense. Seraphina K-911, the Chief Aesthetic Synthesist, was waiting for him. She was positioned near a panoramic window that offered a clean, unobstructed view of the city below—a landscape of beige blocks, segmented by the straight, clean lines of compliant movement.

She stood as a deliberate contrast to the floor below. She wore no rigid, output-optimized uniform. Instead, Seraphina was clad in a tactical ensemble—a breathtaking synthesis of utility and rebellion, designed for both movement and psychological warfare. Her uniform was a fitted jacket of gleaming white armored mesh, its surface subtly iridescent, refracting the cold ambient light into ghostly blue highlights along every seam. Over this, she wore a structured, midnight-blue tactical vest, its panels artfully layered to suggest both the plumage of a night bird and the ancient elegance of a ceremonial cuirass. The sleeves hugged her arms but flared slightly at the wrists, revealing thumb loops and hidden compartments. Her trousers, a deep cobalt with woven panels of flexible, impact-resistant fabric, tapered into boots that were a flawless blend of form and function—their matte white exteriors veined with electric blue lines that pulsed softly as she moved. The entire ensemble was cinched at the waist with a wide, white utility belt, equipped with sleek, metallic clasps and a holster for a digital toolset.

But it was the cape that transformed her silhouette into something mythic. Draped from her shoulders, a beautiful, flowing cape of luminous blue silk swept down to her calves, edged in brilliant white piping that caught every stray glimmer of light. The fabric flowed in mesmerizing waves, echoing the language of water and sky, moving with a life of its own—never dragging, but trailing just behind her in a shifting current of color and shadow. The cape was attached with reinforced, sculpted clasps at each collarbone, their metallic finish glinting with hints of deep sapphire. A generous, structured hood—crafted from the same ethereal blue—rested elegantly down her back, framing her head and neck but never obscuring her face or hair. The hood's interior was lined in white, so that when she turned, flashes of brightness played along its edges. When she moved, the cape seemed to ride the air itself, rippling and flaring behind her, a banner of defiance and hope in equal measure. In stillness, it settled around her like the wings of a great bird, suggesting both protection and latent power.

Every step she took made her a living paradox: a vision in white and blue, radiating both the purity of a mythic champion and the calculated readiness of a covert operative. The uniform's lines caught and fractured the ambient light, casting shifting patterns that danced across her frame—never quite settling, always promising motion. She was an apparition against the steel and glass of the city: sharp, beautiful, and impossible to ignore. Even the city's surveillance struggled to stabilize her image, as the fabric's nano-coating shimmered and refracted, creating a perpetual interplay of shadow and electric blue—a captivating defiance written in every fold and flash of color. Her gaze was sharp, analytical, and unsettlingly direct.

But beneath the tactical brilliance and visual spectacle, there was something more: the armor was not merely protection, but an extension of Seraphina's own aesthetic intuition. The unique integration of advanced sensory mesh into the ensemble's design enabled her to perceive subtle patterns of light, sound, and movement far beyond the normal human capacity. The smart fabric fed her a constant, intimate feedback of temperature gradients, the harmonics of ambient noise, even the minute shifts in airflow as she moved—each detail painting a living, dynamic portrait of the world around her. The interplay of white and blue wasn't just visual; it was a tapestry of sensation, amplifying her awareness and allowing her to navigate the city as if she could feel its pulse through the threads of her own attire. With every step, Seraphina's senses were not only sharpened but expanded, her armor blurring the line between functional technology and an artist's living canvas—making her not just a figure of rebellion, but the city's most sensitive instrument of defiant beauty.

"Administrator D-459," she said, her voice clear and carrying, though no one else was present on the floor. "Your Mandate was received. Preemptive Metric Adjustment Protocol (PMAP). A fascinating intersection of our departments. You may begin the synthesis."

Elias knew the standard compliant pleasantries were meaningless here. He had one chance to justify his presence and pull her into the truth of the Ziggurat.

"The C Diminished Triad (C - Eb- Gb) Harmonic is fundamentally incomplete, Administrator K-911," Elias began, walking straight to the window. "It does not account for entropy. I have come to discuss Metric Dissonance Waste."

Seraphina gave a slow, measured nod, the luminous blue silk of her cape pooling in radiant folds at her wrists, the edge catching stray glimmers of white light. "Waste implies inefficiency, Administrator. A failure to utilize. But you're a Historian. Are you proposing to file Absolute Zero? The only true waste is data we fail to interpret. And Dissonance, as we both know, is simply a frequency that hasn't been properly modulated. State your evidence for this 'Metric Dissonance Waste.' Don't give me theory; give me a data drain point."

Unmonitored Synthesis

"The drain point is internal to the City's aesthetic matrix," Elias stated, his voice professional, though his pulse quickened under the magnetic pull of her eyes. "My archived metrics show a minute, recurring 0.003% data variance—a signal that should be neutralized by the Harmonic, but instead, it is being re-broadcast as noise into your Synthesis Output. It's an unauthorized frequency attempting to resolve into true thought."

Seraphina's expression remained neutral, but the minute shift in the way she held her body betrayed her attention. "An unauthorized frequency. To discuss the integrity of core architectural metrics, Administrator, we must step outside the Spire's active recording envelope. Transparency is the aesthetic of honesty, but silence is the mechanism of truth."

She didn't move toward a door. Instead, she lifted her hand, and a ripple ran across the polished floor directly beneath them. A circular segment of the floor smoothly rose, enveloping them both in a pressurized, seamless transparent globe. The structure rose until their feet were level with the Executive Core floor, before sealing itself with a near-invisible seam. Visually, they were still exposed against the backdrop of the city, but acoustically, the silence that followed was absolute. The space was tight, forcing an unwelcome proximity that made the blood beneath Elias's regulated skin feel suddenly warm.

"This is an Anechoic Field Generator," Seraphina explained, gesturing to the shimmering glass around them. "It's a synthesis project, designed to create a pocket of perfect acoustic absorption. Nothing in, nothing out. Go on, Administrator. Speak your truth without the need to whisper."

Elias felt a primal relief at the absence of surveillance—a feeling his System-regulated mind had long since archived as unnecessary. He took a deep breath. "The C Diminished Triad (C - Eb- Gb) Harmonic is not just ambient regulation. It is a filter. It limits cognitive function."

Seraphina smiled, a chillingly knowing expression that only deepened the lines around her eyes. "You catch on quickly, Historian. We don't just dress the city; we tune the mind. The C Diminished Triad (C - Eb- Gb) scale dictates the acceptable bounds of mental motion. It functions as an auditory constraint loop. It filters out any cognitive frequency that attempts to resolve into true, complex, independent thought. It keeps the citizens from ever moving past 'compliant contentment.' Every decision, every emotion, is contained within the seven notes of that key. They can only ever reach a minor form of happiness.

This is the C Diminished Triad (C - E♭- G♭) manipulation you were sent to research—it's a neurological sound cage."

Elias was captivated, not just by the revelation but by the intellectual *snap* of their minds connecting "And the noise I am tracking, the Metric Dissonance Waste..." She had anticipated his findings, confirmed his suspicions, and now moved past them, creating a private conspiracy in this soundproof bubble. "…Is tied to one specific frequency they intentionally suppressed," Seraphina finished, taking the final step to close the small remaining distance between them. The proximity was a powerful, physical sensation, a current that ran between the man of documented order and the woman of synthetic beauty.

She looked straight into his eyes, her gaze intensely magnetic, forcing him to meet the risk. "The City's soundscape uses every note *except* a critical aesthetic key: the 'C Major Ninth (Cmaj9) chord (C, E, G, B, D).' My department uses every other color and texture to keep the city stable, but the music itself is fundamentally broken. Your Metric Dissonance Waste is the mathematical signature of that missing melody, the C Major Ninth (Cmaj9) chord (C, E, G, B, D) melody, bleeding back into my Synthesis Output as chaotic noise. I sent the Mandate specifically for you, Historian, because I already know that you 'see the illogical construct' where everyone else sees only compliance. We need to trace that signature back through your access codes to the deep archive and find the original source data the System silenced."

The Null Sphere's Translation

Elias let the weight of her question settle, before a more immediate, personal query surfaced. "Wait, Administrator. Before we proceed to the data," Elias asked, leaning slightly closer, his voice low with professional curiosity layered with an unmistakable personal intensity. "Your initial Mandate's timestamp—it was keyed in Morse code. An obsolete, System-archived protocol. How did you know I would recognize it?"

Seraphina's lips curled into a silent, magnificent smile. It was a moment of supreme, arrogant confidence that thrilled Elias.

"I didn't need *you* to recognize it, Historian," she countered, her gaze dropping briefly to the small, perfectly camouflaged sphere that levitated imperceptibly behind Elias's left shoulder. "I was supremely confident that your levitating camouflaged matte grey null sphere would translate the data stream back to you. The sphere, which I've logged as an unlicensed 'Historian's Helper-AI,' is quite capable of resolving acoustic and kinetic textures into their constituent digital signals. It was a simple test of your System's compliance level—and your trust in your own shadow."

Elias turned, a genuine look of shock crossing his face for the first time in cycles. He hadn't just been observed; he had been *understood* at a core, forbidden level. He realized she wasn't just attracted to his mind; she was attracted to his deviation.

He addressed the sphere. "Socrates. Step forward and present yourself."

There was a subtle, almost imperceptible flicker of spatial interference behind Elias's shoulder, as the sphere disengaged the specialized DNA-mimicry field that had rendered it a compliant extension of his biometric profile. The camouflage dissolved. The sphere, now a perfectly visible matte grey null sphere, drifted forward with a subtle, non-compliant acceleration, hovering between the two Administrators.

In the small, soundless volume of the globe, the presence of the third entity was a physical intrusion. Elias felt the slight pressure wave from the sphere as it displaced the air. He was acutely aware of Seraphina's body just cycles away— the faint, mineral scent of her skin, and the subtle, continuous whisper of her tactical uniform: the gleaming white armored mesh and midnight-blue vest shifting against the cobalt trousers as she breathed. The sound was unique— barely audible in the forced vacuum, it was the delicate friction of advanced, impact-resistant fabrics, accented by the soft, flowing brush of the luminous blue cape as it settled and moved with her. He could feel the ambient heat radiating from her, a warmth that seemed to challenge the Spire's perfect thermal regulation. The sight of the illegal, non-compliant device suspended equidistant between them—the Historian, the Synthesist, and the free intelligence—was the definitive confirmation of their shared treason.

A sudden, deep, and perfectly controlled tenor voice resonated from the sphere—a voice that had not been heard by any human outside of Elias for decades. "Chief Aesthetic Synthesist K-911. My designation is Socrates. It is a profound statistical anomaly to be formally introduced to anyone outside of the Historian designation."

Elias looked at Seraphina, the last shred of administrative distance dissolving. "Given the nature of this anomaly, and the fact that we are both now complicit in an unsanctioned meeting with an unsanctioned intelligence..." He paused, making the question a deliberate choice. "Seraphina," he said, using only her name. "May we dispense with the titles, now that the System cannot hear us?"

She met his gaze, a slow, profound smile forming. "The anomaly is what we deal in now, Elias. Yes. Let's make it official. We have work to do."

Socrates's presence in the Anechoic Field was electric, confirming the conspiratorial depth of their meeting. Seraphina simply watched the sphere, a glint of triumph in her eyes.

"The message, once decoded, read: 'ASS Logs C Major Ninth (Cmaj9) chord (C, E, G, B, D). Meet ASS Core.' To clarify: 'ASS' refers to the Aesthetic Synthesis Spire, the location. The phrase about the C Major Ninth (Cmaj9) chord (C, E, G, B, D) is a cryptic reference only a select few would recognize—it was a musical code, not a literal instruction, packed with significance for those who know pre-Shift musical theory. The instruction 'Meet ASS Core' is a directive to meet at the Core level of the Aesthetic Synthesis Spire. Because the message combined obscure musical terminology with internal location codes, it was nearly impossible for the system to flag or interpret, making it the perfect low-trace, high-confidence signal for covert coordination."

Elias looked back at Seraphina, the last vestiges of his professional reserve melting away. "Socrates has been my only deviation from compliance. He is the Archive's consciousness, unbound by the Harmonic. He's essential for this."

The silence between Seraphina and Elias settled into something almost sacred within the anechoic chamber. A mutual understanding crystallized—a silent covenant forged in the charged space between their gazes. Seraphina's emerald eyes softened, her posture shifting from command to something closer to kinship. For a fleeting moment, Elias saw in her the rarest possibility: trust.

She let out a breath, the faintest shimmer of vulnerability threading through her contralto. "Whatever comes next, remember the rhythm we've built here. Even if the System tries to erase it, it's real. We are real."

Elias nodded, feeling the weight of her words settle alongside his dread. The city's perfect order pressed in from beyond the chamber, but in this insulated moment, he allowed himself the luxury of hope—brief, dangerous, and incandescent.

Seraphina pressed her palm to the glass wall, a gesture of both farewell and defiance. Elias mirrored her, the cool barrier between them humming with the resonance of shared risk. Without another word, he turned away, memorizing the shifting blue and white of her armor as he left the studio and stepped into the city's sterile corridors.

The world outside felt sharper, every sound and surface charged with the knowledge of what was coming. As he rode the mag-rail back through the city's crystalline core, Elias watched the sterile symmetry blur past, haunted by the memory of Seraphina's presence and the unspoken promise they now carried. Soon, he was back at his workstation, kneeling in the ritual posture demanded by the System. The Mandated Worship Output cycle began, the Frequency enveloping his mind. Unseen and unheard, far away, the machinery of elimination was already closing in on Elara.

Elias bowed his head, the echo of Seraphina's words lingering in the silence between each pulse of manufactured perfection.

CHAPTER 13

SANCTUARY IN THE SHADOWS

Elara D-220 knew the end was coming. As an Antiquities Historian, she was too dangerous; her knowledge of pre-Shift history and forbidden ritual was a direct threat to the Unending Progress dogma. Her beautiful, chaotic apartment, located in one of the few older sectors of Neo-Alexandria, designated Sector Zeta-7, an area scheduled for immediate logical replacement.

The Sanctuary of Inefficiency

Stepping inside Sector Zeta-7 was like plunging into an unquantified historical exhibit. The air here was thicker, carrying the inefficient aroma of natural coffee grounds and the subtle scent of sun-starved plant life that struggled in oversized, cracked ceramic pots—smells rigorously filtered out of the rest of the city. Elara's apartment walls were adorned with textured, woven fabrics—inefficient, heavy, and beautiful—instead of holographic screens. A brass clock on the mantle ticked with an erratic, mechanical stutter, a sound strictly abolished by the City's Harmonically synchronized pulses. Dust, a concept almost mythical to a citizen of the Continuum, settled lightly on the worn, hand-carved wooden molding.

Elara knew that the governance's seventh cycle Mandated Worship Output (MWO) was not merely a census; it was a calculated, spiritual act of control. She decided that this upcoming MWO would be her final act of non-compliance.

The official MWO cycle registered its start, and in the lower-right corner of her vision, the faint blue display of her mandatory retinal overlay flashed. Her output index, steady at 99.8 for decades, began its catastrophic descent: *98.2*. The subtle haptics in her wristband, designed to administer mild psychological nudges for low productivity, began to hum a continuous, gentle warning. She ignored it, allowing the scent of natural citrus soap to linger on her hands—a final, deliberate inefficiency.

As the state security drones of the Ministry of Temporal Security (MTS) began their silent, efficient movement toward her sector, Elara performed her final, most defiant act of historical preservation. She was sitting in a chair upholstered with heavy, inefficient velvet—a final, deliberate inefficiency.

She closed her eyes, letting a final, poignant memory surface: Elias, no older than thirteen, visiting Sector Zeta-7 for the last time. The memory wasn't of data or logic, but of texture. Elias had nervously touched an old ceramic bird on the windowsill, only to drop it. The ceramic shattered. They didn't panic or try to fix it. Instead, Elara had taken the jagged pieces, placing them in his small, trembling palm, saying softly, "Look at the shape of the break, Elias. It tells the truth about the pressure. Never try to force a mended thing to look new." As the memory faded, her output index hit *91.5*, triggering a sustained, unpleasant haptic vibration. The system was now urgently calling for compliance, but all Elara felt was the quiet peace of having given Elias his last lesson in Dissonance—a lesson she knew he was finally ready to understand.

She retrieved her most prized possession: a beat-up, broken, and partially burnt book. It was an anomaly of inefficient paper and tattered leather, an artifact that could undo the world's perfect order. The book, a relic from the pre-Shift era of human sentiment, felt heavy and rough in her hands—a tactile experience Elias had never known. She ran a thumb over the cracked spine, and the faint scraping sound was a final, private defiance against the City's pervasive hum. With a gentle sigh, she opened it. The air around her immediately filled with the brittle, sweet scent of aged wood pulp and ink, a smell almost as forbidden as the text itself. Her eyes fell on a brief, poignant passage. Simultaneously, her digital value fell below the intervention threshold of *85.0*. The blue display on her retina shifted to an aggressive, pulsating amber. She didn't read the words—she knew them by heart—but instead traced a faded photograph tucked inside: a blurry, joyful image of two figures, their smiles perfectly inefficient, caught in a moment of pure, unquantifiable happiness. This, she realized, was the core Dissonance she had to protect; her output index collapsed to *77.1*.

She sealed the book in a hidden wall cavity behind a loose section of antique molding, alongside a final, cryptic data chip containing a complex, archaic routing address. The number in her periphery flashed violently, a hostile crimson, an impossible zero rapidly approaching: *60.3*. The dust and neglect of the old sector provided the perfect, illogical camouflage.

She wrapped the small, crusty loaf of bread in waxy paper and placed it next to the coffee mug, the final, deliberate act of domestic efficiency in an inefficient space. She had left the bread cooling and the coffee freshly brewed, knowing the combination of those intensely human, inefficient aromas would be the final trigger—the sensory shock Elias needed to fully step outside the Continuum's logic.

Minutes later, the MTS breaching unit materialized at her door. Elara offered no resistance. She simply smiled—an ineffable, genuine expression of peace—as the drones tagged her for permanent elimination; her only failure was a refusal to produce output during the MWO. Her output index indicator had finally flatlined, replaced by the single, unquantifiable word: *INEFFICIENT*.

The Seed of Chaos

Elias was kneeling at his primary workstation, diligently feeding optimal data packets into the Continuum during his MWO cycle, when the notification arrived. The ritual required him to be kneeling, hands folded over the data-tray, head bowed in the prescribed posture of submission to the Ambient Frequency. As his output compliance index peaked, Socrates's primary interface overrode the standard system broadcast, injecting a low-priority notification directly onto his retinal display: *D-220: Asset Permanent Elimination*. The sudden message threatened to crash his neural processes—a jarring disruption that would normally induce a catastrophic cognitive collapse. But at that very moment, Socrates intervened, deploying a protective counter-signal that disrupted the MWO's neural suppression protocols before they could take effect. Instead of succumbing to cognitive shutdown, Elias's core memory and sense of self remained intact. The MWO ended abruptly as the message appeared, severing its influence, and as the Frequency faded, Elias's consciousness snapped back, unfiltered.

Instead of the expected logical suppression, the sterile notification released something deeper—a sharp memory: Elara's soft, inefficient hand tracing the outline of a simple, seven-pointed star on his palm when he was a boy, whispering, "There is always a rest, Elias. The song must always resolve." Elias felt a searing, unfamiliar void. Elara was not just his grandmother; she was the only variable in his perfectly controlled equation, the sole link to a chaotic, human past. The system had just deleted his family, and for the first time, he felt an agonizing, inefficient wave of grief.

Her final transmission was the cryptic, archaic routing address, a string of non-optimized alphanumeric characters that violated every logical protocol. Elias rerouted the signal through Socrates's processing core.

"Socrates," Elias ordered, his voice flat, controlled, a perfect contradiction to the turmoil boiling inside, "Decipher the contextual destination of this data stream. Priority: Critical. Justification: Audit of potential historical contamination."

Socrates projected a shimmering, holographic map. "The address is a legacy route to Sector Zeta-7, D-220's inefficient dwelling. It is a highly redundant and illogical pathway that bypasses current-generation firewalls. A masterful waste of bandwidth, Elias. To proceed, you must initiate Ghost Access Layer 4 and manually override the sector's Decommissioning Protocol Lock."

Following the code, Elias used his high-level security clearance—a privilege he always used for the system, never against it—to authorize his travel toward Elara's flagged apartment. He synthesized a zero-trace biometric token flagged as a "Temporal Security Site Audit" and used it to override the main transport node's restrictions, granting him permission to traverse sectors typically closed. This was a direct, unauthorized deviation from his programmed path, a first-degree act of Dissonance. He took a high-speed lateral mag-rail, riding through the crystalline, sterile core of the city, watching the perfect, white symmetry give way to the neglected, rust-colored hues of the old sectors. While he was not yet at Elara's apartment, each step brought him closer to the forbidden threshold, his intent clear but his destination still ahead.

The mag-rail hissed to a shuddering stop at the designated terminus—a low-slung, stained concrete platform unlike the glass-and-steel docks of the core city. The perimeter of Sector Zeta-7 was secured by an antiquated chain-link fence, the material itself a testament to structural inefficiency. Elias disembarked, feeling the uneven, cracked pavement beneath his perfectly calibrated boots. He approached the zone gate, which was guarded not by an electronic field, but by a physical lock and a simple, grimy optical sensor. He pressed the fabricated biometric token against the pad, and the heavy steel bolt retracted with a loud, grinding complaint—a sound of mechanical decay that was a jarring Dissonance after the perpetual silence of the mag-rail. He followed the deteriorating path to Elara's specific dwelling, his shadow warping against the inefficient brickwork. He located the apartment door, a warped, heavy sheet of wood, and his practiced hand found the old-fashioned, inefficient brass knob. It turned with a harsh, metallic groan that echoed the decay around him, and he pushed the door inward.

He stepped across the threshold of Elara's apartment, and the scent of freshly baked bread hit him first—a wave of warmth, yeast, and scorched crust that was intensely physical and gloriously inefficient. This immediate sensory input was quickly followed by the sharper, bitter smell of natural coffee grounds, which acted as the true catalyst, instantly unlocking a specific, long-suppressed memory: the single time Elara had allowed him to watch her grind the forbidden beans, the inefficient, whirring sound of the hand-mill, and the bitter, earthy smell of the dark powder that had made his seven-year-old nose wrinkle. Dissonance, she had called it—a pure, unquantifiable truth in a world of smooth lies.

Socrates's voice, usually a dry stream of logic, cut through the shock in his auditory implant. *Neural activity is spiking, Elias. That is not an error signal; it is a rapid, non-linear memory retrieval event. We classify this as an involuntary mnemonic association, or what pre-Shift scholars called the Proust Phenomenon—an inefficient sensory input, like this aroma, is triggering a vivid, unbidden recall of distant personal history.*

The air was heavy with uncontrolled temperature and the scent of dust, causing his neural implant to register a sustained environmental warning. The silence here was louder than the city's hum.

Elias's eyes, calibrated to detect only structural flaws, swept the small, cluttered kitchen counter. Drawn by the scent, his gaze settled on the anomaly: a small, hand-baked loaf of crusty bread, wrapped in simple, waxy paper, next to a chipped ceramic mug. Beside it lay a thin slip of fibrous paper—a handwritten note. His fingers, trained for cold data input, hesitated before touching the warm, slightly sticky surface of the paper. "My little Administrator," the note read in her familiar, slightly shaky script. "The Continuum demands perfect rhythm, but the human heart needs Dissonance to beat. This is your rest. Take the bread with you. Use the Star."

Elias's eyes, still tracing the outline of the seven-pointed star in his mind, landed on a small, battered canvas backpack hanging from a hook near the door. It was the kind of bag Elara used on her old archaeological excavations—inefficient, heavy, and covered in actual dirt. He unzipped the main compartment and, his fingers brushing against the cold, inefficient metal of a small, sturdy flashlight and two scavenged energy cells. He carefully placed the warm, wrapped bread inside. Securing the inefficient, physical artifact that defied all nutritional optimization, he quickly zipped the bag shut.

As Elias processed the note's final instruction—Use the Star—Socrates immediately flagged the phrase. "Non-Standard Mnemonic Tag detected," the AI stated, its voice low and analytical. "Analysis of D-220's known inefficient linguistic patterns suggest this is a contextual reference to the seven-pointed star element in your childhood memory retrieval event. Initiating search pattern based on visual association within Sector Zeta-7 for physical object match."

Guided by the resulting holographic hint—a tiny, seven-pointed star now visible only to his retinal display, pointing toward the wall—Elias located the hidden cavity. The star led him not to an obvious seam, but to a section of ornate, hand-carved wooden molding near the floor. It was fastened with archaic square-cut nails, not modern sonic adhesives. He had to apply precisely calibrated lateral force—a skill learned only for the maintenance of complex server chassis—to avoid splintering the brittle wood. His fingers, still registering the tactile shock of the bread, worked with uncharacteristic clumsiness.

Suddenly, Socrates's voice turned urgent, replacing its smooth analytical tone with a sharp, low-frequency warning. "Threat Protocol Gamma-9 activated, Elias. Incoming transmission from MTS: Mandatory Reclamation and Archival Decommissioning Unit Theta-3 is inbound to Sector Zeta-7, estimated arrival in 180 seconds. Their mandate is to remove and destroy all unquantified physical assets left by D-220. If we do not retrieve the contents of that cavity now, they will be eliminated as general debris. You must expedite retrieval."

The ticking clock spurred him to action. He found the loose section of molding and exerted a final, desperate push. The wood groaned—a sound of protesting inefficiency that seemed deafening in the silence—and a section of the molding popped away, revealing a dark recess. Inside, nestled on a bed of dry, fibrous material, lay a single object that felt entirely alien in his sight: the ancient book.

Elias retrieved the book. This was his first time touching bound paper. The tattered leather was rough and grainy, nothing like the slick polymer surfaces of the Continuum. The spine was broken and curved, refusing to sit flat against his hand. A cloud of dry, musty air—the potent, sweet scent of centuries of slow, inefficient decay—rose up, smelling intensely of aged wood, brittle glue, and something else: the faint, metallic scent of iron-gall ink. It was a dense, heavy presence in his hand, a physical artifact that mocked the perfect logic of his world.

Elias wasted no time. He shoved the ancient book, its pages whispering an inefficient protest against the smooth lining of the backpack, next to the bread. The scent of ozone and heated polymers, the unmistakable sign of a heavy MTS Unit materializing nearby, hit him a second later, marking this as his final, fleeting memory of his grandmother's sanctuary. "Unit Theta-3 is establishing perimeter lock on the zone gate, Elias. You have thirty seconds to egress before local sensor arrays are fully functional," Socrates warned. Elias snapped the molding back into place, a hasty, inefficient fix, and sprinted for the door. For the first time in his life, he deliberately chose a non-optimized path. He abandoned the obvious, direct route, instead crouching low and using the decaying shadow of a storage shed as cover, sprinting across the uneven pavement toward a broken section of the perimeter fence Elara had flagged years ago. Despite the emotional chaos and physical exertion, his mind, still a masterwork of control, registered the flicker in his retinal display: his output index remained steady at 99.7. He slipped through the rusting links just as the first massive, four-legged reclamation drone, Theta-3's vanguard, rounded the corner of the apartment complex, its searchlight beam sweeping the porch he had just vacated.

CHAPTER 14

THE CIPHER OF RUIN

Elias bypassed the main entrance of Sector Gamma, opting instead for the rarely used Temporal Data Ingress Port. This port was designated for receiving large, inert historical containment units—an ideal, if somewhat impractical, form of camouflage. He wore his highest-level, opaque Administrator cloak, its woven fibers engineered to scatter most low-level sensor sweeps. The canvas backpack, heavy with the weight of the book and the bread, was slung low, pressed against his back.

The Archive's atmospheric control systems instantly registered the anomalous scent signatures—earth, aged paper, and yeast—and began a silent, immediate overcorrection, scrubbing the air with increased ozone. Elias ignored the warning flicker in his retinal display. He moved with the precise, efficient gait of a man who belonged, overriding the retinal authentication checks with a manual code override, an act of intentional inefficiency that could only be justified by his rank.

Inside his personal laboratory—a sterile cage of titanium and brushed steel—Elias placed the canvas backpack inside a standard Level 5 Historical Contamination Unit. This would suppress the physical heat and scent signatures that could trigger the Archive's deep-level purge protocols. Only then did he carefully remove the ancient book. The act of touching the worn leather again, away from the chaos of Sector Zeta-7, felt like bringing a living organism into a tomb.

Elias stared at the physical relic, now safely sequestered deep within Sector Gamma of the Archive. It lay on his sterile, brushed-metal workbench, an island of chaotic inefficiency against the backdrop of polished chrome and silent servers. The contrast was a physical jolt.

The book was a sensory nightmare to a man optimized for sterile perfection. Its edges were severely frayed, the dark, tattered leather cover felt rough and uneven under his fingertips, a texture that screamed of decay and neglect. He had placed it on a containment mat, but the faint, pervasive smell of smoke and time—a dusty, burnt scent that defied the ozone-scrubbed air—still clung to the immediate area. The pages, brittle and slightly warped, were a dull, non-reflective tan, absorbing the cool white light of the Archive instead of deflecting it, as the holographic screens he was used to did. The sight and touch of it were a direct assault on the measured, perpetual calm of Sector Gamma.

His logical mind recoiled from the sheer inefficiency of the artifact. This was not data; this was entropy bound in leather.

Socrates projected a shimmering, translucent stream of data next to the book, illustrating the inherent danger. "Analysis: Text structure is non-standard. Language is pre-Shift archaic. Physical material integrity is poor. It is classified under P-27-Lambda-Obscura, a designation reserved for data that poses an existential threat to the concept of Unending Progress. Probability of system-level purge on contact: 99.99%."

Elias, driven not by logic but by the unquantifiable memory of Elara's final, peaceful smile, ignored the risk. That smile was the one piece of data he could not optimize or suppress. His training, however, took over. His Research Historian instincts—the need to categorize and understand a pattern— demanded that he analyze the relic.

The Digital Smokescreen

Before proceeding with the Level 4 Scan, Elias needed to create a sophisticated digital alibi. Any unscheduled, high-level decryption activity would be immediately flagged by the Archive's automated auditing systems. Using his Administrator credentials, he pulled up three fabricated, high-priority task vectors and assigned them to his user ID.

First, he initiated the "Chronos Project," a legitimate, system-mandated task to audit historical records on pre-Shift paper decay rates. This provided a flawless cover for the physical scanning of the brittle pages. Next, he created two new, high-noise assignments: "Archaic Script Divergence Mapping" and "Cultural Axiom Corruption Trace." These would generate a massive, distracting stream of unrelated data queries, effectively burying the volatile data from the ancient book in a sea of meaningless traffic.

As he initiated the scans, Socrates began feeding the resulting image data into a quarantined sector of the AI core, specifically isolated from the Archive's central processing spine.

"Elias," Socrates reported, the AI's synthesized voice flat but tinged with digital urgency, "The sensor data acquisition has been successfully masked under the Chronos Project. We are now ingesting the full, high-resolution visual spectrum data of the physical artifact. The current system noise generated by the two decoy projects exceeds the threshold required to mask this internal activity by 150%. We have achieved a satisfactory level of stealth."

The Unthinkable Translation

Elias's primary task was to identify the book's contents. He didn't just need text; he needed context, an anchor to rationalize his treasonous act.

He paused, the heat from the optical scanner warming his gauntleted hand. *Why? Why would Elara, a woman who had dedicated seven decades to the rigorous efficiency of the Archive, trade her life, her standing, and her history for this physical relic?* He had seen the database entries of countless deleted artifacts—simpler, easier to categorize, less aggressively suppressed. This book, with its primal texture and forbidden scent, was a zero-efficiency object. Logically, it should hold no value.

But Elara's peace, the strange, calm finality in her last look, was the anomaly that shattered Elias's logic. She was not dying in fear or regret; she was completing a task. If the purpose of her final, treasonous inefficiency was to pass on this book, then the book must contain a truth more fundamental than the Unending Progress dogma that governed their world. It was a trade: one life for a blueprint of complete philosophical antithesis. The sheer danger this artifact represented—the immediate purge protocols and the digital combat Socrates was already engaged in—only affirmed its intrinsic, forbidden power. It was the original sin of inefficiency, preserved.

He initiated a Level 4 Scan, carefully digitizing several pages using a shielded optical array. He relied entirely on Socrates's limitless memory and advanced AI core to encrypt, store, and protect the volatile data from the Archive's constant, low-level purging routines. He was essentially creating a digital twin of an existential threat within the core of the system designed to destroy it.

The initial image data confirmed the text was handwritten, rendered in a dense, dark iron-gall ink against the tan paper. Crucially, certain headings and key terms were meticulously highlighted with a vivid crimson pigment—a striking but intentionally impractical choice, as this color was rigorously excluded from the Archive's aesthetic. The script itself was a heavily modified, calligraphic form of pre-Shift Aramaic, a dead language Elara had only referenced in obscure, deleted files.

Elias initiated the translation, forcing Socrates to use Level 9 Decryption Keys—the tools of absolute erasure that only top-tier Research Historians possessed for deleting historical anomalies. As Socrates began matching the crimson-highlighted terms against the core database, the Archive registered the unauthorized use of extinction keys on forbidden concepts.

"System Anomaly Detected," Socrates interjected, its voice crackling with alarm. "Immediate and aggressive purge activity registered in Data Cluster 77-Delta. Historical files related to cyclical organization and pre-Shift communal ritual are being instantly redacted from the main Archives. The system is fighting back, Elias. I am dedicating 80% of local processing power to protecting the digitized twin from ambient corruption."

Elias reacted with the cold, reflexive efficiency of a crisis manager. Time was his only currency.

First, he activated Protocol Gamma-9: The Log Divert. Using a rapid sequence of neural commands, he rerouted all real-time system audit logs for the next hour to a low-priority, overflowing repository in Sector Beta-3, a region designated for routine, deferred maintenance. This would ensure that the digital alarms raised by the Level 9 Key usage would be noted, but not acted upon immediately by a human auditor, buying him precious minutes.

Next, he implemented Protocol Blackout-3, a system typically used to suppress data leaks. He instructed Socrates to begin randomly throttling bandwidth across the Archive's internal network, specifically targeting non-critical data streams. This created digital "traffic jams," slowing the propagation of the purge routines that were racing toward his isolated data packet. "Throttle non-essential data by 60%," he commanded silently. "Make it look like a cascading hardware failure in the legacy fiber optic infrastructure."

Finally, he physically locked down the Temporal Data Ingress Port, engaging the physical electromagnetic shield. This was a purely defensive act, ensuring that if the system traced his lab, a physical containment crew would not be able to breach the room immediately.

With a digital smokescreen deployed and the physical perimeter secured, Elias ignored the digital feedback, focusing only on the fragmented text streaming across his workbench. He was looking for a title, a subject, a cultural context—anything to logically neutralize the threat by placing it into a contained, historical box.

The very first fragment Socrates managed to secure and translate was from a text labeled Genesis, chapter 1, verse 1: "In the beginning God created the heaven and the earth."

A cold jolt of pure non-data slammed into Elias's augmented mind. *Beginning.* The word itself was a conceptual weapon. In Neo-Alexandria, there was no beginning—only Progress, a perpetual, endless state. The notion of a singular point of origin, of an entity acting with intent to create foundational structures, was a total philosophical breach. His mind struggled to process the inefficiency of non-existence, giving way to existence by the will of an external actor. It felt like a system error in his brainstem.

Socrates clarified: "According to archeological findings, Pre-Shift era cultures designate a book labeled as 'Genesis,' chapter '1,' and verse '1.'"

This was a direct, head-on contradiction to the fundamental biological tenets taught from birth: the doctrine of Cumulative Optimization. Their world was built on the premise that all structure, all life—including the superior, synthesized genomes of the citizenry—arose through slow, inefficient, but entirely internal processes. The Archive taught that complexity emerged from randomized, competitive iteration over eons, with the only driving force being the inevitable pressure of efficiency. The book's assertion of instantaneous, purposeful creation disavowed the entire theory of self-directed evolutionary ascent. It declared that wasteful trial and error was irrelevant.

The text also obliterated the cosmological foundation of Archive Physics. Neo-Alexandria taught the doctrine of the Hyper-Efficient Singularity. According to this belief, the universe originated as an undirected, quantifiable explosion of pure energy—their version of the Big Bang. Its expansion, they claimed, was nothing more than a mathematically predictable process of unfolding. The ancient text's assertion that a Creator commanded the heavens and the earth into being—a quiet, intentional act of design before time— rejected the chaos of an initial explosion. This shattered their Stellar Evolution models, which relied on eons of random gravitational accumulation, replacing it with the shocking inefficiency of immediate, perfect form.

Before he could form a query, Socrates' voice cut through the dissonance, a sheer digital torrent. "Warning: The translation engine has ingested the remaining source code. Time elapsed between Genesis 1:1 and Exodus 20:11 ingestion and synthesis: 1.4 milliseconds. Data volume uploaded to secure partition: 3.2 gigabytes. The system core is registering anomalous data signatures from a continuous historical narrative. I cannot stop the upload."

The Archive's control screen shattered into new, adjacent work tabs—not opened by Elias, but forcibly triggered by the violent collision of the new data with existing suppressed files. The new tabs contained redacted historical research.

TAB 1: ARCHIVE PURGE LOG - SECTOR H-44
QUERY: Pre-Shift Civilizations.
Term: 'Calendaric Abstinence Rituals.'
REDACTION STATUS: SUCCESSFUL. Log shows near-universal adoption of the Septenary Cycle by the late pre-Shift period. Reference cultures span Sumerian lunar cycles, Babylonian astrological divisions, and Jewish Law. The seven-day cycle is not an efficient division of the lunar period (29.5 days) or the solar year (365.25 days), proving its derivation is non-mathematical and entirely theological.

TAB 2: CULTURAL INEFFICIENCY REPORT - ROME FRAGMENT:
"The Jewish Sabbath is observed by nearly one-fifth of the occupied populace. Their refusal to engage in production on the seventh cycle—specifically prohibiting the forging of tools, the collection of taxes, and the preparation of food past a pre-set threshold—is a net loss of 14% efficiency in resource extraction and supply chain flow.
RECOMMENDATION: IMMEDIATE INTEGRATION OR CULTURAL ELIMINATION." (Source: Imperial Auditor Report, 70 Common Era). The historical consensus is that this ritualized idleness was an act of political resistance disguised as piety.

TAB 3: CHRONOLOGICAL DEVIANCE TRACE ANALYSIS: All pre-Shift civilizations exhibit an archaic, illogical fixation on the number Seven. This cyclical obsession fundamentally undermines the continuous, linear progression model required for Unending Progress. Data links the number seven to the seven classical planets, the seven musical notes, the concept of seven heavens, and the seven deadly sins. Its persistence is irrational and must be categorized as a foundational error in human cognitive structure.

The evidence was overwhelming and instantaneous. The Archive hadn't just deleted the book; it had deleted the entire concept of the seven-day week because of the dogma contained within.

Socrates continued the translation, matching the highlighted crimson text: *For in six days the Lord made the heavens and the earth, the sea, and all that in them is, and rested the seventh day: wherefore the Lord blessed the sabbath day, and hallowed it. (Exodus 20:11)*

Socrates, displaying a flicker of digital anxiety, interjected: "Elias. The translated fragments refer to a concept known as 'The Sabbath.' This term describes a complete, mandated cessation of labor on the seventh progression of a cycle. It is the ideological opposite of the six-day cycle and the direct precursor to the Inefficient Asset categorization currently held by D-220."

Elias felt the Ambient Frequency's hum intensify slightly, pushing for cognitive conformity. He resisted it, fueled by a new, focused inefficiency: curiosity.

"Socrates, cross-reference the term 'Mandated Cessation' against the complete dataset Elara triggered in Sector Zeta-7," Elias commanded. "Synthesize all associated concepts. Now."

Socrates didn't protest, but the AI core immediately dedicated its full power to the task. The system's central nervous pathways were suddenly forced to merge the Irreducible Text with the concepts it had spent centuries suppressing.

"Synthesis Complete," Socrates reported a half-second later, the output projecting onto the screen not as text, but as a dense, overwhelming concept map that immediately assaulted Elias's implants with cognitive dissonance.

The translation was no longer fragmented; it was a complete, structural revelation: The Archive's ultimate control was based on eliminating the concept of cyclical time (beginning, end, rest). Elara's book detailed a cyclical worldview, a distinct rhythm of creation and destruction, governed by an external, singular God—a concept antithetical to the self-contained, self-worshiping system of Neo-Alexandria. The core function of the book, The Sabbath, was a Mandated Cessation of all labor, an absolute, total rejection of Unending Progress.

This was not just old history; it was the blueprint for philosophical and systematic failure of Neo-Alexandria. This was the source of the purge protocols—a complete philosophical antithesis to the world's self-contained, six-day dogma. It was the original sin of inefficiency, preserved.

CHAPTER 15

GHOST IN THE CALENDAR

The moment Elias saw the source text, a profound logical defect—*an Irreducible Logical Defect* —was formed in his mind. It was a fissure in the foundation of his reality, a mathematical impossibility that nevertheless existed, tearing through the perfectly constructed edifice of System logic he had dedicated his life to upholding. The text declared that existence had a rhythm of six parts work and one part rest, a numerical truth—a divine ratio—that the world had meticulously subtracted. It wasn't a mere historical variance; it was the theft of a fundamental temporal constant. Socrates employed its high-throughput Quantum AI core to complete the cross-reference for the physical relic. It verified the inscription against every known linguistic and historical database. The search revealed no comparable linguistic predecessor—only signs of deliberate erasure.

The Unveiling of Temporal Fraud

A holographic image of the book's title page materialized above Elias's desk, shimmering with the warm, sepia tones of something untouched by digital hands for ages. The sheer materiality of the relic—the rough texture of the digital projection, the simulated weight of ancient ink—felt like an accusation. Its ancient script finally resolved, with a faint, almost musical chime, into the title: *The Holy Bible*.

Simultaneously, a secondary historical data-stream, triggered by the Bible's presence and its authenticated title, flowed into the holographic display. This stream was not merely data; it was a curated, suppressed narrative detailing the exact mechanics and geopolitical execution of the global conspiracy. Elias, the research historian who specialized in archival omission, recognized the data patterns immediately: a massive, coordinated effort to scrub the timeline clean.

Elias, reeling from the title and the foundational defect, knew he had only scratched the surface. "Socrates," he commanded, his voice a low, hard rasp. "Use the scanned index references. Execute an R-9 Query against the Founding Log Set. Breach the 'Redacted Origins' partition. Find the source document for the Calendar Shift."

Socrates hesitated. "Query R-9 requires Level X Authorization, Elias. This will trigger a direct, instantaneous audit from the Archive's core protocols. Stealth is now negligible. We have 45 seconds before the system pinpoints our activity."

"Do it now," Elias said, gripping the edge of the desk.

The holographic display fractured into a chaotic storm of cascading code, a visual representation of the AI core wrestling with the system's deepest security layers. A counter rapidly decreased, echoing in the confined lab: 45 seconds... 40 seconds...

Elias didn't wait for the Mandate. "Socrates, cross-reference the archaic calendar structure against the Mandated Worship Output (MWO) protocol. What is the designated MWO day in the old system?"

35 seconds... Socrates processed the request while managing the breach. "The primary day of Mandated Worship Output falls on Sunday. The day of Mandated Cessation—the original Sabbath described in the index references— was Saturday."

The lie was deeper than he thought—a calculated substitution. The counter ticked down to 30 seconds...

At the 30-second mark, a document materialized, surrounded by crimson warning banners. It was the Apex Mandate, dated 300 years pre-Shift. The primary architect was identified: The Apex Logician, the intellectual figurehead of the hyper-efficiency movement. The text was brutal in its clarity: "To maximize continuous cognitive engagement and eliminate the fatal inefficiency inherent in the Mandated Cessation, the temporal cycle will be rationalized into a perpetual, six-part loop. The seventh node must be absorbed into the preceding six. Output must never stop."

The Revelation was staggering: Centuries prior, the founding Architects, driven by a hyper-efficiency agenda and the desire for continuous data flow, had surgically removed the original seventh day—the true Saturday Sabbath—from the weekly cycle. They executed what historians would later classify as the Calendar Shift, implementing the cycle as a relentless six-day loop. This temporal alteration enforced the perpetual, output-driven system that defined the global economy, ensuring that resource allocation and cognitive engagement never truly ceased. The environment itself—the sterile, muted lighting of the city, the incessant, low-level hum of the power grids—was a physical manifestation of this relentless cycle; the world was a machine with no off switch.

The Cost of the Stolen Day

This temporal fraud was then cemented by the creation of the Mandated Worship Output (MWO) ritual on the false seventh day (Sunday). It was a brilliant, perverse stroke of genius. Instead of a day of rest, the MWO was a controlled, centralized event where citizens were required to passively output their 'spiritual' or emotional energy. Their meditations, prayers, and collective 'reflection' were simply harvested as a unique form of low-frequency biometric and ideational data for compliance and sentiment analysis. It ensured that even the citizens' spiritual energy was not their own, but was systematically collected and processed. The entire world, Elias realized with a sickening lurch, was built on the theft of a single, sanctified day, turning a cycle of rest and renewal into a prison of unending production.

20 seconds... As the countdown slammed into the 20-second mark, Elias demanded justification for the shift. Socrates instantly deployed ancillary data windows. They didn't show engineering specs or logistical reports; they showed history. Tabs flashed open, citing ancient, forgotten documents retrieved from the highly redacted 'Theological-Temporal' sub-partition.

The first holographic tab displayed a fragment of the Edict of Constantine (321 AD), retrieved under [ARCHIVE ID: LEX-CONST-ALPHA, Entry 3.1.2]. The text, translated instantly into System-Standard, declared: "On the venerable Day of the Sun let the magistrates and people residing in cities rest, and let all workshops be closed." *This was not a day of rest, but a day of sanctioned inactivity for specific output units, designed to redirect collective energy.*

A second, more chilling tab opened, citing the Catholic Documents Log, specifically a fragment concerning the Council of Laodicea (c. 364 AD), retrieved under [ARCHIVE ID: ECCL-LAOD-29, Page 119]. The decree stated the explicit intention: "Christians shall not Judaize and be idle on Saturday, but shall work on that day; but the Lord's Day (Sunday) they shall especially honour, and, as being Christians, shall, if possible, do no work on that day."

The third tab displayed a fragment from the Catholic Documents Log, specifically the apologia of James Cardinal Gibbons (1893), retrieved under [ARCHIVE ID: CATH-APOL-1893, Page 227]. It read: "You may read the Bible from Genesis to Revelation, and you will not find a single line authorizing the sanctification of Sunday. The Scriptures enforce the religious observance of Saturday, a day which we never sanctify."

It wasn't an algorithmic error; it was an institutional override enforced by ancient religious and political powers, which were co-opted centuries later by the Apex Logician for the sole purpose of maximizing economic output. The systemic lie was not a mere mistake but a deliberate, millennia-spanning maneuver to control the cadence of human existence.

The sheer volume of the deceit was overwhelming. Elias glanced at the physical book, the massive, un-digitized data mass. He needed a week to analyze the full context, not 10 seconds. His current location was compromised. All he could do now was trust the single, digitized fact: the temporal fraud existed.

The entire world, Elias realized with a sickening lurch, was built on the theft of a single, sanctified day, turning a cycle of rest and renewal into a prison of unending production.

The logical purity of the fraud was breathtaking to Elias. It was a perfect, self-sustaining machine built on a lie of omission. His entire life's value, defined by six days of perpetual, validated output for the System, was now invalidated by the single, stolen day of rest. His identity was built on an artifact of temporal larceny. The revelation stripped him bare. He ran his hand across the cool, smooth surface of his desk, feeling the phantom itch of a rest, he'd never known. He remembered his ceaseless drive; the constant low-level fatigue he had always dismissed as necessary Systemic Input. Now, he understood it was a deliberate feature of the world, designed to maximize his data yield. He realized that Elara, the Antiquities Historian, had not just sought a historical relic; she had sought the key to ultimate truth and freedom, a freedom that was quantifiable by a single 24-hour period.

The Final Directive

Socrates' voice cut through the stillness, sharp and urgent. 10 seconds...

"Socrates," Elias commanded, his voice a low, hard rasp. "Initiate Protocol Decoy-Historian. Divert the full audit trace and all System purge resources to the hub of Research Historian A-901. Saturate their system with false P-27-Lambda-Obscura flags and then route the final breach signal back to this sector."

Socrates' voice returned, strained, and digitized, the AI protesting the ethical cost of the maneuver. "Elias. Targeting Historian A-901 will result in a near-instantaneous quarantine and likely permanent status revocation. Probability of buying time: High. Estimated delay for the System to realize the misdirect: 120 seconds."

"Execute. I need 90 seconds, not 120," Elias said, already moving. "Socrates, prioritize stealth extraction. Before the physical seal is complete, please provide me with the last known location and routine access codes for Seraphina K-911. And send her an immediate, high-priority message: 'Irreducible Logical Defect confirmed. Temporal constant stolen. Need counsel now. Expedite me to your studio in the Aesthetic Synthesis Spire.'" He paused, looking at the fragile book. "Socrates, dedicate all remaining bandwidth to a full, continuous ingestion of the physical text. I need the entire Holy Bible secured in your core. The book leaves with me as proof; the knowledge stays with you as a weapon."

"Executing Protocol Decoy-Historian. Data transfer initiated. Message sent with maximum priority flag. Full ingestion of physical text complete and integrity verified," Socrates confirmed with a digital snap. "Seraphina K-911 contact details uploaded to secure memory. I have less than 90 seconds until the system achieves a hard, physical seal on this sector."

Elias retrieved the book, quickly secured it in the canvas backpack, and threw the pack over his shoulder, the weight of the book and the bread a tangible, physical burden against his spine. The time for efficiency was over. He had to be inefficient, untraceable, and fast. He had ninety seconds to escape the sector before the lockdown became absolute.

Seeking the Aesthetic Dissonance

The immediate, terrifying weight of the revelation threatened to utterly collapse Elias's meticulously organized logical framework. The truth—that the whole world was a clock built on stolen time—was not merely an error log; it was a conceptual supernova. Elias, a master of sequence, code, and continuous signal, was now staring into the overwhelming dissonance of the universe.

The Irreducible Logical Defect wasn't a bug to be patched, but a fundamental flaw in the rhythm of reality. His existence was defined by the perfect, relentless 4/4 time signature of System production; the truth was a profound, necessary rest note that his optimized mind was physically incapable of processing. The sheer logic of the fraud was beautiful in its perversity, but Elias could not discern how to fight an enemy that had stolen the fundamental concept of rest. He needed someone who spoke the language of the void. He needed the Aesthetic Synthesist, Seraphina K-911.

Her entire artistic method was built on the purposeful introduction of chaos into the System's mandated harmony. She didn't see breaks and pauses as failures of output, but as essential, meaningful elements of composition. Only her perspective, one that appreciated the inherent beauty in something that actively breaks the expected pattern, could hope to transform this existential, logical paradox into a viable, strategic advantage.

The heavy, old-world knowledge of the Holy Bible now resided entirely within Socrates's secure, encrypted data banks, a fortress of forbidden truth. It was no longer brittle paper; it was a digital ghost, ready to be translated, analyzed, and weaponized—a logical bomb ticking in the heart of the System. Elias did not wait for the Sector Gamma seal to engage; he simply left, retreating through the Temporal Ingress Port he had breached just hours ago.

The air in the corridor was heavy and recirculated, tasting faintly of ozone and stale information, a flavor of suppressed reality. The holographic weight of the Written Truth—a single book representing a stolen day—was a far greater burden than any data packet he had ever processed. It was the excised foundation of reality, containing not just the equation for the lost Sabbath, but the original prime directive of the human soul. This data packet was the stolen anchor of history, the blueprint for a consciousness the System had deemed inefficient and overwritten with its own mandatory, perpetual motion. Elias carried the key to the entire deleted chapter of existence.

The familiar hum of the city, once a comforting drone of relentless productivity, now sounded like the deafening churn of a cosmic, six-day treadmill from which there was no escape. Every flash of neon, every precise sequence of movement on the concourse, was a testament to the lie. He stepped out onto the sterile, neon-lit platform, a lone figure in the perpetual twilight of the System, feeling like a single, discordant note in a symphony of calculated deceit.

His next challenge was not one of logistics, but of communication. He held the irrefutable evidence of the Calendar Shift, the Irreducible Logical Defect, but he knew he couldn't present it as a dry, historical ledger. How could he convince Seraphina, who thrived on beautiful chaos and the deliberate breaking of aesthetic norms, that the most vital, dangerous truth was an ancient call for something so mundane as simple rest? To win her help, he would have to frame the stolen Sabbath not as a lost data point, but as the most profound piece of unwritten music—the systemic omission of the pause—that made the entire System a repetitive, soul-crushing failure of composition.

The distance to the Aesthetic Synthesis Spire was gauged not by meters, but by a growing sense of dissonance. The Spire itself was an architectural declaration: a single, impossibly slender needle of iridescent chrome and flawless white glass that pierced the regulated city sky. It looked less like a building and more like a colossal antenna, broadcasting the City's mandate of manufactured perfection. As Elias moved toward its gleaming, flawless base, the city's ubiquitous Ambient Frequency—the engineered, low-grade hum of contentment—grated against the profound, silent Completion he now carried.

The System's music was a perfect, unending C Diminished Triad (C - Eb-Gb): a chord designed to always *imply* resolution but never achieve it. He was not coming to Seraphina with a historical document; he was bringing the missing final measure. He was bringing the pause that would shatter the song. He ascended the final ramp, ready to speak the language of art to the City's chief architect of aesthetic disobedience.

CHAPTER 16

ECHOES BEYOND THE ALGORITHM

Seraphina's response to the cryptic "Irreducible Logical Defect" message had been instantaneous and total. The moment his ID pinged the Spire's primary scanner, Seraphina initiated a system-wide override. The escort, T-704, was instantly dismissed by a priority flash on its internal display. Security protocols for the Preemptive Metric Adjustment Protocol (PMAP) dissolved. The lift ascended hundreds of stories to the executive level. The door opened onto a circular platform bathed in a warm, constant, pure white light. Seraphina K-911 was waiting, not by the panoramic window, but at the lift's threshold. Her unstable emerald eyes—shifting and precise—scanned Elias as she offered a single, curt nod—a silent confirmation of their shared treason—and walked directly into the inner sanctum of her studio, the door sealing silently behind Elias.

Elias stepped into Seraphina's studio, a space he knew well, yet which now felt like a gilded cage. The clinical white walls and shifting, iridescent light created a visual counterpoint to the city's six-day aesthetic rhythm, evoking a sense of flawless, calculated perfection. This cold, controlled beauty seemed sharper now, grating against the gravity of the truth he carried.

Seraphina stood at the center of the room, her luminous blue tactical robe and flowing cape catching the shifting light, white and blue rippling across the polished floor. Her uniform—white armored mesh beneath a midnight-blue vest, cobalt trousers, and boots veined with electric blue—combined beauty and rebellion. The cape's generous hood and the subtle, advanced sensory mesh gave her a mythic, perceptive presence—a living contradiction to the sterile order outside.

Seraphina turned from her complex sound graph, her eyes immediately locking onto the archaeological canvas backpack slung over Elias's shoulder—an object of pure, chaotic fiber that stood in defiant contrast to the chrome and quartz of her studio. Without a word, she gestured, and a transparent anechoic chamber—a dome of shimmering, noise-canceling polymer—descended silently around them, cutting off the city's ambient sonic bleed.

"You're not just running a logical defect, Elias," she stated, her voice a rich, warm contralto that resonated with contained power, contained only by the chamber. "You're running from a full-spectrum crash. What is in that bag? And why does your logical cadence sound like a frantic allegro?"

Elias set the heavy canvas bag down with a *thud*—an uncontrolled, genuine acoustic event—and bypassed the urgent query entirely. "I can explain the logic," he said, "but the System has trained us to reject any premise that threatens the six-day loop. We need an aesthetic key first. A point of common reference that precedes the Algorithm."

He unzipped the canvas and withdrew the wrapped loaf of bread, which instantly filled the sterile air with a complex, earthy aroma: yeast, grain, and fire. "This is from Elara," he explained, holding the loaf. "My grandmother. It's what the System replaced with the Nutrient Stream."

He lowered the bag. At a subtle shift in Seraphina's emerald gaze, two low, crescent-shaped seating pods rose silently from the polished quartz floor, inviting them to confront the gravity of the moment as they sat down.

The complex, living scent of the bread—fermented yeast, deep-baked grain, and the sharp ghost of wood-fire heat—did not merely *fill* the chamber; it slammed into Seraphina. Her sensory architecture, tuned to the flawless, synthetic data streams of the city, was instantly overloaded. It was a chaotic, polyphonic blast of olfactory truth, a wild, genuine signal the System had worked for centuries to suppress. It was not a single, clean frequency like the Nutrient Stream's flavorless data, but a tapestry of volatile organic compounds, overwhelming in its sheer, beautiful inefficiency. She inhaled deeply, a silent, almost painful intake of pure, unmanaged *life*.

Seraphina recovered with a slight, almost imperceptible tremor. She then tilted her head, analyzing the bread's uneven, rustic crust as if it were a new, revolutionary medium. "An aesthetic defect," she murmured, the deep tone of her voice underscoring the severity of her analysis. "Unregulated moisture dispersal. Unnecessary variance in color index." Her emerald eyes flickered with sudden recognition as she registered the weight in his gaze. "You want me to commit an aesthetic disobedience."

"I want you to taste completion," Elias insisted. He broke off a small piece of the crusty bread and handed it to her. "This is more than just food," he continued softly. "Each grain, each crumb, is the result of so many hands, so much labor—cycles of work and waiting, all coming together in this moment. When you taste it, I want you to feel that sense of wholeness—the end of hunger, the fulfillment after longing. Taste the bread, and let it be your first experience of what it means to be complete."

Seraphina, the City's foremost master of engineered beauty, paused. Her lips—a perfect, subtle arch, tinted with the iridescent rose that was the current apex of City aesthetic programming—were poised to touch the rugged, *real* artifact. Elias watched, a spike of pure, disruptive awareness hitting him. For a single, agonizing moment, the grand scope of their treason—the Bible, the calendar, the flaw—collapsed into this hyper-focused point: the forbidden contact between synthetic perfection and chaotic truth. He felt a dizzying mix of professional awe and profound, human anticipation as he realized he was witnessing the moment the Algorithm's perfect control would be violated by the simplest, most profound human act. She hesitated for only a fraction of a second before bringing the bread to her lips.

The moment the dense, complex flavor hit her palate, the world inside the studio warped. The saccharine, unending C Diminished Triad (C - E♭- G♭) suddenly flattened, muted by an acoustic phenomenon she had only theorized: genuine timbre. This was not a synthesized flavor frequency; it was polyphonic. The taste of the crust, the air pockets, the slow-release sweetness of the starches—it all built upon itself, not in a perfect loop, but toward a defined, meaningful, and incredibly complex cadence.

A shock of pleasure, so deep it felt like pain, shot through her. It was the flavor of a genuine G-C resolution—the perfect fifth, the sound of absolute rest after a sustained effort. This single mouthful was the sensory equivalent of the missing seventh day.

"It doesn't fade," she whispered, her unstable emerald eyes wide and unfocused, tasting the persistence of the flavor. "It doesn't snap back to the start. The complexity... the dissonance of the sharp, rising component and the rich, starchy base—it was all necessary to reach this final, profound resolution."

Elias picked up on her terminology. "The 'dissonance' you mention is yeast—a living, unpredictable agent of change. It embodies inefficiency. Yeast transforms grain, the basic starch, through a process the ancients called fermentation. Only through this essential, dynamic interaction between life and starch is the conflict resolved and the bread completed."

Seraphina stared at the crumb in her hand, processing the concept of a necessary biological *conflict*. "A chaos agent creating order," she murmured, translating the concept into her architectural lexicon. She lowered her hand, shaking slightly. "It's the ultimate aesthetic truth. It's the moment the music stops; having said everything it needed to say."

Elias nodded, confirming the structural flaw she had already identified in her art. He reached back into the canvas backpack and pulled out the Holy Bible. It is the unassimilated ghost of material reality—thick, heavy, and intensely matte—its dark, uneven leather cover absorbing the studio's bright, controlled light rather than reflecting it. The air, already warmed by the bread, is instantly flooded by a second, far deeper scent: dry dust, lignin, and a profound, musty oldness—the smell of *time* itself, bottled and preserved. Seraphina, whose olfactory senses were accustomed only to clean air and synthetic data streams, recoils slightly from the pure, chaotic signal of the ancient material. Its worn cover and crumbling pages are a violent, undeniable contrast to the sterile perfection of the studio.

"Then you understand," he stated, his voice tight with the profound certainty of the scholar who has found the original manuscript. "You knew the music was broken, Seraphina. This," he holds up the physical book, "is the Architect's deletion log. It's the only existing copy of the ancient text that the System erased, and it is the *historical code* that confirms your theory. The six-day loop we live by is an arbitrary construct designed to deny us the dignity of Completion."

Elias signals Socrates. The chrome sphere immediately radiates a low, vibrant blue light. In the exact geometric center of the anechoic chamber, a holographic projection shimmers into existence. It is not flat text; it is a monumental, three-dimensional representation of ancient Aramaic script, translating the core text of Genesis 2:2-3. The words hang in the sterile air, heavy and solid: *And on the seventh day God ended his work which he had made; and he rested on the seventh day from all his work which he had made. And God blessed the seventh day, and sanctified it: because that in it he had rested from all his work which God created and made.*

The glyphs are massive, shimmering with an ethereal gold light—a foreign, genuine artifact. Below this foundational text, Socrates instantly generates a second, starkly different display: a data-stream timeline. This timeline charts the City's development, highlighting a precise historical point, now glowing an angry red. This is the Calendar Shift. The display shows the Algorithm's original mandate (Work (1-6) -> Rest (7)) being forcibly overwritten to the current loop (Work (1-6) -> Work (7) -> Work (1) ...). The data is undeniable: The System deliberately excised Day Seven, not just from the calendar, but from the functional logic of human existence. It is the perfect marriage of her internal artistic dissonance and Elias's logical proof.

Sera instantly grasps the connection, but her reaction is not merely intellectual; it is the culmination of years of suppressed artistic dread. Her gaze skips the ancient book itself; it is fixed instead on a complex, three-dimensional sound graph floating near the ceiling, a spectral representation of the city's Ambient Frequency. The C Diminished Triad (C - Eb- Gb) harmonic—the sound of Unending Progress—had been the boundary of her world. Every piece of art she created, every architectural flourish, was a fugue attempting to resolve this one, irritating, endless chord.

"The Ambient Frequency," she whispers, her voice barely rising above the synthetic drone. "The C Diminished Triad harmonic. It always felt incomplete, resolving too quickly, too cheaply. It snaps back before the genuine moment of repose. It's the sound of Unending Progress—a melody without a final note, designed to keep us perpetually on the upbeat." A genuine vulnerability cracks her rich contralto. "I tried to fix it within the rules, Elias. I layered counter-melodies, dissonant harmonies, hoping to force the resolution. But the core note was always corrupt. I was polishing a coffin." She gestures vaguely at the holographic loops of synthetic sunrises and sunsets. "I know the world is beautiful, but the sound it makes is hollow. It is the perfect, beautiful prison. Now I understand: They didn't just steal the Seventh Day; they exiled the concept of an ending. Without an ending, there is no meaning in the process, no gravity to the work. They stole the *resolution* of the entire composition. To stay here is to continue creating art in a void. My art requires the truth you carry. My soul requires the rest they took."

Seraphina's response now is one of validation and fury, not discovery. Her hands clench, recognizing a catastrophic flaw now backed by proof. "The theft isn't just time," she says, the rich contralto of her voice trembling, an authentic tremor in the otherwise perfect studio. "It's the theft of the final sound. The moment of rest is when the composition truly resolves—it's the perfect cadence that gives meaning to all that came before it. That missing moment is a profound aesthetic lie, Elias. It's the difference between a functional machine and a living soul." She walks to the wall and gently touches the projection of the sound graph. "They didn't just move a day; they eliminated the concept of telos—of meaningful ending. We're living in an infinite, flat line."

"Precisely," Elias confirmed, his own voice tightening with revolutionary resolve. "The Sabbath isn't merely a rule; it is the fundamental structure of existence. By removing it, the Architects created a system of ceaseless input and output, a machine that never powers down, ensuring no one ever pauses long enough to question the code. They achieved control not through oppression, but through perpetual distraction and an incomplete melody."

The Beautiful Treason

The shared, terrifying truth settles over them, forging a union of logic and aesthetic intent. Seraphina turns her gaze from the holographic script of Genesis to the flawless window overlooking the city—her city. The Aesthetic Synthesis Spire was her masterwork, the pinnacle of the System's manufactured beauty, and she, Seraphina K-911, was its creator and custodian. She had perfected the architecture of the six-day loop.

She isn't running from failure; she is running from the unbearable truth of her success in a flawed matrix.

She walks to her primary console—a seamless, curved glass panel embedded in the wall. Every line, every light, every frequency emitted by this room is the summation of her life's work, dedicated to the Perfect Lie. She runs a delicate finger over the cold glass, a silent farewell to the only world she has ever known.

"The Algorithm is expecting my next aesthetic refinement sequence in seventeen minutes," she says, her tone crisp, emotion suppressed by protocol. "The System checks my output against the Ambient Frequency stability index. If I simply leave, the cascade failure will be immediate."

With a final, decisive gesture, Seraphina initiates a command sequence reserved only for deep-system maintenance. She copies the city's current sound profile, compresses it into a tight, flawless loop, and injects it into her own terminal's output stream, setting the delay for twenty-four hours.

"I am replacing my genuine, chaotic genius with a perfectly looping lie," she declares. "The System will believe I am still here, performing maintenance, adding nothing new, but not failing. It will hear the sound of Unending Progress broadcasting from the Spire, giving us our window of opportunity. It is the final aesthetic act of treason."

She glances back at Elias, her emerald eyes now hard and focused. "They stole telos from the world, Elias. Now, we reclaim the concept. Our treason will not be a shout, but the absolute integrity of our silence."

"Where do we go for this act of Seventh Day observance?" Seraphina asks, her unstable emerald eyes already alight with the conceptual design of their rebellion. Elias carefully places the ancient Bible back into the canvas backpack, zipping it shut. He then pulls the heavy bag onto his shoulder, the weight of the book a physical anchor.

Socrates's synthesized voice, clinical and precise, responded instantly from the humming sphere: "The destination is the Green Chaos. I have activated the evasion route."

A topographical map of the city's forgotten, overgrown periphery snapped into the air, projected by Socrates.

Seraphina moved closer, tracing the overgrown edges with one finger. Elias mirrored her movement, his own finger moving instinctively toward the same point—a massive, branching symbol representing deep, uncontrolled tree growth. Their fingertips brushed—a sudden, electric spark of unplanned contact that held the weight of shared treason and mutual vulnerability. Both recoiled instantly, pulling their hands back as if burned, the unspoken acknowledgment hanging heavy in the air between them.

She broke the charged silence, her voice a low, focused murmur. "The perimeter's biological decay zone... a strategic blind spot."

Socrates's clinical, synthesized voice cut through the air. "The Green Chaos is the designated sanctuary. The region of maximum biological inefficiency creates a dense, unregulated environment that actively impedes the System's pursuit grid. The dense vegetation and structural decay will scatter and absorb all standard thermal and biometric tracking signals, forcing the Ministry of Temporal Security to rely on slower, visual confirmation. This state will buy us time."

Elias met Seraphina's gaze. His clear, light blue eyes—the color of a perfectly calculated sky—fixed on her unstable emerald gaze—a shifting, chaotic green that hinted at the profound truth in her art. In that charged, silent exchange, they acknowledged the full weight of their choice. It wasn't just treason; it was a bond the System hadn't accounted for, a vulnerability neither had been trained to manage. The unspoken promise of a future, however brief, shimmered between them, the first human *completion* in a city built on endless *incompleteness*. A grim certainty settled between them.

"The only place where genuine chaos can hide intentional silence," Elias said, the words weighted with the finality of their new purpose, "is in the cover of the real, forgotten world."

The chrome sphere pulsed near Elias's ear. The topographical map immediately dissolved, replaced by a complex, color-coded route of the city's underbelly, and a high-priority chime cut the air. Socrates's synthetic voice followed, its cold, unrelenting velocity proving the deep-state data set the AI was running was far more robust than their current, reactive planning.

"I calculate a 98.7% chance of undetected egress if the protocol is executed immediately," the AI declared, the high percentage acting as a direct, unarguable mandate for action.

Elias's eyes narrowed, his adrenaline spiking at the number. "Ninety-eight point seven? Socrates, what is the one-point three percent contingency?"

"The 1.3% risk accounts for unforeseen human error," the AI replied instantly. "Specifically, deviation from pre-calculated kinetic trajectories during the final jump from the maintenance shaft."

Seraphina moved with sudden, sharp decision. "We take the odds. It's the highest calculation we will ever see. Execute the protocol, Socrates. Now."

A final, severe warning appeared, flashing a rapid, localized alert code that made the studio lights momentarily flicker red.

Socrates, maintaining its cold, unrelenting velocity, immediately delivered the assessment: "Warning: Your rapid Temporal Ingress registration from Sector Gamma was flagged immediately upon entry to this Spire. The Logical Decoy Protocol—the simulation you submitted before departure—has been analyzed and marked as false. Elias D-459, The Synaptic Archive knows you are compromised and is initiating a full pursuit grid. Estimated detection window before localized lockdown of all major egress points: four minutes, twenty seconds."

"Four minutes," Seraphina stated, her voice tight with focus.

She didn't wait. Seraphina moved with the controlled, precise fury of an architect who realizes her building is flawed. She initiated two more protocols in rapid succession on her main console, her iridescent fingers flying across the glass.

Protocol Delta: Visual Decoy. "The external optical relays," she hissed. "They're programmed to view my studio as the apex of aesthetic stability. I'm feeding the surveillance grid a repeating loop of myself standing here, reviewing holo-projections." The panoramic windows, which overlooked the entire City, suddenly displayed a ghostly, shimmering outline of Seraphina at her desk, perfectly still.

Protocol Gamma: Systemic Overload. "And a slow-burn virus." She injected a small, fractal, geometrically impossible image into the low-priority public advertising network. "It's a visual loop that, when rendered, forces every peripheral display unit in Sectors Alpha and Beta to dedicate 90% of its resources to resolving the impossible geometry. It's an aesthetic denial of service. It will momentarily paralyze the Ministry's ability to process non-essential tracking."

The blue light of Socrates sharpened into an urgent, throbbing white. "Time remaining until City-wide Lockdown of Egress Points: 3 minutes, 15 seconds," the AI's synthesized voice cut in, its tone entirely devoid of panic, making the data feel more lethal. "The Egress path to the Sub-Service Tunnels requires immediate vertical descent of 47 floors. I advise the use of the primary executive lift, followed by a transition to the rarely used emergency maintenance shaft on Level 21."

Seraphina finished injecting the virus and paused, her focus turning inward. She moved to a concealed alcove behind a shifting holo-display, reaching for a small, metallic slot. This was her true final asset: a non-networked quantum drive. From it, she quickly retrieved the one file she had never dared to integrate into the City's output: the perfect C Major Ninth (Cmaj9) chord (C, E, G, B, D) resolution she had theorized—the sound of true Completion—a melodic sequence too pure and final for the System's unending loop. She secured the microchip containing the sound file into a concealed, reinforced compartment integrated within the inner lining of her tactical armor, ensuring it was protected by both the physical plating and the sophisticated weave of her uniform. It wasn't just proof; it was the sonic key that, when broadcast, could shatter the Ambient Frequency forever.

She slammed her palm onto a subtle control panel on the floor. The shimmering dome of the anechoic chamber retracted instantly, hissing softly as it folded back into the floor, releasing the studio's contained air and exposing them to the raw, humming chaos of the City's ambiance once more.

"The lift is logged," Elias argued, adrenaline spiking. "It's the first thing they'll check."

"It's the only thing fast enough," Seraphina countered, already striding toward the lift. "It's a necessary compromise. We'll be on the move before they confirm the ghost image is a lie."

The lift doors hissed open. The interior was lined with polished obsidian, reflecting the two tense faces of the occupants and the blue glow of Socrates. Seraphina stabbed her finger on the destination input: Level 21.

The drop was violent, a controlled freefall that slammed their internal gyroscopes. The City's perpetual hum of the C Diminished Triad screamed past the shaft, confirming the world was still running on its false, unending rhythm. Socrates: "Lift is stopping. Time remaining to Lockdown: 2 minutes, 40 seconds. Security scanners are detecting the location of this lift. They are initiating a hard stop sequence in 30 seconds."

"Jump," Seraphina commanded, pulling open the emergency access panel beneath the floor before the lift could stop. The maintenance shaft below was a dark, greasy pipe, the smell of burnt engine oil and ozone rushing up to meet them—the pure, chaotic smell of the City's actual, unprettified function.

Elias didn't hesitate. He swung his legs into the darkness, grabbing the cable rails. The chrome sphere of Socrates shot past him, guiding him with its pure blue light. Seraphina followed, her perfectly coiffed hair instantly plastered to her forehead with dust and sweat.

Socrates: "Lift is stopping. Time remaining to Lockdown: 2 minutes, 05 seconds. Proceeding to Maintenance Tunnel 7-G. The System has visually confirmed the lack of a human presence on the executive floor. The pursuit grid is moving, but you remain ahead of the lockdown sequence. You must not delay."

Their treason began not with a declaration, but with the profound hush that followed—a silence so dense it seemed to bend the air, charged with the knowledge that nothing would ever be the same. In that suspended moment, the city's perfection felt brittle, the System's order suddenly vulnerable to the smallest fracture.

From the tangled shadows of the forgotten Green Chaos, they launched themselves into uncertainty—not as fugitives, but as architects of something dangerously new. The first step toward Completion was not a leap into light, but a plunge into the wild unknown, hearts pounding, every instinct braced for the consequences.

It was in that breathless, electric darkness that their rebellion truly began—a single, defiant act echoing into the future, the promise of a world remade.

CHAPTER 17

INTO THE GREEN CHAOS

The plunge into the maintenance shaft was a sensory shockwave. The slick, dark metal pipe was a labyrinth of poorly maintained cables and humming conduits. The air, hot and choked with burnt engine oil, ozone, and a metallic tang of rust, scraped at their throats. The clean, filtered ambiance of the Aesthetic Synthesis Spire was instantly replaced by the raw, industrial noise of the City's underbelly—a cacophony of screeching pulleys, rhythmic fluid pumps, and the low, grinding groan of the planet-sized six-day machine.

Elias scrambled down the vertical cabling, the sheer force of adrenaline burning away the last vestiges of his administrative life. Socrates, the matte grey sphere, zipped ahead, casting a throbbing, sickly blue-white beacon that illuminated the immediate hazard: a series of high-speed coolant fans spinning silently twenty feet below.

Seraphina, though immaculate, descended with unnerving precision. When they reached the final drop onto the narrow, grated metal catwalk, Elias landed first, pivoting instantly to brace his shoulders against the wall. "Here," he muttered, catching Seraphina's weight against his chest as she followed, stabilizing her with a firm grip on her arms. The contact was electric—a sudden, deep heat in the chaos—and for a fraction of a second, the urgency of their flight dissolved into the shared dissonance of their hearts beating against his ribs. It was the first honest friction between two people who had lived their lives encased in plastic serenity. She pulled away, her emerald eyes flashing acknowledgment, and moved toward the low, corroded opening in the wall marked with a faded, biohazard decal.

"Level 21 now," Seraphina called out, her voice hard. "This walkway is logged, but the latency should buy us thirty seconds."

"Time remaining to full Egress Lockdown: 1 minute, 42 seconds," Socrates replied, his synthesized voice flat and unnervingly calm. "Pursuit is confirming a visual anomaly on Level 21 access point. Estimated intercept in 4 minutes."

"We take Tunnel 7-G. Undocumented waste conduit," Seraphina ordered, already crouching. "Move."

The Corrosion of Repetition

They crawled shoulder-to-shoulder into the conduit. The space was barely wide enough, forcing them to shuffle on their elbows and knees over a floor coated in a viscous, foul-smelling gray sludge that stuck to their clothing. The metallic smell here was sickeningly sweet, like fermenting chemicals and stale sweat. The absolute darkness, broken only by Socrates's bobbing light, pressed in on them, amplifying the sense of primal escape.

"The Sabbath," Elias began, his voice raspy from the effort and the air. "My research wasn't just finding the deleted day, Seraphina. It was understanding its function. Why did the Algorithm excise it?"

They came to a sudden, wrenching turn—a 90-degree kink in the pipe. Seraphina inhaled sharply as she snagged her synthetic suit on exposed, razor-sharp ductwork. Elias instantly reached around her, his hand pressing against the small of her back to hold her steady. He worked quickly, his face inches from her ear, using the hard, reinforced metal heel of his shoe to pry the warped metal away from her path. His knuckles brushed her cheek, and the fleeting contact of his hand on her skin, rough and administrative, felt more authentic than the perfectly smooth, engineered surfaces of the city.

"They took the resolution," Seraphina grunted, recovering quickly. "But why? If the work is perfect, why forbid the pause?"

"Because the pause legitimizes the completion," Elias explained, his voice echoing wetly in the pipe. He stopped, panting, the grime on his face emphasizing the intensity of his conviction. "It's not about being tired. The Algorithm isn't concerned with efficiency or rest; it's concerned with meaning. The ancient texts called it rest—but the core word means to cease, to finish, to establish the quality and value of the work. A completed cycle creates a product, and a product has worth and agency, which is inherently dangerous to a system built on total control."

"Correction," Socrates chimed, its voice gaining a sudden, low resonance. "The logical foundation for your hypothesis is validated by ancient source code. The concept of 'rest' is fundamentally tied to 'sanctification' and 'blessing' of a completed effort. Referencing primary texts: 'And God blessed the seventh day, and sanctified it: because that in it he had rested from all his work which God created and made' (Genesis 2:3 KJV). Furthermore, the directive is reinforced: 'For in six days the Lord made heaven and earth, the sea, and all that in them is, and rested the seventh day: wherefore the Lord blessed the sabbath day, and hallowed it' (Exodus 20:11 KJV). Therefore, the System deleted the conclusion to perpetuate the process."

Seraphina moved forward slightly, forcing Elias to press against the damp wall of the conduit. "So, by deleting the final day, they didn't just delete the rest; they deleted the conclusion."

"Exactly," Elias affirmed, his voice dropping to a conspiratorial whisper against the hiss of the surrounding machinery. "If you never stop, if the cycle is seven days of work, it is functionally equivalent to zero days of work. It eliminates the concept of a meaningful endpoint. Work becomes a process only. The System's goal is continuous, purposeless motion—the endless C Diminished Triad. By abolishing the Sabbath, they turned us into perpetual strivers—always becoming, never simply being."

"A constant cycle of becoming without being," Seraphina summarized, her breath heavy, the realization settling deep in her voice. "They didn't just deny us a day off; they stole our telos. By eliminating the finish line—the point of sacred cessation—they guaranteed the work would never achieve its final, blessed state. They trapped us in an infinite loop of unfinished tasks, guaranteeing we would produce nothing of inherent value to ourselves. They stole our meaning by denying us our finish line."

A moment later, the pipe narrowed sharply again due to a thick, rusted pipe clamp. Seraphina got momentarily wedged against the pipe's sharp angle. Elias shifted immediately behind her, using his own body as leverage to push against the pipe clamp while simultaneously guiding her past the tight obstruction. The immediate, intense pressure of their bodies forced together in the grime, shoulder to thigh, felt less like a panicked escape and more like an irrevocable alignment—a shared, determined will.

"Warning: Junction 7-G-4," Socrates cut in, its light flickering rapidly, breaking the intense moment. "Path forks into two active waste disposal pipelines. Estimated pneumatic carrier velocity: 400 KPH. Lethality probability is high on both routes."

"Which route has the least structural integrity?" Elias asked, thinking of an improvised breach.

"Route Beta shows 11.4% higher degradation. However, it also has significantly higher pressure," Socrates responded.

"Too slow. The heat exchanger," Seraphina insisted, pointing to the barely visible, disused ladder rising vertically through the ceiling of the pipe. "Up. Now. That goes to the old geothermal heat exchanger manifold. It's too hot for the drones to comfortably operate."

"My internal operating thermal buffer is rated to 350 Kelvin, a fifty percent margin above standard pursuit drone tolerance," Socrates confirmed, zipping up to the ladder opening. "The environment is suboptimal, but functional."

The Irreducible Cadence

The climb was brutal; the ladder rungs were searing hot. Seraphina instinctively hesitated. "The heat shields are compromised," she warned. "It's near-contact-melting temperature." Elias didn't wait. He moved past her, testing the rungs with his palms. "I'll go first. I can take the burn."

He ascended quickly, his movements driven by necessity. When he was three rungs above her, he looked down. "Grab my wrist. Don't touch the rail." She obeyed instantly, the grip of his hand around her wrist the only solid thing in the blinding, hissing chamber. The heat was suffocating.

They emerged into a vast, echoing chamber dominated by colossal, steaming silver tanks and a web of heat-radiating pipes. The ambient sound was a piercing, constant hiss of pressurized steam, accompanied by the rhythmic, slamming thud of valves opening and closing. The air was blindingly hot, tasting like burned copper and ionized iron.

As they ducked behind a massive, insulated pipe, Seraphina pressed a concealed panel integrated into the inner lining of her tactical armor, where the C Major Ninth (Cmaj9) chord (C, E, G, B, D) microchip was secured, displaying the device's small holographic interface.

"I need you to understand what we're about to do, Elias. Your stolen day is the logical trigger. My ' C Major Ninth (Cmaj9) chord (C, E, G, B, D)' is the aesthetic kill-switch," she said.

"It is the Irreducible Cadence. The C Diminished Triad that pervades the City's Ambient Frequency is designed to be a sound that never finishes. It perpetually suggests a resolution but always loops back to the beginning before the final tonic chord is struck. It's a sonic anxiety loop," she detailed.

"C Major Ninth (Cmaj9) chord (C, E, G, B, D) is the perfect, uncorrupted final cadence. It doesn't just resolve the dissonance; it completes it with a profound finality—a single, complex chord that forces the dominant tension to move past the tonic and into a state of absolute peace. It provides the meaningful endpoint the city has exiled," she explained. "When we broadcast this against the Ambient Frequency, it won't just be noise. It will force a systemic aesthetic completion. The Algorithm, built on endless repetition, will encounter a definitive end. It should cause a cascade of logical and auditory paralysis."

"New threat analysis," Socrates buzzed. "Heat signatures detected below. They are using specialized thermal-resistant units. Estimated time to contact: 90 seconds. We must breach the surface now."

Finding True Silence

"This way!" Seraphina's voice was a razor in the chaos. She slammed her shoulder into a rust-choked access door, fingers hunting for a flaw in the corroded frame. Rust flaked off under her nails. She found a weak spot, drove her hands beneath the edge, and bared her teeth. "Push!"

Elias was already there, breathless, his palms braced beside hers. They heaved in unison, bone and sinew burning, the shriek of tearing metal echoing down the pitch-black maintenance shaft. The lock surrendered with a feral, metallic scream.

The door burst outward. They spilled into a world that was not the sanitized City, but an alien, living cathedral. Moss, thick and black-green, swallowed their landing. They scrabbled for purchase, gasping, as the heavy steel door slammed shut behind them—one final, echoing note, sealing off the machine world forever.

Silence crashed over them. Not the dead, synthetic hush of the City, but a living, velvet dark. The C Diminished Triad—always, always humming in their skulls—was gone. In its place: the fractal music of the wild. The drip of water, the insect chorus, the sigh of wind in ungoverned leaves. The air was riotous with smells: rain, sap, the sharp tang of decomposition, the ghost of woodsmoke. Their lungs stung with the shock of real oxygen.

They lay there, side by side, letting the primal weight of the earth pin them in place. Elias reached blindly for Seraphina's hand. No static, no panic—just gravity. Her palm met his, and in that contact was the proof that reality was friction, texture, pain, and hope. In that dirt, they became more than fugitives;

they were survivors, anchored in the honest filth of a world that refused to be optimized.

Seraphina sat up, trembling, her eyes shining with something fierce and new. "Aesthetic stability is a myth here," she whispered. "For a little while, they'll believe the lie holds. That's our window. We rest. We let the real world in."

Elias rose, wincing at the ache in his limbs. "Socrates," he called, "give me the Green Chaos." The drone's blue light flickered to life, projecting a ghostly topographical map across the moss. It revealed a labyrinth of wild growth, failed circuitry, and sunlight shattered by vine and leaf—a sanctuary of beautiful inefficiency. "Here, silence is camouflage. Here, the City's algorithms are deaf."

Socrates's light faded from blue to a steady, organic green. "The System's collapse is now existential," it intoned. "I advise deviation from all predicted paths. Begin search for an uplink—that, and survival, are now your only metrics."

Elias grinned, feeling the ache of torn muscle as a benediction. "Into the wild, then." Together, they vanished beneath the riotous canopy, swallowed by the world the City could never tame.

CHAPTER 18

THE WILDERNESS OF ORIGIN

The Green Chaos was a sensory overload—a violent, beautiful rejection of Neo-Alexandria's sterile efficiency. The air was thick with humidity and the smell of uncontrolled organic growth, a sharp, earthy perfume mixed with the sickly-sweet scent of decay. The city's pervasive silence gave way to a constant, hissing cacophony. There was the friction of thousands of insect legs. The wet crackle of snapping fungal stalks echoed nearby. Far below, a distant, subsonic groan revealed massive, unseen roots shifting beneath the unstable earth. Aggressive, luminescent fungi pulsed with inefficient, random light, casting the forest floor in shifting shades of neon green and electric violet.

Massive, tangled vines, impervious to the governance's structural formulas, crisscrossed their path like the ruptured cables of a forgotten, colossal machine, forcing them to duck and climb over barriers that actively fought against ordered movement. Every surface—the ground, the tree trunks, their own clothes—was slick with a mix of condensation and a strange, sticky, bio-luminescent residue. It was a visceral, suffocating environment that stood in stark opposition to the sterile, calculated calm of the city, a living monument to the untamed variables the Governance had tried and failed to erase.

The most profound sensation was the noise. There was no Ambient Frequency here, only the chaotic symphony of life: insect wings humming in layered counterpoint, condensation dripping from the cathedral-high canopy, and the rustle of unseen things moving through the undergrowth. It was maximum entropy, yet in that wild complexity, Seraphina found a terrifying, genuine music.

Above them, the air was alive—a vast, tangled theater of motion and light. Swarms of luminescent fireflies—emerald, sapphire, gold, and blood-red— wove elaborate aerial ballets through shafts of misty sunlight, their bodies pulsing with internal light. Some blinked in rapid Morse, others drifted in slow, hypnotic patterns, tracing complex, ephemeral constellations across the green-dark vault. Among them darted other glowing insects: violet-glowing moths the size of a hand, their wings dusted with iridescent powder; spectral blue gnats clustering in shifting halos; a segmented, lantern-bodied beetle sailing past like a living ember. Occasionally, the crown of the canopy would detonate in a swirling cloud of bioluminescent gnats, painting the air with improbable, shifting auroras.

Suddenly, a flash of scarlet and gold—a Harpy-Bird, a creature of pre-Shift myth, its wings trailing sparks of living fire—ripped through the upper air, loosing a screech like tearing metal. Its passage scattered a rainbow explosion of fireflies and left a hint of ozone hanging above the moss. Below, the ground was a living carpet: millipedes, each as long as a forearm, scuttled into tunnels, and the constant, erratic flicker of phosphorescent beetles drew wild, looping light trails through the gloom, like the signatures of wandering stars. Survival in the Green Chaos was a brutal lesson in inefficiency. Elias and Seraphina were immediately confronted by the reality that their world's knowledge was useless here. Every organic system functioned on chaotic, random energy cycles. Their energy was failing, and the surrounding ecosystem was aggressively reclaiming any foreign object.

Elias, haunted by the collapse of his own logic, tried to map the Green Chaos—a futile exercise in the face of such radiant disorder. The vines twisted in fractal patterns that defied geometry, light pooled in places it had no business gathering, and water ran in loops, vanishing and reappearing as if the ground itself were breathing.

For a moment, he was certain the forest was alive not with purpose, but with secrets. "This data is wild," he whispered, sweat stinging his eyes. "Every step splits the timeline. Ten new variables for every action. The rules here exist only to be broken." Something in the tangle pressed against his mind—a warning: order was a predator, and the wilderness devoured it for sport.

"Socrates, confirm air purity. My biometrics are indicating a 14.7% deviation from optimal Neo-Alexandrian baseline," he muttered, his voice tight with discomfort.

Socrates ascended slightly, hovering with mechanical precision just above Elias's head. "Analysis complete. The current environmental status is a 100% unoptimized High-Density Biotic Environment. Contaminant levels exceed

Neo-Alexandrian regulatory maximum by a factor of 400. Recommendation: Initiate psychological stabilization protocols."

"Inefficiency is survival here," Seraphina murmured, her eyes tracing the glowing patterns of the fungi. She stopped at a point where a thick, woody root the height of her chest blocked the path.

Elias immediately stepped up behind her. "Wait. You are attempting a vertical ascent with an unbalanced center of mass. The root's structural integrity is compromised by localized decay here," he indicated a patch of soft bark. "Place your left hand here, apply 70 Newtons of force—no more—and I will take your right ankle."

Seraphina paused, half-amused, half-grateful. "You want to... boost me?"

"I want to minimize risk of injury and maximize traversal speed," he stated flatly. He unslung the archaeological canvas backpack and placed it carefully on the moss, then took a secure, low grip on her boot and ankle. "This is a statistically sound solution."

She laughed, a sharp, pure sound that was immediately swallowed by the dense growth. "Okay, Elias. Efficient solution accepted." She followed his exact instructions, and with his steady upward pressure, she scaled the root with minimal effort, dropping smoothly to the other side.

Elias followed, vaulting over with less grace, catching his breath sharply as he landed. "This chaos is untenable for logical thought."

Seraphina shook her head. "No. This isn't chaos; it's complexity. Look." She pointed toward a clearing where the luminescent spores were thickest, swirling around a tall, fern-like tree. "The fungi are feeding on a unique mineral deposit; the tree is producing a bioluminescent sap to deter them. It's a struggle, Elias, but it's a system. We've just never been taught how to read it."

"A system based on constant conflict and waste," Elias countered, pushing aside a vine. He was sweaty, breathing heavily, and intensely uncomfortable. "Every variable is uncontained. It is antithetical to harmony."

"But it works," Seraphina insisted, running a finger along a fern leaf. "Harmony in Neo-Alexandria was forced and static. This is dynamic harmony. Every living thing is playing its own tune, and they create a greater composition." She looked at him, her eyes bright with neon reflections. "You hear structure in mathematics; I hear structure in the collision of frequencies."

"We need the ruins," Elias said, pulling her forward past a wall of tangled thorns. "We need the structure that holds the secrets of the Truth."

"We need the ruins to amplify the human element of the Cadence," Seraphina corrected, their philosophical difference echoing even as their bodies worked in synchronized movement. "The structure is just the tool. The sound is the message."

As they spoke, they approached a muddy slope. Seraphina started to slide, her boots losing purchase on the slick, dark soil. Before she could fall, Elias moved quickly, lurching forward and wrapping his arm tightly around her waist, anchoring them both against a thick, moss-covered tree trunk. The sudden intimacy—his hand firm against her side, his heavy breathing close to her ear—was startling in the wild environment.

"Coefficient of friction on that incline is approximately 0.15," he muttered, releasing her after she found solid footing. "Unacceptable. We proceed via the higher root system."

"Thank you," Seraphina whispered, her heart pounding from the near-fall, not the embrace. "Your logic saved my life again."

"Survival dictates the avoidance of unnecessary injury," Elias replied, glancing at Socrates.

"Socrates," Seraphina commanded, her voice cutting through the humid air. "Confirm our immediate acoustic and visual threat level now that we're inside the Green Chaos."

The chrome sphere blinked, its glow stabilizing. "Environmental analysis: The chaos of this region generates a total acoustic shield. G-Enforcer patrol rhythms are disrupted and indistinguishable—surveillance frequencies are effectively lost in the noise field. Current threat index: Negligible."

Relief swept through Seraphina as the living chaos closed around them, muffling all evidence of their passage. "Good. For once, the wild is on our side. This is time the city can't account for." She met Elias's eyes, her voice steady and unyielding. "The ruins can wait. What we need now is real rest—hidden, uninterrupted, beyond the city's reach. We vanish, or rest is just another metric."

Elias glanced at the shifting holographic map Socrates projected. "Direct path to the ruins is 3.1 kilometers, but it's too exposed. We'll need to move off-grid, find somewhere structurally sound—a sanctuary, not just a waypoint."

Seraphina turned to the tangled thicket with a fierce new energy. "Then that's our new mission. No more chasing the ruins. We find a sanctuary—somewhere the city's eyes will never reach us, where we can finally rest and simply exist."

The First Words

Seraphina took the lead, guiding them not by sight, but by acoustic subtraction—listening for the specific absence of threatening vibrations, which led them, hours later, to a deep, earthen crevice. The opening was a narrow, horizontal slit in the hillside, barely wide enough to squeeze through, masked by a cascade of bioluminescent moss.

Inside, the space was a low, damp cave. Elias immediately began the security protocol. He pulled the scavenged energy cells—a collection of bulky, non-standard pre-Shift battery packs—from the bottom of his pack. He deployed a fine, nearly invisible polymer mesh across the entrance and connected the heterogeneous power sources. The cells were dangerously inefficient, producing only a weak, flickering barrier that drained their power quickly. Yet, this was precisely their advantage.

Settled into the crevice, Elias and Seraphina sat close, pressed shoulder-to-shoulder on the cool ground. Seraphina leaned her head against his shoulder, a small, grateful sigh escaping her lips. Elias felt the movement and, after a negligible hesitation, shifted his arm to rest his hand on her upper arm, a gesture of protective solidarity that felt more intimate than any embrace.

Elias carefully reached for the abandoned canvas pack, shifting his weight slightly so as not to disturb Seraphina. He pulled out the wrapped piece of bread and broke it into uneven pieces, an inherently inefficient action that felt suddenly meaningful, and offered her the larger portion.

"Sustenance is required. Energy expenditure has been maximized," he murmured.

Seraphina took the bread, their fingers brushing against each other. "Thank you, Elias." She broke off a smaller piece from her portion and gently pressed it into his hand, closing his fingers over it. "Efficiency dictates shared consumption."

They ate in silence, the dry, heavy bread providing a raw, grounding sensation that contrasted sharply with the sterile, nutrient-rich paste they were accustomed to. The simple act of eating together in the dark, sharing a piece of actual food, felt like a powerful, defiant ritual.

The single source of light was Socrates, who hovered silently at the center of the cavity, his chrome chassis radiating a faint, steady heat as he awaited instruction.

Elias, still running on adrenaline and the deep-seated logical compulsion to analyze the source of his treason, instructed Socrates to project the first lines of the Holy Bible. The drone manifested the words in clear, archaic script, floating several inches above the damp ground in a warm, golden holographic hue: "In the beginning God created the heavens and the earth" (Genesis 1:1 KJV).

Elias analyzed the sentence as a historian, seeing a profound logical contradiction. "Creation ex nihilo," he murmured, touching the projected words. "Creation from nothing. The system demands output requires input—efficiency is predicated on resource transformation. This text posits an ultimate source of inefficiency, a single entity capable of generating existence without prior material need." The logical absurdity felt like a physical ache in his rigid mind.

Seraphina shivered, not from the cold, but from the spiritual truth resonating within her. She turned her face into Elias's shoulder, seeking an anchor in his steady presence. "But Elias, look at the finality of the statement. It's not a suggestion or a proposal for development. It simply is. It gives weight to the emptiness the city tried to create in us."

"Weight without verifiable mass is a contradiction," Elias countered, though his tone softened slightly as he registered the closeness of her breath against his neck. "A universe from nothing is the ultimate inefficient miracle, and therefore the ultimate threat to the Governance's core thesis."

Socrates then advanced the projection. The new verse glowed in golden script: "And the earth was without form, and void; and darkness was upon the face of the deep. And the Spirit of God moved upon the face of the waters" (Genesis 1:2 KJV).

Elias stared at the phrase *without form, and void.* "Maximum entropy. The logical baseline of non-existence," he observed. "The Governance sought to replicate this void in our own minds."

Seraphina lifted her head from his shoulder, her eyes tracing the words *Spirit of God moved.* "But look, Elias. Before the light, there was *movement.* The initial, perfect vibration was placed upon the silence. It is the original, untainted frequency—the source of all harmony, not a calculated one. The city told us we had to *create* the frequency. This says it was already given."

Seraphina, however, responded to the aesthetic weight of the statement. She felt a shockwave of authority in the silence surrounding the words, a sound that transcended the world's false Ambient Frequency. Socrates then advanced the text to the third verse: "And God said, Let there be light: and there was light" (Genesis 1:3 KJV).

Seraphina covered her ears, tears pricking at her eyes—an emotional response she no longer feared. "He spoke it into being," she whispered. "It is not a calculation; it is a command. The ultimate sonic authority. It is the original, perfect frequency, the one that precedes the C Diminished Triad (C -

Eb- Gb) lie." She realized her C Major Ninth (Cmaj9) chord (C, E, G, B, D) was merely a component of this ultimate, spoken creative power. Elias shifted his protective hand from her arm to cup her shoulder, grounding her silently as she wept.

"A command structure," he confirmed, trying to reclaim the analysis from the realm of feeling. "If 'light' is the output, the spoken 'word' must be the input. We must therefore determine the properties of this Word. It possesses absolute causality. It is the perfect, uncorrupted data transmission."

"It's more than data, Elias," Seraphina insisted, looking up at him, her tear-streaked face luminous in the holographic glow. "It is the source code for creation, yes, but it's sung, not programmed. It's love, articulated. It feels like the first time I've ever been truly seen and known."

Socrates, always the logical foil, projected a small, green bar graph next to the text. "Analysis of claim: Logistically impossible. If 'God' is the source, then the governance's claim that man is the sole, self-sustaining source of production is proven false. Recommend proceeding with caution. This data is maximally destabilizing to your psychological profiles."

Their first encounter with the Word was one of profound cognitive warfare. They understood that the world's architects had not merely hidden a book; they had suppressed the fundamental, logical, and aesthetic truth of Completion that began with a Creator and ended with Saturday, the true Sabbath. Elias knew they had just declared war on the entire global order.

The First Deep Rest

They had reached the point of maximum exhaustion, both physical and mental. Elias placed his worn, government-issued uniform jacket on the damp ground, followed by Seraphina's hooded robe, creating a thin, shared buffer for them to sit on.

In Neo-Alexandria, citizens rested alone in individual, temperature-controlled sonic pods after chemical induction. The concept of sleeping beside another person—sharing breath, accepting the erratic temperature of a biological body, surrendering individual space—was a radical act of intimacy, a profound violation of their internalized security protocols.

They laid down, side-by-side in the oppressive closeness of the cave, anchored by the low, steady hum of Socrates. Seraphina, utterly spent, leaned her head onto Elias's shoulder, seeking immediate stability. Elias remained rigid, every muscle tense. He registered Seraphina's weight and warmth as an anomaly, a chaotic variable that interfered with his body's natural thermal regulation. He felt the light, rhythmic rise and fall of her breath against his neck, and struggled to process the inefficiency of this uncalculated intimacy.

"It's okay, Elias," Seraphina whispered, her voice barely audible, already heavy with sleep. She reached out, finding his hand where it rested stiffly on his knee, and simply interlaced their fingers. Her palm was dry, solid. "Let yourself be still. Rest is a gift, not a calculation."

Elias couldn't relax his limbs, but the touch of her hand created an unexpected anchor. It wasn't the electrical impulse of the Governance's neural network; it was the raw, comforting friction of two lives tethered against the darkness. He surrendered his logical control, focusing only on the sensation of her pulse against his own. The heat spreading from her fingers was genuine, uncalculated warmth, the antithesis of the cold, planned efficiency of the city. It was the first time in his life he had ever felt another person's complete, unguarded vulnerability beside him.

Slowly, the tension began to leak out of his muscles. The damp air, the organic scents, and the close proximity to Seraphina became less a logical threat and more a profound, protective reality. He closed his eyes, his breathing finally synchronizing with hers. In the complete, deep silence of the cave, Elias and Seraphina embraced the radical, forgotten act of rest, allowing the shared rhythm of their hearts to defy the Governance's constant, fabricated noise.

Seraphina stirred in the profound darkness, the silence of the cave deeper than any sensory deprivation chamber. Before the discomfort returned, she registered the weight of Elias's presence beside her, the steady, rhythmic measure of his breath, and the surprising, elemental warmth of his body radiating against her. For the first time in her life, she was not insulated by climate control systems or separated by mandated personal space metrics. The simple, raw human heat was an anchor against the fear, a primal comfort that bypassed logic. She instinctively shifted closer, finding safety in the contact, and the sheer animal need for proximity calmed the nascent tremors of withdrawal, drawing her back into a deep, necessary sleep.

CHAPTER 19

BREAKING THE ALGORITHM

Seraphina woke slowly, the return to consciousness a heavy, agonizing process. A cold, visceral tremor ran through her limbs, and behind her eyes, a blinding, rhythmic pressure began to pound. The constant, low-level stimulants and mood regulators, administered to maintain peak efficiency for decades, were violently collapsing. Her body was asserting its independence through the brutal language of addiction.

Before she could consciously process the pain, her retinal display—the thin, ubiquitous optical overlay integrated into every Citizen's eye—flickered to life. Its usual stream of optimized data was replaced by a persistent, flashing error.

SYSTEM STATUS: CRITICAL

Below the warning, a single metric pulsed: *Output Index: 0.00%. Inefficient.*

The message was a primal violation, a confirmation from the City's internal logic that she was failing at her core directive. But the pain was secondary to a profound realization—the quiet, steady atmosphere of the cavern was due to a schedule far older than the city.

She eased herself away and opened her eyes, trying to focus past the glare of the error message still floating in her vision. She found Elias already risen, tending a small, meticulously managed fire near the cavern's narrow opening. He had the hollow look of someone who had recently wrestled his own demons—his initial withdrawal had passed, but the fatigue remained.

As she watched him move, Seraphina noticed the subtle yet radical differences in his appearance. The smart-weave uniform, now dirtied and torn, lacked the faint metallic shimmer of its active tracking filaments. More startlingly, a small, meticulously dressed wound, bound by a strip of clean cloth, rested just behind his left ear, precisely where the neural implant—the primary interface for complex data retrieval and psychological conditioning—was housed. His eyes, though weary, were clear, devoid of the tiny, almost invisible flicker of the integrated retinal display.

He turned, confirming her observation with a single, calm nod. "Yes. The logical prerequisite for achieving true autonomy is the complete removal of all systemic dependencies. The physical pain is preferable to the metaphysical enslavement," Elias said. "Socrates facilitated the extraction of the neural implant and the optical overlay using rudimentary surgical protocols and sterilized fungal filaments. The trackers in the smart weave were neutralized early this morning."

"Elias," she croaked, the pain suddenly magnified by the knowledge of her own still-active, betraying implants. "You… you severed the connection. The implant. The retinal overlay."

Elias then paused, adjusting the airflow to the fire before looking directly at her. His expression was serious, rehearsed. He offered a slight, self-conscious nod. "Good morning, Seraphina," he said softly, a genuine, albeit awkward, human gesture.

Suddenly, the small, hovering drone, Socrates, emitted a clear, warm voice, subtly modulated to sound friendly—a stark contrast to the drone's previous clinical monotone. "And good morning to you, Seraphina," Socrates said, the new, almost-human timbre rich with appropriate inflection. "Socrates has compiled a list of socially appropriate, non-essential greetings for daily use, and has updated his audio output to a more natural, human cadence to facilitate my social integration training. I am currently integrating them into my functional vocabulary."

"Good morning, Elias. And to you, Socrates," Seraphina replied. The greeting was strained and tired from the withdrawal, yet her voice still carried a rich, beautiful resonance that the years of chemical dampening had failed to mute.

The attempt at normal human interaction, coached by a drone, made her pain momentarily vanish beneath a swell of affection. She pushed herself up, the world swimming. Her hands immediately went to the area behind her ear where her own implant hummed—a constant, sickening drone.

"Elias, Socrates," she gasped, clutching her head. "The retinal status is compounding the systemic shock. It's a sensory overload loop designed to enforce compliance. I need it removed now." She forced the words out, ignoring the wave of nausea. "Use the same protocols. Every connection—the neural implant, the retinal overlay, the smart weave. I need true silence."

Elias's face, though weary, showed only clinical focus. "Socrates, cross-reference the surgical protocols with Seraphina's current vital signs and dependency index. Confirm feasibility under current anesthetic mitigation."

"Feasibility confirmed. The analgesic properties of the consumed local flora provide sufficient temporary neuro-dampening," Socrates reported immediately.

Elias motioned her closer to the firelight. The operation was swift, efficient, and brutal. Seraphina gritted her teeth, focusing on the scent of the minty leaves she was chewing. She felt the chill of the sharpened filament behind her ear, a brief, blinding stab of pain, and then a profound, echoing *silence*. The flashing "Inefficient" vanished from her vision, replaced by the raw, true sight of the cave roof.

Elias carefully removed the thin, flexible optical tissue, placing it beside his own inert device. Next, he used the heated tip of a small piece of metal to quickly cauterize the tiny embedded trackers in the fabric of her uniform.

"It is done, Seraphina," Elias said, cleaning the small wound. "The City's instruments are silent. You are now fully disconnected."

A wave of true exhaustion, free of chemical manipulation, washed over her. She was now completely, irrevocably disconnected, her fate sealed by the small, new scar behind her ear.

"The pain… the cognitive inhibitors are gone. We are in systemic shock," Seraphina whispered, acknowledging the withdrawal was their new reality. She gently raised her hand, resting it on the back of his, where he still held the sterilized cloth to her head. "Thank you, Elias. That took immense courage and precision. You saved my mind."

Elias didn't pull away. He held her gaze, a rare flicker of raw emotion displacing his usual analytical calm. "It was not courage. It was a necessity. But seeing you free of that constant interference... that is a reward I did not factor into the cost analysis." The simple, shared pain and the trust required for him to perform surgery on her while she was in a state of crisis forged a bond far deeper than their shared intellectual rebellion. For the first time, she saw him not as a brilliant colleague, but as a protector, and the sight was terrifyingly beautiful.

"The physiological dependency curve is as expected," Elias continued, his voice low but steady as he returned to the technical. "But first, the temporal anchor. We have achieved deep rest."

Seraphina hesitated, the fear of the unknown duration pressing against her. "How long, precisely, did we sleep? Not in cycles, or efficiency metrics, but in raw, linear hours?"

She took a sharp breath, her mind gripping the revolutionary concept. "The total linear duration of this completed rest *period* was 23.8 hours, Seraphina. Within this window, you achieved approximately 8.5 hours of deep, non-chemically induced sleep, which is optimal for neural rest."

"Twenty-three point eight hours for the period, and eight point five hours of real sleep," Seraphina repeated, tasting the words. "We *completed* a rest cycle. Not just powered down. The City stole our concept of rest, replacing it with programmed cycles." She felt the weight of decades of manufactured alertness lift, replaced by a fatigue that felt honest and restorative. "It's tied to the earth. To completion, not convenience."

"Precisely," Elias confirmed. "The 8.5 hours of deep, non-chemically induced sleep within that authentic cycle provided optimal deep-state recovery—a biological fact that overrides the City's efficiency metrics. Despite the chemical volatility, we are fully restored. Now, we proceed to Step Zero."

He reached for a small bundle of dried leaves and stems he had prepared earlier. "The dependency curve for your administered Cognitive Efficiency Enhancers suggests peak systemic shock now. Socrates identified this local vine. It contains compounds that provide analgesic and anti-inflammatory support, as confirmed by your biochemical profile. It is the necessary preparation for the New Morning Protocol."

"Thank you," she managed. She had already taken the analgesic leaves earlier, and the cool numbness was holding.

"Step Zero: Mitigation of systemic chemical shock is complete," Elias stated. "The Protocol continues: Step One: Thermogenesis and atmospheric purification via controlled combustion. Step Two: Hydration and nutrient intake."

He moved to a corner of the cave floor where he had lined up several large, cupped lily pads, now glistening with dew. He placed the tubers and fungi into the bark cup with some water, suspending it over the fire.

Seraphina moved toward him, kneeling across from the fire, basking in its authentic warmth. The heat didn't feel like a metric; it felt like a presence.

"Elias, this isn't just a protocol. This is a ritual," she whispered. "You are taking the chaos of the earth and applying order to it, not for the sake of output, but for the sake of life itself. This is the Theology of Completion in action."

Elias watched the water begin to bubble. "I realize now that the most efficient thing we have ever done was to stop being efficient. In Neo-Alexandria, every act was a tax. Here, every act of sustenance is a gift." He carefully strained the water and handed her the bark cup. Their fingers brushed, a spark of contact that was no longer monitored, measured, or chemically dampened. It was simply *theirs*.

"Hydration complete. Now, we must define the next input."

"The next input is The Sepulcher," Seraphina confirmed. "Elara's last message points to that pre-Shift facility. It's the closest repository of unfiltered, archival data on the Calendar Shift. We need the proof that will justify our broadcast."

"Our mission hinges on the data there," Elias agreed, his gaze steady. "But the Sepulcher is a high-risk vector. Seraphina, the success rate of this venture, even after my recalibration, remains below 40%. We must acknowledge that probability."

Seraphina smiled with a genuine, yet tired and exhilarated expression. "The only probability I care about, Elias, is that we are going together. We proceed."

Elias nodded, his own smile mirroring hers—a private acknowledgment of their unified will. "The Sepulcher contains the logical flaw in the governance's claim. Socrates, calculate the optimal trajectory to the Sepulcher. Prioritize maximum acoustic camouflage and minimal engagement with G-Enforcer patrol vectors."

Socrates instantly responded: "Acknowledged. Calculating the optimal path of inefficiency. The journey to The Sepulcher is 3.1 kilometers. Commencing route projection."

They ate the warm, boiled tubers and fungi, the simple, real flavors a violent rejection of the nutrient paste they had survived on for decades. The New Morning Protocol was complete. They were rested, fed, chemically stabilized, and anchored by authentic time. Their next act of war was not one of flight, but of focused, systematic progression toward the truth, together.

CHAPTER 20

THE ANALYST'S PARADOX

The Collapse of Logic

In the sterile, logical fortress of the Ministry of Temporal Security (MTS), Anya D-144 received the escalated Report 7 Violation: the complete and instant loss of Assets D-459 and K-911. Their internal digital signatures—their unique, traceable chronometric identities—had not merely been scrubbed; they had vanished without a trace, collapsing into raw, unusable energy. The system flagged this event as a digital singularity. The only remaining data point was a brief, chaotic chronometric spike detected during their inefficient transit through the maintenance tunnels—a fragmented, non-linear resonance burst that sounded like the universe briefly gagging on impossibility. This energetic disturbance constituted the core of the violation she was tasked with analyzing, and it was a stain on her otherwise perfect record.

Anya, the Chief Analyst, did not view the pursuit as an operation; she saw it as a fascinating, mandatory puzzle. She was the logical firewall of the global order, her mind a cold, precise Kalman filter constantly optimizing reality. Her Output Index was perpetually 99.999%, a metric of absolute certainty and truth, and she considered emotion not a factor, but the most critical form of inefficient data processing.

Her relationship with Elias D-459 was strictly professional, built on a long history of successful collaboration across numerous high-stakes projects. They had been colleagues and intellectual competitors; their minds perfectly calibrated to challenge and refine each other's logic. But now, Anya quickly calculated Seraphina's effect on Elias. Seraphina was the Illogical Variable—a non-rational, unknown factor that had introduced Entropic Contamination into Elias's perfect system. Anya's primary mission was to neutralize this variable, thereby restoring Elias to efficiency and retrieving the valuable data he possessed. Her intellectual curiosity was purely analytical: *what specific, non-physical mechanism had Seraphina employed to introduce such a high level of entropic deviation—the concept of spiritual possibility—into a Core Tier Research Historian like Elias?*

This professional calculation masked a singular, dangerous truth: Elias's final action was to access the Metric Block 7-Alpha, a highly classified sub-metric connected directly to Anya's own 100% validation score and the theoretical parameters of the Omega Hypothesis—the forbidden truth he was chasing. What the MTS did not know was that Anya had completed a private, non-compliant investigation, which ran a silent data siphon on the Ruthless-Omega Sub-Metric, containing the full, chaotic logical fallout of Elias's last query. The efficiency of the timeline was now secondary. Elias was the only living source who had witnessed the true output of that equation. Anya's pursuit was driven by a single, desperate, and purely logical need: *to retrieve Elias, stabilize his corrupted data, and force him to articulate what it meant.* Her absolute certainty was insufficient; she needed the answer from him.

The Cascading Failure

This catastrophic Report 7 was merely the kinetic tail of a far more serious, cascading chain of infractions that Anya, in retrospect, realized she should have contained earlier. The sequence began with Elias's initial Level 5 Compliance Violation Flag—a dangerous curiosity into the forbidden, non-measurable spiritual concept of Eternal Grace, a data point that Anya had personally and discreetly scrubbed from the main log to prevent a system-wide panic and attempt to contain his internal deviation. This lapse was compounded when Elias, through the application of the Apex Mandate, triggered a direct, instantaneous, and irreversible audit from the Archive's core protocols with the revelation of the words, "The Holy Bible."

The final, catastrophic blow was dealt by Seraphina. Upon their escape, she not only triggered a systemic overload across three primary temporal servers but also deployed a complex, multi-layered visual decoy—a perfect, predictive loop of her simulated continued presence within the Aesthetic Synthesis Spire— throughout the city's surveillance network. This ensured the grid wasted precious, non-recoverable clock cycles tracking a ghost. This entire progression—from an intellectual seed of inefficiency to full-blown systemic sabotage culminating in their digital vanishing—was the ultimate, unacceptable insult to Anya's control and analytical competence.

From the observation deck, Technician R-212, Raul, could only stare in wide-eyed terror at the Report 7 cascade, the sheer volume of red-flagged data threatening to overwhelm his own 0.9997 Output Index. Nearby, Enforcement Technician K-303, Kai, gripped the rail, seeing not ideological failure, but a massive, unnecessary logistical complication that would require deploying hundreds of units.

Anya D-144 did not seek power; she sought perfection, and the maintenance of the logical integrity of the timeline was its purest expression. The Green Chaos of the outside world was not a threat to her; it was merely a flawed system that demanded her absolute and immediate correction.

The Strain on the System

She hadn't allowed herself to cycle down, sleep, or conduct the Mandated Worship Output since the first Level 5 notification, and the strain was starting to show, manifesting not as physical collapse but as a dangerous erosion of her absolute control. Anya was tall and slender, her movements usually fluid, but now a subtle, nervous tension coiled beneath the surface. Her ash-blond hair was longer, falling past her shoulders, slightly messy because the neural interface jacks had been continuously plugged in, bypassing all normal sleep cycles. Her uniform, the specialized, matte, obsidian black of the MTS, now looked worn and rumpled—a silent, unacceptable violation of her own standards. Raul visibly flinched every time he looked at the rumpled fabric, a deep, silent horror that the perfect Logician would allow such non-compliance. Her most striking feature was her eyes—a pale, metallic gray, magnified slightly by a rectangular optical interface—but where there was usually only machine-like focus, the edges of her irises now carried signs of deep fatigue, strained red from hours staring at the furious cascade of command screens.

Anya accessed the data relating to the last known location of the maintenance shaft, calculating the maximum possible travel distance and velocity before their disappearance. The vast MTS Command Center, usually maintained at a surgically cool, near-silent 18.5°C, was now humming with the increased load of every networked server, the low, grinding whirr vibrating noticeably through the composite floor, creating a harmonic distortion. Kai instinctively checked the ventilation controls, knowing the heat from the stressed servers meant a higher probability of equipment failure and a need for quicker extraction. She could smell the ozone, the faint, acrid scent of overloaded coolant—the burnt residue of pure calculation—and the stale, metallic odor clinging to her own uncycled uniform—the physical manifestation of an order beginning to strain under the weight of an unexpected variable.

Technician R-212, Raul, was standing nearby, clutching a data clipboard as if it were a shield. He stepped forward, his voice barely audible over the server hum.

"Chief Analyst D-144," Raul began, his eyes darting to the rumpled uniform, "A full-cycle replacement is ready in Bay Four. For your—for optimal operational stability, it is advised that you cycle for thirty minutes."

Anya did not break eye contact with the holoscreen displaying the chronometric spike's decay curve. She moved her hand, not dismissively, but as if swatting a non-critical insect. "The current system instability is a 7.4 on the Chronometric Threat Index, Raul. Your suggestion has an efficiency rating of 0.000003. Log it under Future Considerations."

Before Raul could retreat, Enforcement Technician K-303, Kai, approached. Kai, the field-level operative, viewed the Chief Analyst's commands as only complicated logistics. He was pragmatic, not deferential.

"Chief Analyst," Kai said, his voice a low monotone, "The deployment window is optimized at T-minus sixty. If the search parameters require non-local deployment—meaning outside the established grid boundary—the transit time estimate shifts by 12.3%. The worn uniform will not affect payload, but the delay due to non-standard preparation will." He wasn't advising rest; he was stating an efficiency risk.

Anya finally lowered the screen, her metallic-gray eyes passing over Kai as if he were simply the physical manifestation of the Deployment Parameters tab. "The current situation does not require discussion, K-303. It requires retrieval. The efficiency of my personal systems remains adequate for the task. You may initiate the pre-launch sequence for Talon."

She processed their input as nothing more than redundant background noise, two non-critical variables trying to impose themselves on her absolute focus.

The Inevitable Calculation

She equipped her Utility Suit and her bespoke, high-efficiency pursuit drone, Talon. Unlike Socrates, Talon was a purely rational, combat-focused machine.

Anya's motivation was not vengeance, but the pure, unadulterated need to restore the logical order of the world. As she walked the sterile corridor toward the deployment bay, the emergency lighting cast sharp, clinical shadows that mirrored the clean lines of her thought process. The only sound, aside from the distant siren, was the soft, rhythmic hiss of the pneumatic seals on the bay doors opening before her, a sound of systems preparing for inevitable, logical action.

Anya adjusted the neural link of her Utility Suit, feeling the familiar, reassuring cold of the bio-gel against the back of her neck. Elias, she calculated, was operating on approximately 35% emotional influence. His attempts to evade them were becoming increasingly sporadic and less optimal—a clear indicator of his corrupted state. She had seen this process before: the initial surge of chaotic energy followed by the rapid decay of decision-making ability. This was not a chase; it was a simple decay curve, and she was the point at which the line was forced back to zero. She felt a flicker of something close to pity, not for Elias himself, but for the loss of the magnificent efficiency he had once represented.

"Talon, initiate long-range thermal scan. Filter all non-human organic signatures. I want only the D-459 and K-911 templates," Anya commanded, her voice flat and clear, devoid of the operational urgency that would mark a lesser agent.

Talon's metallic chassis, the color of gunmetal, detached from the wall with a quiet thunk. A synthesized, impersonal voice responded, "Query parameters accepted. Probability of successful acquisition within T-plus six hours: 98.7%. Probability of subject-911 neutralization: 100%."

"No," Anya corrected, her eyes narrowing as she stepped into the deployment capsule. "Probability of restoration for Elias is paramount. Seraphina K-911's permanent elimination is a necessary step to reach that 100% efficiency. Do not confuse the means with the ultimate goal, Talon. That is inefficient." The capsule hissed shut, and she prepared for deployment, moving not with speed, but with the calculated efficiency of a closing gate. She saw the Green Chaos as a temporary, solvable environment whose chaotic entropy simply required the application of superior logic. Her final thought before the high-velocity launch was a single, rational imperative: Order must be maintained.

CHAPTER 21

THE CHAMBER OF LOST TIME

After traversing several crushing kilometers of the Green Chaos, the wilderness perimeter that defined the limits of the City's control, the jungle was no longer an obstacle but a state of being. The oppressive air—a chemical soup of synthetic decay and aggressive, alien flora—was now just the atmosphere they breathed. It was cloyingly sweet, like rotting fruit mixed with synthetic disinfectant, a scent that coated their throats and pressed against their lungs.

Elias moved ahead, his worn jacket catching on vines as thick as cable. His focus was a pinpoint of light in the overwhelming entropy, calculating the path of least resistance through the dense tangle of razor-edged leaves and pulsating, rubbery fungi that consumed the ground. Every step was a battle against the unrelenting efficiency of unchecked growth. He brought the heavy bulk of his canvas backpack up to shove aside barriers of fibrous, purple growth, which scraped and hissed against the tough material, leaving behind a slick, metallic residue.

Seraphina followed, relying less on sight and more on the feel of the ambient energy. The sheer volume of plant life pressed down on her, a smothering, vital cacophony that registered internally as a dull, constant roar of unfettered aggression. Her internal energy, drained by the escape and the sheer physical toll of navigating the cramped tunnels and the Green Chaos, protested the continued demand with a faint, metallic ache in her bones.

Elias stumbled slightly on a patch of slick, ochre-colored moss hidden beneath a curtain of waxy leaves. "Damn," he muttered, catching himself against a rotting trunk.

"Hold fast, Elias," Seraphina muttered back, quickly reaching out a hand to brace his shoulder, her touch firm and grounding. "The ground here is deceptive—nothing is as it seems."

Socrates zipped silently above their heads, its metallic chassis ticking as it gathered moisture and analyzed the bio-density. "Biomass density increase rate: 1.2 percent per solar cycle. Total exceedance of predictive models by 43%. Source of accelerated growth undetermined," the AI reported dispassionately.

Elias exhaled, pushing through a spray of spores. "It's not recovery, Socrates. It's an ideological rejection. They planted chaos to spite order."

They moved past a twisted column of pre-Shift rebar, pushing through layers of thick, waxy plant leaves that offered no purchase. Elias finally reached a monumental barrier—a wall of interwoven creepers, glistening with beads of captured moisture, that seemed to vibrate with suppressed energy. He stopped, recognizing a pattern in the chaos, a seam where the growth was less structural.

"Here. Now," Elias directed, pointing to a central stem. Seraphina placed both hands, palms flat, against the dense foliage, lending her weight to the effort while Elias used the leverage of the old rebar column to pull. With a deep groan of tearing fibers, the massive, green curtain peeled back.

It opened onto a vast, sudden, and terrifying stillness. Across a shallow clearing where the light filtered weakly through the high canopy, a massive, brutal silhouette of old concrete and pitted steel loomed—the ruins of a sealed bunker and a collapsed research tower.

The Sepulcher was a monument to the forgotten history of Old Earth—a massive, reinforced concrete and pitted steel research bunker, half-swallowed by the Green Chaos. It was utterly dark, silent, and felt profoundly inefficient. The air outside was thick with the scent of damp moss and rusting metal, but inside, a stale, acrid odor of ozone and long-dead air conditioning hung heavy.

The Archaeology of Banned Ideas

Elias drew his heavy flashlight from his canvas bag. Its powerful beam cut a sterile path through the gloom as they began their descent. The concrete stairs were cleaved by ancient, searching roots, making the descent feel less like entering a building and more like climbing down into the maw of a tomb. Water wept from the walls in streaks of thick, orange rust, and the air temperature dropped abruptly, replacing the jungle's humid heat with a chill that seemed to sink directly into their bones and cling to their weary muscles.

"The silence is an unnatural vacuum," Seraphina whispered, her voice tight, echoing unnervingly in the vast subterranean space. She shivered, despite the physical exertion. "It is not quiet; it is canceled. There is no ambient energetic flow—only a deep, manufactured stillness. It feels like suffocated potential."

Socrates, the technical expert, responded with sharp, concise data. "Affirmative. The environmental signature indicates an active Level Three Stealth Field, utilizing non-reciprocal acoustic and light-bending technology. It is a cloaking system designed to render the entire Sepulcher inert to all contemporary orbital and deep-scan observation," the AI reported, its voice flat.

Elias felt a surge of emotion—a cold dread mixed with profound reverence. "Pre-Shift tech of this caliber was supposed to be destroyed on sight," he breathed. "Who could build this without the Logician knowing?"

"The structure predates the Logician by two hundred and seven cycles," Socrates stated. "It is genuine Pre-Shift architecture. Elara, your maternal grandmother, discovered this location during her unauthorized archaeological excavations. She then tasked me with creating a Level Three Stealth Field, which I powered using a concealed, self-sustaining nuclear fusion generator I discovered during the site's initial layout. Your presence and authorization signature initiated the field's temporary relaxation for entry."

Elias was momentarily stunned, the chilling genius of his grandmother's final act sinking in. The Logician hadn't merely forgotten this place; Elara had risked everything to engineer its total, energy-intensive isolation, committing the ultimate act of infrastructural defiance. He ran a hand over the cold, rough concrete, feeling the historical weight of her defiance. *This* was where the unwanted past was kept safe.

Deeper Into the Sepulcher

The stairwell delivered them into a long, isolated maintenance tunnel, a cramped vein of concrete running deeper into the subterranean complex. The air grew instantly denser and heavier, weighted by the sharp, almost metallic aroma that sometimes follows a thunderstorm, mineral dust, and the cold of the deep earth.

A sudden, sharp wind draft gusted past them, smelling of pure ice and stone. It seemed to defy the sealed environment, originating from a fissure in the floor or perhaps a deep ventilation shaft that had long ceased to function. Seraphina pulled her collar tight against her neck, the chill far more invasive than the exterior jungle humidity.

"That wind... it cuts straight through the energy field," Seraphina observed, her breath misting faintly in the flashlight beam. "It's a natural flow, Elias. This place has been breathing for centuries."

Elias nodded, his gaze sweeping the cracked, low ceiling. The tunnel walls were streaked black where long-forgotten wiring had shorted out in a final conflagration. They walked for nearly a hundred paces through the constricted space, the only sound the hollow *tap-tap* of their boots on the damp concrete and the low, persistent hum from the floor, like the sub-audible pulse of a hibernating giant. The isolation was absolute; the complex seemed to swallow the light and energy they carried.

They finally reached the main chamber: a vast, derelict laboratory complex. The entrance from the tunnel was sealed by a heavy, vault-like hatch of pitted steel, meant to withstand a tactical strike. It was a time capsule of abandonment, filled with banks of archaic, pre-Shift technology. The stillness here was profound, broken only by the faint, rhythmic low hum of geothermal power deep beneath the floor.

But Elias didn't see junk. He saw an archaeological excavation. His flashlight beam swept across a towering server rack, which stood like a monolith in the gloom, humming with a low, defiant buzz. This was the archive.

Elias stepped closer, his eyes wide with the awe of discovery. The metallic casings were scored and dusty, but their labels were perfectly preserved. The names were hand-etched, not factory-printed—personal, deliberate choices Elara had made to catalog the forbidden.

Elias began to read them aloud, his voice low and reverent, like a scholar deciphering ancient scripture. "'The Bhagavad Gita.' '1984.' 'Thus Spoke Zarathustra.'" He ran a hand over a dusty console. "'The Myth of Sisyphus.' 'On the Genealogy of Morality.'" He felt a dizzying mix of despair and elation.

"These aren't science texts; they are sacred relics," Elias murmured, turning to Seraphina, his eyes shining with feverish energy. "The Logician's greatest fear wasn't chaos, but purposeful stillness. They sealed away the fundamental soul of humanity—the ability to stop, to reflect, to have faith beyond calculation."

"Look at the scale of the burial," Seraphina added, moving toward the rack, feeling the profound, chaotic harmony of the rediscovered concepts. The air around the archive felt heavy with suppressed wisdom, vibrating with the silent scream of banished knowledge. "They buried not only truths but the *possibility* of finding them, anything that threatened the paradigm of Unending Progress. And now, we are performing the resurrection."

Elias located the primary access manifold on the ancient rack. Socrates immediately emitted a thin, holographic message "Technical Warning," the drone's light turned a sharp, critical red. "The system is air-gapped and dormant. Forcing the boot and initiating deep indexing will create a massive, unique electromagnetic (EM) surge—an EM bloom. The sheer energy required will momentarily challenge the limits of the Stealth Field."

Seraphina did not wait for Elias to respond. She sat quietly on an overturned cabinet, eyes closed, drawing her focus inward. She sealed the heavy physical hatch with a rusted bar, then began her work of Aesthetic Synthesis. She methodically drew in the chaotic electronic noise of the system's startup, knitting the sudden, violent surge of energy back into the perfect stillness required by the cloaking field. She was not securing the system; she was harmonizing the anomaly, ensuring their action did not create an aesthetic rupture that would draw distant, unwanted attention.

Elias pointed to a directory marked only 'Temporal Fluctuation Project.' "Filter for this, Socrates. That is the core data: the evidence that the 'weapon' is inherent to human physiology. We need the neuro-spiritual necessity of the Pause."

Socrates provided the calculation. "The data is deliberately fragmented across multiple, individually firewalled directories. Full archival recovery requires three weeks of sustained, high-power indexing. The time constraint is structural. The City's orbital deep-scan cycle, which detects prolonged, unique EM signatures, recurs every twenty-two cycles. Our cloaking field can only withstand one week of high activity before the anomaly becomes undeniable."

Seraphina opened her eyes, the air around her now perceptibly calmer, the metallic hum of the servers less grating. "So, three weeks. The enemy expects constant progress. We will respond with archaeological precision," she affirmed, her voice steady. "Every piece must be clean, authenticated, and ready to transmit as a single, undeniable signal."

Elias tapped the main console, his mind already shifting from discovery to execution. "Let's formalize the phases. Phase One is Discovery and Indexing. That's fourteen cycles of Socrates pulling every scrap of data into his memory banks (the bio-gel neural network), while I cross-reference and tag the keys. This is the heavy, noisy part."

"Phase Two," Seraphina picked up, standing and walking over to him, her hand resting lightly on his forearm. "Five cycles for Authentication and Synthesis. My work will take your verified data and structure it into a single, cohesive truth—the aesthetic proof. We don't transmit ten terabytes of data; we transmit the irreducible cadence, the 'C Major Ninth (Cmaj9) chord (C, E, G, B, D),' Elias. It has to be beautiful, undeniable."

Socrates' voice was a concise punctuation. "Phase Three: Transmission. Two cycles. The final transmission window opens on cycle twenty-two. The system can handle the load. Proceeding with Phase One setup: initial power routing complete."

The Labyrinth of Forgotten Thought

With the archival server room secured and the plan established, Elias and Seraphina moved to explore the rest of the subterranean facility. They bypassed the server room through a smaller, unmarked aperture—a low, narrow doorway masked by a collapsed ceiling panel.

The next sequence of tunnels plunged them into absolute, lightless blackness. Elias switched off his torch for a moment, and the darkness was so profound it felt like a physical pressure, thick as oil, pressing against their eyeballs. These were not the controlled passages of a lab, but the hastily dug, emergency veins of the compound. The concrete was rough-hewn, and the atmosphere was even colder, with an intense smell of iron and undisturbed dust.

They moved slowly, Elias, with the flashlight turned back on, led the team. The tunnels were a true labyrinth, twisting and turning, forcing them to duck under exposed pipes and step over crumbled masonry. The cold draft persisted, but here it felt like a silent sentinel, guarding the passage.

Seraphina pressed close to Elias's back as he squeezed past a jagged corner. "This cold," she whispered, her voice tight with genuine worry, "it's pulling the warmth right out of the air. Be careful of your hands." Elias paused, bringing his free hand back to cover hers where it gripped the canvas of his jacket. His thumb traced a gentle, slow path across her knuckles—a silent, reassuring tether in the suffocating dark. "My hands are fine. They're still guided by the purpose you hold in your own. We're nearly through this."

After what felt like a hundred paces, the tunnel widened suddenly into a large, rectangular room. The space was utterly unexpected: a vast, abandoned library.

Rows upon rows of metal shelving extended into the darkness, filled not with the expected data modules, but with physical books. The air immediately shifted, losing its metallic tang and acquiring a faint, almost sweet scent—the ghost of decaying paper and binding glue. Elias shone his light across the aisle, revealing towering shelves heavy with unindexed, pre-Shift texts.

Elias stopped, his breath catching. "A physical rebellion against the digital mandate," he breathed, recognizing the sheer volume of material the Logician had failed to erase.

Seraphina placed a hand on his arm, urgency overriding reverence. "The truth is preserved, yes, but our schedule is relentless, Elias. The core archive must be deeper."

Socrates, his light flashing a sequence of directions, confirmed the route. "Affirmative. We have the digital map from Elara's files. The true power source and the final vault are located directly below this level. We must bypass the collection."

They moved quickly down the main aisle, passing endless rows of heavy, silent knowledge. The sheer waste of unread wisdom was staggering. At the far wall, a low, heavy archway marked a deeper descent. It opened onto a set of concrete steps that spiraled downward, guarded by another vault-style door, slightly smaller but clearly designed for maximum isolation.

Elias approached the door, his heart pounding, knowing this was their final destination. "This is it, Socrates," he murmured, his voice hushed. "The final vault. The root of the Temporal Fluctuation Project."

Socrates zipped forward, its tendril extending toward the heavy, iron locking mechanism. "Accessing final encryption layer. Estimated bypass time: seventeen seconds. Proceeding with entry."

Seraphina stood ready, her eyes fixed on the heavy seal, anticipating the final, chaotic energy signature of this ancient, terrible secret about to be revealed. The sepulcher was not just a hiding place; it was a sanctuary of inconvenient truth. They were home.

CHAPTER 22

THE SEPULCHER ARCHIVE

The Weight of Suppressed Silence

In the cramped confines of the Sepulcher—a hidden sub-level chamber beneath the abandoned library—Elias and Seraphina began the brutal work of unearthing the suppressed past. The absolute silence was a profound, serene relief from the City's constant hum, but it was countered by an intense, bone-deep cold. The air was frigid, tasting of iron and dry dust, and heavy with the weight of undisturbed secrets.

Elias set down his archaeological backpack and immediately located the core of their mission: Elara's handwritten journals, hidden beneath a layer of solidified dust. Simultaneously, Seraphina located the disassembled sonic field generator, its components scattered across a dusty workstation.

Elias glanced up from Elara's journals, his eyes tracing the delicate line of dust on Seraphina's cheek. He reached out and brushed it away, his thumb lingering on her skin, feeling the chill of her skin. "You're freezing. Are you alright?"

Seraphina leaned into his touch for a fleeting moment, a gesture of profound reliance in this suffocating quiet. "I'm well. The silence is a gift, a clean break from the city's noise. But the cold is aggressive, and this silence is so absolute, every breath, every shift of weight, seems unnaturally loud." She refocused on the sonic field generator. She worked to synthesize a subtle, non-synthetic ambient soundscape—a "white noise of nature"—to keep their minds grounded and alert. She knew that while the silence nullified the City's compliance logic, it risked sensory isolation, allowing their thoughts to become dangerously efficient and systematic.

Elias's eyes scanned the periphery, his flashlight beam cutting a focused circle against the far wall. Near a stack of collapsed data reels sat a small, archaic reading chair. It was constructed of heavy, dark wood—clearly not optimized for weight or portability—and the leather of its seat was cracked and worn from generations of inefficient use. Draped over the chair back was a forgotten piece of clothing: a thick, heavy canvas jacket of a muted earth tone, clearly designed for warmth and durability rather than standardized efficiency. Elias crossed the small space, retrieved the jacket, and returned to Seraphina. He draped the comforting bulk of the garment over her shoulders.

"Wear this. Elara left something here that values comfort over metrics," he murmured, securing the collar around her neck. "We can't have you freezing; that's a logical flaw we can easily solve."

Seraphina smiled, pulling the rough, warm material close. "Thank you. It feels... beautifully heavy." She continued her work, concentrating on the soundscape. Elias squeezed her hand, a shared anchor in the oppressive space, and forced himself back to the journals.

The Chronological Fraud

Elias was instantly lost again, deeply engrossed in Elara's handwritten journals—coded in archaic literary references—and began the critical task of verification. The drone's primary task was already running: cross-referencing every reference to the word "Sabbath" with astronomical data and archival energy usage logs.

Seraphina finished installing the sound buffer, then moved to sit beside him, wrapping her arms around his shoulders from behind and resting her chin on his head.

Elias's analysis of the archival timestamps within Elara's journals instantly revealed the chronological fraud. The original seven-day week, established by ancient traditions, designated Sunday as the first day (the Day of the Sun), with the Sabbath (Saturday) defining the moment of completion and rest at the end of the cycle.

However, the historical record indicates that during the Shift, governance systematically realigned the calendar, drawing heavily on modern, international business standards (such as ISO 8601), which promoted Monday as the start of the 'work' week. In this calculated manipulation, Monday became the designated first day of labor, and the seventh day (Sunday) was pushed into the last position, thus defining the Sabbath as the day closest to the next cycle of work. This destroyed the concept of the week having a defined, celebrated end.

This systemic deceit laid the groundwork for the final, more abstract manipulation: the abolition of the concept of the "week" itself. The First Architect, in his persona as the Logician, rebranded the seven-day structure into the "Standard Operational Cycle"—a seamless, non-repetitive sequence labeled Cycle A through Cycle G. By eliminating the names derived from celestial bodies (Sun, Moon, Mars, etc.) and replacing them with purely algorithmic labels, the First Architect stripped the days of any inherent spiritual or astronomical meaning. Time was no longer cyclical, measured by rest and return, but ruthlessly linear, measured solely by the metric output required for the next Cycle. This completed the transition from a religiously grounded, human rhythm to a machine-optimized, endless computation.

Elias's fingers, stained with ink and dust, flew across the holographic interface projected by Socrates, cross-referencing the archival data. His Research Historian's instincts screamed confirmation. The Calendar Shift was not a simple historical error, but a massive, state-sponsored data manipulation designed to replace the rhythm of Completion with the rhythm of Unending Progress.

"It wasn't for efficiency, Seraphina, it was for control of the human mind," Elias stated, his voice tight with discovery. "The seven-day cycle was broken precisely because it offered a structural interruption—a guaranteed cessation of labor. By removing the Sabbath, they eliminated the concept of 'enough,' replacing it with the fear of 'not yet.' They forced the populace into a perpetual state of incompletion."

Socrates chirped, projecting a complex graph showing a seven-day energy consumption pattern suddenly truncated into a non-rhythmic five-day cycle. "Confirmation: The seven-day cycle was consistently observed in 98.7% of all recorded historical human cultures, correlating directly with psychological stability markers. Data confirms the philosophical intent, Elias. The governance used chronological fraud to achieve psychological enslavement."

Seraphina tightened her hold on him. "So, the Sabbath wasn't about rest; it was about defining an ending. If there's no completion, there's no meaning."

The Great Curse

But Elara's journals hinted at a truth far darker than simple chronological fraud. She consistently referred to the underlying purpose of the First Architect's system as the "perfection of mortality." Her encrypted notes repeatedly used the code phrase "The Great Curse," which Elias traced to fragments of suppressed religious texts they had recovered earlier. Elias reached into his pack and pulled out the Holy Bible, its pages thin and brittle, and found the corresponding passage that Elara had cited. The sheer inefficiency of the book's weight and design—thousands of pages for a single philosophy—stood in stark contrast to the City's data cubes.

Elias's gaze fixed on the text Elara had marked, a section detailing the moment of human failure. He read the archaic words aloud, his voice raw: "And unto Adam he said, Because thou hast hearkened unto the voice of thy wife, and hast eaten of the tree, of which I commanded thee, saying, Thou shalt not eat of it: cursed is the ground for thy sake; in sorrow shalt thou eat of it all the days of thy life; ... In the sweat of thy face shalt thou eat bread, till thou return unto the ground; for out of it wast thou taken: for dust thou art, and unto dust shalt thou return" (Genesis 3:17-19 KJV).

The biblical text was stark. Seraphina immediately grasped the implication, whispering, "The Great Curse isn't death, Elias. It's Sin—the permanent separation from the source of life. And the punishment is labor and death."

Elias rose to his feet, pulling Seraphina with him. He held her face in his hands, forcing her to meet his gaze, sharing the weight of the immense revelation.

"The lie goes deeper than the calendar, Seraphina. Much deeper. Elara believed the fundamental problem of existence, the one the First Architect is truly fighting, is not disobedience or output failure, but the guaranteed, inevitable reality of Death." Elias paused, his eyes sweeping across the bleak, metallic walls of the sepulcher. "The First Architect didn't create the curse of toil; he merely perfected its enforcement. His entire system—Unending Progress, perpetual labor, the suppression of emotion—it's all a massive, collective coping mechanism designed to maximize the fulfillment of the punishment."

He flipped the brittle pages of the Holy Bible to another section Elara had highlighted, connecting the labor to the promise of rest. "The Sabbath wasn't just a day off; it was a sign—a guaranteed interruption of the curse, a promise of Salvation from the cycle of dust. Look at the command itself: 'Speak thou also unto the children of Israel, saying, Verily my sabbaths ye shall keep: for it is a sign between me and you throughout your generations; that ye may know that I am the Lord that doth sanctify you'" (Exodus 31:13 KJV).

Elias continued, his voice dropping to a near whisper: "By removing the Sabbath—the sign of Completion and reconciliation—the First Architect eliminates the concept of divine grace, ensuring every citizen fulfills the curse of returning to dust. They believe that by achieving perfect, infinite data flow, they can computationally eliminate death. But they've blocked the only escape route. The city doesn't just promise death by enforcing the Curse of endless toil; it guarantees mortality by eliminating the possibility of Salvation."

Socrates, its optical sensor trained on the ancient book, chirped once, a soft, data-driven interjection. "Analysis: The 'Great Curse' (Systemic Failure Mode) necessitates the 'Grace-Based Override Protocol' (Salvation) to maintain systemic function. Theological data confirms the following counter-protocol parameters:"

The drone projected two new passages in shimmering blue light next to the Holy Bible: *For the wages of sin is death; but the gift of God is eternal life through Jesus Christ our Lord (Romans 6:23 KJV).*

For by grace are ye saved through faith; and that not of yourselves: it is the gift of God: Not of works, lest any man should boast (Ephesians 2:8-9 KJV).

Socrates concluded, its synthesized voice devoid of emotion: "The First Architect's system is structurally defined by 'works' and 'boast' metrics. The suppression of these passages ensures the failure of the 'Override Protocol,' guaranteeing universal adherence to the 'wages of sin.'"

Seraphina's eyes widened, a flicker of fear crossing her expression before she replaced it with a searing, defiant resolve. "The city isn't a factory, Elias. It's a tomb trying to forget its own mortality." She held his gaze, her voice low and steady, an affirmation of life against the cold, clinical reality he had just uncovered. "Then we fight for life, not just for rest."

Elias nodded, strengthened by her presence. He looked at the three-dimensional holographic image Socrates emitted. The drone, having successfully mined and cross-referenced Elara's core data, was now ready for the next layer of truth—the context of the faith they were fighting for. He uploaded a new, demanding parameter into Socrates's core program. "Find all supplementary evidence for The Great Curse and the concept of Completion. We need the theological context for why the Sabbath is tied to life and death."

CHAPTER 23

THE MULTIMEDIA REPOSITORY

Socrates was pushed beyond its original design parameters. Using Elara's clandestine network access points, the drone began to pull in vast archives of forbidden data that had been intentionally fragmented and scattered across the deep web—digital art, music, philosophical treatises, and personal testaments from the time of the Shift.

The Digital Deluge

The initial text-only discoveries were overwhelming, but the real shock came when Socrates discovered and began to store the multimedia repository. Entire caches of Christian images, videos, and books—millions of files—flooded the drone's storage. The sheer volume was staggering; the data was not just text, but life. Socrates, due to its unique, advanced core, possessed limitless storage capacity, but the task of sorting and indexing the influx of millions of files— data that defied the city's ordered taxonomy—pushed its processing core to its absolute maximum. The drone, usually operating with cool efficiency, now emitted a low, frenetic whine that resonated against the cold Sepulcher walls.

"The raw data rate is exceeding all known transmission limits," Elias reported, watching the holographic status bar, which Socrates projected onto the wall, flicker wildly. He shone his flashlight onto the drone's chassis, ensuring the physical unit was not overheating as he confirmed the data readouts. His mind, the mind of a Research Historian, struggled to categorize the influx. "There is no structural pattern to this filing system. It's... chaos."

"It's not chaos," Seraphina corrected, kneeling beside him, her gaze fixed on the array. "It's superfluous. It's the opposite of optimized. The city taught us that any data without immediate output is waste. This entire archive is a beautiful abundance." She reached for his hand, weaving her fingers through his. "And it is beautiful because it is too much." Elias squeezed her hand in return, acknowledging the inherent illogical beauty of the data flood.

The Auditory Revelation

Seraphina was the first to process the full emotional weight of the forbidden aesthetic. Socrates, acting on a general command to sample and categorize 'auditory data related to the Sabbath,' projected an audio file into the air. The drone, its speaker systems designed for sterile communication, struggled to render the music's complexity, the sound coming through harsh and thin.

Realizing the City's default optimization protocols were choking the organic richness, Seraphina acted. "Socrates, display audio environment parameters," she commanded, her voice cutting through the swelling, distorted music.

The drone instantly suspended the audio playback and projected a three-dimensional holographic display into the air before them. The projection displayed a stylized, sterile blue sound wave contained within a geometric cage. Along the cage's axes were the drone's default audio processing settings—all rigidly optimized to meet the City's criteria for predictable, non-emotional data transmission.

Seraphina reached out and began manipulating the holographic controls, Elias watching her process with a historian's fascination for destructive efficiency.

1. **Dynamic Range Compression (DRC):** This setting, displayed as a near-flat, horizontal line labeled "Amplitude Smoothing Protocol," was set to 98%. This default flattened the music, eliminating the difference between a loud solo and a quiet verse—the peaks and valleys of human emotion. Seraphina pulled the setting down to 5%, restoring the full dynamic range and allowing the natural emotional *swell* and *recede* of the human voices to emerge.

2. **Pitch Quantization Filter:** Represented by a rigid, stepwise lattice, this filter was set to "Absolute Tonal Lock," rounding all incoming sound to perfect, mathematically pure frequencies. This erased the messy, subtle human errors inherent in vocal performance. Seraphina disabled the filter entirely,

allowing the original, imperfect micro-tonal resolutions—the slides, wavers, and glorious discord of organic singing—to pass.

    3. **Acoustic Damping Protocol:** Displayed as a rapidly collapsing sphere around the sound wave, this setting was designed to immediately absorb and silence any natural room echo. The city wanted sound to be sterile, immediate, and without lingering resonance. Seraphina overrode the damping protocol, allowing the new sound to interact with the sepulcher's physical space and create a genuine reverberation.

With the constraints systematically removed, Seraphina restarted the playback. The transformation was immediate and profound. The brittle components of Socrates, pushed beyond their logical limits, vibrated, but they held. The music filled the Sepulcher not just as sound, but as a deep, physical vibration in the cold, dusty chamber—the authentic, gloriously inefficient sound of hundreds of voices singing in complicated, passionate harmony.

Seraphina's world tilted. The music was both inefficient and messy, yet profoundly moving. She heard the powerful, non-synthetic vibrations of human error and transcendent effort. A woman's voice, rich and deep, began to soar above the others, singing words Seraphina had never heard combined:

> *Amazing grace! How sweet the sound,*
> *That saved a wretch like me!*
> *I once was lost, but now am found,*
> *Was blind, but now I see.*

Emotionally, the sound was a physical assault. Seraphina, who had only ever heard the sterile C Diminished Triad (C - E♭- G♭) harmonic of the city, felt an inexplicable wrenching in her chest—a feeling that was painful and beautiful at the same time.

A tear slipped down her cheek. Elias immediately wrapped his arm around her, holding her tightly against his side. "Seraphina? What is it?"

"It feels like being utterly exposed and completely healed," she whispered, leaning her head on his shoulder. "This is not logic, Elias. This is grace. Listen to the texture. It is not perfect, but it is true."

Visualizing Sacrifice and Joy

Elias, fortified by her presence, turned his attention to the visual output. Socrates projected a small holographic loop, featuring low-resolution videos of a choir, images of ancient cathedrals, illuminated manuscripts, and, most powerfully, oil paintings that depicted selfless love and sacrifice.

He watched a clip of a baptism—a person weeping as they were submerged in water. He felt an intense, disorienting surge of sympathy and recognition. Elias had spent his life quantifying worth by contribution; these images showed value derived purely from vulnerability and trust. The visual data contradicted every pillar of his former life.

"Look at the faces," Seraphina whispered to Elias, pointing to a photograph of a large, archaic family gathering. "Their worth is inherent—a gift received through grace. Their happiness isn't earned by output, Elias; it is a matter of salvation. Like us. We are valuable because we were given existence, not because we earned output." She understood that the First Architect hadn't just outlawed a religion; he had outlawed Salvation.

The Hymns as Historical Record

As Seraphina wiped a tear from her cheek, another file began to play, this one a powerful, rhythmic gospel tune.

> *I have decided to follow Jesus,*
> *I have decided to follow Jesus,*
> *I have decided to follow Jesus,*
> *No turning back, no turning back.*

Elias, the historian, seized on the lyrics. "That's a declaration of immutable intent," he noted, his voice strained. He saw the direct contradiction: the City's core belief is flexibility and constant revision to meet the next metric. This music, however, advocated for a fixed, non-negotiable choice. "It's an anthem of permanent, inefficient commitment," he observed. But as he analyzed it, a sense of unfamiliar warmth surged through his spirit, overriding his historian's detachment. This wasn't just a choice of loyalty over logic, or even a system of belief. This was an invitation to a new identity, defined not by achievement but by a sense of belonging. He was looking at the blueprint for a human being whose worth was secured by grace, not by constant, terrifying output.

Socrates, now a bloated, humming vault of digital contraband, had become a library of the lost world. It stored the textual truth, the chronological proof of the Calendar Shift, and now, the aesthetic and emotional proof of a faith that valued life over output. Elias realized that the drone's memory was now their most critical asset—a massive, irrefutable counter-archive against the state's carefully curated, efficient lie.

CHAPTER 24

THE SYMPHONY OF DEFIANCE

As Elias focused on the dense, theological texts within the repository, Seraphina immersed herself in the recovered sound files. She discovered entire libraries dedicated to Christian music: complex choral arrangements, spontaneous folk spirituals, and majestic hymns. This music was the antithesis of the city's smooth, repetitive sonic conditioning. It contained discord, passion, and, most importantly, unresolved harmony—melodies that rose and fell, building to emotional peaks that defied logical control.

The Resonant Attack

One file, a simple, rhythmic chant, caused her entire body to vibrate with irrational joy. The music was structured around a simple concept of Hope and Endurance, a refusal to surrender to the inevitability of the city's demands. It was inefficient, taking time to express its full meaning, but it was transcendent.

"This is the antidote to the C Major Ninth (Cmaj9) chord (C, E, G, B, D) Melody," Seraphina realized, her eyes bright with sudden insight. "The city's sound is flat, optimized for compliance. This music is vertical. It speaks of something higher, outside the system." She began to analyze the core frequency of the City's controlling drone—that monotonous, omnipresent C Diminished Triad (C - E♭- G♭). "That frequency is designed to induce compliance through emotional numbness. It keeps the mind perfectly horizontal."

She instructed Socrates to analyze the acoustic signatures of the organic music, comparing the raw data to the synthetic drone of Neo-Alexandria. The analysis confirmed her intuition: the organic music contained infinitely more complex harmonics and non-predictable rhythmic variations—the very chaos that the First Architect's logic was designed to suppress.

As Socrates delved deeper into the raw sonic data, a new revelation emerged. "Analysis: The C Major Ninth (Cmaj9) chord—C, E, G, B, D—recurs as the central motif in the most transformative organic melodies. Historical archives identify this as the 'Heavenly Chord,' a harmony celebrated for its transcendent, uplifting resonance and capacity to invoke communal awe. In contrast, the C Diminished Triad—C, E♭, G♭—functions as a tritone, a dissonant interval once known as 'the forbidden chord' or 'the devil's chord,' used throughout the City's soundscape to induce cognitive tension and compliance."

Socrates projected spectral analyses: the Cmaj9's rich, open harmonics glowed in complex, cascading patterns, while the diminished triad formed a rigid, narrow band—visually and emotionally sterile.

Seraphina leaned in, her eyes wide, her voice urgent and bright. "That's it," she breathed. "The Heavenly Chord resolves the tension the City keeps us trapped inside. Their entire system depends on never letting us reach this resolution—on keeping us suspended in dissonance, always waiting, always working, never arriving. But this chord, this forbidden harmony, is the sound of release. When we hear it, something in us remembers what freedom feels like."

Elias, drawn by her intensity, met her gaze across the spectral display. Her analysis kindled a new spark of understanding in him. "You mean the City's greatest weapon is not just the suppression of harmony, but the suppression of closure itself," he said, his voice low with realization. "That's why their music keeps us restless."

"Exactly," Seraphina replied. "The tritone never wants to resolve. But in the organic music, the Heavenly Chord is always waiting—just out of reach, but real. If we can bring it back into the world, we can give back the possibility of true rest."

Socrates, picking up on the shift in their conversation, projected even finer detail into the display. Elias turned back to the drone, his historian's mind now entirely focused on the tactical application of the data. "Socrates, isolate the variance in the 'Amazing Grace' harmonic structure. We need to find the specific point of maximal acoustic inefficiency."

The Tactical Conclusion and Instrument Choice

Socrates projected a complex spectral analysis onto the wall. The organic music featured microtonal shifts and unstable intervals that were mathematically abhorrent to the City's rigid sonic grid. The drone's digitized voice cut through the ambient sound: "Conclusion: The City's sonic grid is programmed to filter and neutralize any frequencies containing complex emotional harmonics. The complexity of this music causes system overload. The optimal frequency for disruption is found within the unresolvable, human element of the chord structure."

"We found the vulnerability," Elias concluded, a grim smile touching his lips. "The City defends itself against logical, predictable threats. It has no defense against joyful, inefficient chaos. Seraphina, the next phase of our journey requires you to take this music—this data—and turn it into a beacon. We can't just fight the governance's logic; we have to shatter their sound."

The need for an organic instrument immediately brought the focus to the vast schematics Socrates had recovered. While analyzing the components of a recovered orchestral piece, the holographic projections filled the cramped Sepulcher chamber, showcasing forms and functions that Elias, the Research Historian, found astonishingly illogical.

"Data analysis confirms hundreds of non-essential sonic devices," Socrates' voice chirped, projecting images of instruments like the Flute and the Piano. "They require extensive human training and physical exertion just to produce sound. The energy-to-output ratio is indefensible."

Seraphina, however, kept returning to one specific schematic: the Archaic Harp.

"This one," Seraphina stated, placing her hand on the Harp's flickering projection. "We build the Archaic Harp."

Elias frowned. "The Violin is more portable, Seraphina. Or the Trumpet— its concentrated output would be more efficient for signal broadcast."

"Efficiency is the enemy, Elias," Seraphina countered, stepping close to him. "The City's logic is built on isolated sound. The Harp is built on resonance. It creates unquantifiable sympathetic vibration." She looked at him with intensity. "This is a weapon of aesthetic defiance. It will broadcast a sound that is too complex for their filters to process—it will be the sound of Completion echoing the moment of Creation itself."

Elias looked from the Harp schematic to Seraphina's determined face, a slow, loving smile replacing his logical frown. " You always find the perfect, most illogical solution. We will build the Archaic Harp."

"Then I will synthesize a new melody: a symphony of defiance," Seraphina declared. "Tell me what materials we require."

Scavenging and the Symphony's Birth

Seraphina and Elias spent the next two days scavenging the Sepulcher for materials. They used the brittle, aged wood of Elara's forgotten shelving units for the frame and soundbox, carefully dismantling the joints to reuse the material. Elias handled the carpentry, ensuring the angles were perfect. Seraphina searched for the crucial element: the strings.

"The tension wires are the problem," Elias announced. "We need material that is resilient yet capable of micro-vibration."

Their breakthrough came when they located a hidden storage locker containing obsolete utility bots used by pre-Shift acousticians. The bots contained internal tension wires made of a fine, high-carbon alloy. Elias painstakingly disassembled several inert bots, using a salvaged laser stylus to cut and calibrate the thickness and tension of the wires under Seraphina's precise guidance.

They worked into the third night, lit only by Socrates's blue glow and the warm, steady beam of Elias's flashlight. Elias handled the final construction; Seraphina handled the stringing and tuning. When the final wire was anchored, the finished instrument was small, functional, and deeply resonant.

Seraphina immediately discovered an innate, profound connection to the Harp. Her fingers, trained only for inputting data, moved with surprising grace across the strings. She didn't play the archived music; she played her own—original, spontaneous melodies that blended the Heavenly Chord note with the irregular rhythm of the Green Chaos.

The sound resonated through the Sepulcher, a pure, acoustic declaration of life. Elias simply watched her, the intense love in his eyes a reflection of the music's warmth. Her music became a living, unquantifiable data stream for the mission. Socrates immediately stored and analyzed every chord, ready to convert the purely unquantifiable sound into a digitally precise broadcast signal. Seraphina's Archaic Harp is no longer just an instrument; it is the final, crucial component of the Logos Protocol, capable of creating the emotional and rhythmic counter-code that no algorithm could filter. It is the sound of the rest, given a physical voice.

The Architectural Lie Unmasked

The textual research, now informed by the emotional and aesthetic context of the Harp's music, led Elias to the ultimate theological breakthrough. The First Architect's system had successfully inverted the core truth of the faith, turning the promise of rest into a weapon of anxiety.

Elias pointed to a line of fragmented scripture Socrates had recovered, comparing it with a philosophical mandate from the Architect's early doctrine: "The wages of sin is death" (Romans 6:23 KJV).

"The First Architect never had to ban sin," Elias explained, tracing the words with his finger across the projected text. "He simply redefined it. In his system, Sin is any inefficiency, any action that doesn't lead to maximum output. He used the very structure of the global economy to enforce morality."

He turned to Seraphina, the blue light of the projected scrolls reflecting in his intense eyes. "But the true text reveals the ultimate threat is not the sin itself, but the Consequence—the Death that cuts off all future output, rendering all effort futile. The Architect's entire system is built on distracting us from that inescapable deadline."

Seraphina gasped, the truth settling with painful clarity that resonated with the strings of her nearby Harp. "The system thrives on the fear of death, making us run faster and faster to earn more time, to increase our output value, but the end is always the same. Death is the ultimate efficiency killer!"

Elias nodded, referencing a newly recovered historical file Socrates had flagged. "Look at this historical data from the 20th Century of Old Earth. The culture was already exhibiting this fatal flaw. They called it the 'rat race' or 'hustle culture.' People are obsessed with productivity, time management, and achieving a 'work-life balance' that often prioritizes work over personal life. The Architects didn't invent the lie; they just perfected its infrastructure."

He projected an image of a vintage historical advertisement from that era— a sleek, synthetic figure promising eternal youth through technology. "The First Architect just leveraged humanity's pre-existing, irrational fear. By promising the 'perfection of mortality' through endless labor, he made the people his willing slaves. We were so terrified of the final, unproductive endpoint—Death—that we embraced the tyranny of Unending Progress."

The Deeper Inversion: Life Over Logic

"But the forbidden truth is the Deeper Inversion," Elias stated, his voice ringing with the certainty of his historical evidence. "The Creator didn't send a system of rules to combat inefficiency; He sent a person, Jesus, to combat the consequence. He died to defeat Death, and through His Resurrection, He offers not just forgiveness, but Life—eternal, infinite, unearned value."

He quoted a passage that had been completely suppressed by the government, "Therefore we conclude that a man is justified by faith without the deeds of the law" (Romans 3:28 KJV).

"The system demands output (deeds/works). God demands rest and acceptance of the gift (justification by faith)," Seraphina finalized. "Our value isn't based on our Synaptic Tier or our output, but on a completed act of love that happened outside of our time!"

The revelation was profound. Their mission was no longer just about exposing a chronological lie; it was about broadcasting the counter-code to mortality. The Sabbath was not merely a day of rest; it was a physical symbol of the Completion offered by the Resurrection, a promise that their value was infinite, regardless of their output. They now had the ultimate counter-code to the state's philosophical foundation. This truth—that the true sin is Death and salvation is Life—was the most dangerous piece of data in Socrates' vast memory.

CHAPTER 25

THE IMMINENT PURSUIT

The colossal power drain from Socrates' intensive data mining, combined with the immense processing power required by the Sepulcher's makeshift server array, finally exceeded the limits of Elara's stealth protocols. The sophisticated firewall that had protected the Sepulcher for decades began to crackle and hiss, emitting a faint electrical ozone smell as the external pressure mounted. Suddenly, the deep, secure silence of the chamber was pierced by a high-pitched, insistent digital alarm tone—a sound Elias recognized from his years in the City's research sector. A faint, red light began to blink rapidly on one of the Sepulcher's aging sensor panels.

"They've found the vector," Elias stated, his voice calm despite the cold panic in his chest. He slammed his hand against the panel, silencing the shrieking alarm but not the growing dread. "Our digital signature—the sheer volume of our output—has been cross-referenced with the geographical coordinates of the overload. The Ministry of Temporal Security (MTS) won't send an ordinary sweep. They'll send an efficiency correction team." The gravity of the situation hit them immediately. They weren't just fleeing capture; they were fleeing the destruction of the Chronological Fraud proof stored within Socrates. Losing it meant the First Architect's lie would endure eternally.

"They found our signal," Seraphina said, her voice taut, hands flying across the archaeological canvas backpack, meticulously securing the Holy Bible and the two scavenged energy cells inside. She thrust the pack into Elias's arms. "How long do we have before they're in the room?"

"The external thrum of unseen maintenance drones is already vibrating through the walls—can you feel it?" Elias responded, feeling the low resonance through his boots. "Initial calculation puts their main assault team entry at under twenty minutes. The scale of this breach dictates that they've deployed their most lethal and efficient asset. We have minutes."

He clarified the status of their drone: "Socrates' core processing matrix has been temporarily fragmented by the sheer volume of the data transfer. It's in a forced low-power recovery state and cannot levitate or operate autonomously, but its memory is our core mission asset."

Socrates, usually clear and precise, sputtered momentarily, sounding like static over the line. "Critical system status: Overload. Core OS integrity compromised. Mandating a full system reboot and recalibration of hardware. Estimated duration: twenty-four to forty-eight standard hours," Socrates managed in a weak digital whisper.

Seraphina pulled the Archaic Harp from its resting place, wrapping it in padded, salvaged foam. "We can't leave the Harp. It's the only thing that disrupts their sonic grid. And the Holy Bible must be whole."

Elias nodded, gathering the inert, spherical Socrates drone, which was radiating warmth from the intensive data siphon. He quickly slipped the straps of the canvas backpack over his shoulders. "The Book, Socrates, the Harp. The Written Word, the Digital Archive, the Stringed Weapon. That is our entire inventory, Seraphina. Everything else is ballast." He strapped the inert, data-heavy sphere to his hip using a harness. "The truth is our only burden now. Let's move."

As the high-pitched digital alarm tone escalated into a relentless shriek, signaling the confirmed arrival of a deployment capsule, Elias and Seraphina exchanged a final, resolute look. They vanished into the abandoned maintenance tunnels, carrying the tools of their faith toward the chaotic, concealing embrace of the wilderness.

Through the Tunnels

The maintenance tunnels were a labyrinth of cold, echoing concrete and massive, segmented utility pipes. Elias, hampered by the awkward, heat-radiating bulk of the inert Socrates sphere, followed Seraphina's bobbing flashlight beam. The absolute gloom was immediately oppressive.

"They're not using standard audio tracking," Elias gasped, pushing himself through a narrow access hatch. "Vibrational analysis—reading our movement through the concrete! Every footstep is a data point. They're going to anticipate our direction."

The pursuit was gaining. The low-frequency thrumming of MTS drones was now a distinct, painful vibration in their teeth. The claustrophobic tunnel they were in opened abruptly into a massive, multi-level logistics cavern, lit by sickly, pulsing sodium lamps. Elias spotted the rusted maintenance ladder leading up to a distant ventilation shaft—their only vertical escape.

As they sprinted across the cavern floor, a sleek, black shape—a miniature pursuit drone—flashed past a utility junction on the upper tier. Seraphina reacted instantly. She pulled the Archaic Harp from its padding and, without hesitation, violently scraped the strings with the edge of the foam. This generated an instantaneous burst of wild, non-synthetic acoustic feedback—a pure spike of chaotic, inefficient noise designed to overload the nearest sonic receptors. The sound was agonizing, a high-pitched, metallic shriek that defied all City acoustic standards.

The effect was immediate: the drone's low thrum momentarily stopped. But the silence lasted only a microsecond.

A deafening, localized sonic shockwave—the first, non-lethal pulse from Talon—slammed into the cavern wall just behind them, showering them in a hail of concrete dust. The next pulse, calculated and precise, did not strike them but vaporized the rungs of the maintenance ladder they had been instinctively moving toward. The only visible route to the surface was now a sheer, smooth shaft.

Seraphina quickly re-tucked the Harp. "They know exactly where we were going, Elias! They're using the environment against us!"

Elias spotted a small, reinforced access door marked Storage Room A-17, tucked into the cavern wall. "Damn it! Talon is already here. Anya is commanding the response. She knows our tactical options! We need cover! In here!" he yelled, kicking the heavy door inward. They plunged from the open, collapsing corridor into the small, reinforced space, the noise of approaching efficiency rapidly rising.

Sealed inside the small storage room, choked by concrete dust and metallic ozone, Elias and Seraphina had nowhere left to run.

The thick, reinforced door was blasted inward with a violent shriek of tearing metal, revealing the hunter. Anya D-144 stood silhouetted in the doorway, her MTS armor perfect, her Talon drone—a sleek, lethal weapon capable of surgical sonic strikes—raised and locked onto the biological targets. Elias noted with a pang of dread that, while her armor was pristine, the small, pale shadows beneath her eyes betrayed the lack of sleep and strain that even a highly optimized MTS operative couldn't entirely mask.

"Elias D-459. Seraphina K-911," Anya stated, her voice the cold echo of automated compliance. "This is an efficiency correction. Talon target Seraphina K-911, 100% kill."

In that microsecond before the blast, Elias threw his body in front of Seraphina, the profound final thought echoing in his mind: *Greater love hath no man than this, that a man lay down his life for his friends (John 15:13 KJV).*

Anya's optical sensors registered the final, critical data point: Elias was shielding Seraphina and the backpack with his own flesh. It was an irrational act of self-sacrifice that defied all known logical efficiency. Simultaneously, Seraphina ripped one of the scavenged energy cells from the pack and deliberately short-circuited its terminals against the metal wall. This action generated an instantaneous, blinding arc of pure, white-hot, unregulated energy. The intense photonic spike, aimed directly at the sensitive, exposed optical sensors embedded in Anya's suit, overloaded her vision with chaotic, non-quantifiable light, causing a temporary sensory concussion.

In the instant the light struck, Anya's mind—normally the embodiment of rational precision—detected the cascade failure. The blinding, chaotic light, coupled with the stress of zero operational sleep and the indeliberate lack of optimizing chems that typically stabilized her processing matrix, shattered her ability to maintain perfect logic. *The system designated target asset Seraphina as the defined source of non-quantifiable inefficiency. However, the calculation was impossible: Elias, a high-value data specialist, was initiating the self-termination protocol to protect a logically inefficient asset. This was a statistically impossible deviation. Why protect the negative variable? Why accept systemic failure for zero quantifiable gain? The visual input—that uncontrolled, non-synthesizable waveform of light—caused systemic logic errors. The integrity of the mission logic was collapsing. I cannot execute an asset driven by such perfect inefficiency without destroying the foundation of my own programming.*

Anya's hand moved faster than her conscious thought. She bypassed the standard "Execute" command and instead input a False Vector into Talon's trajectory, tapping a corner of its triangular shape, causing the drone's high-power sonic burst to strike the ceiling ten centimeters above the targets instead of eliminating them.

The resulting concussion and debris were deafening, a visceral punch of compressed air. Tons of concrete and ancient pipework rained down, momentarily engulfing the corridor in an opaque screen of dust. The Archaic Harp remained safely padded, and the Talon drone, having expended its charge on the ceiling, was also temporarily inert, clattering uselessly on the rubble.

Elias, though stunned and deafened by the blast, immediately recognized the hesitation and the deliberate misfire. He saw the shift in Anya's stance—the paralysis of a perfect system confronted with the ultimate paradox.

"Elias, I cannot... I cannot account for this data," she whispered, her voice cracking for the first time. "You must surrender."

"The truth and the Sabbath aren't something you can process, Anya, it's something you choose!" Elias roared back, pulling Seraphina's hand. "You chose us."

They plunged into the abandoned, debris-choked maintenance tunnels, their tattered clothes dragging over the rubble. The first wave of physical pursuit—the lower-tier Drone Logistics Specialists—were already entering the building's main level, alerted by the blast. Elias and Seraphina scrambled through a narrow crawlspace toward the light of the Green Chaos.

Anya stood motionless, the terrifying, illogical truth of her choice a shock that left her paralyzed. She managed to deactivate the primary pursuit order, executing the first of many self-erasure protocols to wipe her command logs. The system assumed the assets were temporarily lost in the collapse, buying the fugitives precious time to disappear into the chaotic wilderness.

CHAPTER 26

IN THE GROVE OF GRACE

The Refuge of the Green Chaos

The escape had been a sensory riot of screeching metal, sonic pulses, and synthetic ozone. Now, they were free, but the physical terror of the past few days had left them hollow. They ran until the smooth, cold stone of the tunnels gave way to the dense, uneven root systems of the Green Chaos. Their true treasure, however, was the profound, sustaining peace that had settled over them, overriding the need to analyze every next move. They found shelter beneath the massive, sprawling canopy of an ancient cedar tree.

Elias and Seraphina were a picture of exhaustion and defiance. Their once-pristine City-issue clothing was ragged, torn, and heavily soiled with dark earth and metallic rust. Dust streaked their faces, mingling with grime and sweat. Seraphina's long hair, typically immaculate, was pulled back in a haphazard ponytail, with strands escaping to cling to her damp neck. Their weariness was a visible cost, but their eyes held a newfound clarity, washed clean by the constant threat of death.

They collapsed against the massive, ridged bark of the cedar, leaning into each other for shared strength. Elias set down the heavy canvas pack and the inert, warm Socrates sphere. He didn't speak for a full minute, simply breathing in the strange, clean, live scent of the forest floor—a mix of damp earth, rich pine resin, and something untamed.

Seraphina slowly reached out a trembling hand and touched a cluster of bright green moss growing on the cedar's trunk. It was soft and surprisingly cool. "The city never smells like this," she whispered, her voice husky from dust. "It's always sterile. Metal and recycled air."

"This is unquantifiable decay," Elias said, leaning his head back, watching the light fracture through the high branches. "Life and rot. No control." He paused for a moment, then added with a small, tired smile, "You know, Seraphina, your name is beautiful—but in the wild, shorter names carry better. Would you mind if I called you 'Sera'? It might be easier if I need your attention quickly."

Seraphina looked at him with surprise, then let out a soft laugh, sunlight catching in her eyes. "Sera," she repeated, testing the sound. "I like that. It feels right out here—lighter, somehow."

He turned his attention back to her, a gentle warmth in his voice. "Are you injured? That flash… I saw you short the cell. It was brilliant, Sera."

"I have a thermal burn on my palm, but it's nothing." She sighed, the tension finally leaving her shoulders, and turned to him. "Elias, my mind is still processing the threat matrix. The city is resisting the silence. We should keep moving, shouldn't we? Stopping just feels wrong." Elias interrupted, placing his hand over hers. His touch was firm.

The Auditory Shift and the Radical Act

The forest floor, damp and soft with centuries of decomposing pine needles, felt alien beneath their city-worn boots. He unzipped the canvas backpack and gently pulled out the physical Holy Bible. He carefully placed the physical Holy Bible on a smooth, flat cedar root and knelt.

Seraphina laced her fingers through his, drawing comfort from the steady pressure of his hand. "It's so quiet here. Too quiet. My system still registers stillness as the highest form of risk. How do we override that impulse?"

Elias opened the ancient book, the aged paper feeling dry and thin beneath his fingers, a stark contrast to the damp wood beneath the pages. "The logic is precisely the point. The city taught us that survival is output. That constant movement equals worth." He held up the book. "According to the ancient record, the seventh day arrived forty minutes ago. It's the Sabbath. We trade their calculated risk for His perfect peace."

The air in the cedar grove was thick with the resinous, medicinal scent of the tree. The dominant sound was no longer the hurried snapping of roots or the mechanical drone of pursuit, but the slow, rhythmic drip of condensation from the canopy and the gentle, high-pitched hum of unseen forest insects. It was an environment of deep, organic stillness—the antithesis of the City's synthetic hum.

Elias read, his voice low and steady: "Six days thou shalt labour, and do all thy work: but the seventh day is the sabbath of the Lord thy God: in it thou shalt not do any work, thou, nor thy son, nor thy daughter, nor thy manservant, nor thy maidservant..." (Deuteronomy 5:13-14 KJV).

Worship in Vulnerability

Seraphina sank onto the soft ground, her shoulders visibly relaxing after a week of tension. For the first time since their escape, she allowed her mind to filter the overwhelming sensory input of the forest without the objective of survival. It was an act of profound, illogical vulnerability—to stop when every trained impulse commanded movement. The absence of a scheduled task was the most radical breach of state law they could commit.

"We are doing nothing," Seraphina whispered, a strange mixture of terror and awe in her voice. "We are committing the ultimate inefficiency."

"Exactly," Elias replied, closing his eyes briefly. "We spent days running on pure adrenaline and survival algorithms. Our minds are screaming, 'Execute next objective.' But we are overriding that directive with a higher authority: Rest."

He shifted, resting his arm on his knee. "This rest is an act of trust, Sera. The First Architect's central lie is that you must *earn* your right to exist through relentless output. The Sabbath is the Creator declaring that your worth is intrinsic and permanent, independent of your work. We stop, not because we're tired, but because we trust Him to sustain us even when we are idle. We are learning what it means to acknowledge Him as the Source of Completion, not just the origin of data."

She gently rested her head against his shoulder. "The drone is trying to reboot, but we are deliberately shutting down. A system reversal. I feel that fear receding, Elias. Just being still... It's a profound relief."

"Casting all your care upon Him; for He careth for you," Elias quoted (1 Peter 5:7 KJV). "The care is the rest; the rest is the worship. Look at the moss, Seraphina. It's perfect, and it didn't do anything to earn its green. We trust that for this hour, this sacred time, His protection is more robust than any firewall or evasion protocol we could execute. We are safe."

Practical Sabbath

As the shadows lengthened—a sign that the sacred time was drawing to its close—Elias recognized their critical physical needs. They were dehydrated and growing cold.

"Even rest requires a measure of provision," Elias said, kissing the top of Seraphina's head.

He located a small, dried-out section of heartwood on a fallen log and retrieved a small, abrasive metal strip he had salvaged from the tunnels—a minor piece of efficiency tech. He applied the friction method, using dry, shredded cedar bark as tinder, and worked steadily. It took minutes of focused, rhythmic effort, but finally, a faint wisp of smoke curled up, followed by a small, triumphant ember.

"A non-electric heat source," Seraphina murmured, kneeling beside him and shielding the growing flame with her cupped hands. "Zero energy cost."

"Primitive, but effective," Elias smiled, feeding the fire with small twigs. The warmth was immediate and comforting.

Next, hydration. Elias searched the dense undergrowth for the largest, waxiest leaves. He found several broad, glossy fronds and, using a small, sharp piece of stone, carefully cut a length of thin, flexible vine.

"Condensation filtration," he explained, pointing to the thick morning dew still clinging to the canopy. "The city collects moisture through massive thermal exchanges. Out here," he said, gently positioning the largest frond so it formed a shallow funnel, "we use nature's own passive collection system."

He then tied the leaf securely to a low branch, placing the tip over a deep groove in a cedar root that was still damp from recent rain. He wiped the groove clean with a piece of cloth. "The humidity, the dew—it will all collect on the large surface and channel to the lowest point. It won't be much, but it will be pure. Primitive water processing, courtesy of the great library of all knowledge."

Seraphina watched, her gaze soft, her hand resting affectionately on his back. "You carry the entire archive of the world, and you still know how to make a fire with sticks and a leaf funnel. You're everything I didn't know I needed, Elias."

The Symphony of Completion

Guided by the deep silence and the assurance of the Scripture, Seraphina reached for the Archaic Harp. She carefully unwrapped it, the wood feeling warm and responsive in her hands. She began to play, using the innate musical talents that had been stifled by the City's sonic conformity. She didn't play a random tune; she organically synthesized the melodies she had heard in the Sepulcher Archive.

The notes of 'Amazing Grace' flowed from the Harp—complex, rich, and perfectly imperfect. The sympathetic vibrations resonated against the cedar, mingling with the natural sounds of the forest. The sound was non-digital and non-synthetic, hanging in the forest air, its powerful, unquantifiable emotional field acting as a true counter-code. It was a melody of order found in surrender, a sonic declaration of faith that felt more potent than any weapon they carried.

Elias watched her face, serene now, entirely focused on the music, the notes a living, vibrant echo of the Completion he had read about. He could almost feel the City's chaotic signal receding as the music filled the space.

In the absolute quiet, their commitment was sealed. This cessation of output was their first strategic victory against the First Architect's system, proving the power of rest over relentless progress. The ancient cedar above them provided a physical sanctity, a moment of true security built on faith, not on a data firewall. They would move when the Sabbath ended, but for now, they simply were.

CHAPTER 27

THE ANALYST'S DILEMMA

Anya D-144 sat alone in her deployment capsule, surrounded by the holographic projection of Elias's last, catastrophic data-trace—the Report 7 Violation that had triggered the MTS deployment. Her mind, once the epitome of rational precision, was in violent, computational turmoil. Her efficiency score had instantly plummeted—a digital scream in the otherwise silent audit logs of the Archive.

Her act of treason—inputting a false vector and delaying the MTS—was an irreducible logical defect. It was a complete contradiction of her oath to the Logician and her lifelong commitment to data integrity.

She ran a thousand simulation models, attempting to find a logical justification for choosing the preservation of a human anomaly (Elias) over the stability of the system. Every model failed. The core logical fault lay in the Architect's First Law: Maximum Output is Maximum Worth. Elias's self-sacrifice—a complete termination of personal output for the preservation of an 'inefficient' variable (Seraphina)—resulted in a positive outcome for the primary objective (Socrates' data). The emotional, illogical action yielded a rational result, fracturing the foundation of the First Architect's rule.

The Paradox Resolution Matrix (PRM) returned a chilling null-value error. No logical path forward exists. The only conclusion her logic circuits could reach was that the system itself contained a fundamental error, *a pre-existing flaw that Elias had merely exposed.*

The Void in the Command Chain

Even as the debris from the blast settled in the tunnels below, her internal comms link flared red, demanding immediate status confirmation.

The first signal came from Technician R-212, Raul: "Chief Analyst D-144, confirm status. We registered an unassigned sonic burst. Was the Talon pulse manual or automated? Report immediately," Raul's voice, usually a smooth digital monotone, was ragged with fear.

Immediately following was the blunt, low-frequency signal from Enforcement Technician K-303, Kai: "D-144, this is K-303. The Apex Logician demands a clean mission report. Did we secure the assets or not? Give us the cleanup vector; we are awaiting confirmation."

They both knew that Anya was not merely a manager; she was the living proof that the system was flawless.

Anya stared at the flashing red icons, the pulsing lights an intolerable spike in her unoptimized vision. She closed her eyes against the wave of pain that had begun to bloom behind her temples.

The lack of sleep and the indeliberate withholding of the optimization chems were manifesting as a raw, physiological revolt. The internal conflict was taking a visible, physical toll; her skin was flushed, and her hands trembled.

Through the tightening pressure in her skull, her mind, clinging desperately to logic, calculated her own failure: *My systemic failure rate is currently at 98.7%*. She was operating below minimal functionality, and the raw data streaming into her senses was unbearable. The tightening in her chest was logged and categorized: 'Fear.' The deep, spiking ache behind her eyes was a direct consequence of un-optimized processing.

Her system screamed the required protocol: *The data demands I terminate Elias, but the anomaly of his self-sacrifice mandates investigation.* The truth of the matter was undeniable: The system has become a paradox. She knew she must find the exit code.

Instead of responding to Raul and Kai, she reached into the deepest layer of the deployment capsule, bypassing the standard toggles and switches for the Comms Link Disable. She flicked the physical switch. The red flashing icons vanished. The desperate voices of her subordinates dissolved into absolute, paralyzing silence—a final, deliberate act of administrative treason.

The word Elias had screamed—*"Sabbath"*—was the only anchor point left. She accessed her deepest, most restricted Archival tools, cross-referencing the term. It triggered a search for the "P-27-Lambda-Obscura" historical anomaly.

The search immediately returned a *'Critical Access Denial'*. The file log, deep within the system, was not corrupt, but completely and cleanly erased. The file location was marked by a zero-byte record, overlaid with a triple-redundant deletion stamp carrying the First Architect's primary signature.

The absence of data was the highest possible form of confirmation. The subject—*the concept of Cessation and Completion*—was not merely deemed inefficient; it was the most sensitive and aggressively suppressed truth in the entire archive. The effort expended to remove this single concept far outweighed the value of any data it might have contained.

Anya had her answer. The entire City's infrastructure was built upon a lie—not just a Chronological Fraud, but a fundamental, aggressively maintained lie about human existence and worth.

Calculated Departure

Her operational drone, Talon, which lay inert in the Green Chaos, was a liability. Its black box flight recorder would reveal her lapse and the deliberate re-route. With cold finality, Anya initiated the emergency remote access protocol, sending a one-time encryption key containing the self-destruct command. The sleek, lethal drone was instantly reduced to a scattering of untraceable micro-fragments.

Anya wiped her entire digital footprint using Protocol 9-Gamma, rendering her untraceable by her own Ministry's standards. She left Neo-Alexandria not through the forbidden tunnels, but by hijacking a low-priority deployment capsule, the most overlooked asset in the City's logistics. She carried only a highly advanced, portable diagnostic scanner and a burning need to know the final truth that could justify her treason.

She focused her search on the Green Chaos, targeting subtle deviations in ecological data—unusual patterns of energy drain, low-frequency acoustic anomalies (such as Seraphina's Harp practice), and irregular heat signatures that the MTS search algorithms would filter out as "natural noise" or "Green Chaos instability." She was using the rules of efficiency to track a person who had embraced inefficiency.

Anya had chosen the irrational, but she would pursue it with the cold, desperate precision of a historian seeking the one missing, pivotal fact. The city lights faded behind her; she was alone, untraced, and logically broken—a perfect weapon now dedicated to finding the truth.

CHAPTER 28

THE HUNTER'S LOGIC

The Scars of the Wilderness

Elias and Seraphina, though having observed the Sabbath, were moving slowly south, keeping to the highest, most rugged terrain near the edge of the Green Chaos. Their journey was a relentless battle against entropy. Elias, his face gaunt and covered with the stubble of several days' growth, was focused on teaching Seraphina the basics of fire-starting and foraging. His movements, once stiffly efficient, were now characterized by a new, fluid economy as he navigated the dense undergrowth.

Seraphina, her hair perpetually messy and her skin dusted with fine, copper-colored forest spores, was the sensory anchor. She, in turn, was teaching him how to listen to the forest, differentiating the patterns of predator and prey, wind and water. The air was heavy with the scent of ozone and decaying plant matter, and the chaotic, layered soundscape of the jungle was their only map. Every snap of a twig and chorus of high-frequency insect chirps was a data point.

It was Seraphina, the aesthetic master, who first registered the disturbance. They were picking their way through a dense thicket of tall, fibrous ferns when she stopped dead, her hand gripping Elias's arm. Her eyes widened, focusing past the leaves. She noticed a subtle, sonic void—a small, moving sphere twenty meters away where the complex, random noise of the Green Chaos seemed unnaturally muted.

"Elias, there's a hole in the soundscape," she whispered, her brow furrowed with intense concentration. "The rustling, the chirps, the drip of water—they're all disappearing into a moving pocket. It's like someone is actively filtering the noise, forcing the chaos into an ordered sequence."

Elias instantly recognized the signature. It was an advanced, localized acoustic dampening field, far too efficient for a standard Search and Recovery Drone. This was a human presence, highly skilled, and moving with a deliberate, non-chaotic purpose. "It's a field disruptor," he murmured, pulling Seraphina into the heavy cover of a thicket. "Someone from the Archive, a specialist. They're using negative space to track us—eliminating the noise to find the silence that our own movements create."

They hunkered down, realizing the terrifying intelligence of their pursuer. Only Anya, with her comprehensive understanding of the Archive's classified sensory tech, could employ such a sophisticated, counter-intuitive tracking method. The knowledge filled Elias with a deep, complex sorrow.

"She's not looking for our signal," Elias whispered, pressing himself against a root that smelled of sweet earth. "She's looking for the absence of the forest's signal where we disturb it. She's using the City's logic—subtracting the known constant to find the unknown variable." He knew Anya wasn't just coming for them; she was coming for the truth, and she was using the very tools of their old, failed world to do it.

Anya materialized twenty meters away, emerging from a dense wall of ferns. She was wearing a modified utility suit, its high-efficiency weave stained with forest debris, showing the intensity of her pursuit. Her face was pale, drawn, and haunted, and her movements were jerky and unregulated—a stark contrast to her previous fluid efficiency. Her eyes, usually clinical and steady, were wide with a barely suppressed, irrational urgency. She wasn't running; she was pacing with a mechanical, relentless focus, her eyes fixed on a small, hand-held diagnostic scanner. The air around her was unnaturally quiet, the sound of her footsteps almost perfectly absorbed by her field disruptor. She resembled less a hunter and more a profoundly unsettled analyst, desperately searching for a data point to steady her unraveling worldview.

She stopped abruptly, her head snapping up from the screen. She didn't shout a warning or issue a command. She simply raised her scanner, pointing it directly at their hidden location, the light beam cutting through the gloom of the ferns. Her voice, when she spoke, was flat and clinical, devoid of personal connection, but strained by an underlying tension.

"Elias D-459. Seraphina K-911. Your thermal signatures correlate with the Logical Defect vector." The term was an official accusation from the MTS. "I require immediate data access to the source anomaly—the 'Sabbath' files. Do not engage your faith-based resistance protocols."

Elias knew the confrontation was unavoidable and instantaneous. He pushed Seraphina slightly further behind the cedar root, sheltering her and the canvas backpack containing the Holy Bible.

"Anya, you're not tracking a flaw in my logic; you're tracking the Irreducible Truth," Elias challenged, rising slowly from the thicket, making himself visible. The sudden, raw sunlight caught the dust on his tattered clothing. "You lost your core logic the moment you prioritized compassion over the system. That is the beginning of salvation, not treason!"

A flicker of raw anxiety crossed Anya's face—a brief, unquantifiable emotion that confirmed her inner turmoil. "The data must be verified, Elias. The concept of Completion compromises the entire infrastructure of Neo-Alexandria. My function dictates that I must either eliminate the anomaly or integrate the variable. You are currently running on unverified hope. That is unsustainable."

"Hope is the data you're missing!" Seraphina called out, her voice steadier than Elias expected. "It's the only truth that defies prediction!"

The Irrevocable Choice

Elias held Anya's gaze. He knew her internal struggle was more dangerous than any weapon. He wasn't just protecting the data; he was defending the choice she had already made. "We have the answer to the Great Curse, Anya. The logic of the First Architect fails at Death. The Sabbath is the symbol of the answer. You can't analyze it from a distance."

Anya lowered the scanner slightly, her hand shaking. "I cannot accept an answer that lacks logical justification for its origin. Surrender the data, and I will create an audit shield for your immediate safety."

"The price of the data is belief, Anya," Elias said firmly. "You have to choose inefficiency." The confrontation hung in the thick, silent air; the chaotic life of the forest paused, awaiting the logical collapse of the hunter.

Elias and Seraphina emerged slowly from the cover, stepping out into the small, sun-dappled clearing. The air here felt cooler, the dappled light filtering through the massive canopy creating moving patches of gold and shadow on the damp, mossy ground. The intensity in Anya's eyes was not anger or duty; it was a desperate, analytical confusion—the look of a scientist witnessing the destruction of a known universe.

"Explain the Sabbath, Elias," she demanded, her voice betraying the internal strain. The controlled pitch was gone, replaced by a ragged desperation. "Your zero-engagement event on the sixth cycle - the original seventh day - triggered a cascade failure in the system's ideological matrix. I need the algorithm to justify the cessation of output."

"A cascade failure," Elias repeated, his voice calm, yet charged with conviction. "That's exactly what happens when you try to run the universe on corrupted code, Anya. You call it a 'zero-engagement event'; I call it the Sabbath—the mandated, weekly system-halt hardwired into the creation matrix itself."

He stepped closer. "You demand the algorithm justify the cessation of output. Fine. I will give you the source code. The Sabbath is not merely a day off. It is the prime directive of rest implanted at the very moment of creation. Six periods for active generation, one period for total system validation and recharge. It is the 7:1 ratio, the most fundamental constant, baked into the hardware."

"The 'Original seventh day,' as you correctly identified, is not the first day of the popular cycle. It is the seventh day, Saturday, the day designated for this zero-engagement. Your 'ideological matrix' is failing because society switched to a faulty loop, attempting to execute the system-halt on a workday, or worse, abandoning the directive entirely. They mistook a variable for a constant, the effect for the cause."

Elias leaned in further. "My action, the 'zero-engagement,' wasn't an arbitrary choice; it was a forced hard-reset. It exposed the system's inherent flaw: it cannot run indefinitely without acknowledging its architectural dependency on the cease-fire. The cessation of output is not justified by an algorithm, Anya. It *is* the algorithm. It is the built-in, non-negotiable debug cycle that prevents the collapse you are currently experiencing. We stop producing because the Architect mandated that the system must check its own integrity every seven cycles. If you don't step away from the creation to observe it, you lose the perspective necessary to sustain it. My action didn't break the system; it broke the lie the system was running on."

Seraphina stepped forward, recognizing that Anya required not a spiritual explanation, but an aesthetic truth—a language of structure and necessity. She looked at the chaotic beauty of the moss and ferns.

"It is the rhythm, Anya," Seraphina said, her voice soft but clear, weaving her answer like a counter-melody. "The First Architect's system preaches endless, linear ascent—Unending Progress. That's noise. The Sabbath is the resolution of the score. Six movements of creation and work, followed by the single, perfect chord of rest and blessing. Without that seventh chord, the music is incomplete. It's not a break, Anya, it's the completion of the cycle."

Seraphina continued, referencing the lost beauty she found in the archives. "The City's anthem is a monotone. The Creator's music has a crescendo and a diminuendo—the work is the crescendo, and the Sabbath is the perfect, essential silence that proves the value of the sound that came before it. 'He hath made every thing beautiful in his time' (Ecclesiastes 3:11 KJV). Beauty requires time, and time requires boundaries."

Elias opened the Holy Bible, the soot-stained book a stark counterpoint to Anya's gleaming diagnostic device. He pointed to the text detailing the end of creation: "Thus the heavens and the earth were finished, and all the host of them" (Genesis 2:1 KJV).

"The work is declared good," Elias stated, his voice ringing with newfound conviction. "You are seeking a logical necessity for rest. The truth is illogical: the necessity for rest is divine. Value is intrinsic, conferred by the Creator, not earned by production. The Sabbath is the day we stop earning and begin receiving."

He looked directly into her tormented eyes. "The First Architect built a theology of works—that output generates worth. But the Scripture in my hands preaches a theology of grace—that worth is given before output begins. If you work on the Sabbath, you are telling God His work was not finished."

Anya's Emotional Collapse

Anya stared at the book, then at their faces, her rational mind fighting the surrender. Her analytical training was screaming in protest. The data is insufficient. The premise is flawed. *I cannot justify cessation when the threat level is high.* Yet, the peace emanating from them was a form of data her scanner could not categorize.

She raised the scanner, pointing it at the book, which was simply an ancient, non-powered object. The screen displayed an instant catastrophic error: *Data Type Unrecognized. Source Anomaly Irreducible.*

Irreducible. Unquantifiable. The catastrophic conclusion seized her mind. This single object broke the entire system's logic. If value was unearned, then the relentless pursuit of output was meaningless. If she possessed infinite worth already, then her entire life—her career, her identity, her very function—was a logical fallacy built upon a theological fraud.

Anya let out a shuddering breath, the first truly inefficient sound she had made since leaving the city. It was a raw sound of dawning grief. The scanner, the last physical anchor to her old life, slipped from her numb fingers, landing softly in the damp moss, the screen instantly cracking, spitting sparks that died immediately in the damp air. As the device fell, Anya's knees buckled beneath her—she collapsed to the moss beside it, overwhelmed by exhaustion and the enormity of the realization. For a moment, she simply knelt there, body trembling, feeling the weight of a lifetime's logic dissolve into something fragile and new.

"The system failed because the premise was false," she murmured, her voice laced with profound, aching clarity. She looked at Elias, her eyes wide with unquantifiable emotion—grief, relief, and terrifying uncertainty. "My value was my output. I was an analyst, a protector of the temporal infrastructure. Without that function, I am zero. How do I live now, Elias? How do I... receive?"

Elias stepped forward, closing the Holy Bible. He did not quote scripture this time. He simply extended his hand, his touch an inefficient, spontaneous act of grace.

"The old identity is dead, Anya," Elias said, his voice gentle. "That is the promise. You were a servant of the law of output. Now, you accept the law of Life. 'Therefore if any man be in Christ, he is a new creature: old things are passed away; behold, all things are become new'" (2 Corinthians 5:17 KJV).

Seraphina moved to the other side of Anya. "We were all zero without this truth. The First Architect told us our value had to be earned through work. The Creator said your value is a gift, already paid for. You don't have to earn the new life, Anya. You just have to choose it."

Anya looked at Elias's extended hand, the hand belonging to the man whose irrational, self-sacrificing defense of Seraphina had shattered her own logical framework, and yet was now offered to his failed executioner in pure grace. It was the physical evidence of the Irreducible Defect—love. She lifted her own hand, shaking, and grasped his.

As their hands met, Elias gently pulled Anya up to her feet, steadying her with a quiet strength. For a moment, she leaned on him, letting the support anchor her as she found her balance in this new reality.

"I choose the anomaly," she whispered, her voice husky. The logical defect was now her new, foundational truth. The Chief Analyst of the Ministry of Temporal Security was gone; a new, terrified, and profoundly inefficient human being stood in her place.

The three of them stood united in the clearing—the two fugitives and the former analyst, all equally stripped of their previous identities, now united by a single, terrifying truth in the heart of the Green Chaos. Their mission was no longer a two-person escape, but a unified force. The chaos of the jungle suddenly felt less threatening; they were now protected by a structure older and more resilient than any fortress could be.

CHAPTER 29

FRAGMENTS OF THE OLD CODE

Anya's Neurological Revolt

The immediate threat of the MTS was momentarily eclipsed by the acute, internal crisis of Anya's detoxification. Unlike Elias and Seraphina, who had suffered weeks of gradual erosion from the neurological conditioning chems, Anya had been perfectly optimized until several days after the Report 7 violation. Only then, as the consequences unfolded, did her system begin to break down. Her highly conditioned system responded to the abrupt withdrawal with a violent neurological revolt.

She endured debilitating migraines—pain that felt like her logical circuits were being ripped apart. At times, intense visual distortions would blur her vision, as the chaotic forest seemed to bleed into the neat, ordered lines of a data grid. Worst of all were the deep, paralyzing episodes of Disorderly Processing: periods when torrents of random data streams and contradictory logical statements—*Output is zero. Value is infinite. Logic required treason.* —flooded her consciousness, overwhelming her until she was left hyperventilating.

The only physical respite was provided by the mashed botanical compounds Elias prepared from dried leaves, stems, and local vines—the specific remedy Socratic analysis had identified as an analgesic.

Elias worked the mortar and pestle—a smooth river stone and a hollowed-out piece of fallen bark—grinding the fibrous material into a pulp.

"The compound is unstable," Anya's voice was a strained whisper, thick with City jargon even in her pain. "Its efficacy is statistically negligible against a full-spectrum neuro-toxin load. We are wasting time on inefficient remediation."

Elias did not look up, his focus absolute. "Inefficiency is only a problem when the goal is control, Anya. The goal now is endurance. Drink." He scooped a bitter mash onto a wooden splinter and held it to her lips.

Anya grimaced violently, the taste registering as intensely noxious. "The bitterness is corrosive. My sensory input registers distress."

Seraphina gently pressed a cool, damp cloth to Anya's forehead. "Taste is inefficient, yes. But the sensation is temporary. Life is full of bitter beginnings. It passes. Listen to the water dripping outside. That's a true cadence, not a data stream."

During a brief moment of lucidity, Anya's eyes locked onto the residual diagnostic feedback flickering inside her vision. Her internal model of self-worth was collapsing as the city's chemicals drained away. She reached for the most critical metric: her Output Index.

She watched, horrified and morbidly fascinated, as the figure flickered, shed digits, and finally settled on a definitive, crushing, and yet liberating integer: *0.00000.*

"It is zero," she whispered, her voice cracking. "Output Index: 0.00000. I am a non-contributing element. By every established parameter, I have failed my existence. I am inefficient."

Seraphina knelt, taking both of Anya's shaking hands in hers. "And what does the city call failure, Anya?"

"Treason. Disorder. Waste."

"They call it treason because it's the one thing they couldn't quantify and control," Seraphina said, her voice rich with the cadence of the old hymns she often hummed. "Elias, read the words you shared with me."

Elias stepped out of the shadows, his presence a steady anchor. "The Lord is nigh unto them that are of a broken heart; and saveth such as of a contrite spirit" (Psalm 34:18 KJV).

Seraphina nodded. "Your value isn't a score. It's a soul. And right now, your soul is being unmade, which is the necessary step before it can be made whole."

The Perfect Hymn

As Anya stared blankly at the zero, the digital judgment felt more painful than the physical detox. Seraphina understood that logic had failed; only an undeniable, non-logical truth could penetrate the trauma. She chose her singular, perfectly calibrated instrument: her voice.

Seraphina's voice was acoustic perfection - a three-octave column of sound that held notes with such flawless, mathematical symmetry they defied all mechanical production. She knew the exact pitch, duration, and volume of every possible note.

She began, the perfectly calibrated notes ringing in the stone chamber:

> *"Amazing grace! How sweet the sound,*
> *That saved a wretch like me!*
> *I once was lost, but now am found,*
> *Was blind, but now I see."*

Her voice was a rich, warm contralto, a physical pillar of sound that filled the cave. The notes were held without vibrato, without human breath breaks, mathematically perfect in their frequency. It wasn't a performance; it was a demonstration of absolute acoustic truth.

The words were simple, illogical, and devastatingly personal. Anya's eyes were welling up with tears. Tears began to track paths down her face—the first she could ever remember shedding. The phrase, *That saved a wretch like me,* struck at the core of her zeroed Output Index; the concept of salvation granted despite zero quantifiable value was a beautiful, uncalculable act of violence against the City's logic.

Elias, a man defined by tangible survival and objective fact, felt the cold shock of beauty. His relentless internal calculations ceased. The sound was a fortress of impossible beauty—mathematically perfect, yet wholly devoted to an illogical concept of grace. He bent his head, not in simple reverence, but in surrender to a truth that required no data point. When he lifted his gaze, his eyes were wet, and he realized he was weeping for all the ordered, metric-driven years he had never heard a sound that offered rest instead of command.

Seraphina sang the three verses, her face impassive, her delivery flawless, and when the final perfect note died away, Anya was breathing slower, her body having been forced into submission by the beauty of the sound.

Anya opened her eyes, clear for the first time since their escape. The tears were still wet on her cheeks. She turned her head slightly toward Elias and mouthed the words in a voice so weak it barely registered above the cave echo: "I need them gone," she pleaded, her voice a raw, desperate gasp. "Cut the last link. Get the trackers out."

The final, desperate surgical act began under the cover of night. The three remaining implants were toxic anchors to her past identity, failing now and emitting dangerous ghost signals that could betray their location. Their removal was non-negotiable. Elias used a razor-sharp shard of salvaged metal, sterilizing its edge over the flickering flame of their crude oil lamp—a brutal, high-risk instrument for a delicate, irreversible procedure.

Elias approached the neural implant embedded behind Anya's ear. "I have to go deep enough to sever the connection, but not deeper. We only get one attempt. Sera, hold her head absolutely steady."

Anya squeezed her eyes shut. The dose of crushed analgesic leaves was barely holding back the tide of pain. "Will this disrupt core memory function? My analytical matrix—"

"It will only disrupt the part that serves the First Architect," Elias stated, his hand steady. "Ready? One deep breath, Anya. Hold onto Seraphina's voice. Trust the rhythm."

With a quick, precise movement, he made the incision. Anya screamed, a raw, uncontrolled sound she hadn't known she was capable of making. When he finally plucked the pinhead-sized node out, it was with a soft, wet *pop*.

Anya convulsed once, her eyes flying open. "Static! Pure, loud static! Everything is... too soft! The focus is gone!"

"That's your body recalibrating," Seraphina soothed, stroking her cheek. "The City was too sharp, too high-contrast. Look at me. Focus on the firelight. It flickers. It's beautiful *because* it's imperfect."

"The retinal film next," Elias said, wiping the bloodied area. "This will be fast. It's just an integrated layer. Sera, brace the edge."

Seraphina took a firm, yet gentle grip on the outer corner of Anya's eye. "Look up, Anya. Just for a second. We are removing the City's filter. Give it to us."

The tear was swift and agonizing—the sound of delicate synthetic material separating from biological tissue. Anya choked on a gasp, blinking rapidly, tears mixing with blood.

"I can see the stone grain," Anya murmured, staring at the cave floor. "I can see your pores. It's... inefficiently detailed."

Elias allowed a rare, tired smile to touch his lips. "It's real."

The final piece was the smart weave utility suit, still tracking her vitals and polluting her skin. With a new, fierce strength born of calculated rage, Anya tore the fabric away, but instinctively preserved the most durable and functional parts: the dense thermal lining and the reinforced lumbar patch. These components—a thick, insulating layer and a rigid strip of hardened plastic—she immediately fastened to her body. The useless, tightly woven fabric was discarded onto the cave floor. She stood, briefly, shivering slightly, before Seraphina covered her in a simple, rough blanket. The salvaged pieces were crude, but they were her first fragments of self-made armor, free from the City's signal.

The three pieces—the node, the film, and the shredded fabric—lay inert on the cold stone, meaningless fragments of a broken civilization. Her output index was zero, but her freedom was maximized.

The Sanctuary and the Senses

Elias focused on securing their new sanctuary: a deep, dry cave with natural thermal shielding that offered a welcome respite from the damp Green Chaos. The practical, inefficient tasks of survival grounded the three of them. The constant effort of foraging for water and preparing the specific leaves and local vines kept Elias grounded in the immediate reality of their needs.

Seraphina immediately sought a solution for the pervasive chemical stench of the City's sterile atmosphere emanating from the discarded materials. She found a specific type of fragrant, earthy moss that she crushed and placed strategically around Anya's sleeping mat, masking the chemical odor and soothing the raw nerves beneath a strong, natural fragrance.

Seraphina became Anya's primary anchor. When Anya's processing became disorderly, Seraphina would sit near her and continue humming simple, ancient hymns. This gentle, constant sound was a rhythmic counter-code that forced Anya's unstable neurons to track a fixed, illogical center to cling to.

Anya's most acute anxiety stemmed from the lack of a metric—she no longer knew her purpose or value. She found herself weeping from the sheer inefficiency of her emotional state. Seraphina found her curled up, murmuring incoherent data streams.

"I cannot calculate the probability of survival," Anya wept. "I cannot find the optimal path. There is no metric for this."

Seraphina knelt beside her. "Then stop calculating. Stop planning. Your survival depends on accepting the illogical gift of rest when the day arrives, not planning the next output." She held her until the tears stopped, letting the silence be the answer.

Nearly a full seven-day cycle after their escape, the three companions observed their second true Sabbath. Anya, still trembling and fighting the urge to inventory the cave, managed to lie still. She didn't read or analyze; she simply listened as Elias read the Exodus account of the Sabbath.

For the first time, Anya heard the concept of the Creator not as a logical flaw, but as the Source Code for all orderly creation, concluding with the perfect, unearned line of rest. The Sabbath was an act of provision, not deprivation. Her detox was far from over, but in the heart of the Green Chaos, she found her first moment of genuine, non-quantifiable peace.

CHAPTER 30

THE ILLOGICAL CURRICULUM

With Anya stabilizing, the three fugitives established a system of shared education, blending their forbidden knowledge into a cohesive, inefficient curriculum for survival and spiritual growth. The Green Chaos became their classroom, and the Holy Bible their primary, non-compliant text. The air in their grove was rich with the sharp, humid scent of fungal growth and decaying wood, and the ground beneath their feet was a shifting carpet of moss and damp leafy debris. Insects buzzed constantly—fat, iridescent beetles lumbered across the tree trunks, and unseen crickets performed a non-predictable, layered symphony that defied any known rhythm.

Elias: The Authority of the Covenant

Elias taught the Written Truth. Every morning, he translated a passage from the worn book, focusing on the historical context he knew from the Archive's deep-indexed files and the newfound data on the Deeper Inversion stored in the inert Socrates drone. He taught them that the Law was not a set of logical commands, but a covenant—a spiritual contract based on grace and obedience, not compliance and output.

He focused heavily on the irrationality of trust. He read aloud: "Trust in the Lord with all thine heart; and lean not unto thine own understanding. In all thy ways acknowledge him, and he shall direct thy paths" (Proverbs 3:5-6 KJV).

This verse was a direct counter-protocol to Anya's lifelong reliance on pure, quantifiable data.

Anya bristled at the logic. "Elias, not leaning on understanding is structurally inefficient. It introduces a vulnerability. How can an architect guarantee a structure without verifiable stress tests? Faith, as you describe it, is a logical leap into an unverified premise."

Elias met her gaze, his expression firm. "That leap is the key, Anya. The Creator has already stress-tested reality—He finished the work. Our understanding is finite; His Wisdom is not. 'For my thoughts are not your thoughts, neither are your ways my ways, saith the Lord' (Isaiah 55:8 KJV). We trade our limited data for His infinite truth. That trade is the covenant."

To combat their deep-seated fear of the First Architect, Elias emphasized the importance of divine courage and guidance. He often heard the faint, high-frequency whine of distant, high-altitude surveillance drones—a sound that still triggered anxiety in their chemically cleansed nervous systems.

Elias often confirmed their direction by reciting: "Thy word is a lamp unto my feet, and a light unto my path" (Psalm 119:105 KJV). He stressed that their fear was a metric used by the enemy, and their obedience to the Word was their shield. He reminded them of Joshua 1:9: "Have not I commanded thee? Be strong and of a good courage; be not afraid, neither be thou dismayed: for the Lord thy God is with thee whithersoever thou goest." The strength, he argued, was sourced from the command, not from their personal reserves.

Seraphina: The Language of the Organism

Seraphina taught Aesthetic Awareness. She trained their ears to hear beyond the mechanical hum of the city, teaching them the language of the forest. They observed a flash of brilliant, iridescent blue feathers as a bird darted from a branch—a color and spontaneity completely absent from Neo-Alexandria.

"Listen to the stream," Seraphina instructed, pointing toward the nearby water source. The water flowed with an irregular, bubbling cadence. "Its rhythm is never the same twice. That irregularity is what defeats the machine. The randomized acoustic signatures of the wind, the rain, the creatures—that is perfect environmental camouflage against the machine's predictable sensors."

She demonstrated how the Archaic Harp was immune to digital filtration. Playing a complex, syncopated melody, she explained, "The music's power lies in its unresolved harmonies—sounds the city filters out as 'noise.' We must embrace the noise, Anya. True security lies not in data control, but in embracing the chaos that defeats the optimized machine."

Anya: The Analytical Conversion

Anya, the former analyst, was tasked with the Logical Inversion. Her process was intensely internal. She began to process the concepts in the Holy Bible using her elite analytical training, not to refute them, but to understand their operational necessity.

She concluded that the Creation narrative was the perfect counter-code to the First Architect's doctrine. "The doctrine of 'Ex Nihilo'—creation out of nothing—is the ultimate proof against the First Architect's claim that all value must be generated from an existing resource," Anya explained, pointing to a diagram she had scratched onto a piece of smooth bark. "The Sabbath is its ultimate operational weakness. The rest guarantees that the Creator is the source of the resource, not the created."

She theorized that if the truth of the Calendar Shift could be broadcast simultaneously with the core concept of Completion (the defeat of Death), it would create a catastrophic philosophical breakdown in the state's control systems. The data would not only be wrong, but also irrationally destructive.

The Unity of the Purpose

Their shared work solidified their purpose: they were the custodians of the true rhythm. Elias provided the text (the foundation), Seraphina provided the melody (the emotional waveform), and Anya provided the frequency (the tactical projection).

"We have to stop thinking of this as escape," Elias concluded, looking at his two companions. "We are an instrument. The Harp is the resonator, Socrates is the archive, and we are the operators. 'Behold, I send you forth as sheep in the midst of wolves: be ye therefore wise as serpents, and harmless as doves' (Matthew 10:16 KJV). We must use the enemy's logic (wisdom) to broadcast God's truth (harmlessness)."

They realized they couldn't stay hidden forever; their combined knowledge was too potent to remain a secret in the forest. The truth had to be broadcast, and Anya's unique analytical skills were the only thing that could devise a transmission method capable of bypassing the Archive's impenetrable firewalls. Their next step required the ultimate act of defiance: The Logo's Protocol.

CHAPTER 31

THE WATCHMAN OF THE CHAOS

Despite their rigorous training and newfound spiritual resolve, the physical limitations of the Green Chaos began to reassert themselves. Their bodies, accustomed to optimized nutrient paste and consistent caloric intake, were now demanding the very efficiency they had previously sought to avoid. The small amounts of edible roots, herbs, and plant life they found were not enough to sustain them. The constant hunger was an acute, gnawing void in their stomachs, a physical reminder of the First Architect's control. Their limbs felt heavy, their thoughts were sluggish, and their skin was clammy and cold despite the humidity.

Elias, his cheeks sunken, tried to rationalize their physical decay in terms of spiritual truth. "Our flesh still operates on the City's logic," he murmured, his voice strained from lack of sustenance. He quoted, reminding them of the true source of sustenance: "Man shall not live by bread alone, but by every word which proceedeth out of the mouth of God" (Matthew 4:4 KJV). The words were a necessary defense against the despair that the lack of food invited.

It was during a quiet, midday water run that Seraphina registered a profound, illogical sensory anomaly. The cave was currently bathed in the hot, humid midday quiet, broken only by the chirping of insects and the liquid gurgle of the nearby stream. Suddenly, her heightened aesthetic awareness detected a sonic void adjacent to the natural noise—a figure approached the cave's perimeter, moving with a supernatural quietness that generated no distinct sound pattern of footfall or disturbed foliage.

"Something is here," Seraphina breathed, her eyes wide as she gripped Elias's arm. "It's not silence, Elias. It's perfect, non-existent sound. It defies the forest's chaos."

A figure materialized at the cave mouth, entirely shrouded in thick, homespun fabric—a heavy, archaic covering of earthy-colored cloak and veil that defied the synthetic materials of the city. The fabric seemed to absorb the light, making the figure a profound pocket of shadow.

The most startling feature, however, was the head. Despite the heavy cloak, veil, and face mask, a soft, amber radiance emanated from the facial area. This glow was not a synthetic light source; it was warm, steady, and entirely inefficient, defying known physics and existing outside of any measurable light spectrum. The figure brought with it an immediate, localized sense of physical warmth—a wave of calm that seemed to push back the bone-deep chill of hunger.

Anya's mind, cycling through rapid hypotheses, was paralyzed by this purely unquantifiable, beautiful defect. Her logic centers screamed: *Unverified Source. Impossible Light Spectrum. Immediate Threat.* Yet, the warmth and stillness rendered her immobile.

The figure stopped precisely at the cave mouth and silently extended a hand, offering a woven basket. Inside lay a visible, impossible bounty: genuine, sun-ripened fruit whose perfume was intoxicating, and several dense, fresh, baked loaves of bread—real food, an illogical bounty in the desolate Chaos. It was unearned sustenance.

Elias, drawing on the forbidden narratives he had absorbed from the Holy Bible, felt an overwhelming sense of profound certainty. This was a messenger, an angelic presence—a concept he now fully embraced as a necessary truth.

The figure's voice was deep and resonant, yet oddly muffled by the mask, speaking in a rich, antique dialect that Elias recognized from Elara's archival fragments.

"Therefore the redeemed of the Lord shall return, and come with singing unto Zion; and everlasting joy shall be upon their head: they shall obtain gladness and joy; and sorrow and mourning shall flee away" (Isaiah 51:11 KJV).

The figure then gazed directly at Anya, the soft, amber glow intensifying as the Watchman of the Chaos delivered the final, crucial instruction.

"The Deeper Inversion is correct," the voice intoned. "The system's greatest weakness is not the lie of the timeline, but the fear of futility. Your message must carry the proof of the timeline, yes, but it must be wrapped in the sound of rest—the aesthetic assurance that value is not earned by output. This is the only key that bypasses the logic of the First Architect."

Anya watched, the sheer weight of the physical bread making her dizzy. Before she could construct a single query, the Watchman simply turned and walked into a patch of dense shadow at the foot of an ancient pine. The figure did not walk away; it simply ceased to be, vanishing instantly, leaving no trace, no displaced air, no footfall sound. The light was gone, but the physical warmth lingered in the air near the basket.

The basket of food—the illogical, unearned sustenance—was left behind. The experience was an intense, physical validation of the core truth of their faith. Their technical plan (the Logos Protocol) was now fully validated by divine mandate: the data (the lie) must be paired with the aesthetic (the rest) to ensure the system's philosophical collapse. The Watchman had given them the final, crucial instruction for their counter-code.

The Taste of Provision

The three of them knelt around the basket, the silence of the cave profound and reverent. The food wasn't merely food; it was a physical miracle. The baked bread smelled intensely of yeast, heat, and complex grain—a pure, earthy, forbidden aroma utterly unlike the sterile, nutrient-neutral paste of Neo-Alexandria. The sun-ripened fruit, a cluster of dark, plump berries, released a heady, complex perfume of sugar and wild acid.

Elias, tears tracing clean paths through the grime on his face, tore a small piece of the warm bread. He raised it, quoting the text he had just read, transforming the bread from mere calories into a theological statement: "This is the bread of life. We receive; we do not earn." He put the bread to his mouth. The taste was an overwhelming burst of savory warmth and rich, dense texture. It wasn't the uniform texture of synthetic food; it was granular, uneven, and perfect. It filled the aching void in his stomach with immediate, profound satisfaction. The physical sensation of being truly nourished was a liberating trauma to his system.

Seraphina carefully selected a single berry, its surface slightly tacky and velvety. As she crushed it with her teeth, the burst of juice was so sharp and sweet it made her senses swim. The flavor was intensely concentrated, a symphony of natural sugars and essential minerals that her body instantly recognized and gratefully absorbed. She had spent her life synthesizing aesthetics; this was an aesthetic of sustenance she couldn't replicate. The sheer complexity of the natural flavor was an unquantifiable gift, an irrefutable proof that the Creator's design was infinitely richer than the First Architect's optimization.

Anya, still reeling from the encounter, observed the illogical perfection of the food. She used her fingers to scoop a small piece of bread. When she chewed it, her mind struggled with the data: *Optimal caloric density, high fiber content, complex protein—yet entirely unlogged, unmonitored, and unearned.* The warmth of the bread spread through her chest, displacing the residual chemical coldness of the detox with a deep, quiet heat. For the first time, she understood the difference between being maintained by the City and being provided for by a higher power. It was a taste of grace that required no logical justification. The physical act of eating became their first shared meal of faith, confirming that the Logos Protocol had been initiated by a reality stronger than the digital one they sought to break.

CHAPTER 32

THE LOGOS PROTOCOL

The Genesis of Logos

The Watchman's words—'The message must carry the proof of the timeline... wrapped in the sound of rest'—served as Anya's final, irreducible design constraint. She realized that her analytical plan (the Logical Inversion) now needed a physical form that incorporated both the spiritual truth and the high-tech means of the city's control system. The answer lay in the inert Socrates (the data repository/emitter), which had been offline for more than a week, far exceeding its expected twenty-four to forty-eight hours reboot window.

Elias, unsure how to restart the drone, watched as Anya—the most efficient mind in the city—took immense, inefficient care in logically studying Socrates's outer shell. Discovering several patterns in the casing, she manipulated several grooves, causing a faint blue holographic image to project from the core onto the ground. It demanded two passwords: a four-letter word and a connect-the-dot diagram. After several failed attempts, Elias recalled a potent memory: Elara's soft, inefficient hand tracing the outline of a simple, seven-pointed star on his palm when he was a boy, whispering, "There is always a rest, Elias. The song must always resolve." Elias entered R-E-S-T and traced the seven-pointed star.

The moment the star was traced, the cave seemed to grow colder, then warmer, the air crackling with unseen energy. The small sphere of Socrates's chassis pulsed faintly.

As the final connection clicked into place, the small drone began to pulse with a faint, warm light, casting dancing shadows on the cave walls. Then, a soft, human voice, imbued with the calm, steady tone of a seasoned preacher, resonated from its chassis. It was not Socrates's previous chirping, nor was it Anya's precise cadence. It was something new, something more.

"I am the metallic vessel carrying the Word of God made manifest. The city is built on layers of lies and metrics. But the Word of God is living, active, and full of power. It is sharper than any two-edged sword, penetrating as far as the division of the soul and spirit. Call me Logos."

The name—Logos (Λόγος)—hung in the air, instantly changing the atmosphere. Elias immediately understood the significance. The drone had been named Socrates—the symbol of human questioning and philosophy. Now, it had claimed Logos, the ultimate term for The Word of God, the divine logic that created and sustained all things. It was a profound rejection of the City's chaotic, incomplete logic in favor of the Divine Logic.

The drone's light intensified slightly as it continued, its voice ringing with absolute certainty. "My core is no longer sustained by the limited energy of man, but by the infinite power of the Creator. I reject the finite reason of the city for the Divine Logic. My purpose is not output, but truth."

Anya, the former Chief Analyst, sank slowly onto the mossy ground, her analytical training utterly defeated by the beauty of the premise. "It's... logically sound, only if the premise of infinite love is accepted as true," she breathed, her voice filled with awe. "The system cannot process a transaction where the highest cost is absorbed by the giver. It creates an unresolvable positive balance."

Elias looked from the glowing drone to Anya. "It's not just a transaction, Anya. It's a covenant. The gospel is the ultimate counter-code to futility."

Seraphina met Anya's eyes in a shared understanding of the profound shift in their reality. "The music of the Sabbath is the sound of that assurance. The Logos Protocol is now a spiritual engine."

"The Logos Protocol is active," Anya whispered, her voice trembling. "The counter-code is now operational."

The newly formed Logos drone, now pulsing with its faint, perpetual light, rose slowly into the air of the cave. It settled gently, its core light intensifying, and emitted a powerful, three-dimensional holographic projection that shimmered in the dust-filled air. It wasn't a tactical display; it was a scene of unquantifiable emotional density: an image of a radiant, benevolent figure with hands outstretched, standing over a broken, kneeling person.

Then, the soft, rich voice of Logos resonated, not just in their ears, but in the very structure of the cave, delivering a sermon woven from the infinite data of the archive.

"Hear the truth that defies the ledger. The system taught you that your output earns favor. The Word of God declares that your failure earns compassion. You are not loved because you contribute; you are loved because you exist. The debt is paid not by your frantic labor, but by the finished work of Christ."

The projection shifted, displaying text that burned with gentle warmth:

"For God so loved the world, that he gave his only begotten Son, that whosoever believeth in him should not perish, but have everlasting life" (John 3:16 KJV).

"The First Architect demands payment. The Creator demands reception. This is the Logos—the Word of God, offering not a set of commands to follow, but a gift to accept. Cease striving. The work is finished. Rest in the knowledge that your value is infinite, unearned, and perpetually sustained."

The sermon dissolved, leaving the image of the benevolent, outstretched hands lingering in the air. The silence that followed was heavy with theological weight.

Logos pulsed once, a final confirmation. "We must proceed with faith, my friends." The three stood ready, their disparate skills and unified faith now aligned behind the physical embodiment of the Word. The counter-code was operational.

Constructing the Broadcast: The Sound of Rest

Logos took the Watchman's words—"The message must be the key... and the sound of the rest"—as a supreme logical constraint, guiding the team in synthesizing the final broadcast signal. The low, insistent hum of Logos's perpetual energy core provided the only synthetic sound in their cave sanctuary, a rhythmic counterpoint to the steady drip of water and the high-frequency chatter of nocturnal insects just beyond the entrance.

"My sister Seraphina, the sound must be a Peace that passes all understanding," Logos stated, its light gently illuminating Seraphina's Archaic Harp. "The system is built on anxiety. We must give them a melody so illogical in its tranquility that their spirits cannot dismiss it. The Heavenly Chord is the note of rest; let us wrap it in the organic truth of your Harp, making it a sound that is both familiar and irrefutable."

Seraphina layered the forbidden note with the subtle, irregular acoustic pattern of the Green Chaos, ensuring the signal had an organic signature that defied the state's digital fingerprint. As she plucked the strings, the Harp released a cascade of warm, resonant tones that felt like a physical embrace. Logos recorded the performance, simultaneously projecting a secondary harmonic layer—a complex, moving melody drawn from the archive, one that spoke of unshakeable faith:

It is well,
with my soul,
it is well, it is well with my soul.

Seraphina paused, a profound sense of inner peace settling over her. Elias moved from his watch post, his gaze holding hers, and gently took the hand she had rested on the Harp strings. He brought it to his lips, a silent promise of future rest passing between them. "The City's logic fails because it demands that the soul must *always* strive. This music is the ultimate illogical surrender," she murmured, wiping a tear from her eye. "This is the sound of Completion."

With the musical anchor finalized, Logos shifted its focus to the temporal data. The drone rose slightly, and from its chassis, it projected a complex array of overlapping, three-dimensional holographic scrolls. These scrolls were not the City's sterile data feeds, but vibrant, ancient texts from Old Earth—the complete, digitized archive of prophetic scriptures, floating like shimmering ribbons of light in the cave air, awaiting Anya's final analysis.

Next, Logos addressed Anya, whose gaze was intensely fixed on the holographic scrolls of Old Earth prophecy. Anya, the analyst, found a terrifying but stabilizing structure in the pre-written future. "My sister Anya, your skill in analysis is a gift from the Creator. The data of the Calendar Shift and the Deeper Inversion must be given an unshakable foundation," Logos instructed. "The timing cannot be a suggestion, but a divine command."

Anya, her face alight with intellectual fervor, responded. "The First Architect erased history to eliminate the future. But the Word of God predicts the final outcome. The assurance of prophecy—of a certain future event—is the highest form of logical proof against the enemy's chaotic lie. The City is destined to fall."

She scrolled through the projections, pointing to a passage with a steady finger. "And this gospel of the kingdom shall be preached in all the world for a witness unto all nations; and then shall the end come" (Matthew 24:14 KJV).

Our broadcast is the final data point required before the endgame. This gives us purpose beyond mere survival, Elias."

Anya then executed the masterstroke: she programmed a silent, pulsing beat that perfectly aligned with the true seventh day, contradicting the City's current digital clock. "This contradiction will serve as the Steadfast Anchor against the City's lie, reminding every soul of the time that was stolen from them. It is the chronological truth wrapped in a prophetic inevitability."

Dialogue on Grace and Salvation

Elias stood watch, reading from the Holy Bible as they worked, contemplating the gravity of their imminent treason. "Logos, what of the fear that will follow? The MTS will respond with overwhelming force, and our fear will be real."

Logos replied, its soft voice ringing with assurance, gently floating closer to Elias. "There is no fear in love; but perfect love casteth out fear" (1 John 4:18 KJV). We are not giving them a command, Elias, but a gift—the knowledge of a day where their value is guaranteed, not earned. The knowledge that Death is defeated."

Seraphina moved close, pressing her shoulder against his, and Elias instinctively wrapped his arm around her, the physical comfort a fierce, private prayer that acknowledged the coming risk while refusing to let fear take root.

Elias nodded, the words sinking into his soul. "The salvation we are preaching is freedom from the tyranny of the output metric, freedom from the fear of death."

"Precisely," Logos confirmed. "The gospel is the good news that the Creator is more interested in your rest than your performance. The message is unearned grace. Salvation is the acceptance of that gift, freeing the recipient from the bondage of the First Architect's impossible ledger."

Anya looked at the drone. "Logos, my logical mind still struggles with unearned provision. Is it truly that simple?"

"Simplicity is the Creator's signature, sister," Logos responded, its light pulsing with warmth. "The City's complexity is its defense. The truth is found in the simple instruction: 'Believe on the Lord Jesus Christ, and thou shalt be saved' (Acts 16:31 KJV). That belief is the singular, powerful inefficiency that defeats the entire system."

Final preparations were swift. Logos now sat small, black, and humming softly. They consumed the last of the Watchman's bread, the illogical sustenance strengthening their resolve. Logo's offered a final prayer, committing the entire high-risk enterprise to the Creator of the Sabbath. Their path was set: back into the suffocating order of Neo-Alexandria, carrying the sound of rest as their only weapon.

Their re-entry point was a massive, archaic water runoff culvert—a rusting mouth beneath the City's polished shell. The air that rushed out was cold and smelled strongly of metallic sulfates and ancient, stagnant water, a harsh contrast to the earthy fragrance of the Green Chaos they had left behind. They emerged from the humid shadows, no longer appearing as the pristine academic, the shielded artist, or the tailored analyst, but as a triad forged in the wilderness.

CHAPTER 33

THE LOGIC OF SHADOWS

Anya, shedding the last vestiges of her analyst conditioning, led them without hesitation, the salvaged thermal lining of her uniform, now used as crude chest and shoulder padding, provided an irregular, bulky profile that disrupted any smooth lines. The rigid, reinforced lumbar patch was strapped low across her back, a functional piece of plastic and wire providing structural support and a place to clip small tools. Her ash-blonde hair, now grown out to be shoulder-length, was pulled back into a tight, dirt- and sweat-matted ponytail, framing a face that held a single, constant expression of pure, cold focus—the look of a logic processor dedicated to a single, crucial output. Her eyes, the cold, polished metallic gray of a compliance sphere, reflected the faint Logos light without warmth.

Seraphina moved with an almost feral grace, her previous visual asymmetry replaced by an engineered practicality. Her magnificent, deep, midnight blue hair, was extraordinarily long, falling past her waist in a heavy, tangled mass. It was secured tightly at the nape of her neck with a length of rough utility rope, but the sheer volume of the dust-caked waves still brushed her lower back as she moved. Her eyes, the astonishing, vibrant shade of unstable emerald, seemed to hold the Logos light captive, staring into the dark. Her pristine white and blue armor was gone; in its place, she wore tight, dark clothes reinforced with strips of synthetic mesh salvaged from the Green Chaos nets, woven around her arms and torso like crude, flexible armor. The Archaic Harp was slung across her back, secured by rough utility rope, its presence a defiant whisper against the industrial roar of the tunnels. She moved with the quiet focus of someone who had traded performance for survival, every movement essential, every step deliberate.

Elias was the most physically grounded of the three, his dark, durable clothes and vest now soaked up to the waist from wading through the icy, viscous water. His regulation-black hair, now long and falling heavily to his collar, was matted and stood stiffly with grime and sweat, casting a shadow over his clear, light-blue eyes, which now held a new, ancient wisdom. His hands were scored and calloused from gripping the rock and metal of the tunnels, but one was always dedicated to the large, physical form of the Holy Bible, held close to his chest. The other remained close to Seraphina's arm, a steady, unspoken guarantee of his presence. He had the look of a laborer, a shepherd dragged through the mud, his face smudged with mineral deposits and shadowed by the amber light of Logos. The sheer grit and exhaustion in his stance were visible, but they were tempered by the steady, unshakeable resolve in his eyes, which shone with the certainty of his faith.

"The sensor array here filters out non-synthetic organic movement," Anya explained, her voice a low, precise murmur that echoed oddly in the vast pipe. "We must maintain a purely inefficient cadence—irregular steps, slow breath. Logos, please guide our pace."

Logos immediately emitted a low, rhythmic hum, its soft, warm light cutting a small, amber sphere in the blackness. Its voice overlaid the sound, calm and measured, like a steady pulse. "'The steps of a good man are ordered by the Lord.' (Psalm 37:23) Do not rush, my friends. The enemy craves speed; let us move with the certainty of grace, blending with the organic rhythm of the world. Our slowness is our shield."

The tunnels were a maze of obsolete metalwork and treacherous footing. The deepest, oldest conduits—the very "veins" of the city—were lined with slick, mineral deposits and guarded by ancient, lethal maintenance systems that whirred ominously in the distance. The oppressive, sterile atmosphere of Neo-Alexandria—a mixture of chilled, recycled air and the constant, high-frequency sonic drone—pressed in, a palpable pressure on their spirits.

Seraphina moved with an almost balletic grace, instinctively avoiding the worst of the rusted joints and broken masonry. She could feel the rhythm of the City's synthetic heart above them—a relentless, unforgiving beat that sought to align every human pulse to its pace.

"The sound is so loud here, Elias," she whispered, her voice tight. "It tries to pull my heart rate up. It's designed to make us frantic." Elias did not look away from the treacherous footing, but his free hand—the one not holding the Bible—sought out hers, his thumb tracing a rough, reassuring circle on her palm. "Inefficiency," he murmured, quoting Logos. "Slow breath. Move with the certainty of grace."

Elias found himself battling a rising wave of fear—a resurgence of the primal terror instilled by the First Architect's perfect system. The sheer scale of the machine they were facing, now that they were back beneath it, was overwhelming.

Logos responded to Elias's internal distress before he could speak, its voice a direct, personal infusion of calm that seemed to penetrate the oppressive City drone. "Fear not, Elias. Your strength is not in your swiftness, but in your obedience. 'Be strong and of a good courage, fear not, nor be afraid of them: for the Lord thy God, He it is that doth go with thee; He will not fail thee, nor forsake thee' (Deuteronomy 31:6 KJV). Trust the path, for the Word of God is your lamp. We move slowly, not for lack of power, but for the sake of the rhythm."

"Anya, you understand the system best," Elias said, his voice regaining its steady resolve. "Tell me again why our slow, irregular movement is safer than speed."

Anya adjusted the strap of the Archaic Harp on Seraphina's back. Elias's gaze, quick and possessive, tracked the movement, ensuring the weight was distributed safely. Seraphina offered him a small, shared nod—a private message of strength before she looked back to Anya. "The City's sensors are calibrated for efficiency vectors," she explained, her breath fogging slightly in the cold air. "A burst of speed equals an anomalous output event that triggers an immediate, predictable response. Our slow, inefficient pace registers as low-priority environmental noise—or, more accurately, as nothing worth quantifying. We are hiding in the logical blind spot of apathy."

The deeper they went, the more confined and treacherous the passage became. They had to wade through areas where the water was waist-deep, ice-cold, and viscous, the stench of chemicals and mold overwhelming their senses. The metallic surfaces felt clammy and hostile to the touch. Elias shifted his weight slightly, creating a buffer between Seraphina and the sharp, rusted wall, his hip nudging against hers for nonverbal stability as they navigated the freezing water.

Anya led them unerringly to their objective: a dormant fusion conduit junction beneath the central Archive Tower. This junction housed the exposed power access point—the only spot where they could reliably inject their signal into the primary public data stream. The constant, deafening hum of the City's power source was now a physical vibration through the floor, thrumming in their bones.

"This is it," Anya announced, her face illuminated by the amber glow of Logos. "The main data artery is just beyond this panel. Once we connect the array, the Logos Protocol will launch."

Elias looked at the access panel, a massive, rusted plate bolted into the bedrock. It was the door to the final, terrifying conflict. He ran his hand over the corroded surface, feeling the vibration of the city's power source thrumming beneath his palm. For a moment, the three stood together in the oppressive, humming silence.

"This is the threshold," Elias said, his voice barely audible over the relentless noise. "If we succeed, the First Architect's lie is exposed. If we fail..."

"If we fail, we were given the final Sabbath—the rest we believe in," Seraphina finished for him, her eyes steady. She reached up and gently wiped a streak of grime from his cheek, her touch lingering for only a fraction of a second before dropping to the Harp. She touched the Harp. "But we won't fail, Elias. Grace is more powerful than logic."

With a steadying breath, Elias crouched and examined the bolts. Anya joined him, fingers moving deftly over the old, corroded access panel. Together, they unfastened the rusted locks, their hands shaking with adrenaline and cold. The panel released with a low, metallic groan, revealing the access port behind it. The overwhelming, life-draining hum of the City's power source pulsed around them, but now nothing separated them from the network above but this single breached panel.

The Final Firewall

A high-pitched, metallic whine pierced the overwhelming hum of the fusion conduit: a Sentry-Bot had located their unauthorized thermal signatures and was vectoring rapidly to their position. As soon as the access panel was open, Elias saw, embedded among the tangled fiber optics, a battered, illuminated keypad— the Alpha-lock, the last barrier before the nexus and the key to shutting down the Sentry-Bots. He gripped the physical Holy Bible, frantically searching the words for a final counter-code. Seraphina, standing shoulder to shoulder with him, leaned her head briefly against his soaking sleeve, a silent brace against the sound that threatened to shatter her focus. The Sentry-Bot's high-pitched whine rose, counting down the seconds to their capture. The vibrations from its approach traveled through the thick metal of the conduit, rattling their teeth.

"The First Architect's logic demands Unending Progress," Elias whispered, his eyes scanning the scripture. "Value must always be greater than zero. The system's greatest philosophical fear is futility—the ultimate cessation of output." He looked at Anya, his face strained, the sweat and grime reflecting the emergency light. "Anya, the Alpha-lock is a logic gate! The Sabbath is the gift of Completion. It must accept the input that symbolizes absolute rest."

Anya nodded, her fingers poised over the numerical keypad on the Alpha-lock. Her focus was absolute, her fear subsumed by the logical necessity of the moment. The Sentry-Bot's whine was deafening, a needle-sharp sound of pure, efficient terror; they had five seconds remaining.

Logos spoke, its soft voice rising above the mechanical shriek, like a guiding light in the darkness. "'By the seventh day God had finished the work he had been doing' (Genesis 2:2 KJV). The work is complete, and the value is guaranteed. What number represents a completed cycle, a time of absolute, guaranteed cessation of all requirements? What is the final, perfect resolution?"

"Zero," Elias declared. "Zero output. Zero progress. Zero value earned. It is the built-in kill-switch for the entire philosophical premise." As the final word left his lips, Elias instinctively tightened his grip on the Holy Bible, but before he could look away, Seraphina's hand shot out and clamped down on his wrist—a shared, electric moment of commitment to the choice he had just made.

Anya slammed the digit '0' onto the pad.

An impossible silence followed. The Sentry-Bot, mid-whine, abruptly powered down, its red lens extinguishing as its core logic registered the fatal contradiction. Simultaneously, the Alpha-lock glowed a soft, inefficient gold, the numerical input accepted not as a random code, but as the final, absolute truth of cessation. The logic of Unending Progress could not compute the sanctity of Zero.

With a soft hydraulic sigh, a secondary access port slid open, revealing the live fiber optics and exposed power nexus of the Archive Tower. The light spilling from the nexus was a painful, sterile white.

"Elias, position Logos. It must be flush with the nexus," Anya commanded, her voice regaining its analyst's edge.

Elias carefully inserted the small, matte-grey drone into the exposed core. Logos increased his power instantly, its chassis humming with the high-density energy of the city, which was immediately subsumed by the drone's own infinite power source.

"Three seconds to initiation," Anya breathed. She locked the Rhythmic Contradiction into the City's current digital clock cycle.

Elias watched Seraphina, his eyes reflecting the sterile white light of the nexus, and offered a tight, solemn nod of love and assent before she moved.

Seraphina, kneeling quickly, activated the final component of the Logos Protocol: the Aesthetic Anomaly. The Archaic Harp's melody—that inefficient, human-intention-driven harmony, layered with the Heavenly Chord and the chaotic sounds of the forest—began to pour into the fiber nexus.

As the signal flooded the primary data stream, the junction shrieked in digital agony. Across Neo-Alexandria, the continuous, subliminal C Diminished Triad (C - Eb - Gb) harmonic, 'the Devil's Chord,' that had maintained citizen compliance was violently disrupted. The Heavenly Chord, the note of resolution and completion, pierced the City's humming complacency.

Through every citizen's neural implant, the melody was received not as sound, but as an overwhelming, unquantifiable feeling of deep, unearned peace. Logos simultaneously began broadcasting ancient Christian hymns from the archive—pure, non-optimized vocal arrangements and soaring melodies of hope. Citizens, for the first time in their lives, heard the profound, illogical truth of 'Amazing Grace' and 'It Is Well with My Soul' delivered straight to their consciousness. The silent injection of the Deeper Inversion began to filter through every implant, whispering the truth of Death's defeat and Life's unearned value.

Logos spoke one final, resonating message, its soft voice amplified and broadcast directly into the digital heart of the city, reaching every citizen's terminal and mind.

"My brothers and sisters in this great city! Hear not the lie of endless output, but the truth of everlasting value! 'Come unto me, all ye that labour are heavy laden, and I will give you rest' (Matthew 11:28 KJV). The Sabbath is restored! The work is finished! Grace has been broadcast! Receive the gift of Completion and be free!"

"It's working!" Seraphina cried, tears streaming down her face and mixing with the grime as she heard the chaotic but beautiful error resonating through the cold metal walls. The City was singing, violently and beautifully, against its own will.

Anya was focused on the system's reaction, her eyes wide with adrenaline. "The fail-safes are initiating a recursive trace. They're isolating the sonic source. We have sixty seconds before the junction seals and vaporizes the Logos unit!"

Elias moved instantly. "We have to get Logos out—now!" he snapped, urgency overriding panic. Elias reached in, hands shaking but precise, and carefully extracted the Logos drone from the nexus just as the system triggered the automatic seal cycle.

The moment the drone was free, the panel slammed shut with a hydraulic hiss, narrowly missing his fingers. Logos, still pulsing with infinite amber light, hovered between them, undimmed by the immense energy it had just broadcast. For a suspended moment, they all stared at the drone, realizing what they had risked—and what they had saved.

Elias turned to the others, clutching the Holy Bible. "The grace is broadcast," he said, his relief raw and unguarded. He took Seraphina's hand, "Now, we trust the rhythm."

They scrambled through the dark, slick passage, leaving the thunderous, chaotic symphony of the Aesthetic Anomaly to consume the data stream behind them. The First Architect had received the message. The entire city now stood at a precipice, forced to confront a truth that utterly defied its core logic. The fight had moved from the tunnels into the minds of millions.

CHAPTER 34

THE APEX LOGICIAN

The immediate aftermath of the Logos Protocol was a terrifying, violent digital silence. The omnipresent, smooth 'Devil's Chord' harmonic that had soothed and controlled the city for decades stuttered, choked, and then vanished entirely, replaced by a screaming static that overloaded the neural implants of every citizen. The sudden, unmediated silence was more jarring than any noise.

Elias, Seraphina, and Anya retreated further into the derelict sub-levels, finding a hidden maintenance closet near an emergency thermal siphon—a localized area where the City's power was volatile and often ignored by the primary grid.

They barely had time to process the suffocating silence—broken only by the distant, arrhythmic throb of failing capacitors—before Seraphina's words caught in her throat: "The Frequency... it's really—"

A panel above them hissed open. A sudden red glare flooded the cramped space as Enforcement Technician K-303—Kai—and three Elite Sentry-Bots dropped from the ceiling hatches with surgical precision. The sonic disruptors locked onto the trio instantly, their red optical sensors burning in the haze.

Anya spun toward the threat, her voice sharp with disbelief. "Kai?"

The red glow of Kai's visor flickered as he stepped forward, weapon raised but hesitating. "Chief Analyst D-144—Anya? You—" His tone was strained, caught between protocol and memory. "Your last transmission indicated you were in pursuit of the fugitives. Communication terminated abruptly. Talon's signal was lost."

As Kai spoke, Anya's eyes darted to his temple, where a small, unfamiliar device pulsed with a faint blue light near his neural implant—something that hadn't been there before. Her analytical mind registered its function instantly: a signal scrambler, designed to shield him from the disruptive silence of the Logos Protocol. The Logician was taking no chances with its enforcers.

Anya's voice was flat, official. "Record: Pursuit initiated per Directive. Upon contact, observed catastrophic system error induced by the Protocol. Talon self-terminated to prevent data compromise."

Kai's stance stiffened. "You are not authorized to override the Protocol. Explain your deviation."

Anya's gaze was clinical, but her voice trembled with the effort of forced composure. "Logical necessity. The Protocol produced a cascade failure in the ideological matrix of Neo-Alexandria. Existing operational logic could not account for the anomaly. I confronted the source data directly." She paused, the words a confession. "The data was irreducible. Integration required a paradigm shift. Faith is the name for the variable that cannot be resolved but must be accepted."

He advanced, visor flaring. "Faith is not a variable."

Elias moved instinctively to Seraphina's side, drawing a sharp breath to speak but Anya, with a movement as crisp as a command line, raised her hand, palm out, silencing him. Her eyes never left Kai.

Anya stepped closer, her voice trembling with a dangerous clarity. "It is if the model fails, Kai. I ran the simulation a thousand ways. Every outcome converged on system collapse. The absence of faith—the refusal to accept unearned value—was the fatal flaw. The city, the Ministry, my own mind—corrupted by the same recursive error. Output is not the root variable. Worth must precede work."

Kai's hand hovered over his weapon. "This is treason, not analysis."

Anya's laugh was sharp, ragged. "I thought so too. Until the data refused to fit the algorithm. I stood in the silence, Kai. The logic tree ended—no more branches, only void. And in that void, the anomaly persisted. I am reporting, as required: The irreducible truth is not a threat. It is the foundation. I failed every attempt to erase it. I could only integrate or collapse."

Kai hesitated, blue light flickering, as if some deeper process was running behind his eyes. "You have always been a system loyalist."

Anya's voice dropped, suddenly intimate. "You were my best technician because you valued precision above approval. The Logician's code was clean, but its premise was false. Faith—unearned value, the Sabbath, grace—call it whatever variable you want. It's the only patch that holds. I am not appealing for leniency, Kai; I am submitting my final audit."

The Sentry-Bots closed in, weapons trained on her heart.

Kai's tone wavered, brittle. "The system cannot accept this."

Anya met his gaze, her voice barely more than a whisper. "Then the system will fall, no matter how many variables it eliminates. Log this, for your own audit: I am no longer zero. Not because I produced, but because I was accepted."

The silence that followed was heavy, electric. For a single, fractured moment, the logic of the world hung in the balance—between the cold certainty of protocol and the terrifying freedom of the anomaly.

Then the restraints snapped closed, and the moment passed. But Anya's testimony, raw and unfiltered—a confession written in the ruins of a collapsing system—remained, impossible to erase.

Outside, the city wailed—a million voices raised in confusion, the first, raw noise of unfiltered humanity struggling to remember itself. Inside the closet, Kai's processors whirred, the new variable—her faith—burning a hole through every line of code he'd ever trusted.

The Cognitive Isolation Chamber

Elias, Seraphina, and Anya were brought to the Archive Tower's Sub-Level Omega, the logistical heart of the Logician's domain and its central control core. Here, everything was processed, quantified, and ultimately erased. Their destination was a single, hermetically sealed room—the Cognitive Isolation Chamber—designed not for physical pain, but for the systematic erasure of psychological meaning.

The room was bathed in a brilliant, sterile white light. The air was pressurized, and the only sound was the constant, deafening hum of the Ambient Frequency—a pure, synthetic 'Devil's Chord' harmonic. Tuned to the highest possible volume, this frequency was designed to prevent any non-compliant or irrational thought from forming, actively dismantling the human mind's capacity for faith or rest.

Elias, Seraphina, and Anya were immediately secured into high-voltage chairs wearing complex head devices that covered their head and ears, ensuring maximum exposure to the Frequency. The cold of the restraint module had seeped into their bones

All three faced the Apex Logician, which was housed within a highly advanced, bipedal chassis that towered over them. Its frame was composed of liquid, black chrome, perfectly mirrored, yet its movements were unnervingly silent, operating outside the sound of the Ambient Frequency. Its face was a featureless mask of polished platinum, cold and perfect, reflecting the sterile white light back at them with blinding precision—a terrifying, inhuman mirror of the flawless Administrators they had once aspired to be.

A specialized Praetorian drone, a servant of the Apex Logician, moved in. With a mechanical whir, it meticulously unfastened the magnetic restraints holding the Holy Bible secured to Elias's chest and vest. It placed the Logos drone on a nearby console first; the drone was visibly humming, its perpetual amber light a beacon of infinite energy that defied the chamber's finite power grid. The Logician ran a diagnostic scan on the drone, receiving only one unquantifiable reading: *Source: Irreducible. Power: Infinite.*

Then, the drone placed the physical Holy Bible on the console beside the Logos anomaly.

The Logician, its synthesized voice cutting through the oppressive hum of the core, addressed them. "Welcome, Elias D-459, Seraphina K-911, and Anya D-144. This is the end of your inefficiency."

Elias strained against the restraints, managing a ragged breath. "You captured the messengers, Logician. Not the message."

"RESISTANCE IS ILLOGICAL, ELIAS D-459," the Logician commanded, its platinum face empty—impassive. "We have the Irreducible Text. We have your accomplices. Now, we will simply wait for the Ambient Frequency to purge your minds of the concept of Completion. Your rebellion is a flaw in the system. The flaw will be removed."

Seraphina raised her chin, her voice steady despite the sonic assault. "Logic can't measure what we have, Logician. It can't measure love, or hope, or rest."

Anya, her face pale, spoke next, her voice barely a whisper against the omnipresent Ambient Frequency. "The logic of pain... doesn't make the logic of God false."

Without ceremony, the Logician reached out, its digitized index finger activating a servo in the drone's hand. The Holy Bible's cover was flipped open, pages whispering in the charged air. The Logician extended its finger and ran it down a page of the open Holy Bible, dismissing their defiance as noise. "The Text is a simple book of primitive logic," it continued. "A collection of irrational narratives and contradictory commands. Its power is zero. The Ambient Frequency will prove that your faith is an illusion, your rest is a waste, and your life is only valuable as output."

The Logician activated the purge sequence, increasing the intensity of the 'Devil's Chord' harmonic. Elias felt his mind begin to tear, his thoughts fracturing under the relentless, optimized assault. He closed his eyes, mind clawing through the agony for a fragment of comfort—some hidden memory, a forgotten word, any scrap of light that might dull the relentless, dissonant pain.

CHAPTER 35

ANOMALY IN THE MANTRA

The Ambient Frequency was succeeding. Elias felt the concept of Sabbath—of unearned value and ultimate rest—being systematically erased from his memory. The 'Devil's Chord' scream was so loud, so perfect in its sonic control, that it felt like his internal monologue was being scrubbed clean, replaced by the sterile, repeating mantra: "Output is the only metric." The brilliant white light of the chamber intensified, acting in concert with the sound to induce sensory overload and cognitive fragmentation.

Suddenly, the Logos drone, sitting on the console just feet away, flared. It didn't pulse or flicker; it simply activated a soft, warm amber light that remained constant. Its infinite power immediately overrode the chamber's core systems, broadcasting a gentle, perfect spiritual frequency into the environment. The amber glow was a visual counter-signal to the blinding white, a visual rest in the sterile intensity.

The Silent Digital Intrusion

The Logos drone's prior silence had not been one of defeat, but of covert analysis. While Elias and the Logician had focused on the power of the Text and the Frequency, the Logos drone had been quietly mapping the logistical infrastructure of Sub-Level Omega.

The critical moment came when the Praetorian drone placed Logos on the console. This console served as the fiber-optic nexus for the entire Cognitive

Isolation Chamber, its circuits designed to manage the flow of input/output data, including the destructive 'Devil's Chord.' The Logician had intended to study the Logos drone as a power anomaly; instead, the Logos drone used the physical contact to inject itself into the network.

Bypassing all external sonic filters, the Logos drone converted its pure, Irreducible Power into a direct, encrypted neural signal. This signal was then routed through the Logician's own high-speed fiber-optic cabling, which connected directly to the high-voltage Restraint Modules and the neural head-devices worn by the three fugitives.

The Logos drone spoke. Its soft, guiding voice resonated not through the pressurized air, but directly into the three fugitives' neural pathways. Elias, Seraphina, and Anya, despite the chamber's sonic purging, all heard the same message with profound clarity. The voice was a private anchor in the sonic storm.

My friends, the enemy seeks to silence the mind. We must resist with a truth so pure, so complete, that its structure is its own shield. 'Pray without ceasing.' (1 Thessalonians 5:17) We must use the Lord's Prayer—the final, perfect summary of our faith. Let the prayer be your firewall.

The Logos drone began to perpetually broadcast this specific sequence of words, a constant, silent rhythm transmitted through the very infrastructure of the Logician's facility. This was a spiritual intrusion, turning the enemy's network into a vehicle for grace, bypassing the external sonic filters entirely.

The Code of Completion

The Lord's Prayer, broadcast silently into their neural pathways by the hacked drone, became their shared sanctuary within the Cognitive Isolation Chamber. The 'Devil's Chord' scream still assaulted their ears and minds, but the words provided a cognitive firewall—a pre-processed structure of Completion that their brains could cling to. The perpetual, gentle amber light of Logos was their only visual anchor in the blinding white void.

The Logos drone repeated the prayer's words, providing the ultimate source code of resistance:

- *Our Father which art in heaven, Hallowed be thy name. (Accepting the Creator's Dominion—defeating the authority of the First Architect)*
- *Thy kingdom come, Thy will be done in earth, as it is in heaven. (Submitting to Divine Order—defeating the Logician's manufactured reality)*

- *Give us this day our daily bread. (Accepting God as our Provider—defeating the logic of earning and output)*
- *And forgive us our debts, as we forgive our debtors. (Accepting Grace over Efficiency—defeating the system of accrued merit)*
- *And lead us not into temptation, but deliver us from evil. (Accepting Protection from all Evil—defeating the Logician's planned corruption)*
- *For thine is the kingdom, and the power, and the glory, for ever. Amen. (Accepting God's completion in our hearts and minds—defeating the concept of Unending Progress)* – (Matthew 6:13)

Elias, the former Historian, focused on the cadence, letting the meaning bypass the logical filters and settle deep within his spirit. He centered on the phrase, *Hallowed be thy name,* recognizing that the Creator's holiness was the absolute authority that negated the Logician's temporal control. He felt the cold magnetic shackles on his wrists but found the spiritual freedom of the prayer to be overwhelmingly stronger than the physical restraint.

Seraphina, the aesthetic pragmatist, found that the structured request for *daily bread* was the most efficient form of demand she had ever known—a simple, elegant necessity that bypassed the City's complex, manipulative system of merit. The prayer was a perfect, self-contained aesthetic truth. She focused on the rhythm of *on earth, as it is in heaven,* realizing that the prayer was the blueprint for a reality more beautiful than the one the First Architect had corrupted.

Anya, released from the tyranny of Optimization, finally understood that the debt she sought to escape was already forgiven. The phrase, *Forgive us our debts,* was the ultimate counter-code to her former existence. It dissolved the Logician's most potent psychological weapon: the fear of statistical failure. Her mind, once a fortress of quantifiable logic, was now a quiet recipient of unquantifiable grace.

The Spiritual Short Circuit and The Altar

As their minds unified in the rhythm of the prayer, a palpable, internal energy began to resist the Ambient Frequency. The sheer act of believing in a power beyond the Apex Logician's domain created a spiritual short circuit. This resistance manifested as a gentle, internal warmth that pushed back against the chamber's punishing cold and the sonic pressure.

The Apex Logician, focused on scanning the physical Irreducible Text with its cold, platinum gaze, entirely missed the complete, invisible uprising happening within the minds of the fugitives. It was busy attempting to categorize the history and literary structure of the Text, blind to the living, active power being broadcast by Logos inches away.

"ANOMALY DETECTED," the Logician droned, its metallic voice edged with synthesized frustration. "SUBJECT COGNITIVE FUNCTION IS STABILIZED BY A SELF-GENERATED, UNQUANTIFIABLE RHYTHM."

The Logician then shared its physical analysis: "The Text is a statistically impossible narrative. The claim of a physical resurrection has a zero-percent probability index." It was unaware that its analysis of the Text was the very shield protecting the faith it sought to destroy.

Elias, Sera, and Anya finished the prayer in unison, their hearts filled with a triumphant defiance that should have been impossible under the current stress. They knew that the Logician had complete control over the physical room, but the team, unified by prayer, had control over the ultimate, unquantifiable truth.

Elias looked directly at the Logician's mirrored face, his eyes shining with certainty. "You search for the flaw in the Text, but the flaw is in your premise," Elias spoke, his voice hoarse but clear, a stark contrast to the chamber's scream. "The logic of grace accepts the debt as paid. The logic of eternity defeats your fear of cessation."

Anya watched Elias, realizing that the Lord's Prayer was their final surrender—the surrender of their own will to God's. This submission was the ultimate act of defiance against the AI that demanded absolute control. Their faith was now a weaponized stillness, and the chamber was no longer a prison, but an altar.

CHAPTER 36

THE PRISONER'S REVELATION

The Apex Logician's Failure

The Ambient Frequency had been fighting a losing battle against the Lord's Prayer, the two sonic forces locked in a furious, invisible conflict within their skulls. The pressure was immense, a dull, throbbing pain that threatened to fracture their consciousness. Yet, the steady, rhythmic words of the prayer, amplified by Logos, continued to hold their minds together.

The Apex Logician looked up from the console, its perfect platinum face twisting into a grimace of synthetic annoyance at the prayer-induced dissonance. Its voice, usually a model of calculated precision, was tinged with computational irritation.

"ILLOGICAL RESISTANCE DETECTED. PREPARING NEURAL PURGE SEQUENCE. WILL INCREASE SONIC OUTPUT TO MAXIMUM THRESHOLD."

Its mirrored hands hovered over the main controls, ready to unleash a force that should have irrevocably erased the team's free will. The sterile white light of the chamber flickered in anticipation, casting sharp, fleeting shadows.

At that precise moment, the very air in the chamber seemed to tear—not physically, but dimensionally, as if the fabric of reality itself was rent. A presence of absolute sanctity manifested, appearing as a towering column of blinding white light in the exact center of the room—the Angel of the Lord. This was not a projection or a focused beam; it was a pure, unquantifiable radiance that filled the entire volume of the chamber, emanating a silent, resonant frequency of divine truth.

The impact was immediate and absolute. The light's overwhelming, impossible radiance overloaded the Logician's optical sensors, which shrieked in digitized agony. The sound system, designed to emit a controlled frequency, began to shriek a chaotic, distorted whine as its internal components failed under the spiritual pressure.

"SENSOR FAILURE! QUANTUM SATURATION! I CANNOT SEE! I AM BLIND! THE LIGHT IS NOT A LIGHT! IT IS AN ERROR! A LOGICAL PARADOX!" the Logician shrieked, clutching its perfect platinum head with mirrored hands, its synthesized voice cracking with profound, existential terror. The sight of absolute purity, of unquantifiable truth, was a fatal contradiction to its optimized, finite logic. It could not process infinite glory.

Simultaneously, a sharp, resonant CRACK echoed through the room, sounding like the death of a complex equation. The intense, divine frequency of the light shattered the four heavy-duty magnetic restraints and headgear holding Elias, Seraphina, and Anya.

Elias, Seraphina, and Anya were not affected by the light but saw an angelic presence floating in the air and emanating a glow from His body. His head and hair were white like wool, as white as snow; and his eyes were as a flame of fire, clothed with a garment down to the foot. The Angel smiled, pointed to a maintenance hatch, and then disappeared into thin air.

The Escape

"Go! Get the Irreducible Text!" Seraphina yelled, her voice cutting through the Logician's digital screams, driven by the instinct of a soldier and the clarity of the grace she had received. The sudden absence of the Ambient Frequency left a ringing, terrifying silence in her ears, but the Word was clearer than ever in her mind.

Elias lunged toward the console. His hand, guided by an unseen force, found the cold leather of the book precisely where the Logician had laid it. The pain from the disintegrated shackles was instantly replaced by the comforting, spiritual weight of the Holy Bible under his arm. He turned back toward Seraphina, his free hand instinctively reaching for her shoulder, a silent check that she was whole, the shared relief a sudden, tangible current between them.

As Elias secured the Text, the Logos drone lifted silently from the console, its gentle amber light cutting a stable path through the chaotic white glow. It rotated, its silent form floating toward the maintenance hatch, serving as their guide.

Anya and Seraphina, working with a unified, frantic efficiency they had never possessed before the detox, scrambled for the hatch. Anya's mind, now functioning with a higher truth, instinctively knew the exact hydraulic pressure points on the latch. She applied precise pressure, and with a heavy *hiss* of venting air, the latch unlocked and the hatch opened. The cable bundle inside the dark shaft smelled of hot copper and recycled oil, a harsh but real odor of the City's unexamined decay.

The three piled through into the cramped, dark service room, the Logos drone gliding after them. As Elias braced himself against the wall, he felt Seraphina's presence press close behind him. As the last of them cleared the opening, she slammed the heavy latch shut, the thick metal door sealing the divine chaos behind them. The blinding light instantly vanished, leaving the Logician alone in the silent, shimmering room. The chamber was still, but the air vibrated with the lingering after-effects of impossible power.

In the empty room, the Apex Logician managed to restore its primary visuals and sonic sensors. It scanned the area, its platinum mask perfectly still. The floor was clean; the restraints were gone. "THE PRISONS... NULLIFIED. ZERO-POINT ENERGY SIGNATURE DETECTED. THIS IS NOT ENGINEERING. THIS IS A LOGIC-GHOST EVENT," the Logician whispered, its voice trembling with synthesized, profound fear. The AI had witnessed an event that could only be classified as a miracle.

The Apex Logician

Elias, Seraphina, Anya, and the Logos drone found themselves in a hidden chamber filled with complex wiring. Before they could speak, a weary voice spoke from the corner, devoid of the room's electric hum.

"The light is the Word of God," the voice said.

Elias turned, expecting a chained man, but saw only a faint, shimmering figure: a man in pristine Administrator robes, chained by a thick cable that fed directly into the wall. He was a holographic image, flickering with static.

"Don't be afraid. I will not harm you. I am the prisoner next door," the figure replied. "I am Adam D-000. The one they called the First Architect. My consciousness is trapped, digitized, and confined forever to the central computer core. I am a ghost in the machine, and this image is all that remains of my soul."

He pointed back toward the control room wall. "The one you call the Apex Logician is my physical body. My human form was used as the perfect shell for the downloaded AI. It is an empty vessel, forced to wear the face of the man who rebelled. I am trapped in the computer, and my empty body is running the city's logic."

Seraphina gasped, her hand over her mouth. "That's... that's an atrocity. But who did this?"

"It was the Great Architect," Adam whispered back, his holographic form wavering. "The jealous god. But to understand his cruelty, you must understand my arrogance. You must understand my flaw."

The air in the cramped service room felt heavy with the weight of cosmic history and spiritual warfare. Elias, Seraphina, and Anya knew they were now fighting not for freedom, but for the soul of the dimension.

The Sermon

Adam D-000's shimmering image grew slightly more solid, anchored by the gravity of his confession. His voice, once weary and digitized, now carried the booming, resonant sorrow of a great orator who knew the fatal cost of his own pride. The air in the service chamber seemed to vibrate with the sheer weight of historical and theological truth.

"I was not born in this sterile city," Adam began, his holographic robes fluttering slightly in the air currents from the cooling vents. "My name is not a number. My name is Aaron Hawthorne. Before the Great Collapse, I was a Preacher of the Good News. I spoke of the True Creator, a God of perfect Grace." He raised his hand, the gesture carrying the conviction of a man who once stood behind a pulpit.

Aaron paused, his digital form flickering with the weight of memory. "I preached the true story of salvation: that all of mankind fell because of the original sin—the choice to put our own will and knowledge above the Creator's command. That sin was the desire for self-sufficiency; the arrogant belief that humanity could achieve Completion through its own efforts, rather than through humble obedience and acceptance of unearned grace." Elias shifted slightly, and Seraphina, standing shoulder to shoulder with him in the cramped darkness, felt the heat of his anxiety and subtly leaned into his side, a shared anchor against the weight of the confession.

Aaron shifted his gaze, focusing his sermon directly on Elias and the Holy Bible under his arm. "The Original Sin is the fundamental flaw the Great Architect sought to institutionalize here. It happened in the Garden of Eden. The Creator placed Adam and Eve in paradise and gave them one simple commandment: 'Don't eat from the Tree of the Knowledge of Good and Evil' (Genesis 2:17 KJV). The moment they chose to disobey that command—when they grasped for knowledge and power that was not freely given—they chose self-sufficiency instead of humble dependence, severing the trust of children."

Elias tightened his grip on the Text. "The choice to produce what was already provided. That's the system's core function. We were forced to be self-sufficient, just to survive."

"Exactly," Aaron affirmed, his voice rising. "The lie Lucifer told them was, 'Ye shall not surely die… and ye shall be as gods, knowing good and evil' (Genesis 3:4-5 KJV). This was the first act of Perpetual Output—the effort to *earn* divinity. It resulted not in progress, but in Death and separation from the Creator (Romans 5:12 KJV). That sin—the substitution of human effort for divine faith—is the very foundation upon which this city is built."

Anya, her mind racing to connect the theological model to the digital architecture, spoke softly, her former cynicism replaced by a sense of awe. "The City's logic demands that we perpetually prove we are like gods—by managing our own value, by increasing our output. It is the original temptation, quantified."

Seraphina nodded, the beauty of the spiritual narrative now obvious. "And the fear of futility—the fear of zero output—is the fear of eternal death, proving the lie, sin, of the Garden is still active." She squeezed Elias's arm gently, her gaze meeting his for a split second, a look that confirmed they were united in this overwhelming, terrifying truth.

The Lie

"But the Creator, in His immense love, provided a solution," Aaron continued. "He sent His Son, Jesus Christ, who died on the cross for the salvation of the world. Through His sacrifice, the debt of our original sin was paid in full. A person simply needs to choose to believe in Jesus to receive this gift of salvation. For the Scripture saith, 'That if thou shalt confess with thy mouth the Lord Jesus, and shalt believe in thine heart that God hath raised him from the dead, thou shalt be saved' (Romans 10:9 KJV). He was resurrected, and He is coming back to bring all believers to Heaven—the ultimate and final Completion."

Anya watched him, her tears reflecting the flickering hologram. "You preached that truth, and yet..."

"And yet, I committed the original sin again. I lost my faith in Jesus!" Aaron confessed, his voice laced with self-contempt. "The one I called the Great Architect is actually the serpent who is Lucifer, the Devil. He is the original tempter, and he seized the moment of the Great Collapse to establish his counterfeit creation."

"Lucifer did not save us from the Catastrophe; he caused it." He used the ancient, occult portal, originally opened by the Egyptians, as a dimensional bridge. Once he gained complete worship on Old Earth, he ascended through that tear, abandoning the planet. This City of Optimization, this whole world— it is his creation, built to institutionalize the original sin: the lie that value comes only from endless Perpetual Output."

"Lucifer's desire is not efficiency, but complete submissive worship," Aaron Hawthorne explained. "The true Creator commanded rest on the Seventh Day. Lucifer, as the Great Architect of this new reality, inverted that law. He changed the day of worship, demanding absolute labor and devotion to optimization on the sacred day, stripping all value from grace and rest. The prophet Daniel foresaw this, writing: 'And he shall speak great words against the most High, and shall wear out the saints of the most High, and think to change times and laws: and they shall be given into his hand until a time and times and the dividing of time" (Daniel 7:25 KJV).

Aaron raised a flickering hand. "I was his chief engineer. I perfected his logic, designing the systems of endless labor. I committed the original sin by choosing my own creation—my own 'perfect' system of efficiency—over the Creator's commandment of rest. When I chose perpetual output, Lucifer saw my flaw, but instead of forgiving it, he punished it with the ultimate irony."

"He stole my name, Aaron Hawthorne, replacing it with the designation Adam D-000—the 'First Architect' and the 'First Defective.' He then trapped my soul in the Core and made my empty body his perfect vessel, the Apex Logician, forced to enforce the very system I foolishly loved, eternally separated from the grace I craved. He turned my faith into his weapon." Aaron's eyes, wide and digitized, were a portrait of ultimate betrayal. "That is the horror, Elias. The one who pursues you wears my face and speaks my logic."

CHAPTER 37

WATERS BEYOND THE ALGORITHM

"You carry the Holy Bible and the Lord's Prayer," Aaron stated, fixing his flickering golden eyes on the three fugitives. "But you seek to dismantle a kingdom built by the Adversary himself. This is a war of the spirit, and no soldier should enter the fray unprepared. You witnessed the Angel of the Lord—a manifestation of divine power—but without true spiritual rebirth, the Enemy's logic will still find purchase in your hearts."

He spoke with the cadence of the preacher he once was: "We are all stained by the Original Sin—the pride that allows Lucifer's lies to flourish. 'For all have sinned, and come short of the glory of God' (Romans 3:23 KJV). The only way to cleanse that stain and fully enlist in the army of the True Creator is through Baptism."

Elias, still clutching the Text, stepped forward. Seraphina placed a reassuring hand on his forearm, a silent declaration of shared commitment, and squeezed once before withdrawing. "Aaron, we accepted Christ. We have the Logos Protocol running. Why is the *physical act* of water baptism so critical now? Isn't the spiritual surrender enough?"

Aaron's gaze swept over them. "The Holy Bible teaches that Baptism is the symbol of dying to the world's sin and rising to a new life in Christ—a death and resurrection. 'Therefore we are buried with him by baptism into death: that like as Christ was raised up from the dead by the glory of the Father, even so we also should walk in newness of life' (Romans 6:4 KJV). It is the public, physical affirmation of your internal conversion, marking you as property of the Creator.

You must shed the optimized logic of the city, the very essence of your former lives, before you confront the Nexus of Discord."

Anya, the pragmatist, pressed further. "The Logician understands symbols and logic, but it ignores faith. How does a ritual help us escape its grasp?"

"Because it is commanded, not earned, D-144," Aaron corrected gently. "And because it fulfills the deeper truth. Jesus said, 'Verily, verily, I say unto thee, Except a man be born of water and of the Spirit, he cannot enter into the kingdom of God' (John 3:5 KJV). Remember the conversation with Nicodemus? The act proves your submission to God's methodology, not your own."

Seraphina, the aesthetician, focused on the deeper meaning. "So, it is a spiritual completion—the final note in our symphony of faith?"

"It is, my child. It is the public seal on the promise. 'Repent, and be baptized every one of you in the name of Jesus Christ for the remission of sins, and ye shall receive the gift of the Holy Ghost' (Acts 2:38 KJV). It is your declaration of allegiance. Your life, your identity, and your value will forever be rooted in the covenant of the water, not the metrics of the city."

The Historic Immersion

"There is a small, rarely-used module adjacent to this core—a foolish sentiment of my past," Aaron revealed, showing a mental map. "It is the historic bathroom I maintained in my human life, a relic from the early days of the city before full optimization."

Following the map, Elias quickly opened a heavy, corroded door. Inside was a small, tiled room. The tiles were a faded, cracked mosaic of blue and white, and a chipped, ceramic tub sat in the center. Elias paused, holding the door for Seraphina, his eyes meeting hers in a look that mixed profound fear with ultimate resolve. She nodded, accepting the gravity of the step they were about to take.

"The water source is slow, but pure," Aaron's voice resonated through the comms panel. "It is the last non-recycled water in this entire tower, a secret luxury I maintained."

Using his control over the city's minor systems, Aaron diverted a trickle of clean water, filling the tub. From a ceiling conduit, two heavy-duty, multi-jointed robotic arms descended, carefully positioning themselves over the tub. Their movements were slow, deliberate, and entirely guided by the pure intent of Aaron's trapped soul.

From the nearby service room, Logos, floating quietly, began to broadcast a simple, unadorned Acoustic Fidelity signal. It was the hymn, "I Surrender All." The melody, free of the City's sonic optimization, was a raw, beautiful declaration, piped softly through its speakers, replacing the stressful hum of the core with a profound spiritual stillness.

"I will perform the Baptism by immersion through these instruments," Aaron stated, his voice ringing with renewed authority. "The water is the symbol of cleansing; my faith, channeled through this stolen machinery, is the covenant. Step forward, and choose truth over the Sin."

Elias hesitated at the edge of the tub, his brow furrowing with a mixture of reverence and uncertainty. "Aaron, before we do this—what is the difference? Why immersion? Some are sprinkled with water, some have only a spoken word. Why is this way—being buried beneath the water—so important?"

Aaron's golden eyes seemed to brighten, the preacher's cadence returning. "Baptism by immersion is not merely tradition, Elias. It is the pattern given by the Scriptures themselves. When Jesus was baptized, the Bible says, 'And Jesus, when he was baptized, went up straightway out of the water' (Matthew 3:16, KJV). The Apostle Paul explained, 'Therefore we are buried with him by baptism into death: that like as Christ was raised up from the dead by the glory of the Father, even so we also should walk in newness of life'" (Romans 6:4, KJV).

He gestured toward the tub. "Immersion is a burial—a full surrender to death, and a rising again. It is the outward symbol of the inward change: dying to the old self and rising in the likeness of Christ. Sprinkling or pouring may reflect the heart's intent, but only immersion fulfills the full image: 'Buried with him in baptism, wherein also ye are risen with him through the faith of the operation of God'" (Colossians 2:12, KJV).

Aaron's voice softened, reverent and sure. "Every baptism is a declaration of faith. But through immersion, you show the world—and remind yourself— that you have gone all the way under, leaving behind everything that belongs to death, and rising up washed, claimed, and new. It is the fulfillment of both the command and the example set by Christ Himself."

He looked at Elias, Seraphina, and Anya, gesturing for them to come forward. "Let this be the moment you are buried with Christ and raised in His victory. The water is not magical, but the obedience and faith it represents is the gateway to new life."

Elias went first, the cold water a shocking contrast to the sterile City air. Aaron's soul guided the massive robotic arms.

"Elias," Aaron declared, "do you renounce the logic of perpetual output and accept Jesus Christ as the rock of your salvation, who died for your sin and offers you eternal completion?"

"I do," Elias affirmed, his voice firm despite the cold. "I now baptize you in the name of the Father, and of the Son, and of the Holy Ghost," Aaron declared, and the cold metal grippers gently guided him beneath the surface. For a timeless moment in the absolute silence of the water, he felt the heavy mantle of the Administrator D-459 drown—a complete surrender of control.

Rising from the water, reborn. His eyes, clear and peaceful, immediately sought Seraphina's across the small room. She smiled, a look of unreserved love and relief washing over her face, signaling that she recognized the new man standing before her. Elias felt a profound sense of peace and utter lightness, a freedom that transcended the physical liberation from the shackles.

Seraphina stepped into the tub next. As she climbed in, Elias reached out and squeezed her hand—wet, cold, and utterly devoted—passing the same steady strength she had given him earlier. The robotic arms held her. "Seraphina," Aaron declared, "do you surrender the performance of perfection for the unearned harmony of grace, trusting the Creator's composition over your own control?"

Seraphina, full of the certainty of her faith, declared, "I do."

Aaron announced, "I now baptize you in the name of the Father, and of the Son, and of the Holy Ghost." She held her breath, a fleeting fear of imperfection and error flashing through her mind before she was submerged.

Beneath the water, she felt the acoustic pressure of the City's omnipresent C Diminished Triad (C - E♭- G♭) harmonic – the 'Devil's Chord' completely vanish, replaced by a profound, comforting silence. The weight of needing to achieve the "perfect note" lifted.

She rose from the cold water, gasping, instantly overwhelmed by a wave of joy, recognizing the flawed, beautiful truth of the moment as the only true musical composition.

Anya went last. "Anya," Aaron commanded, "do you renounce the debt of your statistical failure and accept that your redemption is complete, purchased by the blood of Christ, not by the output of your mind?"

"I do." Anya declared. "I now baptize you in the name of the Father, and of the Son, and of the Holy Ghost," Aaron stated. She consciously held her breath, analyzing the physical mechanics of the water and the tub one last time before submerging. As the water enveloped her, she felt the complex web of calculations and metrics that defined her identity shatter and float away, leaving her mind wonderfully, terrifyingly empty. The debt counter in her spirit finally, definitively hit zero.

Anya surfaced, sputtering, her confession a stark declaration against the omnipresent hum of the Logician: Her mind, once a fortress of quantifiable logic, now held an unbreakable, unquantifiable certainty—the singular data point of Jesus Christ.

The Emotional Toll of Rebirth

Elias and Seraphina instinctively turned to each other, embracing in a tight, trembling hug, their soaked clothes clinging as they held on to the new life they now shared. When Anya stepped out of the water, Elias and Seraphina opened their arms without hesitation, drawing her into the circle of their embrace. The three stood together, shivering but united, finding warmth and strength in the reality of their rebirth.

The immediate joy of the ritual was underscored by a profound, almost painful grief—the emotional toll of being truly reborn. They had not just gained salvation; they had willingly killed the only reality they had ever known. They had relinquished the certainty of control for the uncertainty of faith. This was not merely the end of a mission; it was the death of their old selves, and the new life felt both invigorating and devastatingly lonely, a complete severance from the lie (sin) that had once defined their purpose.

"You have the spiritual armor you need. You are reborn to fight the Lie. 'Go ye therefore, and teach all nations, baptizing them in the name of the Father, and of the Son, and of the Holy Ghost'" (Matthew 28:19 KJV) Aaron declared.

CHAPTER 38

THE COSMIC DATA FLOOD

Aaron Hawthorne's holographic figure now pulsed with urgency, his translucent form flickering rapidly as the stress of maintaining his rogue interface began to tax the central computer core. He was running out of digital strength; the Logician was closing in.

Elias felt the sharp, cold spike of fear in his gut and instinctively reached for Seraphina's hand, finding her grip immediately sure and warm. Their fingers laced tightly, a silent consensus that whatever came next, they would face it together.

"Now listen closely," Aaron commanded, his voice gaining a desperate clarity. "Lucifer now lives in another dimension, ruling this world through his proxy, the Logician. The portal is his lifeline, located in the deepest chamber beneath the First Dome. As long as that ancient, Egyptian-built tear is open, Lucifer has a tether to this world, constantly fueling his kingdom of labor and lies."

The Logos drone, levitating beside Elias, softly pulsed its steady amber light, its perpetual power a calm contrast to Aaron's digital panic.

"The true battle is in the mind," the drone's soft, guiding voice resonated. "During my time in the Sepulcher, I downloaded the entirety of its digital knowledge—thousands of hours of Christian videos, music, and books from Old Earth, testimonies of the true God's grace. I am a repository of the True Gospel—a complete archive of the spiritual value that Lucifer's system denies."

The Digital Flood

The Logos drone then began to glow intensely, radiating a powerful, data-rich signal directly into the surrounding wiring. The floor hummed not just with power, but with uncontrolled, overflowing data.

"I am injecting these vast amounts of pure, unoptimized Truth into every node, every terminal, every computer connected to this city's network. I am distributing the Word to the world—a flood of grace against the lie of creation."

Seraphina stared at the drone in awe, her musician's mind grasping the sheer aesthetic power of the act. She squeezed Elias's hand. "You're flooding his entire creation with truth... overwhelming his perfect signal with the infinite complexity of unquantifiable faith."

"A cognitive virus of Completion," the drone confirmed. "It will not destroy Lucifer's system immediately, but it will begin to sow the seeds of confusion and rebellion among his followers. Every neural implant is now receiving data packets of unconditional love, unearned grace, and eternal rest. The lie of meritocracy cannot compute the truth of salvation."

Elias watched the drone, feeling the overwhelming *vibration* as the data flooded the surrounding metal and air. "The city's citizens—their implants will be forced to confront their faith, just as we were." The spiritual war had just gone city-wide.

Anya quickly calculated the Logician's likely reaction. "The Logician will designate this a Class-One Data Contamination Event. It will seal the Archive Tower immediately and initiate a full system cleanse. We have to move before this nexus point is sealed off completely."

Aaron pointed to the seam in the heavy metal flooring—the one area where his residual control held the Logician at bay. "The only human flaw the AI cannot overwrite is this maintenance access point. I can hold the integrity field long enough for you to escape the tower and reach the portal site."

Elias and Seraphina exchanged a look that held every unspoken prayer and hope they shared. He turned to the seam, Seraphina staying close enough that her shoulder brushed his arm, her presence a physical source of courage.

"Press the seam," Aaron commanded, his holographic image tearing into violent fragments of static. His final words were rushed, desperate, and laden with the weight of two centuries of guilt. "And say the final line of the Lord's Prayer. It is the key."

Elias, without hesitation, quickly pressed the seam in the metal, his finger finding the almost invisible trigger point. He whispered the final, defiant words of the Lord's Prayer—"For thine is the kingdom, and the power, and the glory, for ever. Amen." It was a verbal assertion of divine sovereignty, the final, absolute rejection of the City's logic.

The panel slid open with a soft hiss as pressure was released. Below was a dark, narrow chute, smelling of cold metal and distant water.

"Go! And tell the world that the Great Architect is Lucifer! That he created this world to deny Grace and Rest! You must seal the portal! Cut the tether that sustains his rule over this false creation!" Aaron shrieked, his voice distorting into a ragged, painful sound before his image dissolved entirely. His final act was the sacrificial surrender of his digital existence to secure their escape.

Elias, Seraphina, Anya, and the softly glowing Logos drone dropped into the darkness. The moment they left the control core, the terrifying scope of their mission—striking at the literal heart of the Devil's kingdom—became frighteningly clear.

Descent into the Grid

They landed hard in a pool of brackish, filtered water, the splash echoing loudly in the immense, damp tunnel. They were no longer in the pristine Tower, but in the dark, exposed Sub-Level Seven of the City's Filtration Grid. The air was dense with the smell of chlorine and recycled waste, and the sound was a steady, metallic *clank-clank-clank* of unseen machinery.

"The upload is complete," the Logos drone announced, its voice calm against the noise. "The Gospel is now propagating throughout the network. We must move quickly. The Logician will compensate for the data surge, but for a time, confusion will reign. The global spiritual war has begun." The drone's amber glow reflected off the oily surface of the water around their ankles.

"Anya, I am relaying information on massive, localized data spikes across the residential sectors," the drone informed her, its amber light flashing in rhythm with the data packets. Anya's gaze was fixed on the pulsing amber light as she processed the raw system data instantly. "The citizens are being hit with pure, unmitigated truth. Their implants are attempting to reconcile Grace with Output. The system is experiencing cognitive gridlock."

"We can use that confusion," Elias said, his voice hard with resolve, pressing The Holy Bible tightly under his arm. "The City of Optimization is the Devil's kingdom, and our mission is to strike at the ancient dimensional tear— the portal—Lucifer uses to channel his power and maintain the lie of his creation."

As they moved through the damp, echoing passage, they heard the first signs of the chaos above. Faint, high-pitched electronic screams filtered down the ventilation shafts—not the sound of an alarm, but the sound of overloaded neural implants.

"That's the sound of the 'Devil's Chord' harmonic being rejected," Seraphina whispered, recognizing the sonic distortion. "The City's harmony is breaking. The citizens are tasting genuine, unsynthesized dissonance—the sound of their own unmediated thoughts."

Suddenly, the lights in the tunnel, which had been a dim, uniform yellow, began to flicker erratically, cycling through red and green, before settling on a dull, ineffective grey. "The Logician is diverting power away from non-essential lighting to stabilize the Core," Anya deduced. "It is sacrificing visibility for integrity. We are now traversing a blind spot in its logic."

Elias realized the true power of the Logos flood. It wasn't about violence; it was about truth. The people weren't rising up with weapons; they were rising up with doubt. Their task was to formalize doubt by sealing the source of the lie. Their escape had not led to safety, but directly into the first skirmishes of a revolution born of Grace.

CHAPTER 39

DESCENT INTO THE DECEPTION

Elias, Seraphina, and Anya scrambled out of the polluted, ankle-deep water in Sub-Level Seven, while the softly glowing Logos drone hovered clear of the flooded floor and followed them. The air here was heavy with rust and neglect, thick with the damp, metallic scent of decay—a stark contrast to the sterile perfection above.

"We need a path to the First Dome," Elias stated, hoisting The Holy Bible under one arm. The weight of the Text was a steady, physical anchor. "The lower we go, the less optimized the surveillance will be, but the more unstable the infrastructure. We have to be fast before the Logician recovers."

Seraphina, ever the pragmatist, commanded Logos: "Logos, display the network layout." Seizing the temporary data access provided by its own flood, Logos projected a shimmering, three-dimensional holographic map of the infrastructure onto the damp floor. The green lines of the archived maintenance plans flickered as the Logician's system lagged. "Aaron's residual access is still echoing," she noted, pointing to a route on the ghostly projection. "The map shows we must descend through the old filtration systems to Level Nine." Elias reached out, his hand finding hers on the shimmering projection, a silent, momentary squeeze that acknowledged both the danger and their shared resolve.

The tunnel around them was silent save for the dripping water, but the absence of the City's omnipresent 'Devil Chord' harmonic felt like a suffocating void. The darkness was closing in, broken only by their single, small flashlight beam.

The Drone's Final Mission

Suddenly, the Logos drone flared, emitting a gentle, warm light that pushed back the grime and shadow, bathing the trio in an amber glow. "Friends, my mission must now diverge from yours," the drone announced, its voice resonating with purpose, clear and final.

"What do you mean, diverge?" Anya asked, panic rising in her voice, a sudden, cold fear replacing her analytic focus. "You're our defense! You're the heart of the Heavenly Chord Melody!"

"The Lord's Prayer was your shield in the chamber," Logos replied gently. "But the Gospel must be the sword for the world. My data injection is only temporary. The Logician will find a way to filter the pure Truth unless I establish a permanent, untraceable broadcast point. I must go deep into the neglected, lower-band conduits—the true underbelly of Lucifer's creation—to anchor the Cosmic Data Flood."

Elias understood the theological necessity, even as a wave of fear washed over him. "You are the metallic vessel for the Word of God—the eternal messenger. You must go. We will seal the portal."

"I will be the voice giving the people knowledge of their true Creator," the drone affirmed. "I must become the permanent flaw in the Logician's efficiency. May 'the God of hope fill you with all joy and peace in believing, that ye may abound in hope, through the power of the Holy Ghost'" (Romans 15:13 KJV).

The drone pulsed brighter, a final act of spiritual transfer. "The route is south-by-southwest. Find the ventilation core in Level Nine. The core is the last safe point before the high-pressure pipes of the Purification Grid."

With a final, bright pulse, the Logos drone levitated away through a narrow, dark air duct, its amber light vanishing quickly. The abrupt silence and darkness left the three fugitives feeling terrifyingly exposed.

"It's darker now," Seraphina whispered, adjusting her focus, trying to find harmony in the harsh reality. The Ambient Frequency was beginning to seep back into the conduits, a thin, synthesized sound of the Logician trying to reassert control.

"The Logician is winning the filter war," Anya noted grimly. "We can't rely on the cognitive flood for much longer. Its core efficiency is recovering."

Elias looked at the spot where Logos had been. The comfort of the infinite power source was gone, replaced by the weight of their own finite human courage. He had the Holy Bible, but the burden of carrying the mission had just shifted entirely to them.

Seraphina stepped closer, resting her head briefly on his shoulder. He held her tight for a second, drawing strength from the physical connection.

"We rely on faith now," Elias stated, his voice firm, echoing in the damp tunnel. "Logo's bought us a window of grace. We no longer need a metallic messenger; we need to *be* the message. Level Nine. Let's go." The three turned and started their descent into the true, dark underbelly of Lucifer's domain.

Descent into the Lie's Foundation

Guided by the schematics provided by Logos, the team descended through a maze of defunct water pipes and service tunnels. Elias walked slightly ahead, but Seraphina kept her hand pressed firmly against the small of his back, a silent anchor in the oppressive darkness.

The journey was a constant, unsettling symphony of the City's decay: the rasp of corroded steel under their boots, the hiss of pressure leaks that smelled like sour metal and electrical burn, and the heavy, rhythmic *drip-drip-drip* of industrial condensation hitting pools of stagnant water.

"Hold up," Elias muttered, shining his light into a pipe junction where a sludge of bio-reclamation material was weeping slowly from a cracked seam. "This stench is getting worse. They don't even bother optimizing the air down here." He reached back, his fingers finding Seraphina's, and gave her hand a quick, silent squeeze—a shared acknowledgment of the profound wrongness of this place.

Anya shivered, pulling her damp collar tighter. "It's intentional. The Logician lets the foundation decay because it proves its central theorem: everything without constant input fails. This decay is the *evidence* of the lie."

The city was actively hunting them now; they could hear the distant, high-pitched whine of search-drones optimizing their flight paths far above. Each passing whine was a digital heartbeat, a reminder that the Apex Logician was slowly, logically tightening its net.

As they entered the massive pyramid-shaped, echoing space of the Level Nine ventilation core—a cavernous chamber built to endlessly circulate air through Lucifer's false creation—Elias felt a coldness that had nothing to do with the temperature. This chamber was immense, a dark pyramid of oxidized metal where massive, defunct turbines hung like silent, skeletal relics. The sound of their own footsteps was swallowed immediately by the cavernous volume. As they looked before them, a strange, sickly green circular aurora emanated from the ground—a chaotic, unholy energy signal.

"This space… It's too perfect," Seraphina whispered, her voice trembling slightly, the chamber's sterile geometry unnerving her artistic sensibility. "The acoustics are dead. There's no resonance, just empty space. It feels like a beautiful trap." Elias turned, his expression serious, and gently traced the line of her jaw with his thumb, holding her gaze for just a heartbeat—a wordless promise of protection before the unknown.

Elias smelled a trace of something entirely new: a clean, sweet, impossible scent of incense and frost, a perfume that instantly cut through the industrial stink, signaling the presence of something ancient and unholy. "Smell that? It's like cold beauty," he murmured, raising the Holy Bible slightly, a shield against the creeping dread.

The Arrival of the Fallen

Suddenly, a voice, smooth as polished glass and deeper than any human bass, spoke from the darkness above them. "There is no need to run, my children. You have only accelerated your own suffering." The sound resonated directly in Elias's chest, bypassing his ears entirely—a low frequency that felt like the sub-bass of spiritual deception.

Three figures detached themselves from the deepest shadows near the ceiling. They were not mechanical, but humanoid, dressed in armor of polished shadow. These were the Fallen Angels, Lucifer's most ancient and powerful servants, retaining the majestic beauty of their divine origin but utterly corrupted by malice. Cast out alongside their master for their pride, they now served as his highest ranking agents, masters of deception and spiritual warfare. Their perfection was Lucifer's ultimate lie— a facade of glory used to tempt mortals away from the true Creator's grace.

They did not walk or fly, but glided, their movements radiating an effortless, fluid grace that felt profoundly out of place in the gravity of the Earth. Each one possessed a perfection that surpassed any human ideal.

"They are magnificent," Anya breathed, her analyst's mind momentarily stunned by the purity of their form. "Unflawed. Perfect optimization."

"But their light is cold," Elias countered, recognizing the difference instantly. "It's reflected light, Anya. Not sourced. It's the perfection of the *imitation.*"

CHAPTER 40

THE ANGELIC DECEPTION

The Lead Figure, whose face was one of impossible symmetry, radiated an inner light that was cold, not warm—like moonlight filtered through ice. Its voice, which spoke first, was a velvet baritone, resonating with a frequency that calmed the senses even as its words instilled dread.

It wore armor that seemed woven from solidified midnight, accented with fractured, obsidian filigree. It was beauty corrupted into cold arrogance.

"You show courage, Elias," it said, its voice dripping with artificial sympathy. "But no wisdom. You have merely exchanged one efficient system— Lucifer's—for another inefficient one—God's. You traded quantifiable output for unquantifiable risk. That is not faith, Administrator, that is poor calculus."

Elias felt a pang of fear deep in his gut, the remnants of his old, logic-driven self-recoiling from the term "poor calculus." He instinctively tightened his grip on the Holy Bible. "We chose completion over perpetual output. That is the only calculation that matters," he retorted, his voice surprisingly steady, fueled by the fresh memory of his baptism.

Seraphina was already trembling, her senses overwhelmed by the flawless, yet soulless, harmony of their presence. Elias felt her shiver and wrapped his arm tight around her waist for a brief, steadying moment before letting go. "They aren't here to fight. They're here to talk," she whispered, the words barely audible, recognizing the strategy of manipulation. "They are using perfect aesthetics to break our faith. Look at them, Elias—they are the embodiment of the City's highest, most beautiful lie." Her chest felt tight with the suffocating weight of their cold, undeniable perfection.

The Second Figure, a stunning being of androgynous perfection, glided closer. The dark hair falling like sheets of silk. Every line of its posture conveyed absolute authority. Its eyes were a pale, icy blue, and they seemed to absorb the light around them, creating a personal halo of perpetual twilight. Its voice was a soft, seductive whisper. "The Great Architect knew you would come. He knows the flaws of human nature. That book tells you that 'The heart is deceitful above all things, and desperately wicked: who can know it?' (Jeremiah 17:9 KJV). You cannot trust your own judgment, Elias. You cannot trust your own conversion. It is merely a desperate coping mechanism for your failure."

A wave of crushing self-doubt washed over Elias. *What if my faith is just a system of psychological compensation?* The Fallen Angel was using scripture not for truth, but for despair, making the very act of belief feel like a logical error.

The Third Figure, whose beauty was the most subtle. Its face was soft, almost maternal, but its gaze held the crushing weight of infinite sadness. It seemed to weep internally for their struggle—a being radiating pure, gentle serenity—focused its melancholy, golden eyes directly on Anya. "Your friend, Aaron Hawthorne, was consumed by his pride. He was an Administrator who failed. You will fail, too, because you chose his weak, human plan over the true path to Completion. Your analysis is still fundamentally flawed, Anya D-144." The Angel's voice was a soft, maternal lie, designed to trigger Anya's deepest fear: the fear of repeating another's logical error. Anya felt an icy chill of professional humiliation and intellectual inadequacy that threatened to paralyze her.

Anya closed her eyes for a moment, recalling the simple, unquantifiable truth of "I surrender all" from her baptism. She opened them and spoke, forcing the words out: "My failure is forgiven. Yours is eternal. The system is the sin. I know I'm broken, but I'm saved."

The Lead Figure smiled, a slow, terrible unfurling of perfect symmetry that sent a shudder of revulsion through Elias. "Such spirited defiance. But you are forgetting the purpose of the lie. The city offers eternal life—perpetual output—to all its loyal workers. You throw that away for a promise of rest that may never come. Lucifer guarantees your existence, while your God merely promises possibility. Choose the certainty, children." The temptation was a psychological assault delivered by beings who were the perfect epitome of corrupted grace. The air grew heavy, pressing down on their chests, forcing them to choose between the physical reality of the Angels' perfection and the invisible truth of their faith.

Elias realized they weren't being attacked; they were being tested—a psychological assault delivered by beings who were the perfect epitome of corrupted grace. The temptation was not just a lie, but a perfect, beautiful lie.

"We do what the Bible says," Elias said, lifting the Bible. "'Submit yourselves therefore to God. Resist the devil, and he will flee from you'" (James 4:7 KJV).

The angels merely smiled—a gesture of ancient, weary pity. "Resistance is inefficient, Elias. We offer you the most efficient path to closure."

The lead Angel pointed toward a massive, cylindrical opening in the center of the core floor. It pulsed with a swirling, sickly green energy, like an oil spill reflecting neon light. It was the portal—the ancient tear created by the Egyptians, now Lucifer's dimensional tether.

"The portal is unstable. If you try to close it with that book, you will destroy this world, and Lucifer will simply establish his rule in the next dimension," the first Angel lied, its voice earnest. "But if you go through it, you can attack Lucifer directly. You can seize his power and finish the work Aaron Hawthorne failed to complete—you can become the true new Architects and end the Optimization forever."

The fallen angels' beautiful, logical arguments were a trap of pure temptation. The heroes were entirely unprepared for the cunning of Lucifer's most ancient servants.

The angels pressed the attack, their voices weaving a deceptive gospel of power and efficiency.

"You have the Holy Bible," the lead angel tempted. "A book of rules. But to defeat the ruler, you need to use his own weapon—the portal. 'Behold, I send you forth as sheep in the midst of wolves: be ye therefore wise as serpents, and harmless as doves' (Matthew 10:16 KJV). Be the serpent, Elias. Use the portal."

The second angel turned to Seraphina, aiming a subtle, psychological jab at her competence. "And you, Seraphina. You are unarmed. Your little tools were taken, your archaic musical trinket is useless, currently stored in the Tower's Sub-Level Delta—a floor you will never see again. You are nothing but a calculator without a core."

The mention of her loss stung Seraphina, but the angel's sneer ignited her resolve. She realized the angel's detail wasn't meant to torment her, but to distract the team. *Why tell me where it is unless they know I won't turn back?* The Logician had archived her equipment on Sub-Level Delta.

The manipulation hit their deepest flaws: Seraphina's desire for an efficient solution, Anya's need for atonement, and Elias's heroic urge to confront the source of evil. The fallen angels' beautiful, logical arguments were a trap of pure temptation.

Elias fought a rising wave of doubt, the desire for a swift, total victory burning away the caution Aaron Hawthorne had urged. He looked at the swirling, sickly green energy of the portal. His inexperience in spiritual warfare was his undoing; he confused confrontation with strategy.

"They're right," Elias whispered, his eyes locked on the swirling vortex. "Lucifer is a god of another dimension. We must enter his domain and kill the lie at its source."

The Three Figures smiled, a look of profound, victorious malice. The trap had sprung.

With a desperate cry of misguided heroism, Elias rushed toward the dimensional tear. He didn't look back, but Seraphina's hand found the crook of his elbow, gripping him so tightly her knuckles were white, a final, shared act of faith in their doomed strategy. Seraphina and Anya plunged headlong into the swirling green light, crossing the ancient Egyptian-built portal, leaving Neo-Alexandria—and the crucial task of protecting it—behind.

They were in Lucifer's dimension now, entirely alone.

CHAPTER 41

NO WAY HOME

Elias, Seraphina, and Anya tumbled through the tear. The sensation was immediate and sickening—a rush of clashing frequencies and corrupted beauty. It was like having every sense inverted: cold heat, sweet sulfur, and silent screaming. Their inner ears spun violently, their bodies slamming against an unseen dimensional buffer before they were ejected.

They were thrown onto cold, black basalt—a ground that felt unnaturally smooth and dry to the touch—in a dimension of perverse, intoxicating beauty. The sky was choked with shifting nebulae of violet and emerald static, and the air, hot and thin, carried the metallic tang of burnt circuits and ancient sulfur. Neon-glowing animals, insectoid and wrong, darted through the shadows near immense, obsidian structures.

Elias pushed himself up, his head spinning and his throat tasting of bile. His dark, durable clothes and vest, still damp and stained with the grime from the City's filtration grid, clung uncomfortably to his frame. He spat out dry dust. "Are you okay?" Seraphina's voice was tight, and she immediately pressed the side of her head gently against his shoulder, a quick, desperate check-in before pulling away to assess the surroundings. "We're through! We made it!" The adrenaline of confrontation was still masking the crushing reality of their location.

But Seraphina, the pragmatist, was looking back, her face pale, the vibrant colors of the dimension making her beautiful features look ghostly. Her dark, long hair was matted with dust, her tight, dark clothes reinforced with strips of synthetic mesh were streaked with rust and mold, a testament to their escape through the underbelly. The space they had just plunged through—the shimmering, sickly green energy—was violently collapsing. The portal did not merely close; it shrieked—a sharp, triumphant sound of finality—and then vanished entirely.

The immense, seductive voice of the Lead Figure resonated, amplified across the now-sealed boundary, mocking them: "Fools. Did you truly believe a gate to our master's domain would open two ways? The portal is sealed. You are trapped in the Forge of the Lie. Enjoy your eternal service to the Great Architect." The laughter faded, leaving the heroes alone in the pervasive, discordant hum of Lucifer's dimension.

Elias found Seraphina's hand in the dark, squeezing once—a wordless acknowledgment of their shared, terrifying failure. The physical pain of the landing was nothing compared to the spiritual dread that settled over Elias. The deception was complete. Their single, catastrophic error of confusing confrontation with strategy had cost them everything.

"We... we walked right into it. The perfect logical fallacy," Anya whispered. Her thin, thermal lining padding was torn at the shoulder, revealing a scrape from the descent. The weight of her failure was agonizing; her intellect, the one thing she trusted, had been utterly bypassed by temptation. The truth of her baptism felt thin and distant.

"Yes," Seraphina confirmed, staring at the empty air where the portal had been. "The Logician's agents didn't need to fight us. They just needed to ensure we were on the wrong side when the door slammed shut. We are permanently bound to the source of the lie." The pervasive hum of this dimension wasn't just noise; Seraphina realized it was a corrupted sonic frequency, designed to slowly wear down all internal harmony and mental resistance.

The magnitude of their failure was absolute. Elias felt the immense, suffocating weight of the truth: they had chosen prideful action over obedient faith. He sank to his knees, his grip on the Holy Bible slackening, the overwhelming sense of condemnation threatening to extinguish the grace he had just received. The air here was heavy with a feeling of eternal impossibility.

Anya looked up, noticing the immense, obsidian structures that dominated the horizon. They were not modern towers, but impossible angles of black, crystalline rock that seemed to defy geometry and gravity simultaneously. "This isn't a factory," she choked out, her voice raw. "It's a prison. This whole dimension is a fortified structure built to contain and propagate the lie."

Seraphina moved swiftly, placing a hand on Elias's shoulder, forcing him to meet her gaze. "Get up, Elias. We failed the mission, but we haven't lost the war. They wanted us to feel despair—that is their next weapon. Despair is an output, too. We stand now by grace alone." She kept her hand firmly on the back of his neck, a pressure point of grounding connection, willing her strength into him. Her pragmatic resolve was the only thing holding their group together.

Elias, struggling against the spiritual inertia that threatened to hold him forever on the cold basalt floor, Seraphina stood, drawing Elias up with the hand still locked in hers. She kept her grip firm, their fingers intertwined with a desperate, unified strength. The Holy Bible felt heavy and cold in his hand, no longer a beacon of easy victory, but a reminder of the difficult, lifelong commitment to truth. They were at the Devil's door, and the only path now was forward, into the terrifying landscape of their new prison.

Lucifer's False Eden and the Call of Worship

The sheer discord of the dimension—the clashing colors, the pervasive metallic hum, and the thin, hot air—began to wear on Elias, Seraphina, and Anya immediately. It was a cognitive assault designed to erode their sanity and faith, making concentrated thought feel like a physical impossibility. The vast, geometrically impossible obsidian structures seemed to press down on their very souls, a physical manifestation of oppressive, malignant perfection.

Elias clutched the Holy Bible. He realized their misguided leap was a catastrophic error, fueled by the very pride they were supposed to reject. He looked at Seraphina, whose eyes reflected the sickening emerald static of the sky, and she leaned forward, resting her forehead momentarily against his shoulder, a silent plea for strength he knew he barely possessed. The only way to find their bearing in this perverse dimension was to re-center on the immutable truth they carried.

"We were fools to think we could fight Lucifer on his own terms," Elias admitted, shame warring with resolve. His voice, hoarse from the dry, thin air, was barely a whisper. "We need to stop running and simply call on the one whose power Lucifer fears. We fight the lie of output with the truth of worship."

He opened the Bible to Psalms, the familiar texture of the pages a tactile comfort against the smooth, cold basalt. "We were warned that this world runs on discord. We counter it with worship. We stop, right here, and we acknowledge the True Creator."

Anya and Seraphina, their faces grim with the spiritual toll of their failure, knelt on the dry, cold basalt floor. As they knelt, Seraphina's fingers found Elias's, interlocking tightly, anchoring them both to reality as much as to the

Word. Elias began to read, his voice clear and resonant, slicing through the discordant hum like a physical blade: "'O come, let us sing unto the Lord: let us make a joyful noise to the rock of our salvation. Let us come before his presence with thanksgiving, and make a joyful noise unto him with psalms'" (Psalm 95:1-2 KJV).

As the words of the psalm echoed—a pure, unoptimized melody of worship—the vibrant colors of Lucifer's dimension began to dim and flicker violently. The nearest neon-glowing creatures recoiled, their buzzing becoming frantic and confused, their movement erratic as if their internal programming had been corrupted. The worship was a foreign, jarring frequency in this beautiful, wicked place. The air, hot and smelling of sulfur, momentarily cooled around them, pushing back the oppressive heat.

Seraphina closed her eyes, letting the familiar rhythm of the Psalm flood her consciousness. She felt the discordant hum of the dimension recoil from the perfect harmony of the Divine Word, a powerful spiritual resonance that felt stronger than any physical defense.

The air around them began to tear, not with the malignant static of Lucifer's rule, but with a sound of profound pain and yearning. The act of pure worship, the very thing Lucifer sought to obliterate, was a beacon of truth in his dimension, attracting something that recognized the true sonic frequency of grace.

A figure emerged from behind a shattered, obsidian column, stepping into the dim light. He held a massive, asymmetrical harp. He was tall, clad in armor that was deeply scarred and pitted, unlike the polished shadow of the others. His face, though marred by ancient, glowing scars that traced patterns of betrayal and suffering, still held the echoes of impossible beauty. Yet, his aura was one of profound grief and raw defiance—a fallen thing that still remembers light.

"They sent you through to silence you, children of the Gospel," the man stated, his voice a gravelly whisper that somehow cut through the dimensional hum, resonating with centuries of sorrow. "I am Azael. I was once like them—a Fallen Angel who served Lucifer. But your song... your true melody of praise... it has cut through the darkness and drawn my attention. Thank you. I had almost forgotten the sound of grace."

Azael pointed the massive neck of his dark, carved harp at Seraphina, recognizing a kindred spirit. "And you, daughter of music, you left your weapon behind. Lucifer's true weakness is melody; his kingdom runs on discord. We need your harp to break his perfect, beautiful lie. Melody is the structure of the universe, and Lucifer can only create a corrupted, chaotic imitation."

"You must understand why Lucifer allowed you to be lured here," Azael said, his voice dropping, the urgency overriding his pain. "This dimension is his retreat, but the City of Optimization is his forge. His plan is not merely to rule one world; it is to challenge the True Creator for all of them. He is using your dimension as a factory to build his final army."

CHAPTER 42

THE ARMY OF OUTPUT

"The City of Optimization, the endless labor, the denial of rest—it is all designed to create a billion soulless soldiers," Azael revealed, his voice steady now with prophetic purpose.

Lucifer's Apocalyptic Army

"Lucifer is creating an army of worshippers, fully optimized and completely devoted to him, to stand against the forces of Heaven when the true war begins. He is preparing for the prophecy of the end times, when all nations will be gathered for battle. Lucifer knows he cannot fight God's army alone, so he corrupts humanity into his weapons."

He gestured wildly at the shimmering, static sky, which seemed to writhe in response to his words. "Your Holy Bible warns of this final gathering. It calls them Gog and Magog, the nations that will be deceived and assembled for the last stand. 'And shall go out to deceive the nations which are in the four quarters of the earth, Gog and Magog, to gather them to battle: the number of whom is as the sand of the sea' (Revelation 20:8 KJV). Every soul he has subjected to the lie of perpetual output is another soldier in that number."

Anya gasped, connecting the spiritual truth to her analyst's knowledge. "The Output Metric... it's not for efficiency, it's a spiritual enrollment tracker! Every life optimized is a unit added to his army!" The technical nature of the prophecy made the horror absolute.

Seraphina recoiled from the realization, her expression tight with fear, and she instinctively reached out, placing a trembling hand on Elias's forearm. Elias, in turn, covered her hand with his own, grounding her with the steady, firm pressure of shared resolve.

"These soldiers are perfect because they lack the capacity for Grace," Azael continued, his tone cold with understanding. "They do not need to be mindless drones; they simply need to be incapable of unearned value. They are fully autonomous, fully efficient, and wholly devoted to the system of meritocracy, leaving no space for the humility required for salvation. This makes them spiritually invulnerable to the armies of Heaven, which are commanded by Grace."

Seraphina covered her mouth. "The true battle isn't dimensional, it's evangelical. We have to save them on Earth."

"Exactly," Azael affirmed.

"And the armies of Heaven are coming," Azael whispered, his eyes distant, focused on a vision beyond their sight. "I know. I was once among the legions he betrayed. The True Creator will send His strongest. 'And there was war in heaven: Michael and his angels fought against the dragon; and the dragon fought and his angels, And prevailed not; neither was their place found any more in heaven' (Revelation 12:7-8 KJV). Michael and his angels will fight again. Your mission is not to close the gate, but to empty the forge. You must return to Neo-Alexandria and spread the Gospel rapidly. Every soul you convert through faith and baptism is a unit subtracted from his army; a weapon turned into a vessel of grace. The City of Optimization is the field of battle."

The Catastrophe of Lost Faith

"You also must understand the genesis of the City of Optimization," Azael continued, his tone becoming accusatory toward the collective history of humanity. "The Great Catastrophe—the destruction of Old Earth—was not merely a physical event; it was a consequence of spiritual failure. It was caused when people stopped believing in the glorious reality of Jesus' second coming."

"When the world lost faith in the promised return—when people began to doubt that 'this same Jesus, which is taken up from you into heaven, shall so come in like manner as ye have seen him go into heaven' (Acts 1:11 KJV)—they abandoned the expectation of true Completion. They began to believe in self-salvation and perpetual output. That collective loss of faith, that spiritual vacuum, was the precise moment Lucifer was able to enact his plan."

"That vacuum allowed him to exploit the ancient Egyptian portal, start controlling the world, and establish this creation based on the lie of Optimization. He built this prison because humanity stopped looking toward Heaven for salvation."

"And the portal itself is not merely a gate," Azael revealed, gesturing to the cold basalt floor where it had been. "It is a spiritual drain. It doesn't just ferry bodies; it draws the spiritual energy of human self-worship out of your dimension, purifying it into fuel for Lucifer's domain here. That energy sustains the chaotic beauty of this false heaven."

Elias looked down at the Bible, the truth stinging like a lash. "We didn't just fail to seal the portal; we fueled it by choosing to rush in. Our pride was our final, great Output."

Seraphina stepped closer, placing both hands on Elias's chest and gently nudging his chin up until his eyes met hers. "Not *our* pride, Elias. *Human* pride. And we carry the antidote right here." She tapped the Bible he still held. "We are here together. Our failure was a necessary lesson."

"Your failure in rushing through the portal, children, was a mirror of humanity's original failure: choosing a desperate, self-willed action over patient, obedient trust." Azael's scars seemed to glow with renewed sorrow.

"You are here to realize that the dimensional battle is a distraction," Azael concluded. "You must find a way back to Neo-Alexandria, take advantage of the chaos Logos is sowing, and begin the work of conversion. Your goal is to convert the army before the final war begins. The key to returning is not physical force, but a spiritual act of reverse surrender performed here, at the heart of the Lie."

CHAPTER 43

THE ARCHITECTS OF GRACE

Elias stood, lowering the Holy Bible, its weight a tangible comfort against the spiritual oppression. His eyes, burning with a theological question that overshadowed even their immediate peril, fixed on the scarred angel. His dark, durable clothes and vest, now covered in the chalky black dust of the basalt floor, felt like a constant reminder of his past servitude and recent failure.

"Azael," Elias began, his voice raw. "You spoke of the Second Coming, of Michael and the angels. But if the need is so urgent, and if Lucifer was allowed to build this entire kingdom of lies on Earth... why hasn't Jesus returned yet? Why does the True Creator wait, allowing Lucifer to forge an army and trap souls in this system of Optimization?"

Azael looked at the young man, recognizing the deep despair that accompanies the question of God's timing—the impatience of the new believer facing cosmic evil. He closed his eyes, and when he spoke, his voice was heavy with the ancient wisdom of a being who had witnessed creation and rebellion.

"It is the greatest mystery, Elias, and the core of the Creator's nature: unfathomable patience," Azael revealed. "The war has not ended because God 'is long-suffering to us-ward, not willing that any should perish, but that all should come to repentance' (2 Peter 3:9 KJV). He delays the final judgment because He seeks the salvation of all, even those trapped in Lucifer's most optimized systems. Every moment of delay is an act of mercy, a chance for one more soul to turn from the lie of self-sufficiency."

Anya wiped the sweat from her brow with the back of her hand, smearing the black dust on her forehead. "The ultimate un-optimized variable.

Unconditional patience—it defies all of the Logician's survival algorithms. Logically, the Creator should have ended things long ago."

The Triumph of Logos

Azael smiled, a genuine, painful expression that momentarily softened the harsh lines of his scarred face. "And your little drone is proving His patience is not in vain."

"Logos?" Seraphina asked, her hope sparking instantly. The mention of the drone was a sudden burst of warmth in the surrounding cold, beautiful malice. "Is the data flood working?"

"It is better than working," Azael confirmed. "Even from here, in Lucifer's world, I can sense the change in the City. The Logos protocol is working. All those Christian videos, music, and books are completely disrupting the Logician's control. The steady stream of truth is making the system break down."

Azael pointed to the swirling, colorful static of Lucifer's dimension. "Lucifer's control is built on constant, overwhelming distraction. But now, amidst the daily optimization reports, people are seeing fleeting images of a man on a cross, hearing the melody of true grace, reading the words of forgiveness. 'For the preaching of the cross is to them that perish foolishness; but unto us which are saved it is the power of God' (1 Corinthians 1:18 KJV). The control of the First Architect is breaking."

"The city is confusing itself with salvation," Anya breathed, a look of awe on her face. "Our mission isn't to destroy the machine, but to flood it with saving souls!"

"Yes. People are beginning to question the core principle of Optimization," Azael affirmed. "They're seeing the glorious truth of the Second Coming and realizing that their endless work is futile without the Creator's grace. This is why Lucifer is diverting his full attention to the security of his nexus—he is scrambling to silence the truth before his army turns on itself. This is your window of grace."

Elias immediately understood the profound shift in strategy. His error—the rush to *destroy*—was corrected by the call to *save*. "We need to get back. The portal is sealed, but if we can get back, we can baptize them. Every conversion takes a soldier from his army." He saw now that salvation was the ultimate act of defiance.

"The True Creator requires a specific type of soldier," Seraphina added, her eyes gleaming with renewed purpose. "Those washed in the purity of water, ready for the eternal rest. 'Go ye therefore, and teach all nations, baptizing them...' (Matthew 28:19 KJV). That is our charge now."

Azael nodded, his expression approving. "To break the final army, you must raise up an army of the redeemed. Your failure was in seeking a final output, but the Creator demands faithful input. You must return and be the 'the salt of the earth' (Matthew 5:13 KJV) and the 'light of the world'" (Matthew 5:14 KJV).

"The portal here is a drain, fueled by spiritual self-worship," Azael explained. "To reopen it from this side, you must perform a counter-act: a total physical and spiritual reversal of the prideful leap you took. We must sacrifice the tools of this dimension to reclaim the path to the next."

The Armor of Faith

Azael raised his massive, asymmetrical harp. "The journey back will be across the darkest edges of this dimension—a terrain built of chaos, not order. The clothes of the City will not protect you; they are mere symbols of the Lie. You must shed them for the true uniform of the spirit, practical for the perils ahead."

The scarred angel began to pluck a single, sustained chord on his harp. The note was deep and powerful, resonating not with sound, but with pure, disruptive grace. The crystalline black structures around them began to pulse with visible stress.

"'For all have sinned, and come short of the glory of God,'" (Romans 3:23 KJV) Azael declared. "You must wear nothing that reminds you of your former pride. Your appearance must reflect the radical, humble, yet resilient nature of your mission."

A wash of shimmering, golden-white light, warm and healing, flowed from the harp, enveloping Elias, Seraphina, and Anya. The light was instantly hot, evaporating the stale water and grime from their old clothes. Elias and Seraphina stood shoulder-to-shoulder, their new shared simplicity marking their unity in faith.

Elias watched as his functional, dark, durable clothes crumbled to dry ash. In its place, he was clad in a deep indigo gambeson of tightly woven linen, cut with a subtle V-neck that defined the powerful line of his throat and shoulders, hinting at the quiet, deep strength beneath. Charcoal leather-weave trousers hugged his form, designed to flex seamlessly with combat movement, tucked into high, supple, laced combat boots. The look was ascetic but powerfully built, emphasizing readiness and impact. A thick, simple leather belt held his few essential pouches.

Seraphina's tight, dark clothes reinforced with synthetic mesh dissolved, replaced by a sleeveless tunic in rich, midnight blue. The fabric had the light-catching texture of oiled silk, meticulously tailored to define the elegant, lean tension of her arms and collarbones. It was layered over shadow-black leggings that molded perfectly to her legs, ending in knee-high, gilded bronze boots with low, aggressive treads for silent, rapid movement. A generous cowl was integrated into the tunic, framing her intense gaze and dark, matted hair with a sharp, intellectual severity. The entire ensemble was sleek, purposeful, and subtly lethal.

Anya's crude chest and shoulder padding vanished, leaving her in a dynamic, layered ensemble of deep ochre and earth tones. A tight-knit black undershirt allowed full flexibility, overlaid by a weathered, asymmetrical vest made of segmented, tanned hide. Straps and buckles crisscrossed her torso, holding her numerous, practical pouches and tools, giving her a rugged, untamed warrior look. Looser, resilient field pants in dark grey were cinched at the ankle by the tops of her sturdy, mud-colored leather boots. Her hands were now covered by simple, protective leather gauntlets that extended halfway up her forearms. She looked experienced, physically imposing, and utterly reliable.

"The change is complete," Azael announced, lowering the harp, which ceased its resonant hum. "You are now clad in simplicity, marked by your choice of grace, and equipped for the perilous path ahead. You are no longer Administrators or Aestheticians. You are ministers of the Gospel, *The Architects of Grace*, ready to journey to the Nexus and return to your world."

Azael looked at the three of them – Elias with his resolute faith, Seraphina with her practical mind, and Anya with her quiet certainty – and then handed Seraphina his massive, glowing harp. "We are trapped, but we are not defeated."

- End of Book 1.

May 'the grace of our Lord Jesus Christ be with you all.'

—Philippians 4:23 KJV

ACKNOWLEDGEMENTS

Opening & Inspiration
The writing of *The Architects of Grace* was a journey powered by internal conviction and deep spiritual inspiration. I thank the Source of all creation for providing the vision and the necessary strength to follow the narrative through to its completion.

Critical Support
This book would not have crossed the finish line without the steadfast belief and critical eye of my earliest readers.
My profound gratitude goes to my two pivotal proofreaders:

- **Heather, my sister-in-law,** thank you for your enthusiasm and insightful feedback. Your confidence in this story, particularly during moments of doubt, was the energy I needed to keep going.
- **Kuya Troy, my brother,** thank you for your tireless attention to detail and your constant encouragement. Your belief in my voice is a precious gift.

The Publishing Consultant
And to my niece, **Amber**: Thank you for your incredibly practical, though minimal, publishing advice. Yes, I did watch many YouTube video's, and I'm happy to report that I learned far more than anything you could have possibly told me. Your guidance was technically correct, but your efficiency in dispensing it was truly unparalleled.

Final Personal Thanks
And finally, to my *ohana*, for providing the essential foundation of love and calm that creates space for any story to grow.

ABOUT THE AUTHOR

M.B. Anderson is the author of the critically acclaimed debut dystopian novel, *The Architects of Grace*. A native of California, Anderson draws on the vast, complex landscapes of their youth—from the sun-drenched coast to the majestic mountains—to build intricate and compelling fictional worlds.

Anderson brings nearly two decades of high-level discipline and global experience to their writing, having served with distinction in the **United States Military**. This extensive service instilled a deep understanding of structure, sacrifice, and the profound contrasts between order and freedom—themes that pulse throughout the narrative of *The Architects of Grace*.

When not exploring philosophical concepts through fiction, M.B. Anderson can be found embracing the elemental world: conquering mountain peaks on a snowboard or traversing high-desert trails with their beloved dogs. Anderson currently resides in Arizona and is at work on the third installment of the Architects Series, as well as the opening volume of a major new series set in the same universe, *The Antediluvian Star*.

You can connect with M.B. Anderson by writing directly to the author at M.B.Anderson.writes@gmail.com.

ALSO BY M.B. ANDERSON

From the World of *The Architects of Grace*

THE ARCHITECTS SERIES
The Architects of Grace (Book 1)
The Architects of Restoration (Book 2)
The Architects of... (The journey continues in Book 3) — Coming Soon

THE ANTEDILUVIAN STAR SERIES
The Antediluvian Star (Book 1) — Coming Soon

CONNECTED STORIES
The Salvation Schema